# HUBOT

*Also by Joseph P. Cody*

# The Tiger's Fury

During the late 1990s, the president of the United States is looking for an excuse to renew the Gulf War and remove the Iraqi leadership. At the same time, Iraq is engaged in a sinister program to produce terror weapons that will find every American whether they live in the largest city or the most remote backwater.

Two men caught up in these plans are Ed Breckon, a skilled engineer, and Capt. Tom Rebic, the commander of a company of Abrams M1 tanks. Unexpected events put both men in Iraq to be sacrificed as they are drawn into an ever tightening vortex of international intrigue.

Breckon, as a prisoner, is beaten and abused as each day becomes harder than the one before. He knows he will live only as long as he continues to do the engineering his captors demand. Having prayed for various things during his life, he finds that when he is reduced to praying for deliverance he has hit bottom. Will his desperate plea be heard?

# Dragon Fang

A breakthrough in nanotechnology is poised to change the world. The CIA has obtained a secret protocol thought to give China's strategic plans in the matter. To the CIA's dismay, the agent carrying it is killed when the airliner bringing him to the United States is destroyed in flight.

The placid world of engineer Ed Breckon is thrown into chaos as he finds himself in China on business. Through a case of mistaken identity, a package is thrust into his hand by a man who moments later is killed. The CIA as well as the Chinese State Police know he received something, but Breckon isn't talking.

Greg Daley of the NSA has identified a mole in his agency. If the wrong people learn of his finding he'll be killed. He links the mole to Breckon's China trip and goes to Breckon for help. Together they look for answers that will save their lives. The clues lead them into the Beartooth Wilderness in the high mountains of Montana where they face their own innermost fears as duplicity, confusion, and high-tech satellite weaponry reign.

Along the way, these two men are forced to ask the question: if God is good, why is there evil in the world? Through bitter torment, they learn the meaning of divine providence.

# HUBOT

---

## JOSEPH P. CODY

## A Thriller

Autotech Industries

St. Paul, Minnesota

This is a work of fiction. Any resemblance to persons living or dead is purely coincidental. Names, characters, places and events, except where noted, are products of the author's imagination and are fictional. The views expressed herein are solely those of the author and do not necessarily represent the position of Autotech Industries.

This book is written, printed, and bound in the United States of America

First Edition: June 2009

ISBN-13: 978-0-9791167-4-2
ISBN-10: 0-9791167-4-0

A Publication of:

Autotech Industries
688 – 11th Avenue NW
St. Paul, Minnesota 55112
www.AutotechInd.com

To my wife for help with ideas and editing.

# — Prolog —

**Fifteenth day of the first month, 6,341 BC**

It was a clear day without a cloud in the sky as Shamis looked toward the sun. Its location was known by a spot of yellow brighter than the surrounding yellow sky. It hovered above the horizon in the heavy moisture laden atmosphere. He rested his forearms on the stone parapet slightly more than waist height, and stared at the indistinct shadows moving on the surface of the sea ten feet below. The lapping of the waves and the warm breeze carrying the smell of salt water hardly registered on his consciousness.

Thoughts of what had come to pass thrashed about in his mind. If the past were even a poor predictor of the future, if even the best scenario he could devise came to be, what was to come filled him with foreboding.

Absentmindedly, he glanced to his left for the fifth time in as many minutes hoping to see his friend, Quentin, coming down the stone steps twenty feet away. Quentin was a leading scientist and the two of them frequently met to discuss the issues of the day. Today in particular, Shamis hoped for a sympathetic ear and assurances on a particularly perplexing situation.

Shamis, a master of philosophy, the prince of the academicians, was in torment. He was in danger of falling from his lauded position by supporting a small but vocal movement intent upon shutting down the energy cylinders in an attempt to arrest the decline of society. If the course of events didn't change, though, his position wouldn't matter much. The number of serious students was dwindling each year. Far too many were willing to forgo the learning of the ages and follow charlatans who promised the easy path to pleasure and personal enlightenment.

The promenade where Shamis stood should have been filled with street vendors and shoppers at this hour, everyone being careful of the other's rights and congenial to all they met. He had always liked this small market and had sent a message to Quentin with an urgent request to meet him here. When Shamis had arrived ten minutes before there were fewer people about than was normal for the hour, but he gave it little thought assuming others would be arriving shortly. His intense concentration was broken by shrieks behind them. Turning, he saw two men chasing a woman who appeared to be running for her life. And, what was this? No vendors . . . no people. The place was deserted.

Off to his right he heard a male voice, "There's one. He's from the academy. Get him!"

Shamis ran for the steps to his left and started up two at a time. The scuffing of footfalls closing behind him increased his fright. His breath was coming hard as he reached the top of his climb and dashed for an open doorway. Through the portal, he was in a large public room used for weddings and similar gatherings. Sprinting to the right he slipped into a food preparation room and ducked behind the serving counter. Struggling to control his breathing lest the slightest sound give him away, he heard voices and then steps enter the room. Fortunately, they continued on to adjoining halls. He waited, unmoving, his mind refusing to believe what had happened. But, it had occurred. If ever there was proof of his concern, this was it. Alert for any indications that his pursuers might be returning, he waited.

In recent memory, the level of violence, crime, and depravity had increased alarmingly. It had started with the invention of the energy cylinders a little more than a century before. These devices provided limitless power that could readily be beamed to any point of use. The availability of vast amounts of cheap energy brought a technology revolution to a society ill prepared for it. Generally, the rulers saw nothing to be gained from technology or anything else that might upset their dynasties. The farms and sea produced an adequate supply of food as long as the people applied themselves with the primitive tools available. Hard working people were tired after a long day, and tired people were easy to control as was the case in all unindustrialized societies.

The time since the introduction of the energy cylinders was a small part of an average lifetime, so most people remembered the *hard life* as it became known. No one was willing to go back to those days.

With an atmospheric pressure of over three bar, people easily lived for five hundred years, and more commonly approached a thousand. This air pressure made it possible for the human body to repair itself quickly and completely. The practical result of this was any person doing the same thing for most of his lifetime became a true expert in his occupation. When this was applied to science the results could be earth shattering. That had happened.

A man named Henton Glasser invented some clever devices that made the life of his well heeled master more comfortable. After that, he was given leeway and funds to pursue other areas of interest to him. In between coming up with gadgets for his master's household, he fought ahead on a pioneering project. Given hundreds of years of hard driving curiosity, not to mention some lucky guesses, he found a way to create magnetic vortices in ceramic cylinders that tapped the energy of what is normally known as empty space. He had the insight to see that the idea of empty space was not valid. We all moved about in it, and it held the universe together, so it had to have structure. He reasoned that with the proper application of science and technology, the energy this structure represented could be tapped. Since it had never been discussed before, he called it *basic energy*.

After due consideration, those who governed decided to use this invention to provide light in the dwellings of the populace. In retrospect, they saw this as a huge mistake because soon the source of the limitless energy was known to all. With this knowledge, the exhausted, benign masses demanded to know what besides lighting could be achieved with this basic energy. The leaders were caught off guard.

In a few short decades, machines were doing most of the grueling work. The people now had free time and boundless energy. Many embraced athletic activities or artistic pursuits, but in the end, there was mass boredom. The listless population slid into physical addictions. The use of alcohol, that had been used only in limited quantities for ceremonial occasions, came into common use. Drugs, long known for their medical properties, were also widely abused. Worst of all, these substances were mostly used in seclusion owing to the centuries of sanctions against their abuse.

To counter these addictions the leaders promoted more socializing by means of recreations of diverse kinds. Once again, it produced undesirable results. Previously, there had been limited fraternizing due to the long days of work so the people were not equipped to handle so much interaction. This combined with the use of drugs and alcohol led to promiscuity, and sexual deviations of all kinds.

These, what could be called psychological addictions, led to the greatest problem of all, spiritual obsessions. Seances and many varieties of sorcery came into vogue. The evil spirits, at first invoked for laughs and thrills, soon possessed those who dared to cross the void. There was no lack of fervor on the part of the hapless individuals now under the control of demons to pressure others to join. Those standing firm in their conviction that this was evil were laughed to scorn, and ostracized from professional and even family circles. Before the energy cylinders, when the sun went down, darkness settled over the city and little stirred. Now the city never slept. Bathed in perpetual light, the night resounded with screaming, howling, and discord.

As a philosopher of renown, Shamis was a relentlessly out-spoken critic of the demonic. In less than a hundred years, it had gone from a shunned practice of savages to the latest fad. However, unlike a fad, it had not died out. With each year, it became more prevalent until it had an iron grip on all of the city-states.

These thoughts brought Shamis back to his present situation. He wondered where Quentin was. If his friend knew how bad it had gotten in this part of the city, he would not be coming this evening, though he had to check. Having heard no voices or movement for several minutes, he crept from his hiding place. Cautiously, he made his way out the door and then to the top of the steps. On the plaza below was a familiar broad shouldered figure, more stooped than normal, it seemed. Shamis waved and descended the stairs toward him. As he approached he saw the gray eyes, deep set in the wide face, were not smiling. The haggard expression lightened slightly as he approached. They met grasping one another's arms.

"You look like you carry the world's problems on your shoulders," Shamis said forgetting his own plight.

"And more, I feel," Quinton replied.

"We will discuss it. But, first we must leave this place." As they hurried away, Shamis told Quentin about how he had been chased.

When they were in a place of relative safety Shamis asked, "What is it? What could cause you such disquiet? You are the one man of my acquaintance who seemed to be above that affliction."

"Aye. So, perhaps, did I."

"Tell me if you can, what is it that concerns you."

"It's technically involved, but I'll try to give you the meat of it. There has always been some fear of the cylinders that generate the energy. On the surface, you could say it was simply that it seemed illogical that we could get so much for so little, well, for nothing, really. Yet, we could find no inkling of a down side. Using an aspect of a new theory of physics, we constructed a measuring device. We believe it measures the asymmetry in the form of subspace from which we draw the energy. We expected there would be some small disruption in the immediate vicinity of the cylinders. However, this asymmetry extends far beyond what we thought. Though, for the present, it seemingly is not causing any problems."

"Wait. What do you mean you *believe* it measures? Don't you know?"

Quentin frowned. "Yes. That's what I mean. That Glasser was a great tinkerer. He'd be livid if he knew I referred to him that way, but that's what he was. He learned how to make the cylinders, get the energy generation started, and invented the means of beaming it to the point of use. But, neither he nor anyone else really knows how or why it all works. That's what concerns me. Some of us believe the asymmetry these measurements reveal will eventually have dire consequences."

Shamis still putting aside his problems concentrated on what Quentin was saying. "Do you see anything unusual happening near the cylinders? Are plants dying or anything of the sort?"

"No. I doubt the manifestation would be of that nature. That's the problem, though. There are no instruments that show the slightest thing wrong, other than this new one that shows this asymmetry appears to grow in distance from the cylinders in proportion to the accumulated amount of energy produced. One would think that this imbalance would immediately be nullified from the sea of basic energy like the lake rushing in to replace the water drawn out in a bucket."

Shamis listened attentively but was growing uneasy. "I feel we must leave. I don't think we are safe. Can we meet again tomorrow? I'm deeply worried about the growing instability of society, and I would like to discuss it with you."

"That won't be possible," Quentin replied. "For the next several days I will be with a team to map this asymmetry over our whole province as reference measurements. I'll notify you when I return. We could meet in the alcove on the second floor of the hall of writings."

"Agreed."

With that, both men warily made their separate ways home.

**Eleventh day of the second month**

It had been some time since their last meeting. Shamis and Quentin spoke in hushed tones on the second floor of the hall of writings. Shamis was saying, "I've put together a plan to organize the few sane people I can find in an effort to bring a petition to the Governor. He must shut down the energy cylinders, or at least the majority of them. It's a harsh measure, but is necessary to return to the normalcy we had before the lighting project. Crime and sorcery are out of control. The food supply is not safe even with the machines. The workers only think about their leisure activities after they leave their place of employment. Anyone who doesn't go along with the lazy mentality is shut off from his coworkers, and eventually dismissed from his job for not being a group worker."

Quint listened in silence with his arms resting on the table. He raised his hand at the wrist indicating he wanted to say something. Shamis paused. "While I agree that is what should happen, I see no possibility the Governor would agree to it. There would be mass rebellion. In addition, it may not be a simple task to shut down the cylinders."

"I don't understand. We started them. Why wouldn't we know how to stop them?"

"It's not that we don't know *how* to stop them, it's that we may not *want* to stop them even if the Governor approved."

Shamis looked askance at his friend. "Please, explain what you mean."

"As you might guess, we have completed our survey of the asymmetry of subspace caused by the operation of the cylinders. It was not necessary to go a complete mapping because after several days a pattern developed. It is true that the anomalous subspace covers an area around each cylinder whose size is proportional to the amount of energy that has been withdrawn. Actually, we're talking about spheres since space is above and below them as well as in the horizontal plane. The spheres are now beginning to overlap. That in itself does not appear to cause a problem. It seems that as long as the withdrawal of the energy does not change things are all right. We surmise that when it is decreased or stopped, a shock wave, for lack of a better term, is generated. Since the shock involves the space in which everything in our world exists, anything could happen."

"Or, nothing. Isn't that a possibility?"

Quentin scratched his head in agitation. "Maybe."

Shamis's eyes widened. "You're starting to alarm me. What does 'maybe' mean?"

"There was an incident at the site of the first cylinder that went into energy production. As you know, that was a prototype and hence is one-fifth the size of each of the others. A young technician became confused and did some routine maintenance procedures in the wrong sequence. The power output of the cylinder fell by one percent. Coincident with the fall in power there was an earth tremor. Tremors of this size are not common, but not unknown, either. The structure of the cylinders is made to withstand considerably greater movement than that represented, so there was no danger of damage.

"Herein lies the problem with the work of Mr. Glasser. Not knowing much about why or how the cylinders generate power, he made no means to throttle them. We simply start them and they produce power at a rate proportional to their size. This technician stumbled onto a possible method to vary the power output. Unfortunately, we don't know why that happened, either.

"I mentioned to others involved in the operation of the cylinders that the power reduction might have caused the tremor. Nearly everyone put it off as a random coincidence. I didn't think it was."

Shamis closed his eyes in thought. Then he said, "The logic of what you said is that there is a danger of very large earth tremors if all of the cylinders were to be shut down."

Quentin nodded. "That's the idea. But, the danger I see is far worse than that. I calculated the total energy withdrawn to date by the cylinders and compared it to the amount the accidental power reduction represented. If they all went down, it would cause an earthquake of unprecedented proportions." He paused and let out a long breath. "On the other hand, the tremor might have been coincidental after all."

Shamis said, "It brings back that nagging feeling that it was all too good to be true. What will happen to us?"

Quentin sat back and laughed lightly. "There'll be some of us left, I'm sure of that. We went way up north to the border of our province to get baseline readings as far away from the cylinders as possible. We've all heard about the old coot back in that valley who's building the big boat. Several decades ago we tried to convince him to get a power receiver back in there. It was as an experiment to see if the distance effected the power beam. He refused. They still do everything like we did in the days of the *hard life*."

"Yeah, him. He comes up in discussions at times. Seems he heard voices that ordered him to build the boat. Sounds like a nutty affair all around. There he is building his boat in the middle of a valley far from the sea. He'll never be able to launch it. He's been at it for nigh onto a hundred years, so they say. Think about it. That was back when the machines began to be widely used, and for the first time the people were freed from the long hours of hard work."

Quentin continued. "Our team showed up and he stopped what he was doing and extended us every courtesy. His location cuts him off from wider society so strangers bring news of what's happening outside his valley. He likes to visit. As he relates it, God has gotten angry about the depravity of the human race and the boat is to save a few of the good ones when He sends a flood to cover the whole earth. So, he's not concerned about launching the boat because he expects the water will come to him. When he was first told to begin the project he didn't start right away thinking God would relent and give us another chance. Anyway, God got after him to get started, so he did. After twenty years of humping his butt, he stopped for several years, and God was back, so to speak, cracking the whip. This continued on and off until in the last ten years he really had a fire lit under him. The thing's all but done now. It's really something to see. You should go out there and have a look if you can break away."

"I don't feel like going on a sightseeing vacation about now. We have a real dilemma. Shutting down the cylinders seems like the only way to return sanity to our society. Yet, you're suggesting that's the one thing we can't do."

### Thirteenth day of the second month

The tremors were first felt throughout the city two days before. Since then they occurred almost constantly, and were getting stronger. Nerves were raw causing more than the usual number of altercations among the citizens. Added to this the rainy season had started early, and the rain was more intense than normal.

Shamis looked up as he heard the rush curtain that served as a door to his chamber pushed aside. Quentin appeared with water still dripping from his cloak. Shamis was surprised to see him because they rarely dropped in on one another unannounced.

"I have an urgent request to make of you," Quentin blurted out as he entered. "There may be a calamity in the offing and someone should make a survivable record of what happened to us."

Shamis had been concerned about the tremors, but this shook him. "What are you saying? These tremors aren't without precedent. And the rains," he shrugged, "the streets are paved and the roofs are strong. We won't wash away."

Quentin eyed his friend. "That's not the point. It's the tremors and what's causing them that counts. It's being kept quiet, but after we spoke last some of the engineers, dismissing the tremor at the small cylinder, tried to make further adjustment to the output. After a few tries they were able to duplicate the exact sequence of operations that produced the first power reduction. Immediately worse quaking began. Being concerned now, they tried to return power to the one-hundred percent level. They failed, but with each attempt, the situation grew worse. Then it was hands off until this was figured out.

"From other observations we can see that these are not normal earth-quake-like movements. It has something to do with the mixing or col-lapse—we don't know what to call it—of the subspace. Here again, the official attitude is that when subspace gets finished adjusting itself, things will settle down."

Shamis couldn't dismiss his friend's expression of near panic. "I think I'm hearing that you don't go along with that reasoning."

Seeming to ignore the statement Quentin continued. "As I mentioned last time, the areas of subspace asymmetry have grown around each power plant to where they overlap. The next nearest generator, a full sized one, had a dip in its power output during one of the adjustments on the small one. The change was so slight as to be almost undetectable. However, since then it has not regained its normal steady performance. In fact, the anomalous behavior has gotten worse. I believe the ground movement will increase until one of the big cylinders cracks and stops producing completely. There could follow a chain reaction and all the cylinders will be affected. You can follow the logic from there."

"I should be shocked by this news. But, since I've been expecting it for so long, now that it's happening, it's almost anticlimactic. What type of record do you propose?"

"If the worst happens, it could be the end of the our race, certainly our civilization. If any are left they will be few which means that it'll be mil-lennia before the human race recovers to a point of caring about repeating our mistakes. The record must be made in clay tablets and then fired. After that, they should be transported to the highlands. It's reasonable to assume this area would be at the bottom of the sea. We don't want to include enough information for anyone to make a cylinder. I wouldn't feel right doing that to a future society."

Quentin left as quickly as he had arrived leaving Shamis thinking his friend could hardly be serious. In his heart, though, he knew he was.

**Sixteenth day of the second month**

Quinton had invited his life long friend, Shamis, to his home. After greetings, they sat for a few moments in silence. The torrential rain beat relentlessly on the roof. The only good thing one could say about the interminable rain was the roar of it impinging on the streets and buildings helped to deaden the sound of what was happening to the people.

Through the din, a scream was heard. "Will they never make an end to their demonic debauchery?" Shamis seethed.

He was, of course, referring to the surge in tumult throughout the city. To stem the sense of impending doom that had befallen the citizenry, they pursued their already deep addiction to the occult with renewed fervor. The movement of the ground had not affected the buildings like an earthquake would have. Land and buildings moved together. So far, only the people were affected. It would have been easier to accept in the form of normal earthquakes.

The news that this was being caused by the energy generators had yielded a mixture of fear and anger. Of these, the anger was the more dangerous because the cult leaders could play on it to convince the people that the rulers were deliberately causing the quaking in an attempt to put the energy genie back in the bottle. Turn off the power and the people would be forced to go back to the *hard life* or starve. Rumors of a revolution to replace the rulers and gain control of the power cylinders were growing.

Quentin sat back in his chair and said. "It seems so long, but it's only been four days since the small cylinder up the river went down completely. The tremors started in earnest then. Each attempt to restart it to stem the earth's movements failed and only exacerbated the problem. The theory, that only a few of us believed at first, is now widely accepted. In addition, the shifts in subspace affect not only the earth, but also the atmosphere."

"The tremors in the earth? Yes. I've come to accept that. But, in the atmosphere? Oh! The rains!" Shamis said incredulously. "The power plant problems are causing the rains? How can that be?"

The look of shock on the thin face of Shamis startled Quentin. "You did not know?" Quentin asked in surprise. "Of course not. How could you? We only put it together ourselves a few days ago. The heavy rains are yet another aspect of the disturbance caused by stopping the use of basic energy. I've told you about the subspace imbalance and what we have learned about it, how it is a sphere around the cylinders. Space is space whether it is occupied by rocks or trees or atmosphere.

"It seems likely that sooner or later, probably sooner, one of the large plants will go down. The pool of instability will expand until they are all down. If we extrapolate what we have seen so far to just those plants in our city, there will be enough dislocation in space so the earth will split open and the atmosphere will give up its water. In the end, water will cover everything. I did that calculation after the first power deviation in the small cylinder. Sadly, I was correct. It will be the end of us my friend."

Shamis said, "Maybe some of the backward people in the highlands will be spared. Can we modify boats so at least some of us in the city could be saved?"

"It's possible some highlanders will be spared. As for boats, I doubt there'll be time. The people in the old guy's boat could be the only ones to make it. The survivors would have a tough go of it, though. Our thinking is that with virtually the entire planet covered with water, it will not just evaporate into the atmosphere again, but it will be lost to space. A new much lighter air will be left. Whether people will be able to live in it is the question. From what we have seen of the highlanders, a lower atmospheric pressure will be hard on life. People will not heal as well as we do, and they will wear down and die in the space of less than a hundred years. It's hard to imagine, I know."

Quentin's voice now changed from alarmist to sadness. "Shamis, have you have time to write a history of what has happened to us in the last hundred years and inscribe it on clay tablets like I asked? You know I'm a believer in survival, and I'm hoping someone will make it. Sometime in the distant future the human race might face this again. Basic energy is there to be discovered. I'd hate to see our fate go to no good use."

Shamis nodded. "Inscribing the tablets turned out to be the easy part. A loyal student helped me with describing the cylinders at the beginning of the narrative. I felt there had to be enough information so someone in the future would know what we were talking about. He didn't give details only the procedure we use to make the cylinders and start the energy. He was an articulate lad who seemed to have a firm grasp of the subject.

"With everything so wet, we had a difficult time with the kiln, though. We were unable to get the temperature high enough to properly fire the tablets. Since you were so certain they had to be done quickly, we sent them off to the highlands as they were.

"I hope you didn't give too many details, or we may have passed our problems on to the future."

The ashen look on Shamis's face portrayed that he only now fully accepted Quentin's verdict. "You are certain this will happen, aren't you?"

"Yes, my friend, I am. The oldest of the large cylinders is not accepting the movement of the land at all well. We estimate it's a matter of days, even hours, before it shuts down."

Shamis shook his head. "At best, there will only be a few backward highlanders to continue the human race."

Quentin managed a wry smile. "Yes. And, we can only hope any survivors are backward enough to know nothing about energy cylinders."

**Seventeenth day of the second month**

"Why haven't you moved inland?" Quinton asked upon being admitted to Shamis's home. Quentin had been searching for his friend and was surprised to find him here of all places. The building was located near the sea.

"I am not a scientist, but even I can see that leaving is likely to be a pointless effort given the rate at which the water is rising."

Shamis showed Quentin to a chair in his eating area after which he placed a candle on the table. The power transmission had become so erratic that Shamis had reverted to this means of illumination from the *hard life*.

"And you? Why are you still here? Is it that you, too, know flight is futile?"

"Aye. I suppose I do.

After a pause Shamis asked, "What is the latest news of the energy cylinders?"

"The fact that you are still here tells me that you suspect the answer. Power has started to fall in the large cylinder that is nearest the small one that went down. A crack will form in it shortly and with that complete power cessation. Other cylinders will follow that course in short order." He almost choked as he added, "This is the last day."

Shamis nodded accepting the judgment. "In that case we must make a toast. I'll return in a moment." Shamis proceeded to a back room where he kept his wines. Shortly thereafter, the amber fluid flowed from the wine bottle as Shamis filled two short stemmed glasses half full. Raising his glass in the toast Shamis said, "To future generations. May there be some."

They clinked the edges of the crystal vessels and each took a swallow of the contents.

"This is fine wine, my friend. Am I correct in assuming it is your finest?" Quentin knew Shamis was a collector of rare wines.

"That it is. And, why not? It's pointless to save it." He stared at the flickering of the candle flame reflected in his wine. In a melancholy tone he continued. "We had it so good. Why couldn't people see that? We had it all. Each man and woman was free to become the best they could be. Why did so many find it necessary to become the worst?"

"I cannot answer that," Quinton replied. "Now, I have a toast. To future generations. May they do better than we did."

Clink!

> In the six hundredth year of Noe's life, on the seventeenth day of the second month, on that very day all the fountains of the deep burst forth, and the floodgates of the heavens were opened. Genesis 7:11

# — 1 —

**Present Day, China**

In Hua Chen's dream, he was floating above the city. At will he could come lower and touch the ground. From there he could spring up and float through the air for hundreds of feet. He presently found himself drawn to a large brick building. With an effortless jump he zoomed up to the third floor and passed through the closed and barred window. There he saw himself sleeping on that funny table with a sphere covering his head. What a pity to have to return from such a resplendent journey. Something told him it was time so he rejoined his body. He found he was no longer in a bed, but suspended in a pool of water with waves gently rolling him from side to side. This was not in the least alarming. The seamless transition from one condition to another in dreams was expected. He thought he should be suffocating since the waves were lapping over his face, but his breath came effortlessly. His state was sublime until he became aware of a hum. It was not an irritating sound, rather an agreeable one that seemed to be associated with an unknown force releasing its hold on his brain. It was as if thousands of tendrils were relaxing their grip on something, he knew not what, and going away. Suddenly, the hum was punctuated by sharp noises. The loud sounds vexed him because they interrupted his pleasant reverie. Finally, a particularly loud sound made him realize that he was hearing a human voice. In fact, it was only one side of a conversation.

" . . . told you those wild claims would get us into trouble. You should have been more reserved in you comments. We have no idea how close we are to success. If we are to have any chance to save our jobs, even our lives, you stay out of my way, and don't tell me how to do my job." Pause. "If the first tests aren't promising, we kill him and try again just like all the other times. We'll do one a day for weeks if necessary, just keep the subjects coming." Pause. "He was dead, I'm sure. We had him in a vegetative state for eighteen hours with no brain wave activity at all." Another pause. "Don't worry. I know a test to tell if he has any free will, and the less you know about it the better. If I succeed, then I'll tell you." Pause. "Screw the nano treaty. I know they failed to stop it. So, the Foreign Service people have their noses bent out of shape. Sure the pressure is on. Just keep them off my back for a few weeks and I'll give you one that's smart and totally obedient." Pause. "Now leave us. It's time to revive this one."

A heavy door opened and clanged shut. "That General Dong will get us all killed if he keeps talking like we had this process perfected," the harsh voice continued.

---

HB-23 lay still on the modified hospital bed located in the center of laboratory room 347C. The respirator inflated the man's chest at a rhythmic sixteen times a minute. The monitors all showed nominal vital signs. His head extended into a spherical device that upon first glance looked like an oversized hair dryer. Actually, the inside surface that pressed against the subject's shaved head contained thousands of micro-miniature magnetic coils. Electronic control circuits steered the focused magnetic field produced by each set of three coils from one brain cell to another. The patient, or laboratory animal, which was closer to the truth, was in the final stages of cognitive remapping by means of the multiple magnetic vortex generators covering his head.

Each member of the laboratory staff tried not to think of the subject on the table who twenty-one hours before had been a robust Chinese man of twenty-four whose name was Hua Chen. Would they be forced to "pull the plug" on this one, too?

The lead scientists and doctors were under tremendous pressure to deliver a lucid, healthy, HB, and had no compassion for their failures. If HB-23 were successful, he would have no rivals since the first twenty-two, having failed in one way or another, were dead.

All hoped this HB, for "hubot" which grew out of "human robot," would be the successful test. The brain remapping had proven to be much more difficult in humans than in animals. It was even being suggested by some of the scientists that it had never been successful with animals. Since communicating with animals is marginal at best, the argument went, maybe they had failed to kill the animal in the first place, so had not remapped it at all. If remapping were possible, it would turn modern day civilization in a new direction.

---

Chen lay still afraid to move as one does after waking from a nightmare. The respirator stopped and it took a few seconds for his muscles to realize that they were now needed for the work of respiration. "Good," the voice boomed, "he can at least breathe on his own."

Something rubbed on his cheeks moving in the direction of the top of his head to reveal a typical Chinese face. Chen's ancestry was from the northern part of China, so he had traits showing the Russian influence. He was tall, almost six feet, had high cheekbones, a strong jaw line, and straight nose. His complexion was light since he spent little time out doors. In typical of the Chinese, he carried little fat.

He saw red and realized his eyes were shut and a bright light was shining on his face. Then it came to him. He was awaking from what the doctors had called the memory enhancement experiment.

"Turn off the over head light." It was the loud voice again. He recognized it as the one he heard as he was regaining consciousness. It had not been a part of his dream as he had thought. This voice had said those words while standing beside his bed, and he, Chen, was the subject of them!

"How's he doing?" the voice boomed. The voice was so loud! Was everyone else deaf?

"Vital signs normal," said a voice in the distance.

"Brain patterns are close to normal," came another faint voice. "The synaptic rate is elevated, though. Might be due to disorientation upon waking, or he's just thinking faster."

Chen heard movements as someone shook his arm. A soft female voice said, "Can you open your eyes for us?"

Blinking, he opened them and looked at the face of a middle-aged woman peering intently at him. Her features were typically Asian, the complexion smooth and almost white. "Can you tell us how you feel?" He watched her lips move. The lower one was dry with small particles of loose skin about to fall off. It had a crack in it that had bled recently.

His first attempt at speech resulted in odd sounds. Then closing his eyes and swallowing hard he looked at her again and made a determined effort. "Maa . . . my mouth is stiff, dry."

"Good, you can talk for us. How are the vital signs," she said turning her head.

"Signs are stable."

"I think we can take the respirator away," she said to someone else.

Others were now near his bed. There was some commotion, as hushed comments were exchanged. Then he felt his bed raising under his head and under his knees. "Here, take a sip of water," the woman said offering him a container with a straw sticking out of it. "If this works, we will remove the intravenous feeding tubes shortly."

After Chen had taken a few sips the woman said, "There. That better?"

"Yes," he managed to say.

Then from further away the loud voice, "Well, do we have one?"

There was a rustle of clothing and the woman's face disappeared. He heard a hushed rapid voice, the woman's. Then some gruff snarls, the loud man. The woman, "Give me some time to reorient him. You'll scare him to death."

More gruff snarls were followed by the door opening and clanging shut.

More hushed voices and the woman appeared again. "Hello, I'm Dr. Mingchang, do you remember why you are here?"

"Um, memory tests," Chen managed to say. Actually, his life before entering the Medical Research Institute seemed hidden in a sort of fog so if memory enhancement was the object he had gone the wrong way.

"Good. We performed an experiment to see if we could enhance your memory. Do you remember that?"

"Yes." But, making me an animal with no free will was not part of anything I would have agreed to, he did not say.

"Now we will put some probes on your head to make some measurements to see if you are just as you were, or have some improvement. We made a very mild probe so it is possible there will be no noticeable improvement." In this, she lied, but everything else was a lie so it caused her to feel no guilt.

Chen remembered that his head had been shaved so it was not surprising to feel the cool swabs as they prepared to stick the probes on his skin. Moments later a faint voice said, "Connections are good, calibrating." There was a long pause, then, "You might want to look at this, doctor."

More hushed tones were exchanged. Then the woman reappeared. She proceeded to ask him simple questions starting with his name and birth date, where he went to school, and other events in his life. This was all information from the forms he had filled out. He found it odd that it was like he was reading the forms, but could not remember the actual events. Then she disappeared again.

After the woman had gone, Hua Chen was helped onto another bed that was complete. The one he was on when he awoke had only a narrow slat that supported his head to leave room for the spherical apparatus that had been surrounding his head during the remapping.

When Dr. Mingchang returned, she said he appeared quite normal. Now there would be some simple tests. She held up a sheet of paper in front of him with a single paragraph filling half the page. She held it there for just two seconds. Then she said, "Can you tell me what was on the paper, or as much of it as you can recall."

At first, Chen was put off. What a silly question. He had only glanced at it.

"Come now. Any part of it you can remember," the woman coaxed.

Without knowing how he could do it, he repeated the entire text verbatim, with no hesitation, no errors. He knew there were no errors.

"Very, very good. Almost perfect. Only one mistake," the woman said.

"No mistakes," Chen rejoined. "There is an error in the sixth character, on the eighth line."

The woman almost snapped the paper in front of her face. Slowly the paper fell revealing a strange expression. "Yes . . . of course, the mistake. We wondered if you would catch that."

She almost sprang away from her position near the bed. Again, rapid hushed exchanges could be heard. Some minutes passed. The woman was back. I have a page here she said. I want you to look at it just as you did the last page. Okay?"

"Fine."

She held it in front of him for just two seconds. "Can you tell me what type of page this is?"

"Yes. It is a page out of a telephone book."

"Good." She was moving her finger down the page as if counting lines. "Now, can you tell me what is on the thirty-second line in the right column?"

When he replied with the information, the woman just stared at him. Finally, her voice absent any of the inflection of before, she said, "That is correct. You must relax now. We will bring you some food."

The woman disappeared. He heard the door open and clang shut.

---

After leaving the recovery room as HB-23 was waking up, General Jia Dong had gone to his office on the floor above. The hubot experiments were not progressing nearly as well as the doctors had promised. This worried him a little, but not as much as he let on to the doctors by means of his demanding demeanor. His plan could progress for the present without a hubot, though in the end he'd almost surely need one, maybe two.

He was deeply into the latest report from Dr. Lung, who was part of the hubot project he led, when a knock on the door interrupted his concentration.

"Yes. Enter." He expected it to be Dr. Mingchang with preliminary results of the latest hubot so when the door opened her appearance was not unexpected.

"Good news," were her first words, though entirely unnecessary as her bright expression said that and more. "HB-23 is awake, lucid, and from two preliminary tests has a photographic memory." Before Dong could make any comment, she continued. "We tested him extensively before the procedure, as we do all the subjects, so we'd know if there were even a slight enhancement of mental powers. This is a clear and extensive improvement."

General Dong was pleased and complimented Dr. Mingchang. After a brief discussion of the next tests and HB-23's schedule for the rest of the day, she left. Alone again, the general took the half-smoked cigar from the ashtray and lit it. He leaned back with a satisfied smile. His plan just might work.

When those above him noted how ambitious he was, and taking into account the fact that he had come from the lowly merchant class, he was shunted into what appeared to be a dead-end job by being assigned the hubot program. Then one day, General Dong chanced to meet Dr. Anfa Luan. Comparing notes, it became obvious that Luan was working on another project that used the same physical theories as those at the heart of the hubot program. Due to the way the two bureaucracies guarded their turf, it was clear that they were the only two men who knew of this connection. Through contacts in their respective communities, Dr. Luan became assigned to the hubot program under General Dong. They both saw the benefit of Luan secretly maintaining his rapport with a few colleagues on his former project, especially a bright young physicist, Heng Lu.

After Dr. Luan was under Dong's direction, it didn't take long to discover why it had been relatively easy to affect his transfer. Dr. Luan was mad. Well, he wasn't really mad, extremely quirky was closer to the truth. There were all those stories in which a mad scientist plotted to take over the world. In this case, it wasn't the mad scientist who'd take over the world, but General Dong, himself. The mad scientist would simply supply the enabling science. Being somewhat honest, the whole world was a bit much even for Dong's inflated ego. However, controlling the PLA and, hence, a large part of China was not out of the question.

His plans were not as hypothetical as it might appear to most people in the world. The People's Liberation Army (PLA), which consisted of China's navy and air force as well as the army, owned most of the Chinese arms industry. This meant the man who commanded the PLA was one of the strongest men in China having not only the military but also a large part of the economy at his command.

It wasn't all clear sailing for General Dong, though. He had to finesse the many parts of his plan in just the right way if he were to achieve the desired outcome. First, he had to be sure the two traits of his mad scientist were genuine. Of the first, he felt certain. Lumping Dr. Luan's fetishes together came close enough to equaling mad that Dong didn't care to split the difference. The madness, he found, was surprisingly easy to control. Besides being more than a few meters off the deep end, Luan was also an alcoholic with a craving for French Cognac. Dong kept a supply at hand and doled it out as needed to keep the scientific results coming in.

His own tastes in alcohol were far more eclectic. When he and some of his old friends got together and partied the form in which alcohol was administrated made no difference to him. The corner of his mouth curled in half a smile. It amused him how, as those evenings wore on, the conversation would become increasingly philosophical. They'd wax eloquent about the grand future of China, and how they were in the right place in history to make it happen as far as position, talent, and intelligence went. It was something of a joke for most of them, he had always known. In his own case, it was obvious. He *was* abnormally intelligent. It didn't take a genius to see that.

As far as Dr. Luan being a super scientist, actually physicist, was concerned Dong was still guarded. True, Luan, at least according to his peers, was one of a group of Chinese men that could be counted on one hand who had done ground breaking work in theoretical physics. Unfortunately, for the moment the physicists were stalled at something called "the quantum conjecture," or simply referred to as "the conjecture." The latter term was used as a code in the theoretical physics community in China. Dr. Luan was one of the physicists who believed the conjecture was true. There were several other outstanding physicists who supported that position. However, there was a healthy amount of skepticism, too. Unfortunately, the gainsayers were mostly from the ruling class so China's leaders gave their opinions more weight. Dong's plans for rapid advancement depended on the conjecture being true.

In Dong's opinion it had been little more than an odd coincidence that he had been given control of the hubot program, met Dr. Luan, and become indirectly involved in deciding the truth of the conjecture. However, when one day Dr. Luan came up with an hypothesis where the hubot experiments could be the means of resolving the conjecture he saw the stars were aligned in his favor.

# — 2 —

On a philosophical level, it was curious that the development of the collective bank of human knowledge in any society was a random thing each society developed in a unique way. Frequently this was based on specific inventions. For example, the Chinese discovered a mixture of chemicals that exploded and used it to construct small noise making devices for ceremonial occasions. Yet, they never made a gun. Technically, they invented firecrackers, not gunpowder. The present day scientific and engineering advancements in electricity and magnetism leaned heavily toward the electrical leaving magnetism as an orphan. Recently, that changed. Research being done around the world by amateurs as well as sophisticated laboratories had advanced the field dramatically. Magnetic vortices in particular were of interest to the Chinese scientific community because they gave hints of being a way to connect to the zero point energy both for scientific research and as a means of commercial power generation. An ambitious research program into the latter was under way in China even as the researchers in this Medical Institute struggled with hubots.

Zero point energy (zpe) equated to empty space that pervaded the universe. Beyond the edge of the universe, if there were such a place, the emptiness would be substantially different from interstellar space, and the space in which we lived. The zpe was also known as the Casimir force after Hendrik B. G. Casimir who wrote a pioneering paper on it in 1948. Since then, it had been definitively proven to exist in laboratory experiments. Calculations showed that there was a tremendous energy content in each small chunk of space. Scientists got their first glimpse of zpe as they observed subatomic particles and their mirror antiparticles fleetingly pop into existence in our observable universe, and then immediately annihilated one another. The fact that this energy existed even at the temperature of absolute zero gave rise to the term *zero point energy*.

The hubot research was based on the idea of the animal soul. What was the difference between an animal, say a dog, that was alive and one that was dead? Alive it runs around sniffing things, barking at perceived intruders, and wagging its tail when called by its master. At the moment of death, perhaps with a bullet through the head, it twitched for a short time and then all bodily functions ceased. Immediately decay started. All of the chemicals were still present so what was missing form the dead dog? It was the strange thing called the animal's soul. The animal got it from its parents at the moment of conception. At least, there was no other obvious place it could come from. Little else had ever been learned about it.

Secret research into this mystery by the Chinese led to a startling discovery. It seemed there was a quantum mechanical connection between the helix of the DNA molecule in the nucleus of living cells to zero point energy. The researchers measured microscopic magnetic vortices in the DNA of living cells that were not there in dead cells. The theory said that the vortices were powered by zpe. The extremely complex DNA molecule at the heart of each living cell was wound into a tight helix. If this helix were to be unwound, it would be six feet long. In the human brain alone there were estimated to be one hundred billion neuron cells, and five to ten times that many glia, or support cells. Each had its own six-foot long strand of DNA coiled up in its nucleus.

The successful hubot would be a being between an animal and a human. More precisely, it would be a human that had no free will, and yet had greatly expanded memory and reasoning powers. It would be akin to brainwashing someone, except it would take only a few days rather than many months. These subjects could be used as totally obedient soldiers or, with minor modifications, used as assassins at home and abroad.

The work in this lab at the Medical Research Institute was to kill a human being while keeping his body alive artificially. Then the researchers would attempt to restart the magnetic vortices in the DNA of his brain cells. This would leave a human being without a human soul. The burning question revolved about whether he would retain his cognitive powers, while at the same time have no free will.

---

After the woman had gone for the second time, Hua Chen lay with his eyes shut, thinking. There was no question he was different. Though he could remember little of his life from before the test, he sensed that if he had always had a photographic memory, total recall, the doctor would not have been so surprised. He could remember every word of the conversation going on beside his bed as he awoke. He could also remember every character on the phone book page. He even tried a mental game of jumbling up the characters on the page to see if after time he would become less certain of them. However, each time the page was still there, not really a picture, but the effect was the same. Well, he could certainly adjust to living with that.

Then it occurred him. If they had achieved this goal, had they achieved the other? Did he have a free will? Was he nothing more than a smart tool? He began at once trying to figure out how he could test this. At first, it seemed it would be easy. He decided he would make a fist out of his left hand, and then gave the command to do it. The hand made a fist. There, that settled it. He had free will.

He continued his cogitation. Well, did it? What happens when a dog feels an itch and scratches it? Does he just do it, or does he think, "I feel an itch, guess I'll scratch it," and then does it. Nobody knew what went on in a dog's head. Nah, he just scratched it. Animals did what they wanted when the stimulus appeared. But then, what about a trained dog? A wild dog relieves itself whenever it feels the need. A house-trained dog doesn't. Maybe, he thought, I'm now just a house-trained animal in human form. Maybe the *me* from before the experiment is dead, and this brain in my head has been restarted as a very smart animal just as they planned. If they restarted all of my brain cells I would certainly know how to *act* like a human being, having been one for a good many years.

Wait a minute, I'm self-aware, I'm thinking about myself. That must mean it's still *me*. What if it's possible to write a program for a very large computer that would analyze not only a problem, but also how it managed to solve the problem? It would start with the logic it used, and proceed to the instructions that formed the logic, to the shift registers, and memory addressing modes that got the data, to the ones and zeros that formed the data, to the silicone that held the ones and zeros. Maybe that's what I'm doing. What does self-aware mean, anyway?

Chen intended to take the mental examination of himself further, but he fell asleep. After all, he still had his "animal" body that required sleep. That had not changed.

---

The gentle shaking awoke Chen. "You have had a nice rest, at least you appeared to sleep soundly. No REM sleep at all." It was the cracked-lip doctor speaking. "Do you feel refreshed, any dreams, or discomfort you remember?"

As the head of his bed was raised he replied, "No problems. No dreams. And, yes, I do feel rested. Can I get up?"

"Vital signs?" the woman asked turning her head.

"Signs normal," was the reply from across the room.

At this report, the monitoring devices were disconnected, but the sensors were left sticking to his skin. He was given a robe and slippers, and allowed to sit at a table where he ate a meal of boiled eggs, toast, and tea. It tasted good as he ate in silence. After that he walked around, sat, and then was connected for more tests. Everything was as expected.

"You are doing very well," the woman said. "Before we go any further I have something for you."

Chen saw her hold out a stainless steel bead chain with a strange pendant hanging from it. It was octagonal, about five centimeters across and a half-centimeter thick. There were several gold stripes on each edge that looked like electrical contacts. On one face was a small digital display.

"You are to wear this around your neck at all times," the woman said. "It is entirely waterproof so don't worry about taking it off to shower. It will help us monitor the state of your health. From time to time we will take it and see if it has recorded anything unusual about your condition. To make it useful to you personally, the display you see on it shows the time."

Chen noted a sternness in the woman's voice that he had not heard before. He was not being asked to wear the pendant, he was being ordered to wear it.

She continued, "I see no reason why we cannot remove the sensors and give you some normal clothes to wear. Then we will continue to test your memory improvement. From your first tests, it appears there is a definite improvement. We will want to know if it is permanent or not, and to measure it more exactly. Are you with us on this?"

"Oh yes, certainly. But, what will happen to me in the long run?"

"It sort of depends on the amount of improvement, how long it lasts, and of course on your desires. If your memory is much better than for other people and long lasting, you will be able to command any number of well paying positions. Your government will expect some amount of service from you because we gave you this ability, and at a considerable expense, I might add. That was part of the agreement you signed."

Chen had mixed emotions about what he had just heard. He could not remember signing such an agreement, but had to believe he had. For the first time, he dwelled on the fact that he could remember very little about his life before coming to the Institute. In actuality, he had received two years of training in electronics, programming, and machine controls. This meant he had a reasonably good life as long as he managed to stay out of trouble, which he had done. The hours were long and the pay meager, but he faired better than the majority of his countrymen. When his father un-expectedly died a year ago, and with his mother in poor health he had looked for a way to help the family. His mother, for the time being, could take care of herself, but was unable to work. She received only a small pension. His younger brother had not gotten any training, so it fell to him to help his mother when other sources of income fell short. That is why he agreed to be a test subject.

———————

Dr. Anfa Luan was working on plans to develop the results of a test presently being set up half a world away. In about a month, that experiment would definitively prove the conjecture to be true.

He was fortunate in having been assigned to General Jia Dong's project. It used the same physical principles as the energy research he had been engaged in. Only here, he was the lead scientist. Moreover, the general seemed to have a knack of indirectly exerting influence in the right places when it came to funding. Luan was torn at times by having to work for a general which meant his theoretical work would immediately be pushed into military applications. It seemed this had always been the case, though. Leonardo da Vinci, a man of monumental intellect, found himself in a similar position. Having him spend time designing siege machines, and devising efficient ways to move dirt for military fortifications just so he could eat regularly was such a waste. Welcome to the real world. He realized that most of what he wanted to do would be used for military purposes at first no matter who did it so there was no point in getting worked up about it.

At least, having a patron as dumb and egotistical as Dong made his life easy—easy as long as he could come up with reasonable sounding results regularly. The fact that he was considered mad by the man stung, but as long as he was given a free hand with his research, he tolerated it. He hated to dump so much of that good Cognac down the drain, but when the general thought he was on a bender he was left alone and managed to do his best work.

While on his former project to develop a process to make power from zero point energy, Dr. Lung had stumbled upon information in an unexpected place. Though this source gave few details, it clearly showed the entirely unlikely sequence of operations needed to achieve power generation from zpe. With Dr. Heng Lu, he put together the apparatus that led to the first successful experiments. In typical fashion, the senior men on the project took most of the credit.

With power generation *fait accompli*, the conjecture reared its ugly head. Dr. Luan's own work showed that the conjecture was most likely true. In addition, the source he had found that pointed the way to building the power generator in the first place, also corroborated his position on the conjecture.

This source, which he closely held to himself, was, of all things, ancient writings. The civilization described in the Vedas of India made reference to the use of zero point energy many thousands of years ago, though it was not clear whether it was used to drive their flying vehicles, employed as a weapon, or both. Those texts had been largely deciphered for many years. Recently though, experts in China had decoded other ancient writings. The scholarly study of this treasure-trove was in the historical and cultural veins. He had been drawn to the science they described. Making a few educated guesses as to the meaning of certain words and phrases, it was clear they had figured out how to use zero point energy to generate power. Except, they had not learned how to deal with the anomaly now called the conjecture. Imagine the dismay of his colleagues who had staked their reputations on this premise being false.

---

"You do your job, and I'll do mine," Dr. Fei Hongi harangued in his normal booming voice. Indeed, she was the psychiatrist tasked with determining the disorders, pathologies, or even improvements the procedure had caused in the subjects. Hongi was the psychologist whose job it was almost exclusively to discover what if any free will remained. Each of these branches of study involved the human mind, though each looked down on the other. This did little to ease the relationship between these two people, which under the best of conditions could easily be brought to a point of incandescent mutual annihilation.

"We have what appears to be at least temporary memory improvement," he continued. "But we must determine if we are dealing with a smart human, or a very smart animal. You remember that the goal was to make a human robot, the ideal soldier. If mental powers were enhanced as the data suggested it might, that was only a bonus, not the objective. Smart robots are the goal, but only if they are totally obedient. Nobody wants something or someone around who is smarter than they are. One day they could decide to stop following the orders of their less smart bosses, and take over."

Dr. Mingchang was uncomfortable and irritated as she always was in the presence of this man. She resented the bullying attitude of Dr. Hongi. His large muscular physique matched his voice. In addition, his hard craggy face, very unlike the typical Chinese features, made him intimidating. She knew that as a boy his facial features caused him no little ridicule. When he grew to size, he fought back with his imposing strength, as at the same time his voice became deeper and stronger.

At his first pause Dr. Mingchang said, "If the first twenty-two HBs taught us anything, it is that they are vulnerable under pressure at this stage. We don't know if this characteristic wears off because none of them lived long enough, or were allowed to live long enough, for us to find out. I feel you terminated some of them too soon. We could have learned more and would actually be further ahead."

"You are forgetting that we don't have facilities and staff to house, feed, and test more than two hubots. What else were we to do? The time schedule has been moved up. I'd say this one's the most robust we've had so far and can be pushed. Meanwhile, be sure he wears his pendant at all times. I don't want that General Dong dropping in unexpectedly and finding we're not following his orders. I doubt that it'll be needed, though. It's more like wishful thinking on the part of the general. It sounds to me like he wants a remote control on-off switch for these things."

Dr. Mingchang nodded her head as she got up. "But, you agree. We'll go easy until we are sure we can reproduce the results just in case we don't know how we got this far. Then, we'll advance to harder testing."

"Yes, yes. I agree. I'm sure we can reproduce the results, but we'll use a light hand on twenty-three for now. HB-24 will be done with cognitive remapping in two days. I must say, you aren't forming an attachment to twenty-three already are you?"

Mingchang gave a just audible snort as she turned and left.

---

As she walked to her office, Dr. Mingchang had to ask herself if she were forming an attachment. It was a thought that haunted her ever since HB-23 woke up somewhat normal. In spite of how she had driven herself to get to where she was, she was still a little bit human, or so she tried to believe. The competition had been intense as she was getting her training, and she had used every means at her disposal. Having to deal with those old lecherous men had been the hardest until it seemed there was no shred of humanity left in her. She herself had felt like a robot. At first, the concept of these tests had seemed like a cruel joke. This inhuman society produced robots by the millions. What was the point of doing it scientifically?

With HB-23 came the first sign of hope. Their prior results had been ugly. To see those healthy young men come in, be lied to, and then be subjected to this treatment was harder than she had expected. The ones that simply never woke up were the easiest. But, there were the others. Some of them were vegetables, others human appearing, able to walk and eat, but dumb as a rock. The insane ones were the hardest. They were whacked immediately. What if twenty-three were human? It seemed he could be controlled and allowed to live. They certainly could use some brains on this project. Surely Hongi was not terribly well endowed in that department.

# — 3 —

The following two days were filled with more and more demanding tests. HB-23 took them in stride and Dr. Mingchang documented the proof of his enhanced mental powers. Surely, human or not he would be allowed to live. She passed the information on to those higher in the chain of command. Finally, she was given a real world abstract cognitive skills test to administer. It involved an espionage case that had been solved. HB-23 was given the first information the counterespionage directorate came across, and he was fed more facts just as the people working the case had received them. They wanted to see if HB-23 could solve the case before their crack counterespionage team did. They were pleased with the results. In retrospect, the answer should have been obvious much sooner, but due to built in prejudices, the staff had not seen it. HB-23 appeared to have no such bigotries.

---

Some hours after HB-24 was to be out of cognitive remapping HB-23 received a visit from Dr. Hongi. In his most authoritarian voice he addressed twenty-three. "You have no objection to addressing me as 'sir' do you?"

The hubot answered immediately, "No sir. Certainly not."

"Good. Do you question my authority over you?"

"No sir."

"Would you do absolutely anything I ordered you to do?"

HB-23 hesitated for an instant. "There might be some conditions where I would question your orders."

"What!" boomed Hongi. "You sit there and tell me you would be insubordinate!" Got the little beggar, thought Hongi. However it happened, the little piece of dirt didn't die in the remapping even with the higher settings. He's still an obstinate scumbag like most of the chattels that inhabit this country. It crossed his mind that never had the decision to ruthlessly crush the Tiananmen Square uprising in 1989 seemed more justified.

Pleadingly HB-23 looked at Hongi. "Sir, what if you ordered me to harm you, or even Dr. Mingchang? That would seem counter-productive. You did not disallow those possibilities from your proposition."

Hongi was shaken, but tried mightily to hide it. "Well, hell no man! Why would I order such a thing?" He instantly closed his mouth and grimaced. There I went and did it, he thought. It was to be an iron rule, his rule, never to address the hubots in any term that would imply they were human. All right, we'll see how good this *animal* is.

"HB-23," Hongi said with solemn authority, "I am having a fixture made where you will extend the first joint of the little finger of your left hand through a hole in a vertical board. The finger will rest on a chopping block. At some future time, you will be asked to use this fixture. You will be given an axe, and on my command, you will chop off your finger. Do you think you will be able to do that?"

"That would hurt, but yes, if you ordered it, I would do it."

We'll see, Hongi thought. He was using as a test the psychology of pain in humans verses the very different pain in animals. Animals lived in a very short period of time, if it could even be called that. There was some sense of when they had their last meal, and when the next might come. Beyond that, they did not have a concept of the past other than a type of learning of what to avoid, and what to attempt when finding food.

People often anguish about the thought of an animal, say a deer, that has been wounded by a hunter. It could no longer move from its hiding place to find grass so would starve to death. However, the animal did not think about the pain already suffered, or the imagined much more severe pain to come. Only humans did that. Animals only suffered the pain of the now.

This was Hongi's plan. Give this hubot time to think about what was to come. If he were an animal and totally obedient, it would have no effect on him. However, if he were human and faking that he was an animal, as Hongi suspected, it would show.

A few days passed during which HB-23 worked with Doctors Mingchang and Hongi, usually only one at a time. Even though nothing was said, he began to understand that the two of them did not get along. The tests, especially those of Hongi, made it clear he was above all trying to find a test that would prove whether or not his subject had free will.

Through sleepless hours at night, Chen worked on the same problem. Most of the time he felt certain he was human. Some of the tests made him wonder, though. Mostly his expanded mental powers were becoming a concern to him because they might prove he was a machine. He even wondered if he could call them mental powers at all. Did he have a mind?

---

On the sixth day after he had awakened from his experiment, HB-23 was left alone the whole day. In the mid-morning a strange sensation came over him. It took only seconds to recognize it as the same feeling he had as he was waking up from his memory enhancement test. At first, the thought gripped him that it meant his mental powers were slipping away. In spite of his questions about being human, he had grown to cling to his new abilities. After several minutes, it became apparent this perception was not coming from him. It was an easy connection to understand that it was the machine he could feel, and they were doing the experiment on another subject. A tint of jealousy tugged at him. But, why shouldn't there be others? From the way he had been treated, the feeling was unmistakable that he was unique up until now.

---

After HB-23 had turned out so well, the scientists and doctors thought they had finally leapt the last of the hurdles and could start making hubots on demand. Sadly for them, it had not turned out that way. The next four were complete failures. None of them regained consciousness. Then they had a stand-down for a day to recalibrate the equipment and instruments.

HB-27 had proceeded with all parameters at nominal. He matched HB-23 as closely as possible and now they were nearing the moment of truth.

"Remapping complete in ten seconds," sounded the male voice of the technician intent on his computer monitor. "Two, one, now!" There was a click of a switch and that was all.

"Respirator off," came a woman's voice. "Normal respiration started, vital signs within acceptable limits, moving toward normal."

Two men removed the vortex generator from the subject's head. Quan Peng opened his eyes and saw Dr. Mingchang looking into them. He tried to orient himself but was not succeeding.

Quan Peng's parents had come from the south of China so his face was roundish, and his nose fairly flat. The eyes were almond shaped and his hair black, though for the test his head had been shaved. He had a stout build and would have put on weight easily if he had always eaten regularly.

"Hello. I am Dr. Mingchang. Do you remember me? You are at the Medical Research Institute and we have just completed a mild memory test. Do you remember that? If you have a little difficulty speaking, do not be alarmed. That is normal at first."

The testing part came back to Peng. What he was not connecting was *why* he was involved with a memory test. In fact, his whole life before the "Medical Research Institute" seemed to be gone. He closed his eyes and all he felt was extreme fatigue. Opening them again he tried to form words. After several tries, he managed to get out, "Very sleepy, need to sleep, then answer questions." His eyelids closed and he slept.

Dr. Mingchang walked over to Dr. Hongi, and said in a hushed voice, "At least he woke up and he is not a wild man. That is close to the same response we had from HB-23 as he was waking up. I say we let him sleep for awhile and not push him."

Hongi's disagreement did not surprise Mingchang. "No need for that. We found that some of the vortex generators were out of calibration and we over-dosed those last four, fried the bastards' brains," he said with his characteristic disregard for the subjects. "He'll be all right. I say we see what we have. A hubot that is no more robust than that, and must get his beauty rest is of no value. I'm going to roust him out. Don't forget, we have to start another one in three hours if he's no good."

"Oh, I wish you wouldn't just yet," Mingchang entreated Hongi.

"Bah! We must know if we can use him."

With that, he walked over to where Peng was lying, and shook his arm. Then he lightly slapped his hand on his cheek. "Okay, time to rise and shine, I'm Dr. Hongi, remember me?" Hongi boomed. "We've got work to do. Are you any good or not?"

There was no response. Hongi slapped Peng's cheek harder this time so it stung. Peng winced and tried to lift his hand. It met with restraints. A large hand gripped his face and squeezed in his cheeks making his mouth pucker as his head was rolled from side to side. The voice was back. "Come on guy, time to hit the deck. We have tests for you. If you don't measure up we'll have to dump you in a cremation box like the rest."

Hongi had no difficulty speaking this way because if this were a successful hubot he would be totally obedient and nothing Hongi said would make any difference. Dr. Mingchang stood by wringing her hands. She was of the opinion that it would be better to let them gradually come to understand that they were obedient, and accept it as a well brought up child expects to obey his parents.

---

Quan Peng felt the sting on his cheek and heard the ugly voice. Now, his face was being squeezed and his head rolled from side to side. In shock he thought he had been caught by the mob or the drug enforcement police, it didn't matter which. Either would torture him until he talked and then he'd be killed. The blank spaces were filling in fast even as the voice continued to boom. He had gotten out of Shanghai, where he had spent most of his life, just ahead of his drug boss. A rival gang had hijacked a load of meth precursor from him. Of course, nobody would believe that, although this sort of thing was common enough.

When he got to Beijing, he had seen the ad in the newspaper for test subjects at a Medical Research Institute. It was a two to four week live-in situation, and looked benign enough. Free food, a place to sleep, and out of circulation. What could be better? He needed time to figure out what had gone wrong and what he could do about it.

From the Institute's point of view, Peng was the perfect subject. He was strong and healthy, and reasonably intelligent. He listed no relatives other than a couple of aunts, and some cousins living in a rural area. There would be nobody to come looking for him.

On the forms, Peng gave the answers that would not raise questions. He concealed that he was brought up on the streets of Shanghai. As a youngster, he had never known his mother. His father, suffering from a lung disease, had made him hustle foreigners on the street outside large hotels begging for handouts. Looking as pathetic as possible he'd speak in broken English or worse French as the case demanded. His language skills were minimal but he'd score often enough so his father kept him at it. When he was having a dry spell, he and another boy would team up to pick pockets, one causing a distraction while the other did the deed. Some times they'd be lucky, other times they'd get caught. Getting caught was no fun because the police had no time to run in juveniles, so he'd get a good whipping and be set free. For the next few days, he wouldn't sit down much, but that was part of life growing up in the teeming swirl of humanity he called home.

As he grew from a street-smart kid to an even more street-smart young man, he branched out into the obvious career path, illegal activities. He had no marketable skills for a legitimate job, so the underworld sucked him in. The market-socialism in China was to all appearances a fantastic success with the economy growing at ten percent a year. Not reported was that some sectors had degenerated into gangsterism. Peng worked any angle that would generate a profit. The one with the highest payoff, and also the highest risk, was where he had landed. It was illegal drugs. Growing up he had seen there was little hope of living a long life. Now at twenty-two he had already come to the end of his string. There was no way he could come up with payment for the stolen goods. He had to disappear.

Now, what did these dung-for-brains doctors want from him? And, what was that part about the cremation box? Talk about disappearing, very thorough, but not while Quan Peng was still alive and able. One thing was obvious. This guy was a control freak, so best to suck up to his bloated ego.

———————————

"Quan, can you hear me?" the voice boomed again.

"Ye-Yes sir. I'm waking up. I seem groggy, though. I'll be ready to answer questions in a minute. Must have been real tired. Is it possible I could have some water, sir?"

Well, this looks promising, Hongi thought. "Bring some water," he snapped. "See Dr. Mingchang, he's doing fine. No need to coddle a fit young subject. He appears ready for duty, aren't you?"

"Yes, sir. Ready for duty, sir," Peng responded as crisply as he could manage.

———————————

The following day Hua Chen, HB-23, mentioned to Dr. Mingchang what he had felt the morning before. She dismissed it as unimportant, though she decidedly did not say there were no others.

The next day *the fixture* showed up. It just sat there and nothing was said. The day after that Hongi had him put his finger through the hole to be sure it would work. That was all. Strangely, this did not seem to bother him. Why?

The tests from Dr. Mingchang grew more complex. He was given one in international diplomacy. Though he was told it was hypothetical, he suspected differently. Each time he worked with it, she would come back a day or two later to add new information and counter moves, as it were, by the opposing government. The timing was the give-away. There was just enough time between sessions to allow the results to be tried on the opposition.

Along the way a combination diplomacy – espionage problem was presented. It dealt with a nanotechnology treaty to which China was party, that was now concluded, with China getting little of what it wanted out of it. It seemed there was a foreign agent, an American, who had caused carefully crafted plans to go awry. This enigma of a man could not be placed. He was at once an agent for the Israeli's Mossad, a deep cover operative of the CIA, working for the Russian GRU, and a none-of-the-above ho-hum electrical engineer who managed to stick his nose in places where he shouldn't. Edmund Beckon. The ILD, International Liaison Department, China's equivalent of the American CIA, had a thick file on this agent. Not a *really* thick file because there seemed to be little to say about the man. If he were somebody's agent it was the best job of deep cover ever done.

The mystery of this Mr. Beckon took HB-23's fancy. Along with each problem, Hu, as he began to be called, asked for more data. They had dropped his given name, Hua, at Hongi's insistence. It might give twenty-three the feeling he was human. Hu, short for hubot, would ask for phone numbers, airline schedules, even books on foreign languages. His uncle knew English, and had spoken it frequently to Chen as he was growing up so he had a basic feel for the language though now did not understand where he had acquired this ability. Memorizing grammar books and dictionaries was not difficult, so with some effort he managed to put together a working use of the language.

Dr. Hongi continued to work away at him. One day he took Chen down several floors to the basement. They walked down well-lit corridors turning first this way and then that until they came to a door that had AUTOPSY on a plaque near it. Hongi entered at once. There were no other people in the brightly-lit room. Chen noticed immaculately clean tile floors, and walls. The covers over the floor drains were even shinny. Along the walls were stainless steel surfaces with turned up edges also equipped with drains. On the walls were faucets, and hoses with spray nozzles. Moreover, there on a worktable was *the fixture*, and beside it lay a butcher's axe.

"HB-23," said Dr. Hongi in the most conversational tone he had ever used, "there is the fixture and the axe, do you know what I want you to do?"

Chen stared it the implements. "Yes. You will ask me to chop off my finger."

"Yes. That is so," Hongi replied. "Do it now."

HB-23 nodded, walked over to the fixture, put his little finger through the hole in the board so only the first joint protruded. He picked up the axe, and using the vertical board as a guide, swung the blade down in a sharp blow severing his finger.

*Pain!* His mind went black with pain. He heard his screams as if off in the distance. Dropping the axe he grabbed his finger and squeezed it to stop the bleeding. Blood was spraying in all directions.

Immediately Hongi was beside him with a string which he wound around the tip of what remained of his finger to stop the bleeding. Then he wrapped cotton gauze over the bloody stump. Hongi had Chen sit on a stool as he took a hose with a high-pressure spray nozzle and washed the area down after which he put away the utensils.

While Hongi was about his job, Chen rocked back and forth trying to absorb the pain. He looked about trying to find anything to take his mind off his finger. His eyes fell on a long bag lying on a gurney. A tag hung from the zipper pull. Written on it in large letters was HB-28. Wow, he thought. The fifth try in the ten days since I woke up. Were any of them still alive?

The pain imposed itself again. Glancing around frantically he noticed a wooden box with a label on it stating in bold letters CREMATION COMPATIBLE. Before he could make anything of it, Hongi was beside him again.

"Now," Hongi said, "when asked about this you will say this was a silly accident, and luckily I was nearby to keep you from bleeding to death. Do you understand?"

Chen nodded still trembling with pain.

"Good. I will take you to a surgery unit where we will get your finger professionally cared for. In this, I will do all the talking."

---

Late into the night, Chen lay awake. The local anesthetic had worn off. They would not give him a general narcotic based painkiller for fear of it affecting his memory. There was a small post attached to his bed where his forearm was held in the upright position by means of straps. This lessened the pain, but sleep was elusive. The thing that bothered him most about the day's events was his total lack of hesitation in cutting off his finger. On the way to surgery, Hongi asked if it hurt more than he had expected. His answer was, of course, much more. Hongi then said that on some future day Chen would be told to cut off another finger. Chen didn't know if he should believe it or not, though it made sense. The first time it was understandable that he would not correctly estimate the amount of pain. The second time he'd know what was coming and the human reaction would be to do nearly anything to avoid it. Yet, the disturbing part was he felt certain he would not hesitate even the second time.

It took until after midnight before it finally occurred to Chen what was upsetting him most. Whether or not he, himself, was human, it was certain that Hongi was an animal, at least in the metaphorical sense. There was no escaping the glee the man took in that whole episode. If he were under pressure to prove that Chen would be disobedient, he had failed. Chen was certain he had not flinched in the slightest. If that sadist thought this technique made sense, and there could be differences of opinion on that, then he would devise ever more cruel tortures.

Then an even more painful thought came to Chen. What if Hongi told him to kill myself? Clearly if he refused, he would be disobeying an order, shown to be a failure, and killed. If he obeyed the order, the result would be the same. Hongi would, of course, plan to intervene it he obeyed. The means of death would have to be credible, though. It would be something like being shown a hangman's noose, being told to grab it with his hands and pull himself up. This would prove it was strong and not rigged. Then, he'd be told to stand on a stool and put it around his neck, after which, he'd be ordered to step off the stool. Hongi would have a secret way to cut the rope at the last instant so he wouldn't die— maybe. What if something went wrong? Or, what if that nut-case got his jollies watching people kill themselves? The conclusion was undeniable, he must escape.

But, how? Where would he go? If he did manage to escape, they would surely retaliate against his family, if he had one. He had to make them think he was dead. From what he knew about the other HB experiments, they were not having much luck, so his premature death would not be too surprising. But, how to do it? And still, where would he go? It all seemed desperately impossible.

As the night wore on, he reverted to thinking about whether he was human. He certainly thought he was. Still there were nagging questions. His seeming willingness to do anything he was told bothered him. Then there was the fact that he could remember everything that he learned after the experiment with total recall, and still could not remember events about his past, like his childhood. This was practically all gone. Eventually, he had to admit that he knew too little about what it meant to be human. He, like billions of others, simply took himself as a given complete with phobias and neuroses.

A strange thought appeared out of nowhere. Did it matter if he were human or not? He was smart and had a perfect memory. He couldn't complain about that. Surely, if he could get away from those two doctors, he'd get the hang of making decisions on his own. As for his family, he remembered his mother's address from the forms. If he could get back to familiar surroundings, maybe his past would come back, too. Yet, what was it that gnawed at him about the importance of being human? If it didn't matter, why did he keep thinking about it? These thoughts continued to bounce around in Chen's head until at some point, unexpectedly, sleep came.

At dawn, he awoke with a start. His left arm and hand were cold and tingled like a thousand needles were being jammed into them. He twisted his body until he could reach the straps holding it against the post. With his arm free, he sat on the edge of the bed slowly massaging his forearm. As life began to return to his limb, the throbbing returned to his finger. As a diversion, he walked to the window that had a pull-down shade, but no curtains. As always, the view was unspectacular. The building he was in consisted of a central rib of corridors and offices with several wings extending out from it at right angles all four stories high. He didn't know which wing he was in but across from him was another one. To the left was the main building, and to the right he could see a boulevard lined with trees. The surface between the wings was completely paved and ended in a loading dock at the main building.

As he watched a truck backed into the space between the wings from the street. It stopped at the dock. Wang's Funeral Services was painted on the side. He had seen this on two other occasions when he had awakened early. The driver got out and was met by another man pushing a handcart with a wooden box on it. Chen remembered the shape of the box from the autopsy room. They removed the lid that lay loose on the box and compared the tag on the contents with a sheet of paper on the clipboard carried by the man from the Institute. The driver nodded and signed the paper. The two men then roughly wrestled the box into the truck. He imagined they must be passing comments about how the occupant of the box didn't mind being jostled around. The business done they stood a moment and passed pleasantries. They suddenly burst into laughter. Mortuary humor, Chen thought. The early hour for this procedure was not unexpected. If this were a serious medical research institute, it would be indecorous for people to see bodies being hauled away at regular intervals.

# — 4 —

The day after Hongi's "finger test" Dr. Mingchang appeared briefly. She asked for Chen's pendant and left. An hour later she returned it with hardly a word. The same was true on the following day. Chen passed it off as them giving time for his finger to heal and checking the pendant for baseline data since he wasn't doing any demanding mental activity.

On the third day, Dr. Hongi had Chen take a lie detector test. Chen thought of lying to some of the questions just to see if the test would detect it. Strangely, he did not. He wasn't sure if it was fear that if he did lie, and it was detected, he would be killed, or if he simply could not disobey the order to tell the truth. It was odd, he thought, if he had not been ordered to tell the truth, maybe he would have lied.

During the questioning, he was even asked if he had thought of escaping from the Institute to which he said yes. Through a series of additional questions, all with yes or no answers, he conveyed the truth that he knew it to be impossible. After the test, he was turned over to Dr. Mingchang.

Her line of inquiry was different this day. At first, it was about how he felt about his situation at the Research Institute. He said he understood the need for the various tests and projects he was asked to work on with the exception of Dr. Hongi and the finger test.

"That was unfortunate," she replied but took it no further.

Chen did not let it pass, though. "I worry that it is possible that he will become more severe. What if he asks me to kill myself?"

Dr. Mingchang looked startled. "I can't imagine why you would think that. What purpose would that serve? Put it out of your mind. That will never happen."

The response was too emphatic, Chen thought at first. After he pondered it for a few seconds, he had to agree it would serve no purpose. It was too silly an idea to receive any more of a response that that. He told her as much and they started on to the main topic of the day.

There was an espionage case that differed from the previous ones. On the other cases, he had been given documents containing the initial information he was to use to solve the case. This time there were no documents. He was told the facts of the case in narrative form. A man who had access to vital secrets had disappeared from a guarded complex. No one had seen him leave, and he was not to be found on the premises. Though this man was of average intelligence, or a little more, he had no privilege. He had no credit cards, or passport, and little money. The authorities had questioned all of his known relatives and associates, and had learned nothing of his whereabouts.

Chen knew all too well what *authorities* meant. It was the MSS, the dreaded PRC's internal security directorate, like the FBI in the United States. The difference here was there were no rules governing its operation other than to get results. If the MSS had come up empty handed, this guy had done a good job. Chen's assignment was to develop possible scenarios the man could have used to avoid detection as he left the complex.

Chen thought about it for awhile as Dr. Mingchang waited patiently. Then Chen said, "I will need access to information of diverse kinds to learn of possible subterfuges he could have used. Is it possible that I could get access to the Internet?" In China, the Internet was really the *Intranet*. The whole country was one net, like one huge company. That way all traffic into and out of the country was checked for viruses, or so the story went. Actually, all the traffic was monitored by the government for whatever they wanted to look for.

"That can be arranged. Is there anything else?"

Chen thought again. "Yes, there is. Can you get me access to a shop with an assortment of small tools? I can work at night if it is otherwise used during the day."

"We have such a shop in the Institute that I could arrange to have you use, but why?"

Chen looked at her honestly, "It seems obvious that if this man disappeared he changed something about himself—the way he looked, the way he acted, what he had. You have seen movies, I presume, where the hero on the run does things. One scene shows him starting to make something, change some wiring in a control system, or similar thing. In the next scene it is done. You simply assume that he is exceptionally talented.

To help you, I must see if various options I think of are reasonably possible. Whatever he did, it would have to be done rather quickly, and with tools and supplies readily available. Along the way I may ask you to buy items that he might have purchased locally and brought into the complex where he worked with no questions. I have an average ability with tools, so if I can do it we could assume he could."

Dr. Mingchang nodded slowly, "Yes, that does make sense. You can start working on ideas now, and I will arrange for the services you requested. We must, of course, continue working on your normal tests and diplomatic cases. And, right now, I must take your pendant for a short time."

---

Each time Dr. Mingchang took Chen's pendant, she brought it to Dr. Anfa Luan. The device was something Luan developed when he came to work for General Dong. It measured and recorded the human energy field of the wearer. On the early hubots who recovered, he saw a steady decline in their energy fields which caused them eventually to become erratic mentally, physically, or both. He soon saw that the device had to act as a feedback mechanism to boost the subject's energy field. With this improvement to the pendants, three of the subjects had a longer period of stability before they became uncontrollable and had to be killed. After a few more adjustments HB-23 appeared. With the cognitive remapping apparatus adjusted to the right energy level, and the pendant programmed to boost his energy field, they had achieved success.

His theory that involved using the hubots to assist with proving or disproving the conjecture used this energy field. Proving the conjecture required generating useful energy from the zero point energy background. From his previous work on that project, Dr. Lung knew their main problem was getting a large enough magnetic vortex started to make the initial connection to zero point. If the pendant were configured properly, it could use every cell in the hubot's body to assist in starting the magnet vortex. It didn't make sense on the superficial level, but on the quantum mechanical level of subatomic particles it did—sort of.

Upon reading out the energy levels from HB-23's pendant a few days before, he was shocked to see a spike that was impossible to explain. Upon questioning Dr. Mingchang, he learned about the finger test. This was yet another twist he had not expected, and immediately he saw the possibilities.

---

Chen's first approach to solving the missing man case was to assume someone on the lam would make himself look like a cripple. He got the idea from what he saw from his window. He had seen people on the boulevard coming and going with various physical maladies. This was a medical institute so that was expected.

He was given access to a workshop after seven o'clock in the evening. First, he made a crutch that had a single aluminum tube that extended up to about four inches below his elbow. At the upper end was a U-shaped bracket that cradled the forearm. Extending out from the tube at right angles was a second tube for his hand to grasp as it supported his weight. There was a non-slip rubber knob on the bottom. He glued rubber pads on it to soften the contact with his hand and arm. He took care to scratch the aluminum, and file, rub, and wear the rubber parts so they looked well used.

At his ankle, he made metal bars that extended into his shoe with leather straps and lacing. It gave the appearance of metal braces that strengthened a leg and ankle that were deformed. Next, he made a pad of sponge rubber that he put in his trousers to give the appearance of a deformed hip. He practiced walking by swinging the deformed hip and leg as if they were hardly functioning.

After three days, he was ready to test his disguise. At first it occurred to him to try walking out the front door and see how far he would get. In spite of the security at the main entrance, he thought it was possible he would make it. Once out, though, what would he do? He might not be able to get back in. If he really did plan to escape there was no place for him to go, at least, no place where the MSS wouldn't find him. Being found and returned was not something he wanted to think about. He'd be at the mercy of Hongi and that meant no mercy.

So, he decided on a different, much less drastic, tactic. Being careful not to be observed, he took his devices to his room. Using talcum power, he grayed his hair, and with a grease pencil he lined and darkened his face and hands to give the appearance of age. Donning disheveled pants and a shirt he had found, he was ready. He knew Dr. Mingchang would be in her office, so he shambled down the hall making grunting noises. Mingchang's door was open and her desk faced the door. She could not help but see the figure pass by.

"Hey you," she said. "You are not supposed to be in this wing. Come in here this minute." Chen kept going. It was not an order directed at him, but at some old cripple. She was beside him in a second and grabbed his left arm. "I told you to stop."

Using a dialect used in his home when he was a child, he looked sidewise at her and said in a deepened voice. "I know what I'm about. You cannot stop me."

Dr. Mingchang jerked him around and looked into the haggard face with strands of gray hair hanging over it. A faded patch covered the right eye. "Stay where you are. I intend to call security."

"That will not be necessary, Dr. Mingchang," the gravely voice retorted. "They will only bring me back to you."

Mingchang looked in bewilderment at the shriveled up man in the too large pants, puckered around his waist by a well-weathered belt.

After a long moment Chen said in his normal voice, "It's me Dr. Mingchang, HB-23."

A slow smile crept across the face that rarely used that set of muscles. Nodding she said, "Oh, this is excellent, most excellent. I have someone who must see your little act."

Chen was not surprised when several minutes later he was told to walk past an office that had "Head Of Security" on the placard beside it. The result was the same. Chen was returned to his room where he was told to clean himself up and put on normal clothes. After that, he was returned to the security department so everyone there could see the before and after appearance. A stern man, obviously the one in charge, nodded and gave a genuinely appreciative thanks to Dr. Mingchang.

As he followed the doctor back to their wing, the obvious conclusion occurred to Chen. This was not simply some abstract espionage case in some far away complex. Someone important had escaped from this Institute. A test subject. Unwittingly he had done what none of them had expected. He had, as it were, hidden in plain sight. It was equally obvious that if he had wanted to walk out the front door he could have.

---

Back in her office, Dr. Mingchang looked at Chen. "You have done well. I am now thinking of another question that I know others are asking at this very moment. And, that is, how does a severely crippled man get along out there?" she asked with a slight twitch of her head indicating the outside world.

"You are asking, how does a crippled man who is not really crippled manage to live in society, where does he go, how does he find work, that sort of thing."

"Yes, that is it precisely."

"The answer is simple. He doesn't. He assumes those looking for him will have figured out his first disguise." Chen did not mention anything about escaping, because he had not been told the subject had escaped from anywhere, only that he had disappeared. "The thing to figure out is what would be his next appearance."

It was apparent to Chen that these people were not accustomed to living in the real world of China. They lived in their closed pressure-cooker environment where food was served, rooms heated, clothes laundered, and all the rest. They were the elite who paid the price of their office by missing a large slice of life. Yes, the life of the masses was hard, but these people were in touch with reality. Hunger and pain were real, but so was the satisfaction of knowing they lived by their own wits and hands. Nothing that actually benefited the individual was a given. Anything you had, you had gotten by your own resources.

Looking a little embarrassed, Dr. Mingchang nodded. "Your thinking has merit. Proceed as you did before. See what you can come up with. If you need anything, be sure to ask."

---

Immediately after the noon meal, Dr. Hongi took Chen back down to the autopsy room. Chen knew what to expect, but as they entered, *the fixture* was not to be seen. Instead, there was a large block of wood on one of the tables. Hongi produced a small handgun from his pocket.

"Do you know what this is?" Hongi asked.

"It is a gun," Chen answered without emotion.

"Yes. It is a revolver. See this cylinder has six holes in it for six bullets." He proceeded to spin the cylinder and showed how each time the trigger was pulled the cylinder advanced a position ready to fire the next bullet. Then he dumped a box of cartridges out on the table and put six in the holes. He then proceeded to shoot the six small caliber slugs into the block. After this he spun the cylinder again and pulled the trigger. Nothing happened. He then removed the empty casings from the cylinder.

"Do you understand how this works?"

Chen nodded.

"Good." Handing the gun to Chen he said, "Now, let me see you load it."

Chen selected six bullets, slipped them into the six holes, and snapped the cylinder into firing position. He slowly lowered the hammer into the safe position.

"That is very good," Hongi said. "Pull the hammer back and spin the cylinder like I did."

Chen complied.

"Now shoot five times into the block."

This Chen did.

Hongi nodded. Watching Chen intently he said, "Now pull the hammer back and spin the cylinder." This done Hongi said, "Aim the barrel of the gun at the side of your head and pull the trigger one time.

Without hesitation, Chen did as he was told. Click was all that happened.

"You can remove the gun from the side of your head, and point it at the block."

This done, Hongi said, "Now pull the trigger." Click.

"Again." Bam!

"Now, you can give me the gun."

Chen handed it to Hongi.

"This is an interesting game, don't you think? We shall play it again one day."

Unemotionally Chen replied, "If the cylinder had stopped two places later I would be dead."

"You are to do as you are told at all times. That is all you must know. We are finished for today. I will take you back to your quarters."

# — 5 —

With Hongi gone, Chen walked to the window and absentmindedly looked out. Everything was hazy. They were having an all too frequent sandstorm. The winds blew in from the desert to the northwest and Beijing was blanketed with a fine choking dust. Dying before his time from air pollution was not on Chen's mind. Dying in the next few days at the hand of that mad man was. It was imperative that he escape. Human or not, he had the animal instinct to live. He walked back to his little table and sat in the chair. The table now supported a computer terminal. This had been supplied after he asked for permission to use the Internet. It did not have Internet access. Rather, it only allowed him to see a limited number of databases. But, it had given him a feel for how the computer system at the Medical Institute operated. With his elbows on the table, he rested his forehead in his hands. In pain, he realized that he had closed his only avenue of escape. Making the disguise to look like a cripple had been nothing but an assignment, almost a game, to him. With it, he had thrown away his chance to live. If animals experienced despair, then he felt like a trapped animal.

He was further irritated by a knock at his door. It was an orderly there to take his pendant for a brief time. He was beginning to wonder if the doctors were more interested in that device than in him.

Alone again, he threw himself on his bed and looked at the ceiling. Eventually, he became interested in a spider on its web that extended between the light fixture and the wall. How did that little bug manage that, he wondered? He looked at the ways it could be done and come up with nothing. If he had been asked about it, he would have said it was impossible. Yet, there it was. Suddenly the dawn broke across the landscape of his consciousness. He was as smart as a spider. He had a problem to solve just like that little animal. His problem had a solution and he'd find it.

He got up and started pacing the floor thinking of everything he knew about the Medical Institute. It was little enough, but he had made no effort to learn anything either. He intended to use his computer terminal to learn what he could about this Institute, magnet vortex technology, and anything else that even remotely connected to his situation.

In the middle of his strategy planning, Chen was interrupted by another knock on the door. An orderly told him to follow. With some trepidation, he hoped he was not being called to another meeting with Dr. Hongi. He was taken to an office down the hall from Dr. Mingchang's. She was there with a man.

"Hu, this is Seng Kejian of the MSS," she began. "He would like to ask you some questions as a follow-up to what you told me about the missing man problem." As an after thought, she produced his pendant which he took and, putting the chain around his neck, let it fall behind his shirt.

Kejian began by producing and, in a practiced fashion, flipping open an impressive picture identification and badge. "I'm with the MSS and I expect your cooperation." There was no reason for this display other than the habitual use of its intimidating capacity made the user dependant upon it.

In the second the credential was visible Chen concentrated his attention on it since he had never had the dubious honor of being under the eye of the MSS. It was a leather wallet affair with a fold in the middle. One half had a picture ID, and on the other was a silver badge.

"Mr. Kejian has asked to speak to you alone," Dr. Mingchang said a little apprehensively. "He will inform me when your meeting is over." Dr. Mingchang left the room.

The wielder of this bureaucratic sword looked singularly disjunct from its power. This was the most emaciated, sickly looking man Chen had ever seen. His taught facial skin accentuated his cheekbones. His sunken black eyes beset with dark rings looked like two holes burned in a blanket. His voice was sharp and his demeanor gave the impression he blamed Chen for his physical state.

"We are looking for a man at large in our society," Kejian began. "You have shown some initiative in demonstrating how he may have . . . " here he paused as if searching for an noncommittal phrase . . . "eluded our surveillance."

A nice euphemism for having escaped your clutches, Chen thought.

"If I understand correctly, you think he would have disguised himself as a cripple to lose himself, but immediately revert to yet another deception. Explain your reasoning and his likely present appearance."

For the first time since waking up from the memory experiment, Chen felt true, deep anger. It was obvious this worm of a man had succeeded in his job precisely because he had an appalling ability to make those before him grovel. With difficulty, he fought the impulse to submit. "I never suggested this man used the appearance of a cripple to disappear. I merely demonstrated that with simple tools and supplies, that can be purchased without raising suspicion, a man could change his appearance. He may have disappeared looking like a policeman, and now looks like a cripple. Is there any reason to assume one disguise would be preferred over another for his initial disappearance?"

"You do not ask the questions, I do!" Chen's interrogator shot back.

"Yes sir," Chen responded meekly.

The interview went on for an hour. It was ludicrous as far as Chen could see. Surely, the MSS and other police agencies were far more experienced then he in locating someone who was trying to avoid detection.

After the session, Chen was returned to his room. Kejian's line of questioning led strongly to the conclusion the missing man had escaped from a hospital or similar institution. Since the MSS had made a point of speaking to him, he began to suspect they believed they might learn something unique about how a hubot thought as if it were a hubot who had escaped. Since he was desperately looking for a way to escape himself, it would be helpful to learn if they had made another successful hubot. The autopsy room might have records of the HBs that didn't make it and were sent out for cremation. This evening he would go to the shop and from there sneak down the hall and look for records in the autopsy room. If he found there were more surviving hubots, it might mean one of them had escaped.

Chen had developed some ideas about what he would do after he was out of the Institute, but none that he liked. He spent part of the remainder of the day trying to devise something to tell his bosses if they continued on the missing man theme. Along the way, he searched the computer for a variety of subjects. He informed Dr. Mingchang he would be spending some time in the shop that evening, to which she readily agreed.

At eight o'clock, he went to begin work on an idea that had come to him. At ten o'clock, he went to the autopsy room. The records indicated there were many hubot failures. The HBs shipped to the crematorium did not go in order indicating that some of them lasted longer than others, some nearly as long as he had. However, from HB-28 on they were all in order. This indicated the test program had taken a turn for the worse. The shipping sheet left two unaccounted for, himself and HB-27. He wondered if perhaps HB-27 had escaped and that was the reason for the MSS interest.

With a sudden pang of fear bordering on despair, Chen thought that if the past were any indication of the future, both he and twenty-seven would show up on the shipment log in time. That thought sparked an idea, and immediately a ray of hope. As he stood there, piece after piece fell into place. It was still rough, but he had a plan, and a renewed will to live. Did that mean he was human? Or, was it simply what a caged animal felt when it found the door unlatched and gained its freedom? Not so fast. He had to pull himself back. He wasn't out yet, and getting out of the Institute was only the first step.

Back in the shop, he applied himself with a concentration and fervor he didn't know he possessed. Finally, he had to hide his work and get back to his quarters before he fell asleep. The next morning an orderly had to roust him out for his first meal of the day. To his chagrin, they had a full schedule for him this day. Dr. Mingchang spent several hours with him on memory tests, and mood assessments. He was tired from the night before and she mentioned he seemed less concentrated than he had been. He shrugged it off and she said no more about it. Then another man, elderly, and appearing wise in the ways of the world, was introduced to him for "diplomatic" problems. To Chen's relief Hongi did not appear.

After his evening meal, Spartan but adequate, he thought about his real problem. It was taking shape, but he absolutely needed one item to make it work. He had thoroughly searched the shop and not found it. That evening he resolved to go to the shop and from there go to search the autopsy room. It was his only hope. After that, he would have to return to his room and get some sleep. To his delight, he found what he needed almost immediately. An instant camera. Obviously, it was used to document certain findings during autopsies. With relief, he went back and slept well.

The next day his mentor with diplomatic problems was on the Beckon case, the second man to employ it. They had a real thing about that guy. Their main concern was finding out who he worked for, and to see if there were any possibility of turning him into a double agent for them. However, without knowing his allegiances, that would be difficult. Chen was given access to a rather large body of sensitive information in the hope that his ability to remember masses of data would permit him to put together connections they had missed. It was interesting work and Chen applied himself.

This went on for a few days where he saw Dr. Mingchang only briefly in the morning and Hongi not at all. He assumed they had a new hubot to concentrate on. In fact, he seemed to be nearly forgotten. Each evening he returned to the shop to work on his project, now nearing completion, and none too soon. During the afternoon, he was told he had a meeting with Dr. Hongi at ten the following morning. So, this was it. That evening he went to the autopsy room. He was struck with feelings of relief and dismay to see the room had been used during the day. There was a wooden crate with a body bag in it prepared for removal with HB-36 on the tag. They were having a run of bad luck, But, HB-27 still had not appeared on the log. The plan he had prepared relied on a shipment to the crematorium the following morning. The first in a series of events that had to work in his favor had fallen into place. He took some pictures of himself with the instant camera. He chose the best two and put the others and the scrap materials in the bag he had prepared. The tools selected and hidden previously were collected and put in the place he had planned.

At a little before eleven, he went to the computer terminal in the autopsy room. He had seen Hongi log on to the Internet once, and from his finger movements remembered his password. He only hoped Hongi was not logged on at this time. It went okay as far as he could tell. As he had expected, using Hongi's password he could get into databases with critical information that had been locked out to him. The most important was the guest logs of the major hotels in Beijing. He started with the Hilton and had what he needed in a few minutes. As a precaution he tried one more in case there was something wrong with the Hilton like a fire, drug bust, whatever. If it could happen, it would. When all was in order he returned to his room. Through it all, he was much calmer than he had expected to be.

———————————

As five o'clock the following morning approached, Chen was up and dressed in the clothes he normally wore. They had allowed him street clothes because it was thought everyone's purpose would be served if he were given the sense that he was more of an employee of the state than an inmate. This was yet another attempt get him to lower his guard and reveal that he was human rather than a smart animal. It also made the relationship with those from outside the Institute that used his services less strained.

He knew a guard walked the halls at regular intervals. He left his room at a time to avoid any meeting and the inevitable questions. Several minutes later, he was in the autopsy room. The crate with HB-36 in it was exactly as it had been the night before. Quickly he took a second box laid it by the first on the handcart and put a body bag in it. There was a good supply of bags as though they anticipated a lot more failures. The dispatch form had one line filled in. He added another. He took the large felt tip pen from the table and marked another tag, HB-23. The string of the tag was affixed to the zipper pull on the body bag exactly as on the other one. The note he had prepared went in an inconspicuous place as planned. Almost running, he retrieved the package he had stashed. The clock on the wall said five-forty when he heard a sound. Quickly he climbed into the box and slipped into the bag. Twisting around, he made a slit in the back of the bag and stuck a plastic tube through it. He laid down, slid the box cover over him, and pulled the zipper closed. The bags were meant to be nearly airtight when fully zipped so the tube was needed for breathing.

He heard the door on the other side of the room open. This was it. Soon he felt the movement of the cart. The wheels bumped as they went over seams in the floor. Getting the hang of breathing wasn't as easy as he had anticipated. He found he had to exhale out of the tube too or the bag stated to inflate. The first half breath of air consisted of exhaled air that had to be sucked in before he got to the new air. He could hear muffled voices as he was loaded into the truck, being tipped this way and that. At one moment, he thought they might drop him.

His breathing was interrupted by the sharp sounds of a hammer. Someone was nailing the lid on. A total of four nails. Okay, he could handle that. At least they weren't screws. Screws would be the worst. He had planned on the possibility of nails, and it wasn't all bad if his plan were to work. The back door of the panel van slammed shut. Moments later, the vibration of the motor was felt, followed by the sensation of acceleration.

Now, the biggest risk of his plan was in play. He counted heartbeats as a timing mechanism. He estimated twenty minutes of driving to the mortuary, if the driver did not deviate. Deviation was what Chen counted on. On the logs, he had seen pickups at a few minutes before six most times. In that, today was normal. The returned certification of receipt was signed showing arrival at the crematorium shortly after eight. His plan hinged on his assumption that the driver stopped some place along the way, perhaps for breakfast, or maybe to meet with a woman. He had all along accepted the possibility that the driver would go directly to his destination, the boxes fired immediately, and the certification signed later when the supervisor arrived. In that event, it was possible he could make noise and get out before being roasted alive. That would mean he'd be returned to the Institute. Or, he would not be heard, and cooked.

Between breathing and counting heartbeats, he lost count so many times he didn't know where he was. There was no back light on the time display of his pendant so that was of no use. It seemed they had traveled twice as long as necessary to get to the destination when the van stopped, and the vibration of the motor ceased. The front door slammed. The air in the box outside the bag was getting bad. He counted a minute's worth of beats. Okay. He got the package open and felt for the craft knife. It was more cramped working in the bag than he had expected, but he managed to slit open the bag. Next, he got the small flat bar used to open crates and began working at the lid. The driver had done a good job with the nails. Exerting himself he realized how well sealed the box was—he was running out of air fast. He felt along the corner between the wall and the lid looking for a flaw in the boards where his pry bar could gain purchase. With nearly his last try, he managed to wedge the bar into a defect and produce a crack of light. He pressed his mouth to the slit and took a deep breath, then another. He worked the bar again. The nearest nail complained with a rasping creak. Cool air flooded over him as he methodically worked the lid off. Sitting up, he realized he was soaked in perspiration. Fearing the driver's return he quickly sorted out what he would leave in the box, things that would burn, and left the rest in the bag. Using the pry bar as a hammer, he nailed the cover back on.

Glancing out the windows in the rear doors, he saw the narrow street of a residential neighborhood. Satisfied he was not at the mortuary, he ran his hands through his black hair to remove the unkempt look, and shook his shirt free of his skin where the sweat pasted it to him. As he settled down to wait, he went through what would happen next.

The waiting was hard, though it gave him a chance to dry out. It was light enough in the rear of the van so he could keep track of the time using his pendant. A few minutes before eight o'clock, he heard a key in the lock and the driver got in. Chen crouched behind the front seat. After they had driven for a minute, he could tell by the sounds and the movement of the vehicle that they were on a main thoroughfare. Getting up on his knees and leaning over the passenger side seat he said, "Just keep driving normally, and you will be all right." The man jerked his head.

Chen said in as authoritative a voice as he could, "Watch the road. I am with the MSS." As the traffic cleared momentarily, he extended his hand across the passenger seat holding his badge. He flipped it open in imitation of the agent who had questioned him. The MSS identification was the patient work of all those nights in the shop. He had remembered the badge of the MSS officer, and duplicated it as nearly as he could. In this case, it would pass without close scrutiny. The big test was yet to come.

The driver glanced at the credential. Chen snapped it shut and withdrew his arm. "I am going to get into the passenger seat beside you. Just keep driving." Chen could see the driver's complexion had gone a shade whiter. Few were the people who had not engaged in one illegal activity or another. A person never knew when these activities would cross paths with big time operators who would not hesitate to let some small fish take the fall for them.

"Relax," Chen said. "You are not be in any trouble from me if you listen carefully. We are working on an espionage case back at the Institute where you made this pickup. The people we are after are engaged in activities that will warrant the death penalty if they are found guilty. They are very resourceful and desperate, so don't let them draw you into their schemes."

"If they are sending stuff to someone at the mortuary where I work, I know nothing of it. I only do as I'm told." The driver was on the verge of breaking down.

Chen had not expected such an extreme reaction. He responded based on the desperation he began to feel. "No, no. You did not listen." Chen fought to keep his voice firm and professional as if the man's reaction were to be expected. "You are in no trouble, and neither is anyone at the place where you work. The people we are after use some of these boxes to destroy incriminating evidence. Cremation. Very thorough, very clever, don't you think?" Wow! That's pretty good, Chen thought. "But, now *we* have the evidence. Don't you see?"

The driver hit the brakes extra hard at a yellow light as it went to red. He let out a long breath. "Okay. Yes. That *is* very clever of them." Chen understood that whether or not the driver believed it didn't matter as long as his attention was off him.

Chen let the man gather his composure. When they started to move again he said, "We have removed something from one of the boxes in the back, so . . . oh, make a right at the next corner. By driving another kilometer you can help me to meet with my partner." The driver made the turn. "When you reach your destination one box will be lighter than when you loaded it. No one is to open either one. While mentioning as little of this to others as possible, burn them both as soon as you can. It is likely someone from the Institute will call asking if the boxes have been cremated. If they are not, it will produce complications. Doing the job quickly will put you in the clear. Now a left, and stop at the next corner. The weight will have to be falsified, so your supervisor may have to become involved. However, the fewer that know the better. Did you understand what I told you?"

This street was crowded so the driver inched along. The relief he felt was evident in his voice, "Yes. I understand."

Chen, again in a gruff voice, said, "Good. Remember, you are one of the few people who knows about what is happing. Letting you in on it was unavoidable. We will need time to examine the materials we removed to connect others to the plot so you must keep knowledge of this from getting out. Tell no one. If certain people are tipped off, we will know who to come to." He paused again to let the words sink in and then in a pleasant voice said, "Now stop here and I will leave you." As Chen was about to step out, he said, "You are serving your country, as is your duty." Chen got out, closed the door, and immediately blended into the crowd of humanity.

Glancing over his shoulder, he saw the van turn on to the main artery. As it disappeared from view he slowed his pace and leaned against a building. The stress of this business is intense, he thought. At least I'm out, but for how long, who knows. For a robot, though, I'm doing pretty good. This caused a smile to cross his face, the first in a long time.

He had managed to filch a few yuan here and there in the time since he decided to escape so he stopped at a street vendor and bought a plate of food, and a bottle of water. As he ate, he thought of the Institute and how there would be an uproar when he wasn't there. His mind saw it as a cartoon building with puffs of smoke emanating from it, not as people hurrying about looking for him. And, just as importantly, concocting stories to protect them from blame. He was a little disturbed that he felt no association with any people there, good or bad.

# — 6 —

When he had eaten, Chen started walking the half-kilometer to the Hilton Hotel. He took his time because he wanted to be sure his target had left his room for the day, and for the hotel lobby to be less congested. In sight of the hotel, he loitered until eight-thirty all the time rehearsing in his mind what he would say. He was encouraged by how well it had gone with the driver. This did not fool him into thinking the hotel would be as easy. The driver had in all probably never encountered the MSS, though he would have heard of its reputation. The manager of the hotel would be different. It was part of his job to deal with the authorities at all levels.

Finally, the time was right. He had a lot to do before ten o'clock when he was scheduled to meet with Hongi. For certain, he would be missed then, if the hunt for him had not begun already. He mechanically put one foot in front of the other. As he approached the entry to the Hilton he clenched his teeth and set his face to the hardest most indifferent expression he could muster. There were a half-dozen taxi drivers standing about in small groups waiting for fares. A few of them looked his way. The uniformed doorman courteously opened the door. Chen nodded curtly in return. As soon as he was through the door, he wondered if he should have even acknowledged the doorman.

As Chen walked across the wide lobby, he could not keep from admiring the opulence of the setting. The spacious reception area gave a feeling of openness and freedom. He swallowed hard as he approached the front desk. A young uniformed woman greeted him.

"I want to speak with the manager," he said flatly.

"May I ask the nature of your business," the woman said pleasantly, but not as a question.

Chen drew in a breath and slowly let it out to still his jitters, but hoping it came off as a sign of boredom merging with impatience.

Leaning over the counter he said in a low voice, "It is police business, and rather urgent. Now, is he available?"

"The hotel manager will not be starting his business day for another hour, but the shift manager is here. If you wish, I will call him."

That was a dumb way to start, Chen thought. He imagined that, of course, the actual manager of the hotel would live in a lavish suite on the top floor, and would never meet with anyone, in his equally lavish office, until they had gone through a series of underlings.

Chen gave a slight smirk and replied, "I will start there. Call him."

The woman pushed a few keys on the phone pad and said, "Mr. Chow, there is someone from the police here to see you."

Out of the corner of his eye, he saw heads turn. Damn that woman. A routine person in the hotel lobby had become a public figure. They would remember him. The man arrived and Chen asked if they could speak privately for a few minutes. Mr. Chow showed him to a modestly furnished office to the side of the front desk.

As soon as the door was closed, Chen looked right into the eyes of the manager as he reached for his badge. "This is a most serious case. I am from the MSS . . . " By this time he had the badge out. He casually let it fall open a little out of the line of sight of the man before him. Chow broke eye contact with Chen and looked intently at the credential. "We must move quickly to make connections to several members of a well organized group managed by the CIA of the United States. I am expecting your prompt . . . "

"I have seen MSS badges before," Chow broke in, "and they looked different . . . "

"The badge design changes periodically to prevent counterfeiting. This is a recent issue . . . I am expecting your prompt assistance. Do you understand?" With that, Chen snapped the badge closed and returned it to his pocket. "We are endeavoring to alert as few people as possible to what is happening today." He left that hanging in the air to give the impression that this was the culmination of a long investigation. "Well?"

Chow nodded.

"Good. I need access to the rooms of two of your guests, and to the personal safe in each room. It is not my intent to remove anything—these are small fish—but I must learn their contacts. Here are the two guests." Chen showed a slip of paper to Chow, but did not give it to him.

Chow seemed to recover from his initial shock. Though he had seemed unshaken, his hands trembled. "Oh, certainly. I should be able to get the information we need from my terminal here." Turning he sat at the desk and started inputting commands. Periodically he jotted down a number on a sip of paper. "This is all we need. Come with me."

When the safe of the first room was open, Chen told the manager to wait in the hall and alert him if anyone were coming. Swiftly he went through the contents of the safe. Yes, exactly what he needed: an American passport, Visa and Corporate American Express credit cards, a small wad of American dollars, and some yuan. No point in pushing his luck. He stuffed these in his pockets, closed the safe, and made sure it was locked.

Returning to the hall giving the appearance of making some notes on a small pad of paper, he saw the manger waiting. "I had my choice of the two. This was the correct one. The case is moving quickly and time is short. Please accompany me to the lobby for appearance sake. It will look better for you." After that, Chen remained aloof. The man tried to start some small talk in the elevator to which Chen responded, "After I have left, you must inform the staff at the front desk that this was a minor matter of a pickpocket operating among your foreign guests. Do you understand that?"

Mr. Chow nodded.

At the door to the street Chen said a perfunctory thank you and hailed one on the waiting taxis.

He stayed in the taxi only a few blocks, paid, and got out. He walked a block, got in a second taxi and relaxed a little. He directed the driver to the neighborhood where the application forms at the Institute said he had formerly lived. As he had hoped, some of it began to look vaguely familiar so he asked to be dropped off.

Coming out of a store after buying a few common supplies, his eyes fell on a restaurant across the street that had failed. He knew the place. It was comforting to realize that at least some of his former memories were coming back. From the alley behind the building, he knew he could gain entry. He needed a place to work unobserved.

Inside he found a rag and wiped off a table and chair. He pulled out the American passport in the name of Zhu Sun who lived in Chicago. Examining it carefully, he could see his job would be difficult. There were several anti-counterfeiting strategies built into it. At first, he felt fortunate in that it was due to expire in less than a year. This meant the picture of Mr. Sun was nine years out of date. After due consideration, he concluded he could not pass himself off as Sun. He would have to put his picture over Sun's. Then, he would go to a nearby shop he had seen from the taxi where the window poster offered self-service laminating. There he'd put a layer of lamination over the whole page that happened to be the inside of the front cover. If it didn't work, it was the end of the line for him.

There was scrollwork that lapped over the top of Sun's photo. Nice touch, he thought, and hard to duplicate. His picture was certainly as good as the one on the passport so that was okay. With a pen he duplicated the blue scrollwork as well as he could.

In the store that offered laminating, he said he had a special medical identification card he wanted to laminate. This was accepted without question. The attendant used a blank card to demonstrate the procedure. When alone Chen carefully laid the materials together and held his breath as the machine sealed the laminate on the passport. Opening the foil cover over the laminated page, he involuntarily let out a groan. The photo had slipped. The passport was ruined. He felt his life ebbing away. The sensation he had in the dark cremation box a short time before engulfed him. It had gone so well up until now.

His mind raced. There was the possibility he could try the MSS badge on the second hotel, but it was a long shot. The Institute would be looking for him. He doubted the ruse of suicide would last long. With his head hanging, he tried to focus on his situation as the black continued to close in. He was not prepared to live under cover for even a day, let alone the indefinite future. He had done no planning for that. Speed and success at every step were vital to his plan.

Without knowing what was happening, he felt a tug at his sleeve. A small man of many summers past sixty, with a thin gray beard, and watery gray eyes was looking at the corner of what Chen had clutched in his right hand. "Frequently the first try is not successful," he said in a soothing ancient sounding voice. "If it is a particularly valued photograph you tried to laminate and it didn't work, I have two talented assistants who might be able to recover it. We would have to charge a fee, but we would be honored if you would accept our assistance." Ever so gently, Chen was guided by the man through a curtained door into a stock room. Without knowing how, Chen was sitting in a chair beside a small table.

"May I see your photograph?" the man asked.

Chen's head hung so his chin nearly touched his chest. "Not a photograph," he uttered with despair in his voice. "I am a dead man walking."

He released the passport so the rolled up document with a dark blue cover lay on the table.

"May I see?" the old man asked again.

"Why not? Nothing matters now. Call the police and make an end to it."

The old man looked at the passport. If Chen had been watching, he would have seen an old eyebrow lift. "Your situation seems dire, and as before, I offer to assist you if you tell me your story."

Chen did not respond. The old man snapped his fingers in front of him.

It was like a shot. Mechanically Chen lifted his head and was alert. "You may not want to know my story after you hear. I am the result of an experiment at the Medical Research Institute. They are killing men and bringing them back to life as animals, smart animals. However, not really animals, more like human robots. They cannot seem to strike the right balance. Either the subjects are dumb animals, or are still human. As far as I can tell I was the closest to what they wanted, with the exception of one other who may not even exist, but I infer that he does. All failures, human or animal, are killed. The fact that I escaped shows that I am a failure in the human direction, though not fully human. If I am returned I will be terminated."

The intrigue felt by the old man was painted in his expression. "In what way are you not human? Allowing for your situation as you describe it, you seem human enough."

"On the positive side my memory is vastly expanded. They estimate I can remember at least a hundred times more than the number of my brain cells would allow. This puzzles them. On the other side, I do not seem to have the ability to refuse an order. See this," Chen said holding up his finger. "I was told to chop off my finger to prove I was totally obedient. I did it without hesitation. Yet, against their wishes, though not against any direct order, I escaped. The memories I have of what it is to be human apparently are left from before the experiment, so if I am an android I know how to pretend to be human. All memories of my family are gone. The forms I filled out before the test tell of a mother and a younger brother. I dare not contact them, or they will be killed, if they are not already dead . . . if they ever existed."

The curiosity in the old man was pushing him to ask things he should not ask in his line of work. "If I may, how *did* you escape. That Institute is like a vault."

Offhandedly Chen replied, "I committed suicide, and had myself cremated this morning."

The old man drew back a bit. Then his eyes started to smile. This was no ordinary man sitting before him. "That was very inventive. Very final, no remains. There will be no manhunt. Where did you get this passport?" He was over the line anyway so he pushed ahead.

"I took it out of the safe in the hotel room of Mr. Zhu Sun."

"How did your do that?"

"The hotel manager opened the room door and the safe for me." This seemed so elementary Chen was getting bored.

"And that, why would he do that?"

"This." Chen pulled the MSS ID from his pocket and tossed it in front of the old man.

Opening it, he sucked in a breath and said, "Young man, you have brass balls as big as coconuts!" He shook his head. This was one thing nobody, no matter how desperate they were, tried to do.

"Is there anything else you got from Mr. Sun's safe?" the old man asked.

Chen dumped the contents of his pockets on the table. To his surprise, the old man ignored the yuan and dollars, and snatched the credit cards. "How long ago did your get these cards?"

"Less than thirty minutes. Sun spends long days at a food plant."

"You must come with me." As soon as the man saw the "means of payment," the atmosphere changed from that of an intriguing story to business.

The man rose and took Chen by the arm. Pushing on a storage rack the whole thing slid to the side and the old man guided Chen into the next room. The wall panel slid back into place. Chen now understood the old man's interest. This was a counterfeiting business, and from the computers, cameras, and other paraphernalia, it had been in operation for a long time. With truly professional help like this man could offer there was still a chance.

The old man handed Chen's MSS ID to a young woman. "Li, radically dispose of this."

She took it and looking at it said, "Hmm . . . Yes. I expect so."

"She will shred it, shred the shreds, and burn what is left."

In minutes Li returned from an adjoining room. Holding up the Visa and American Express cards, the man said, "Li, time to go shopping.

These are less than a half hour old, owner doesn't know they're missing, and gone for the day."

She smiled, "Shopping spree! Can I keep something?"

"Only if it doesn't show." This was the standard warning. In this country people could not be seen as having more goods than the pay from their job could justify. Being assistant manager in an establishment that provided copying services would not warrant a diamond bracelet. This "back room" had connections with high-end retail stores where they would buy expensive merchandise with stolen credit cards and not take delivery. The money from the transaction was split even up.

Turning his attention to Chen the old man said, "And, now Mister . . . what do I call you?"

"They call me Hu. That is short for hubot, which is a contraction of human robot." Chen made a shrugging gesture. "That's what I am I guess. Hua Chen is my name from the forms."

"All right, Mr. Chen, why the United States? How did you pick Zhu Sun's room, or was that an accident?"

"Not an accident. It must be the U.S. There is a man there I must find. I must leave today. They will figure out that I was not cremated soon enough. I must call United Airlines and change Zhu Sun's return flight to the soonest one available. He is having a family emergency so must go home early. I need his passport with my picture on it."

"It is difficult getting into that country after that incident with the World Trade Towers in 2001. I can fix the passport so you will leave China easily enough, but you might have trouble in the U.S. You have been very inventive so far. You will make it. But, we need the credit cards to change the airline reservation, and Li has them."

"I remember everything I see. I will tell you all the information on the credit cards."

The old man called a middle-aged man working at a computer in the corner of the room and spoke rapidly in hushed tones. In minutes they had new passport quality photos of Chen, and his signature."

"There is the matter of luggage. You will need some sign that you are a legitimate business traveler."

"My son is ill so I must rush home. I am having a colleague arrange to have my luggage packed and sent by Federal Express to my home. I need a brief case or small bag that I would have taken to the job with me. What do you think? Will that work?"

The old man smiled, "It'll work if you believe it enough to make it work, and I think you can do it. We'll come up with what you need." The business of providing false documents usually meant the recipients were desperate in one way or another. The key to his survival, as the supplier, had been to accurately size up which ones would succeed. If he sensed they would fail, get caught, and be forced to tell where they had gotten the counterfeit goods, he refused to serve them. This man would succeed, at least as far as getting out of China, of that he was certain.

# — 7 —

Dr. Fei Hongi opened the door of Dr. Mingchang's office without knocking and strode in with his usual air of superiority. Expecting to see Chen setting passively on the chair beside the desk taking instructions from her, he stopped short. In as many blinks, he snapped his head to the left and the right taking in the whole room.

"He's not here," he said in a tone between a question and a statement.

"Of course not. He is scheduled for more of your *tests*." She said it with venom in her voice. "He has been working on a project for the MSS in the shop. Have you looked there?"

"Just came from there. I've had two orderlies scouring the place, too. Your door is normally open, so I thought with it closed you were attending to personal matters. When we couldn't find him anywhere else, it became obvious this was where he had to be. When's the last time you saw him?"

"Yesterday afternoon about four . . . you're not telling me we lost another one!" She was off her chair and out the door. Dr. Hongi hurried to catch up.

"So, you know where he is? How about letting me in on it?"
Shooting a glance at him as they started down a staircase, "No, I don't. But, he's smart. If he could fool us with his disguise as a cripple, he could do it again. How, I don't know, but the answer is in the shop."

They spent twenty minutes looking in every cabinet, wastepaper basket, nook and cranny. There was no sign of any project. "Got an idea," Hongi said. Now she was hurrying to catch him as he headed to the autopsy room. It was shinny and spotless as it always was. Again, they went through all the drawers, and storage cabinets.

"Oh! Look at this!" Mingchang screeched. She was holding the dispatch log for bodies going to the crematorium. Hongi looked over her shoulder at her finger pressed beneath the entry for HB-23.

"The bastard sneaked out in one of those crates. Okay, he can't have gotten far." He opened a file drawer and snatched out a folder with invoices from the mortuary. In a second, he punched in the phone number printed at the top of the form. "Hello, who is in charge of cremations? This is Dr. Hongi at the Medical Research Institute. Yes, that's right. Yes, put him on." After a pause. "Yes, that's right, Dr. Hongi. Did you process two crates this morning for cremation? Yeah, I bet you did. Did you personally handle them? You did? One was empty, am I right?" Another pause. "You're sure? Both the normal weight. I see. You charge by the kilogram, so you weigh them. There's no mistake? Yes, yes, I know our boxes are rough. They limit our budgets. But . . . yes, I see. No one else would think of using something so cheap. Okay, okay, thank you."

The look on Mingchang's face showed she understood what Hongi had learned. He sank into the swivel chair in front of the desk pressed up against the wall. She pulled up a stool and sat down. Both minds were racing to figure how to cover themselves. She said, "He was our best result by far, and so healthy. He had a complete physical a few days ago. Failure of a vital organ would be unlikely, and darn it, we don't have an autopsy." Medical doctors always did the autopsies. That was part of the scientific data collected from each of the subjects. It was important to know if the magnetic vortex resonator harmed the rest of the body as it did its work on the brain. A human robot with a damaged or sickly body was pointless.

Dr. Mingchang paced about the room. "Why would he do it?" She said it repeatedly in a drum beat cadence with her steps. Finally, her eyes focused in a folded paper pinched between the back of a small tool chest and the wall. Curiously she tugged the paper free of its perch and unfolded it.

After scanning the sheet, she read deliberately out loud. "You want to see how long I will go before I fail one test. When I fail you will kill me. No more tests, no more games. No more cut off the finger. No more spin the gun and shoot my head. I will save you the trouble. I will save you the mess."

Mingchang's eyes flashed. "You bastard! You made him play Russian roulette! Well, you're going down, big guy."

Mingchang started for the door. Hongi said, "Wait!" as he sprang from his chair to stand in her route of egress. His mind raced at panic speed like it had not done since he was a boy being pursued by a gang of big kids. "He's not dead! Can't you see this is a put-up? He's too smart.

Why would he kill himself when he's sly enough to escape?" Hongi didn't have a clue as to how Chen managed to do it. He only knew that if this woman walked out of that door he'd be lucky to lose only his job.

"Okay, bright guy. How did he escape? The man at the crematorium told you they burned two boxes, both of normal weight. Am I right? If one had been filled with rocks he would have mentioned it." Without waiting for a reply she continued, "To pull that off he would have needed accomplices. He had no access to the phones, and we watched his use of the computer databases. I'm waiting. How did he do it?"

Hongi edged her to the swivel chair and he sat on the stool. He smiled a sort of conspiratorial smile as he started. "Okay, think about it. He spent a lot of time in the shop and there is not a thing to show for it. Isn't that strange? What do you think he was making?" Still Hongi had no hint of an answer. "What would he need?"

Dr. Mingchang started to seriously consider it. "He'd need something to open doors."

Hongi snapped onto the idea. Of course. Chen was making one or several keys. He pictured him working away for hours on a piece of brass with small files. If he got a good look at any key, he'd remember how to make it. "Yeah, you got it," he said slowly. "He was making . . . "

Mingchang finished his sentence, " . . . an MSS identification."

Bam! That was much better. What would open any door, any place, but on MSS ID. He snatched onto the idea as if he had known it all along. "That's obvious, isn't it?"

Then she continued, "That MSS agent that interviewed him showed his badge. I thought at the time, how pointless that was. *I* told Chen he was MSS. What else was needed?"

"It's the intimidation factor. They always do it. Once HB-23 had seen the ID, he knew what to make. It didn't matter that he couldn't reproduce the holograms, and all the other high-tech anti-forgery features. He only had to flash it at people, just like the real agent did to him."

Mingchang leaned back in the swivel chair and began to laugh, not a funny laugh, more of an hysterical laugh. "Not only did we fail to order him *not* to escape, we practically gave him an order *to* escape. After the cripple disguise, he knew what HB-27 had used to escape so he needed a different plan. Something in law enforcement was perfect. And, what was the only law enforcement ID he had seen since he got his perfect recall powers?"

Hongi answered the rhetorical question, "The MSS badge." After a pause, he continued, "And it's even better than that. If someone had stumbled on to his project, he had the perfect excuse. He was simply doing his assignment." Hongi was breathing a lot easier. This still left many unanswered questions. For starters, how had Chen managed to keep from being fried at the crematorium? What was in the box the weighed as much as a man? In addition, whatever it was had to leave the same ashes as a man. But, the woman seemed firmly off the idea that her subject was dead. He could see from her expression that she was acting like someone who had been told a family member was recovering from a critical illness.

This was going in the right direction but the momentum must not be lost. "So, what does a man on the lam do with an MSS badge?"

She was lost in thought, her fingertips slowly tapped the top of the desk in a rolling sequence. "No, no. That's too direct. It has to be more subtle. Since this is the second one that got away, we have to present the case that these are very special, rare creatures. Hanging onto them is like keeping track of a sack of frog's hair. It's a whole new thing that no one has ever encountered before, and we were caught off guard. This level of cleverness was never suspected."

Oh boy, Hongi thought. This girl is good. When it comes to raw survival skills, she's at the head of the pack.

---

The little team managed to get Chen on a flight leaving at four in the afternoon, grabbing one of the last two seats in "cattle class." As the Boeing 777 left the ground only fifteen minutes late, he relaxed a little. The cabin seating was arranged with two rows along the windows on each side and five in the center. Getting one of the last seats, he was in a center seat of the five. He watched the flight progress on the little view screen in the back of the seat in front of him. Heading northeast, they were staying over China. He would not feel the slightest bit safe until they were out of China's airspace. So intently was he watching their progress that he was irritated when his neighbor on the right nudged him and said in English, "Mister, you want to eat?" He looked at the boy of about twelve peering at him.

Chen blinked. It didn't register at first. Even though he had memorized an American English dictionary, and read several books of English grammar, retaining a copy of each page in his mind, he had not heard the language spoken in years. "Do you want dinner?" the boy asked again very deliberately. It was coming to him when the stewardess asked in Chinese. Chen was flustered as he was asked if the wanted the chicken or the beef. Meanwhile the boy reached up and flipped the lever that lowered Chen's tray.

"What are you wanting?" he asked the boy.

"I'm having the chicken," came the answer.

"I'm having the chicken," Chen said.

Chen had missed the drink cart that had come along before so the boy asked the stewardess if she would bring a bottle of water when she had time. Chen inhaled the food like a starving man. "You are nice for me," Chen said.

"You say it 'you are nice *to* me,'" the boy replied.

"Helpful to me, you. I know English words, but have no speaking chance. When traveling, you, me talk?" Chen said pointing to the boy and then to himself. "Very much help for me."

"Sure. It's a long flight and the movies aren't very good. My name is Jason Finley. What's yours?"

Pointing to himself Chen said, "Hua Chen is called me." They took it from there and spent two hours conversing. Finley commented on how fast Chen was catching on, although many times Finley's use of idioms threw Chen off. Jason had never heard the word "idiom" and Chen recited the dictionary meaning of it.

At times Finley said words that Chen did not understand and Finley did the best he could to spell it out. When they got close Chen would mention several spellings. Finley would say, "Yeah. I think that's it." Chen would proceed, much to Finley's amazement, to "read out" the dictionary definition as he had with idiom.

When Finley asked personal things Chen said he preferred to stay with didactic topics. Finley did not know that word. Chen said, "Is like the word pedantic."

"Never heard of that one either."

Chen paused a few seconds, then said, "Is academic a word you know? That also is what I mean."

"Yeah, I know that. How do you know all those words and the exact dictionary meanings?"

Chen sank back in his seat and quietly said, "Is a thing I learned." Chen was tired from the stress of the last day and could stay awake no longer. "I am awake for much time. Please, I sleep."

Two and a half hours later he awoke as Finley was returning to his seat. A woman had the aisle seat. "I'll be glad to get home and see my mother."

"That is not your mother?" Chen said pointing to the woman in the aisle seat.

"Oh no. I'm traveling alone."

"You are small for that?"

"I do it sometimes. My father works for the American Embassy in Beijing. I spend some time in China so I will learn your culture, and he thinks I'll learn the language. But, it's hard. I think it's easier for you to learn English than for me to learn Chinese. What do you think?"

Chen nodded. "Tell your father, I agree."

"May I ask you what brings you to the United States?"

Chen looked away as something occurred to him. Here he was traveling with a dark blue passport, and this kid knew that when he got on the plane he could not speak a sentence of English without messing it up. Finley would get off the plane with him and could easily end up in the same Immigration and Naturalization line. And, the kid was the son of some sort of diplomat. This could mean trouble in Chicago. Chen was unaware that there was always a separate, and short, line for diplomatic personnel.

Chen said, "I must ask if you please and the woman make space for me to get to the aisle. I must visit the toilet." As he ambled to the rear of the plane, he thought through what he could say. He guessed that since they were both traveling alone the kid would stick with him, if for no other reason than to help him. It was too painfully clear that Chen had never been out of China before. He occupied himself for some time figuring out how things worked in the toilet. It was all so new to him. After that, he stood in the rear of the plane to get the circulation in his legs going again.

As he worked it through, he started with the truth. First, he was escaping death. Second, he was going to tell secret information to Edmund Beckon, the CIA agent. He had convinced himself of Breckon's allegiance from the thick dossier.

When Chen returned to his seat Finley said, "I didn't mean to pry into your business. If you prefer not to tell me why you are traveling, I understand."

The boy looked so sincere it hurt Chen. "I go to see a man. I have information for him." That seemed innocent enough, Chen thought. Not having dealt with a boy for years, Chen forgot how naturally inquisitive they could be.

"Does he work for the government?"

Chen looked away again, and then said, "I think, might."

Finley leaned very close to Chen and whispered, "Are you a spy?"

Chen snapped his head and stared at Finley. "Not, ah, no. I am not!" and immediately looked away again, and sank as deeply in his seat as he could.

The flight was fourteen hours and they alternately snoozed and watched the viewer. At one point to get his mind off his plight, Chen began talking to Jason again.

"Tell some, if you can, of what you like at your home."

Jason wondered why his seatmate had been so quiet, but didn't mind telling something of his family. "Christmas is coming and I like that. My father will be home in a few days so we'll all be together. That's nice all by itself. We give each other gifts on Christmas morning. During the day, relatives and friends of my parents come over. But, I like summer best. That's when some of by favorite cousins visit. We have a good time together. My father cooks brats on the grill outside on the patio. I like them in a bun with sauerkraut."

Hua interrupted. "What is brat?"

"Brat, b-r-a-t. Maybe you don't have them in China."

"Brat is impudent, unruly child, usually with tattered clothing. You sure you eat them?"

"No, no. I mean brat. That's short for bratwurst, a kind of sausage."

"Oh. Words with same letters but say differently. That good. You not cannibal."

Jason laughed. "Our cultures sure are different. There are things I learned about China that are different, too."

It began to wear on Chen how disappointed the boy would be if he was found to be an imposter, traveling with a stolen passport, and hauled away by the police. Oddly, he began to fear the boy's disapproval more than what would happen to him. It had been so long since anyone had taken an interest in him other than as a laboratory curiosity that he was beginning to identify himself with the kid.

Suddenly, he remembered something from before the experiment. As a teenager, he had read a book called *Do Androids Dream of Electric Sheep*. In it, androids that melded in with earth's population were sought out for extermination. He did not remember why this was so. However, the test to see if a subject was a person or an android was to determine if they had empathy. He had just felt empathy for the boy. As quickly as his moment of hope came, it began to die. In the book humans manufactured the androids, and had not gotten the knack of adding empathy. Once again, he had to face the fact that he was different. He had started out with empathy and all the other things that made a human, and in the vortex treatment, presumably, some of those things were subtracted. It appeared empathy was one thing that was still with him.

Chen had been watching the line on the viewer that depicted the progress of the airplane from Beijing to Chicago grow longer until they were nearly at their destination. He pulled his pendant out from his shirt and looked at the time. It showed 0135. Leaning over to Jason, he asked, "What does the watch on your arm say the time in Chicago?"

Jason held up his wrist and said, "I always reset my watch to the destination time zone after the plane is in the air. It is now three-thirty-five in Chicago. We should be starting our descent pretty soon."

Chen looked at the pendant and saw no way of resetting the time.

Jason took an interest in the device and inquired as to what it was. "It doesn't look like any watch I've ever seen."

"Telling the time is part of it. This is, doctors say, to make me in fine health. Some part of it is to work with my energy field. Works at four times in a day. Not sure if it helps. Don't feel any different most times. Start at ten in morning in China. Now in United States, it must work at eight in morning and following at six hours after that."

Jason held out his hand and Hua leaned over and let him take it in his hand. "How do you reset the time? I don't see any little buttons to press. What are the gold tabs on the edges for?"

Hua pulled it back, not too hastily he hoped, and slipped it back behind his shirt. "Only doctor is able to change it. I keep track of time difference in my mind. Not difficult."

Finally, the drone of the engines that had been an invariant background sound for more than half a day changed. They were about to land.

The sounds of machinery could be heard as the flaps extended and finally the landing gear came down—with a thump. Chen stiffened and said a strange word. Finley looked at him and said, "Don't worry. That's the normal sound of the landing gear coming down."

Finley's parents had mentioned how this or that person was afraid to fly for one reason or another.

At the gate Chen sort of woke up and looked at Finley. "Okay now," was all he said.

———————

Drs. Mingchang and Hongi were seated in a small conference room when Seng Kejian entered. He reached into his sport coat that he wore without a tie, and pulled out his MSS ID casually flipping it open.

"Never do that again in this Institute," Mingchang said in an admonishing tone.

They both saw him start to bristle. "And, why not," he said expecting to go into a tirade about how they had better show respect.

Before he could say another word Dr. Mingchang cut in. "We have put together a plausible hypothesis that when you did that to HB-23 you gave him the means to escape. As part of his assignment to figure out what HB-27 would have done after he got out the door posing as a crippled man, HB-23 put together a realistic enough MSS badge to fool people if it were presented as you just did. He based it on his photographic mental image of your badge. Then he used it himself. We are dealing with an entirely new type of being here, and we had no idea they could be so resourceful." It took fifteen minutes of wrangling before Kejian could be brought to accept this conclusion.

Kejian's normally sour expression did not improve with his acceptance of their reasoning. He started to tongue-lash the two doctors about how keeping custody of the test subjects was their problem but Hongi cut him short. "We do not know how he managed to evade being burned to death since he went out in a box that was cremated. However, there was an unauthorized use of the computer system using my password that gives a pretty good idea of what he did with the ID."

"Are you so careless!" was the first rejoinder Kejian got in.

"He apparently watched my finger movements when I logged on to the system at some point. It's hard to get used to the idea that they remember everything. Anyway, he checked the guest lists of two of the main hotels in Beijing. If you take his picture to them, you'll find out what he was up to. We need him back, or if there is no other way, he must be killed. He had access to classified information. When we lost HB-27, we should have been more vigilant, except that twenty-three was so very subservient. In contrast, twenty-seven was no great loss being entirely too willful, even though highly intelligent."

Looking up from making notes, the MSS agent said, "Willful is what you say, a vicious murderer is more like what you made. And, diabolically strong. What do you feed these things? We are not positive, but witnesses have described a man very similar to your HB-27. If it were he, he has killed five times as far as we know. He bodily threw a man five meters and wrapped him around a post. We think he eventually got across the border to the west."

Both doctors were somewhat amused at Kejian's reference to the devil, and Dr. Mingchang mentioned it to him.

Kejian retorted. "When you spend your life dealing with the worst that humans can offer, you begin to wonder. I believe in no religion, or gods. But, there are times when people do things that are beyond being extremely greedy, or cruel. Either there is a dark evil corner in every man, or there is something outside of us that can take over and make a person go beyond merely human evil. I prefer to think it is something from outside. If reports can be trusted, this thing you have made has a demon." He paused for a moment, then continued. "Be assured, we will find them both sooner or later. In the meantime, if either of them contacts you, inform me at once."

Both doctors nodded their agreement and rose to leave before Kejian could lecture them on yet another subject. They passed stiff pleasantries and left as the agent finished his notes.

# — 8 —

In the days immediately after Quan Peng, HB-27, awoke from his cognitive remapping Dr. Mingchang and Dr. Hongi put him through a rigorous test program. Peng played along because he feared if he were not a good test subject he would be dismissed from his haven. Dr. Mingchang had given him various intelligence tests as part of his preparation for the memory experiment. These he remembered doing poorly on, never having encountered such tests before. Now, he was asked to answer the same questions. For some reason, his mentor acted like this would be entirely new to him. To his surprise, he could solve most of the problems easily. In addition, he was given enormous amounts of information to memorize, and he soaked it up. He was more delighted then the doctors were, though he tried not to show it.

Some nights he would lie awake and think about the events that landed him here. Unlike HB-23, Peng had lost none of his memories from before the test. Bringing together the information he knew about his last days on the street, he figured out that his boss had probably stolen the meth precursor. It all fit. As he began to apply his new mental powers to other things in his life, he found he could make further deductions. Soon his mind was whipping through all the little unconnected facts he had stored away. Something that always puzzled him was who worked for whom in the drug organization, and who was really in charge. At once, it was clear. Wow! All he had to do was get out of here and he'd have it made! No more being a patsy, used today, eliminated tomorrow. Knowledge was power, and he had a lot of it. In addition, he had the burning desire to use it for profit and revenge.

Unfortunately, his eagerness to get out of the Institute and back into his life caused him to slip at times and not be the soft putty to be molded as the two doctors seemed to want. He particularly chafed at Hongi's officious attitude. It was becoming apparent to both of them that Peng was the smarter of the two. However, in spite of Peng's hard won lessons in street fighting, Hongi's size was imposing. Hongi would likely win in a knock down, drag out.

When Quan was in his room this particular afternoon, a strange sensation overtook him. It was familiar, but he couldn't quite place it. It drew him, yet remained tantalizingly out of reach. Finally, he lay on his bunk so he could relax. Then he identified it. It was the feeling he had experienced as he awoke from the experiment.

Lying still, he heard someone moving around in the next room. He had known there was someone there, but now there were quick movements and at times moans. Ah yes, another HB experiment. They could feel one another's presence at times. That made sense. But, why now? Why not on other days? Maybe the other guy had been injured or something. Then, he remembered that earlier in the day he felt a short strong episode of this same feeling. It happened when he was engaged in a demanding cognitive skills test with Dr. Mingchang.

The next morning Peng was left alone and told to rest. This was agreeable since it would give him more time to plan for when he left the Institute. No sooner had he set to work when there were two knocks on his door after which it opened. An orderly entered and laid three folders on the table. "I was told to deliver these folders to you." With that, he left.

Odd, Peng thought. What do I care about some folders? Not one to pass up an opportunity he sat down at his table with the folders stacked in front of him. A note paper-clipped to the top one said, "Deliver to HB-23." Obviously, that was a clerical error. He proceeded to rapidly leaf though the assortment of memos, reports, and communiqués in the first folder. It appeared like an extremely involved mental test until in the second folder the nanotechnology treaty was mentioned. He began to see that the information in the folders dealt with a real world case, because there was information not reported in the press that he had heard about through his underworld connections. It did not make sense that these files were in this part of the building, or in this Medical Institute at all.

Clipped to the cover of the third folder was a note on a quarter sheet of paper. It said, "Hu, Review the information in the yellow folders in relation to the new information in the green folder. We urgently need your assessment of the current situation." He made the connection that Hu was HB-23. Peng knew he was HB-27. So, there was another HB! This twenty-three not only existed, but was being given special real jobs to do. He had special privileges! They even addressed him by name rather than his HB number. He slammed the folder shut and started pacing the room as jealousy swept over him. His vision turned black as rage engulfed his mind. How dare they prefer another to me!

Some minutes later Peng was getting his emotions under control when there was another double knock at the door and the orderly reappeared. He entered and went to the table and picked up the folders. "Delivered these to the wrong room." The door closed behind him.

The wheels were turning in Peng's head. He'd have to eliminate his rival and then he'd get the special treatment he deserved. For some time, he thought through the possibilities. It would be hard to commit murder in a placed as closed as this. It would have to be the perfect crime, but with his experience in street survival and his expanded metal powers he was convinced there was nothing he couldn't do.

Of a sudden, that feeling was back. He tried to shake it off and get back to his task only this time the feeling was much stronger than the day before. They were either making another hubot and were nearing the end of the process, or had found a way to enhance the powers of his rival in the next room. Neither alternative was to his liking, but he had to know which it was. If it were his rival, it would be more difficult getting rid of him. HB-23 might even have advanced to where he could read the thoughts of others, though Peng had not had the slightest indication that he himself might have such a power. His arrogance was fueling a paranoia that was taking control of him and making it hard for him to collect his thoughts. His mind thrashed about for a solution to his dilemma.

He had learned the layout of the floor and located the room containing the machine used to mess with men's brains. It was down the hallway to his right as he left his room and then on a short hall at right angles to the main corridor. He resolved to go in that direction to determine if the sensation grew stronger. He'd be in trouble if he were caught out of his room without permission, but it didn't matter. Logical thinking was difficult under the combined pull of the invitation and his paranoia.

He opened his door. No one was in sight so he hurried down the hall to where the short one led to the remapping room. He stopped at the corner. About to proceed, he heard a voice, a woman's, speaking just above a whisper. The reply left no doubt that the man was Dr. Hongi. That meant the woman had to be Dr. Mingchang. Here, the tug of the invitation was stronger. In a way, it was a relief to know they were making another, and his rival had not progressed in his powers. Straining to hear, he at first only picked out a few words, and then he was hearing both sides of the conversation.

" . . . not do at all," Hongi was saying in a low voice. It was doubtful the man could even whisper. As he tried to tone down the volume of his voice it rattled annoyingly, though was understandable. "I tell you he is not obedient! What you see is an act. He even snapped at me yesterday. He's smart and has a great memory, I'll give you that. What's more, I did a little checking. If I am not mistaken, Quan Peng matches a man who the drug enforcement police are after. It would appear he is, or was, in the illegal drug business. That's why I insisted we start HB-28. We can handle testing and evaluation of two of them. With HB-23 doing well, we have room for one more. As soon as we know twenty-eight has tuned out, twenty-seven gets cyanide with his next meal."

Mingchang's reply was too hushed for Peng to hear.

"By the way," Hongi asked. "Did you direct the orderly to deliver those file folders first to HB-27 and then pretend there was a mistake and take them from him and give them to HB-23? That general is an odd man. I hope he knows what he's doing. If twenty-eight is successful it won't matter, though."

"Yes. It was done exactly as he said. No matter what happens, I want to be able to honestly say we followed his orders," Dr. Mingchang said forcefully. The general instilled as much fear in the two doctors as Hongi did in Peng. "I, too, think it was a mistake giving that information to twenty-seven. We should have used another case for him. What's the point? Anyway, I still think twenty-seven is a good subject and that starting twenty-eight will only cause conflicts." The conversation wrangled on with the woman taking Peng's side where she could. Obedience came up several more times. They were both obsessed with being certain the subjects possessed this trait above all else.

Peng became aware that the pull had been lessening for several minutes. It had to be near the time when the next hubot would be done with this remapping business. There was the sound of feet moving and a door opening. The sound of it clanging shut caused Peng to return to his room. All thought of HB-23 was gone. "What if the new hubot turns out better than me!" Quan said half aloud. He knew there was only so long that he could go without eating. In addition, if he refused to eat, they had only to inject him with some poison. Escape was imperative! How long did he have? Pacing his room, he thought about how they had handled him at first. They would spend at least one full day to be sure HB-28 was what they wanted.

In his free time, Peng had watched the comings and goings of the Medical Institute from his window. There were many crippled people that came using canes. Others were helped along in wheelchairs, and there were all combinations in between. He also noticed the staff. The doctors were professionally dressed as they came and went, but they always wore lab coats once at work. He reasoned there had to be a locker room where they hung their suit coats and donned their work attire. The plan was simple. He had noticed that there were extra lab coats hanging around here and there, probably as spares in case one became soiled. The next time he was left alone in an office between tests, as happened frequently, he'd put on a lab coat. He'd head for the lowest floor where he hoped he'd find a locker room and some street clothes that would fit. In the meantime, he'd act like the most humble *and obedient* man ever born.

---

The next morning at eight o'clock Hongi was around to pick up Peng. Hongi said he was scheduled for a special test, and that was all. They ended up in the autopsy room. Hongi showed Peng the fixture on the table and explained its purpose. "There comes a time when we must know if you will follow orders," Hongi said, "and now is the time. You are ordered to chop off the little finger of your left hand."

Peng realized two things at once. The first was to his relief. The hubot of yesterday had been a failure. Second, if he were to remain alive he had no choice but to go through with this. Consciously refraining from clenching his teeth he raised the axe and brought it down on the block. During his life, he had been whipped, beaten, and abused, but nothing had hurt like this. Yet, he dare not lash back. In his present agony, he could have easily killed Hongi. With will power on the keen edge of breaking, he bore it.

An hour later the novocaine had him feeling no pain. The shortened little finger on his left hand was expertly sutured and bandaged. Through all of this, it was apparent to Peng that Hongi was feeling quite pleased with himself. On their way back to his room, Peng asked pleadingly if he would be allowed to stop at the dining room and have a cup of coffee.

"You are permitted thirty minutes, and then proceed directly to your room. Is that clear?"

"Oh. Yes, sir," Quan answered. "I'll be back to my quarters in less time than that."

Hongi nodded in satisfaction, obviously feeling no fear of disobedience from Peng.

The dining room was on the first floor. On their way to the autopsy, room Peng had seen no sign of a locker room. Sipping his coffee, he glanced around the room. On the wall near the door were some lab coats on pegs. In five minutes he had finished his coffee, and put his cup on the stainless steel drain board where it would be picked up to be washed. He eyed the coats and casually took the one most likely to fit.

In a few seconds he was near the front door looking at the directory with the room numbers of the various doctors and departments. No locker rooms were listed. What to do? "Prosthetics" caught his eye. Hmm. People take off clothes to try on mechanical limbs, he thought. Okay, second floor, Room 214. He set out for it.

He heard voices emanating from the prosthetics room. As he entered a young woman looked aside from the man with graying temples who faced her. She asked the nature of his business, obviously not recognizing him.

"Checking on the progress of my patient," he responded. "There, I see him." She nodded and turned her attention once again to the man.

It was a large room with chairs and work tables nearest the door. Tall shelves, nearly to the ceiling, extended from the walls to the center aisle in the back of the room. He stopped by a lone man with a leg off just below the knee apparently waiting for his artificial limb. Passing a pleasantry, he glanced back toward the woman. The man had left and she was flipping through some charts. Proceeding on he disappeared among the shelves. It was taking shape in his mind. He'd leave as a cripple.

Walking among the racks, he took inventory. Everything he needed was there. A second door at the back of the room would make a convenient exit. He checked it. It was unlocked.

Gathering what he needed, he proceeded out the back door and down the hall. A few people passed him walking in the opposite direction, but a man in a lab coat carrying a pair of crutches and other materials, was not out of place here. He descended to the main floor and entered a janitor's closet. He adjusted the crutches to his height. Working with no feeling in his left hand was awkward. He was using more time than he wanted. Hongi might check his room to see if he had returned as another obedience test. What was it about that guy and his obsession with obedience?

There had been some cans of talcum powder in the prosthetics room obviously used to prevent chaffing where artificial limbs met real skin. He had taken one and now used the powder to gray his hair and give his complexion a white sickly appearance. He took off his right shoe and put on a leather contraption whose use he could only guess. A coat and cap hung on a hook in the small room. The janitor will be miffed, he thought. He removed the lab coat, rolled it up, and placed it far back on a high shelf. The coat was a little large, and the cap nearly fit. For the final touch, he put on a pair of spectacles he had taken from a box on one of the shelves. The lenses made him squint but they'd definitely add to the effect. Looking at himself in a small scratched mirror, he was satisfied he had done all that was possible. He almost forgot to put his right shoe in the coat pocket. Not only would he need a good pair of shoes, but he had paid blood for this pair of Nikes, one of his prized positions.

He slowly opened the door a crack and waited until two orderlies, deep in conversation, passed. He took a deep breath and exited the room. If someone were to question why a crippled man was coming out of the janitor's closet, it would be over. There was no one to notice.

In the main lobby, he started to he door. A voice called out, "Hey. You there!"

Peng froze. Slowly he looked in the direction of the command. A guard motioned to him. "You forgot to sign out."

Quan turned with the crutches and saw an elevated desk where the guard sat on a high stool so the sign-in ledger was at convenient height for someone standing. Using crutches when they were not needed would normally have been so easy for Peng as to make it look like he was faking. The numb hand made all the difference. He could feel the crutch under his armpit, and feel the arm moving, but had no sensation of having a grip on it with his left hand. His brain was having trouble sorting out the inconsistent nerve impulses. The net result was he truly looked like a cripple.

He hobbled the few steps to the guard desk. "Sorry. It was forgetful of me," Quan said. "Wouldn't want either of us to get into trouble. They gave me a second crutch today. Seems like I can't make it on one anymore."

The guard mumbled and looked away. Peng immediately realized that here was a man who heard more of other people's troubles than he cared for. Peng kept talking.

"The doctor said the tendons on one side of my foot are weakening, and if I were to step on it wrong they might break. You know what that means? Well, I'd be in a world of hurt." Peng just kept jabbering on as a woman walked up to the desk. The guard was more than happy to divert his attention from Peng.

Peng went through the motions but signed nothing. "There," he said laying the pen down, "now I'm straight with the world."

The guard, giving directions to the woman, totally ignored Peng as he coaxed the crutches out the door and down the steps. Realizing he might be watched from an office window, he continued to slowly make his way along the sidewalk. He felt like taking off at a run, but the thing on his right foot prevented that. On the corner he crossed at the traffic light, and proceeded away from the Institute. This was a rather bad part of town, he noticed. There were a few storefronts, but mostly warehouse type buildings. Halfway down the next block, he slipped into an alley and looked about him. It was free of people with prying eyes so he proceeded some distance and stopped. Immediately, he removed the thing from his foot and put on his shoe. That felt good.

He was about to jettison his crutches when he saw a man enter the alley. Resting his weight on the crutches with his left foot off the ground, Peng waited as the figure slowly made his way toward him. Closer now, Peng could see he was young, maybe fifteen or sixteen, and obviously a tough. He reminded Peng of himself at that age. "Hey old man," the fresh faced youth called out when ten paces away, "gimme your goods, and maybe I'll let you live."

He continued advancing sensing an easy mark. When he was the right distance away, Peng dropped one crutch and rammed the other into the thug's groin. Just as quickly, he swung it overhead attempting to smash his assailant's head, but the left hand wasn't doing its job. The crutch struck a glancing blow. The teenager went down on one knee. At this point Peng could have made his escape. All his life he had feinted around the edges of evil, and the power of the netherworld. Now, with the arrogance that had been building in him over the past days because of his enhanced mental powers, to say nothing of his clever escape, he totally gave in to the call of the evil one. Peng jabbed the foot of the crutch into the face of his attacker hitting an eye. Following this he whacked him on the head again and again until he lay dead on the ground. Peng had never killed anyone before. Unexpectedly, he felt dark elation. His heart beat faster as the only thing he could think of was power and invincibility.

The passion passed. Still aware of his precarious position, Peng quickly rifled the youth's pockets. He gathered up the pieces of the crutch that had splintered in his onslaught, and the foot brace. Off at a trot, he arrived at the far end of the alley. Moving from alley to alley, he deposited the ambulatory devices in a trash bin a half kilometer away. He wanted to be sure the corpse in the alley would not be connected to the Medical Institute, and him.

Looking about he smiled. He was in his element. Moving quickly to put distance between himself and his captors, a tingling sensation in his hand announced the novocaine was wearing off. Having no delusions about the amount of pain that would visit him when the anesthetic wore off, he looked for a store that sold pain remedies. His eyes fell on what he needed across the street and down the block. It was one of those stores that were common in China. It was a single building containing a variety of departments selling everything from furniture, to motor cycles, to cosmetics, to electronics, to pharmaceuticals and gifts. Though it looked like one big department store, each category was a separate business requiring a separate checkout for each type of merchandise.

He did not try to cross the street in the center of the block. That was suicide. No problem with jaywalkers here, the traffic was impossibly heavy. He reached the corner just as the light turned green and crossed. Using some money taken from his would-be assailant, he bought two large Snicker bars, a plastic bottle of water, a small bottle of hydrogen peroxide, and some extra-strength Tylenol. He'd try for a stronger painkiller later. For now, he dare not draw attention to himself.

Outside he found an unused doorway set back into the building. He gulped down three of the capsules and slowly ate one of the bars. The relief of being away from that madman Hongi was replaced by the anxiety about what to do next. The words of Dr. Hongi in the hallway the day before came back to him. It made sense that the police would be after him. If his drug boss had set him up—and he now felt certain that was the case—it stood to reason there would be tips to the police so that if the mob didn't get him the authorities would.

The conclusion forced upon him was a heavy load. Sinking to a sitting position, he stared at the scene in front of him. Legs of all shapes and sizes flashed past on the busy sidewalk. He was halfway through the second Snicker unaware of how it had happened. This had been intended for an emergency source of energy later, if needed. Might as well finish it now,

he thought. The chocolate would melt in his pocket anyway, he rational-
ized, so screw it. He finished the confection, and emptied the water.

Now the conclusion—leave town. Leave everything he had ever
known. Leave the country. So what? he thought. Had this been so great?
One step ahead of the police, a half step ahead of the mob's enforcers,
beating people up, being beaten up. When he thought about it, his life
had been nothing but giving or receiving pain. And, face it, that hurt. He
was about ready to chuckle about the whole sorry mess except his finger
now asserted itself. Either those pills had not taken effect yet, or they
were filled with sugar after all. He had long suspected the whole pain
reliever industry was a hoax. In fairness though, continuing on the
thought path that avoided his real problem, they were meant for head-
aches and sore muscles, not major surgery.

Back to the conclusion. He had to get out of Beijing, and he could not
go back to Shanghai. The airports would be watched. Getting on a ship
was out of the question. If someone were to recognize him while on a
ship, he'd be trapped. So, head west young man, head west. Rail was the
logical means, and he had been around rail yards and passenger stations
as a kid.

# — 9 —

A healthy man traveling west would not be questioned if he were headed for Xinjiang Province. By the turning of the twenty-first century, the Chinese Politburo saw that it had a potential disaster brewing in the vast western reaches of China. The Uighurs and other ethnic minorities made up less than six percent of the total one-point-three billion population of China. However, this small group occupied more than half of the Chinese territory. In typical totalitarian fashion, the leaders took the direct approach in solving the problem. They were forcibly transplanting millions of Han Chinese to the region. The migration of a large number of people, for whatever reason, always drew those who hoped to make profit from it. Peng would be one of these as he decided to make his way to Urumqi the largest city in the province. Once there, he'd see what developed.

He stood up and started out. With a few inquiries, and the use of a taxi, he got to the rail depot. He bought a ticket to take him a hundred kilometers. From there, he would do whatever was necessary to keep moving. This meant spotting someone his size, and hopefully, that looked something like him, and luring him to a secluded place. There he'd kill him and take his money, identification, and what clothes might happen to fit. Beyond that his plan was simple—stay ahead of the police. Moving from province to province there would be a time lag before the connection was made that he was leaving a trail of dead men in his wake. The thought of killing had no effect on him. In fact, he began to look forward to the next time. On the other hand, he was smart enough to know that of all the things that could cause a man trouble, killing was the worst. If he were lucky, there would be need for few killings. He had never been lucky.

It took Peng six days to get to Urumqi, and lady luck had not been a companion for one single kilometer of the trip. Little had gone right. At one point, he had found a target matching his appearance. When he tried to take him, Peng discovered he was a martial arts expert. They fought with Peng using his punch and gouge techniques against a trained and disciplined adversary. Onlookers gathered. Peng was about beaten when his opponent chanced to grab his left hand and squeezed his finger. The pain produced a desire to kill so intense a black power engulfed him. He managed to get hold of his foe's forearm and in spite of clever counter moves of leverage and balance Peng broke his arm. In stunned shock, the man lost his concentration. He then grabbed his opponent by the belt and tossed him five meters through the air against a post breaking his back as his body folded around it. Peng was as amazed at his strength as was the man or any of the bystanders. The witnesses vanished like a pack of rats exposed to a sudden light in a darkened room, though they would remember this unusual man.

In Urumqi, Peng stayed out of sight. He had accumulated enough money in his journey to get by. He was saving most of it for transportation out of China since chances of establishing a new life here were slim to none. When police from the various provinces put together that one man had caused all the mayhem, he would be intensely hunted.

The city was in two parts, the Han Chinese district, and the older part of town where the Uighur lived. The two did not mix. He bought clothes to match the local populace and mingled with the less fortunate of the forced migrants. With so many new people arriving daily, his appearance on the scene was taken in stride by the locals. This allowed him to learn the local politics of the underground economy.

The city had an adequate airport with scheduled service to the eastern parts of China, and off and on service to other points of the compass. He used most of his cash to purchase passage to Deli, India, on a small freighter where few questions were asked. It was a gamble that was unavoidable. For once, he had a measure of good fortune. The poorly maintained plane did not crash, and it reached its destination after dark. He was off the plane as soon as the door opened and disappeared into the shadows. From here his plan was to make his way to Mumbai, steal some identification, get cleaned up, and get on a plane to some place there the spoken language was either English or French, with English preferred. Dawn found him in the train depot. Relying on pickpocket skills from his youth, he managed to lift a wallet with enough money to purchase a train ticket and a meal.

In Mumbai, his real challenge began. He walked the streets in front of large hotels looking for a mark. When he saw a Chinese man that resembled him, he would ask directions of him in English, failing that he tried French. If he got a response in either language, he made a point of remembering the face, time, and hotel. He worked the sidewalks for two days and came up with several possibilities. His goal was to spot one of them coming out of the hotel alone after dark. It was hard because foreigners usually left by means of taxis. On the third night Quan spotted his mark, hailed a taxi, and followed him. The taxi stopped at a posh restaurant and Peng was at his side before he was halfway across the sidewalk. Putting his arm around him like and old friend, Peng forced him to the shadows where, in seconds, he had him strangled. Peng carried him along with one arm around his waist, and the other holding the limp arm around his neck. At the street corner Peng waved down a cab and made an excuse for his inebriated friend.

Nearing the industrial waterfront, Peng paid the driver and took his friend out for some fresh air. This had been his number one target due to their similar appearance and size. The down side was he had responded in French. Once in France, he would figure out what to do.

He dragged his charge around a warehouse and saw the black water of the port. Lights from the far side shimmered off the nighttime ripples. There was activity off to his far right where a large machine was sorting shipping containers. When he was out of the lights and shielded from prying eyes, not an easy thing in a city with so many very poor people, he gently deposited the man on the concrete. It was necessary to keep from damaging the suit, something he intended to use. He stripped the clothes from his prey as well as himself right down to the socks and underwear. With the man dressed in Peng's clothes and himself in underwear, he beat the face against the pavement and dumped him into the water.

Dressing himself in the man's clothes, he found the shoes were a little small, but in general, he was pleased. He had little time to lose. If the man were meeting others for dinner, he would be missed. Hurrying some distance from the wharf, he hailed another taxi. While in transit, he went through the pockets of the other man's clothing he was wearing. He found only a credit card, presumably to pay for dinner, and his room key-card. Contrary to instructions he had written his room number on it so he wouldn't forget. Another lucky break. Were things turning for him?

Back at the hotel, he entered by a side door, and arriving at the room, opened it with the key-card from the body. Immediately, he took a shower. Then he set about getting into the small room safe. From the instructions, he saw the code was four digits. There was not enough time to try them all. He was becoming desperate until he found a copy of the man's passport in a special pocket of the suit coat. Twenty minutes later he hit on the code as part of his home address which, as it turned out, was in Quebec, Canada. The lady of luck kept smiling, if only for awhile. There was some bills of Indian currency, rupees. He remembered as a rough conversion there were five rupees to a Chinese yuan. There was at least three hundred in Canadian dollars.

He locked the safe, and went through the man's luggage making sure there was nothing that would cause problems at security checkpoints or customs. Using the staff entrance, he was on the street by nine-fifteen, and at the airport by ten. He managed a late flight to Cairo that left at eleven forty-five. The following morning he was on his way to Paris, from there to Toronto, and then on to Winnipeg. Why Winnipeg? He could get an immediate connecting flight. At first, he thought of paying for it in cash, but decided if anyone wanted to trace him the name would do it anyway. Besides, he didn't have much cash. From Winnipeg, he intended to continue on to Vancouver, British Columbia, without giving much thought to exactly where he wanted to finally settle for awhile. Once on the run, it was hard to stop.

On the ground in Winnipeg, he discovered he was enormously tired. It was time to rest for a few days. Although it was a small city, he could just as easily go to the U.S. from here as from any place else, if the mood struck him. From the temperature they announced before the plane landed, it seemed certain he'd be heading south.

He took a cab from the airport to a cheap motel on the south side of town. After showering he found Ma's Kitchen a short walk away, and ordered a hot meal, the special of the day. The food was culture shock. Mashed potatoes and gravy were new to him. The roast beef was okay, but what was that yellow stuff? From the menu, the only unidentified "thing" was corn. He was hungry, and he could see others eating it, so he managed to get it down, and keep it down, barely. The cherry pie was good, he thought. The coffee was different, but acceptable.

Back in his room, he succumbed to the combination of jet leg, and fatigue from being on the go for just shy of two weeks. He sat back in the easy chair for a minute feeling relaxed and safe for the first time in as

long as he could remember. His eyelids started to droop and the bed
started to look better and better. At first, he was amused to think the bed
was actually drawing him to it. His eyes popped open. It was that feeling! What was happening? Were they making hubots here, too? No. It
was not the same, and much weaker. The last time he had been only a
few rooms away, so it would naturally be weaker here. He tried to determine the direction it was coming from. That was not clear, but if he
had to say, the source seemed to be south of him. It had built slowly as
he became aware of it. It ended abruptly with nothing left but his fatigue.
Falling into bed fully clothed, he slept.

# — 10 —

**Minneapolis, Minnesota**

The St. Anthony Falls Laboratory was operated by the Civil Engineering, and Geology and Geophysics Departments of the University of Minnesota. In it, engineering, environmental, and geophysical fluid dynamics research was performed. Referred to as SAFL by the researchers and students who worked there, its scientists published many scientific papers each year.

Founded in 1938 on Hennepin Island in the Mississippi River, it was located at the head of St. Anthony Falls in downtown Minneapolis, Minnesota. In the mid-eighteen hundreds, it was the site of saw mills using the power of the falls to produce lumber for the small but growing city of St. Paul. The berg of Minneapolis grew up around these mills. Later Minneapolis became known as the Mill City as companies with names like Washburn (the forerunner of General Mills) and Pillsbury used the falls to operate flour mills.

The SAFL was considered a world class facility partly due to its location at the falls. The forty-nine foot drop from the inlet at the falls' headpool to the outlet flume permitted its laboratory space to use some of the natural power of the falls for experimental purposes. Of the eight thousand cubic feet of water per second that tumbled over St. Anthony Falls, only a fraction of it could be ported through the lab. It entered the lab at two levels in a small building to the north of the facility on the island. The main flume running through the second and third levels of the test spaces could handle a flow of three hundred cubic feet of water per second. That may seem like a small percentage of all the water available at that point in the Mississippi, but it was a huge amount to be precisely controlled to do the bidding of the researchers.

The other reason for the lab's fame was its ability to attract top quality personnel from around the world. The many renowned scientists, permanent as well as visiting, who made use of its facilities attested to its world reputation.

With this in mind it was no surprise when the People's Republic of China approached the University of Minnesota with a proposal, and funds, to do some research in the lab. Modeling studies for some of the largest dams in the world as well as similar environmental hydraulics projects had been conducted there, so the staff was pleased to put its expertise at the service of the PRC. At first, it appeared to be a study of water dynamics for a civil engineering project. However, as the plans developed it became less rather than more clear as to what exactly was the objective of the work. With each step in the negotiations new levels of security and secrecy were first suggested, and then demanded. Finally, it was the extremely generous offer of fees that decided the issue in favor of the Chinese.

It was suspected by some of the permanent staff at the lab that the tests would be a preliminary study of a hydroelectric project that could have major environmental effects in China and this was the reason for the secrecy. If the tests were positive they would, of course, be published to demonstrate what a good world citizen China was. However, if, as the objections went, the tests showed severe ecosystem disruptions this information would be closely held until the project was completed, at which time, it would be too late to do any thing about it. Based on this line of reasoning, there were efforts made to stop the tests until the true purpose was divulged.

Counter arguments said that since the trials involved the large flume it had to be some other type of engineering test altogether. Therefore, there should be no concern. This latter speculation eventually won out since at times the Chinese let slip terms like magnetic vortex and magnetic heating. In fact, that was close to correct, except that there was still the possibility of an environmental impact, a serious one. Only the danger was not to China, but rather to that of the Minneapolis metropolitan area. The whole program was part of an international game being played out between arguably the two most powerful nations on earth, the United States and China. However, only China knew this phase of the contest was about to begin.

On the second of four levels of the experimental area beneath the headwaters of the St. Anthony Falls, the Chinese had a space walled off at the side of the major flume. The doors to this space were fitted with special locks the Chinese brought with them. With enough persuasion in the form of money, Jian Niu, the senior man on the project, had also procured the use of an office in the east wing of that part of the facility. It was situated at the level of the parking lot. This too was fitted with a special lock.

The first modification was to change the shape of the main flume. The test needed the water to come with as much speed as possible into a pool where the experimental apparatus would be located. The flow of water would be ported though specially constructed heat exchangers and then vented out into the pool and hence over a weir and out of the facility. During the work on the water channel, heavy crates were brought into the area, not the easiest thing considering the ungainly layout of the experimental space. After weeks of toil the equipment was installed, the water in the main flume was flowing at capacity, and hopes were high for a good first test.

"We have the generator on line," Hang Lu said to Jian Niu, who was leaning over his shoulder. "According to the agreed upon procedure for this first test, we will proceed to the point of positive power generation barring any fault conditions." Positive power was the point where more power was generated by the apparatus than was consumed. "We are ready to begin." Lu and Niu were both theoretical physicists. Lu was also a fair-to-middling engineer, skills Niu lacked. Niu had an international reputation. Lu was well known in China, but not beyond its borders. However, both had equal rank on this project as far as the science was concerned. Since any organization needed one person in charge, Niu had been selected due to his greater stature among scientists, which was primarily the result of his position as one of the upper class in China. At sixty-three he was nearly twice the age of Lu. Niu also came from the ruling class of China and Lu did not. This would forever keep Lu from gaining the stature Niu had attained regardless of the merits of his scientific contribution. This rankled Lu, though there was no disputing the social and political landscape.

The reason for this project at the St. Anthony Falls Lab was to settle the scientific argument going on in China about "the conjecture." Over the past half century there was a gradually increasing awareness among theoretical physicists around the world that there was a thing called zero point energy, zpe for short. At times, depending on the precise use of the term, it was called zero point force, zpf. Physicists calculated that if this structure of space could be tapped vast amounts of "free energy" could be realized. The estimates of the amount of this energy varied wildly. The smallest most miserly estimate said that each cubic millimeter of space contained energy equivalent to that which would be released by burning ten billion gallons of gasoline. Ten billion is ten raised to the tenth power. Other estimates suggested that the equivalent of ten raised to the hundredth power of gallons of gasoline were available per cubic millimeter. With this energy, machines that were more than one hundred percent efficient, or commonly called perpetual motion machines, could be built. The trick was to build a device that could bring this "background energy" into the "foreground" where we lived. A decade ago China had put a small but committed program in place to determine if zero point energy could be harnessed.

Lu had made significant contributions to this work. This did not go down well with some of the scientists from the upper class who held the view that zpe was nothing more that a useful mathematical construct to help explain quantum mechanical phenomena. Yet, with each passing year the case for zpe grew. Then, two years before, the hoped for breakthrough had been made by the strange physicist, Dr. Anfa Luan. He seemed to have had help, but would not divulge his source. The development produced expectations not unlike the promise of nuclear energy in the early decades of the twentieth century. The implications were so fantastic that it was immediately covered with one of the heaviest clouds of secrecy ever imposed by any organization.

After the invention of the first zpe device, those who doubted it was possible had to admit they were wrong. To compensate, they suggested an immediate program to commercialize the discovery before other countries did. Almost immediately Heng Lu found himself immersed in another controversy over something called the "quantum conjecture" or now simply referred to as "the conjecture." Those in the field of theoretical physics in China were aware of what the abbreviated term referred to. Before this, the conjecture was little more than a footnote in a few obscure scientific papers. Those now pressing to proceed with the development of the technology fluffed it off as silly while the other camp was making increasingly convincing arguments for it. There was even the slimmest evidence in tests run to date that suggested it was true. The dispute had grown increasingly rancorous with both sides adopting a do-or-die position.

Since the scientists could not agree on the validity of the conjecture, the political leaders felt helpless to intervene directly. The promise of the zpe device was breathtaking. However, before vast sums of money were spent on development, the issue raised by the conjecture had to be decided. Time was of the essence since the blanket of secrecy could not last forever. As a result, a typically political decision was made. Take the necessary equipment to a neutral site. Procure mundane equipment locally if that speeded things up. Have two competent scientists at the site, one holding each view of the conjecture. Then perform a master test with both scientists in agreement that it was a fair and legitimate test. The results would be the last word on the matter as far as a crash program was concerned. If it were decided not to proceed with full scale development, research would of course continue, but with no over-reaching world advantage expected.

The politicians true to their nature also had their own agenda. Their biggest worry was that the conjecture was so obviously true that other countries had made the break-through, perhaps years before, and were quietly working on ways to circumvent it. If China went ahead with a major program, it would come to the world's attention. The folly of their incompetent scientists would be extremely embarrassing. However, this partisan debate must be ended now! It would be best if it could be stopped without chopping the heads off half of China's scientists . . . but, it would be stopped.

Jian Niu was of the view the conjecture was without merit, and the master test was a waste of his time and China's money. He had plans in place to have a commercial power plant under construction in a year. His homeland would rule the world. Yet, here he was in this sleepy little city trying to convince the politburo that something that did not exist did, in fact, not exist. He had no choice but to make Heng Lu at least think it was a fair test. This was proving most difficult.

Lu had the opposite problem. All of the heavy lifting fell on his shoulders. Niu could win his case simply by doing nothing. Lu had to be totally certain he had not overlooked the slightest detail that could invalidate the test. With the generator they had built for the test operating at full power, by far the largest ever attempted, they could produce up to one-hundred megawatts of power with fifty being the nominal target. Even the most pessimistic proponents of the conjecture agreed that this level of power production would be enough to settle the issue.

As Lu had prepared for the test, he thought how interesting it was that they had been able to obtain the use of this particular lab. It could direct three hundred cubic feet of water per second through their test apparatus. It was "free" water in the sense that otherwise it fell the forty-nine feet over the upper St. Anthony Falls dam. As a result, it could be allowed to run through the facility as much as necessary at no cost. At fifty megawatts of power generation, that flow of water would be heated less than two degrees Centigrade. The locals would never notice. Lu had precise temperature sensors that would measure the rise of the water temperature as it went through the heat exchangers. There were many other instruments, but the rise in water temperature was the only means of measuring the actual, effective, usable power being extracted from zpe. With this in mind, there were three sensors up stream and three down stream from the experiment. Their outputs were read by a computer. The signals from each set of three were compared and averaged. If one deviated from the other two by one or more percent, it was not used. Lu was in charge of calibrating the sensors since the proof of his position depended on them.

On the wall, they had placed a large digital display of the differential temperature referred to as Delta-T, that is, change in temperature. It showed Delta-T in thousandths of a degree centigrade. Since it would take thirty-five megawatts to heat the flow of water one degree, a thousandth of a degree represented thirty-five kilowatts. To the left of the decimal point on the display was a single digit. No more were needed. If the Delta-T went as high as nine degrees, it would mean over three-hundred megawatts were being generated, far beyond the capacity of the apparatus. Even three degrees was beyond the safe limit of the heat transfer system. The digital meter now rested at all zeros.

Lu was noticeably stressed as Niu hovered about him squinting at the instruments and computer monitors through thick spectacles. In addition to the two scientists, there was an engineer, Wu Zheng, and two technicians. Jianli Huang, the only woman of the crew, was one of the technicians, and Ju Feng the other. Of the four under the administrative direction of Niu, Jianli had suggested a pool to guess who of the four would be the one to finally strangle Niu. The statement was ignored by the other three because they all harbored resentments toward Niu. To give cognitive form to their feelings produced temptations they wished to avoid.

"You act like a child afraid of the night, Lu. If your science and the combined engineering talent of you and Zheng are correct, why are you so cautious? This is only a low power test. Proceed."

Lu wanted to retort with "Did you ever hear of Murphy's Law? For a pencil jockey like you this law says that if something can go wrong it will. And, some say Murphy was an optimist. What he did say was, "We are embarking on an entirely new technology. While we have done small-scale tests in Beijing, this machine at full rated power will produce thousands of times more power than we have ever attempted. We have no way of knowing how perfectly symmetrical the vortex field must be to achieve the level of positive energy generation we expect. Things could go wrong that we have no way of guessing. Don't forget, the conjecture could be true. In that case, even at low power, this test could influence the local power grid, the telephone lines, or something else. Anything out of the ordinary could cause local officials to investigate what we are doing here. That is why everything must be reserved for the master test. We will proceed slowly and methodically to the point of positive power generation."

Here Niu had to back down because the orders were very specific on that point. However, this first low power test was a milestone that had to be met before the final piece of equipment would be delivered. The Chinese leadership seemed to be taking no chances. When working perfectly, the equipment they had could produce slightly more energy than was being put into the device, positive power generation. However, that was not nearly enough to prove the conjecture. When all was ready, a courier would arrive with something called the "keystone device." They all knew there was a receptacle for an octagonal device five centimeters across and a half-centimeter thick. It was commonly thought this device contained a code that enabled the generator to go to full power.

"Feng," Lu said in a commanding voice much too forcefully. Niu was pushing the stress level off the charts. "Are we clear?"

"We've been clear for thirty minutes." Being clear meant having the University of Minnesota graduate students cleared out for testing. They were bright enough, but seemed easily persuaded that the purpose of these experiments was to research magnetic vortex generation for industrial processes. "Everything is calibrated for start."

Niu was pacing back and forth behind the workstations that would record the test. "Test will start on my mark, three, two, one, mark." Lu pressed a lighted green button. There was no sound, but computer displays

showed a variety of data. Jianli Huang's monitor showed a three dimensional display of the thermodynamics separating different parameters by
color. The basic form of the heat transfer from the ceramic cylinder
through the heat exchangers to the water appeared solidly symmetrical.
Slowly the sidebars of symmetry coefficients showed sector eight was
getting out of shape by one part in six thousand. "Symmetry being lost in
thermo transfer coefficients," she called out.

The team of worker bees let out a collective sub-audible "damn." So
much for dictating science from the top down. Niu had given the order to
accept the design of the last heat exchanger section used to transfer the
power generated from zpe in the ceramic cylinder to the flow of water.
Lu and Niu had a heated argument about Niu overstepping his authority,
but had been overruled. The issue of symmetry had been raised but Niu
had passed it off as close enough. Changing the design at that point
would have delayed the first test by a few days, and Niu's schedule had a
date for the first test. That date was today. He had met every other milestone on the schedule and this one would be met, too. No exceptions.

"Preparing to stop test," Lu called out.

"Negative," Niu command. "We will run for one hour as planned to
insure the equipment has no weak parts that could terminate the master
test early."

Ju Feng was intently monitoring the energy flow. Finally, much
against his wishes, he stated in a level voice, "Energy flow is surging."

Immediately Jianli Huang called out. "Temperature is raising in the
vicinity of a thermo asymmetry due to nucleate boiling on the ceramic.
Steam produced cavitation imminent. Recommend terminating test."

Two seconds later she added with increased tension in her voice,
"Symmetry is being lost in sectors one and seven now, too." They all
knew there was enough energy flowing through the device to cause serious damage if steam were produced.

Suddenly, they felt a low frequency thumping as parts began to shift.
"Terminating test!" Lu said as he punched the emergency stop button.
This initiated an automatic sequence of actions thought to be the best
way to stop an out-of-control experiment. The building shuddered once
and all was quiet. Lu pulled a handkerchief from his pocket and wiped
the sweat off his face.

Niu was momentarily silent to the relief of the other four. After a long
pause while each of the technical people verified their data files were
intact and backed up he said, "Well?"

Four heads turned to him. "Did we learn anything?"

Lu and Zheng spoke at the same time. "You first," Zheng said.

"We learned nothing," Lu said as evenly as he could, "other than that last heat exchanger section should not have been used. The asymmetry was large enough to account for the data we collected, and what you felt and heard. It's unlikely the conjecture contributed to it even though we were slightly into positive power generation for a few seconds. All of the instruments we have to measure the sought after effects were affected by the known defect in the apparatus."

"I concur," Zheng cut in. "Some of the power being produced was coming from zero point. The equipment and instruments appeared to operate as expected. This run was a valuable first step. We must rebuild that heat exchanger section to more exacting standards." He hoped this last statement was euphemistic enough to deflect a direct reference of Niu's stupid decision.

# — 11 —

As soon as the airplane stopped at the gate at O'Hare Airport the fasten seatbelt light went off and the aisles were instantly filled with people. Chen stayed in his seat. Finley did too. "If I got up now I'd get trampled," Jason said with a laugh. Chen managed a smile with his mouth, but his eyes were not smiling. He knew that the next half-hour would determine the rest of his life.

When the aisle cleared, those few people who had remained in their seats got up and collected their things. Jason stood reaching up trying to get his carry-on bag out of the overhead compartment. Chen helped him, fumbling as he appeared to nearly drop it. Then he reached for his own. It was December and most of the passengers had a coat, as did Jason. Chen wore only the Oxford shirt he had from the Institute.

"You should have remembered to bring a coat. It's fifteen above outside," Jason remarked.

"Fifteen degrees above freezing of water not cold."

"That's not right. You're in the U.S. now. I mean it is fifteen degrees Fahrenheit. That's well below the freezing point of water."

"Oh." Hua shrugged. "I don't have a coat, so it can't concern me. Wishing will not bring me a coat."

Jason gave Hua a long look as they walked up the jet way with the stragglers. Chen looked straight ahead and tried to fall behind but Finley kept looking back. He stopped and waited for Chen to catch up. "You look worried. What's the matter?" Jason asked.

Chen smiled a little. "I think about the cold outside, no coat."

"I think you have never traveled to the United States before, and are worried about getting through immigration and then customs. I'll show you where to go."

When they got to the Immigration and Naturalization hall, the lines were all long except the one that said "Diplomatic and Airline Personnel."

Jason tugged at Hua's sleeve and pulled him toward the diplomatic line. "If we wait until the end of this short line I will tell the agent you are my friend from China. Since this man has nothing to do after the diplomats and airline people go through, he will not mind letting you use this line. It will save you time."

"I do not want to be special. No reason. I go to line with other people."

"Don't be silly. Nobody will care."

Chen was stuck. The kid would not let go of his sleeve. It would draw attention to him if he insisted and jerked away.

When the last person in front of them was showing his passport to the agent Jason said, "Get your passport out."

Jason looked at him oddly as he hesitated. Slowly Chen pulled the passport out. Instead of the red cover of the Chinese, it had the dark blue cover of the U.S. Finley put his hand slowly to his mouth, and his eyes got very wide. His hand dropped to reveal a look of surprise mixed with bewilderment.

"Next," the agent said. He had to say it again.

"Oh, yes." Jason said as he moved across the line on the floor with the words by it saying "Do not cross until you are called."

As the agent examined the passport Jason waved to Hua to join him. Chen was hesitant. "Is that gentleman with you, Mr. Finley?" he asked.

"We met on the plane and he works for the Federal Government so I thought if he came with me at the end of the line you wouldn't mind saving him from the long lines."

"Well, we don't like to do that, but I guess there's no harm." Jason waved again and Hua timidly advanced, and handed his passport to the agent. "I not special. Should go in long line like rest of others."

Opening the passport the agent said, "That's okay Mr. Sun." Then looking Chen in the eye he asked, "what part of the Federal Government do you work for?"

Chen looked blank for a second while he held eye contact with the agent. Then it registered that he had Zhu Sun's stolen passport. "I um, I so, you must know . . . I not work for. CIA wants information I have. Important . . . they say it is. I think it is only my job, so why? But, they want it much a lot." Chen was twisting his hands together having given up all hope of succeeding in his subterfuge, though as he continued looking at the man he felt a pleasant sense of control in the situation. He wanted to be asked questions about the passport which was the only information he knew well enough to answer without sounding evasive. In a last desperation effort he momentarily flipped his hands palms up, and said, "All I say." He paused and added, "I say more if your want, but not of interested CIA information."

The agent looked a little perplexed. "What is your birth date?" Chen had the image of the passport in his mind, and easily answered each of the questions that followed. The agent thumbed through the passport and asked about other travels. Chen could have answered with no hesitation, but paused as if thinking a couple of times. Finally, the agent said, "I suppose you are in an uncomfortable position. You're right, it must be urgent. You made such a long trip to China and then came back long before your planned date."

The agent twitched his mouth as if uncertain as to what to do. Chen waited as he felt his life about to end. Finally the hand lifted and the passport came to Chen. "Welcome home, Mr. Sun."

Chen nodded. He stooped to pick up his carry-on bag. While his head was below the top of the counter, he managed a slight smile from the relief. Passing through the door, Jason turned to him. "You don't have a coat because you had to leave in a hurry, isn't that it?"

Hua smiled, "You are young, and have imagine of much things. I like if we are friends. Okay for you?"

"Oh, yes. We'll always be friends. My mother will meet me. Before we leave the airport, you must meet her."

They were nearing the luggage carrousel but no luggage had appeared yet. Hua turned to Jason, "No luggage. Must go now, much urgently."

Jason protested, "No, no. Please wait. I don't know how to find you." Chen was already at the customs point. The line was short and having only a carry-on bag there were few questions. Then, he was past his last hurdle. He was inside the United States, a free man!

The signs in the terminal directing him were easy. They were of only a few words each. He could translate them instantly and unambiguously. He followed the signs to Ground Transportation. On his way, he passed a currency exchange window. Stopping he changed all of the yuan he had taken from the safe which netted him another one-hundred-forty dollars. This brought his cash total to nearly a thousand dollars. It seemed like a lot, but he had no idea what he'd do when it was gone.

He had only a vague idea of how he would get from Chicago to Minneapolis. A bus or train seemed the only means available. He could not risk an airplane even if he could afford it because all he had for identification was the passport. The man who made it for him warned about never using it again if he were lucky enough to get through the airport.

He found himself walking past the car rental agencies. He had driven a company van in China, but had no driver's license in the name of Zhu Sun. The old man had not had time to make one. He watched the people. It was five-thirty in the afternoon and there were lines at every counter. The airline magazine on the airplane told of the subway train that ran from the airport to the center of the city. An advertisement along the concourse told of the Greyhound Bus Line. That was probably his best bet, though he didn't like the idea of any form of public transportation. Someone from China might already be looking for him in the U.S.

By chance, he saw a woman with a girl of four or five in tow arguing with an attendant at one of the rental counters. At issue appeared to be a credit card. Finally, the woman stepped aside, picked up one suitcase and gripped the handle of the one on wheels and said, "Come on, Jenny. We have to find a bus to get us to Hudson. They won't take my credit card."

Chen, having heard the exchange, went through in his mind what he knew about this area. There was Hudson, Wisconsin, that was near Minneapolis. It was worth a try. Some distance from the rental counter he approached the woman. "Madam," he said, "Do you not rent a car for lack of money? Might be we can help us both. Do you go to Hudson that is in Wisconsin?"

She stopped uncertain of what to do, nodding slightly. "I lost wallet on airplane, no credit card, no ID with picture. Can not get on airplane, not train without ID with picture. I carried near five-hundred dollars cash in other pocket, so still have. We drive same car, might be? I go to Minneapolis. Most urgent. Mother very sick."

The woman maneuvered the suitcases to the side of the concourse out of the river of humanity swirling about them. He could see the wheels turning. It sounded too good to be true, and such things usually were. "Is there someone I could call to verify this?"

She was a canny one, Chen thought. Slowly shaking his head he said, "Don't think so. Her friend called me. Don't know friend's phone to call." More hesitation. She fidgeted with her coat button. "You not trust me. Okay. See no gun no knife, no coat even. You look in bag. Okay by me. You drive, I am in back, I drive, you are in back. I buy fuel. We get there fast."

It was decision time and the woman knew it. "Let's see the bag."

She was stalling, Chen could tell. She opened it. Chen had all but forgotten about the bag on the flight and never looked in it himself. One of the assistants at the place that made his passport put it together for him. He assumed there would be nothing incriminating. It had an extra shirt and pants, and a pair of clean socks. To his delight there was a light jacket that looked like it might even fit. There was a can of shaving cream, a throw-away razor, and a small pack of women's facial tissue. They must have really scraped to throw this together, he thought.

She pulled out the jacket and said, "No coat, huh? You'd better put this on. It's cold out. Here's my problem. There's no bus until morning, and I must get home for my Friday work shift. They don't like my credit card because it's maxed-out. If I have cash payment, they will accept the credit card and my driver's license as a guarantee of them getting their car back."

Chen searched all he knew and could not find "maxed" or "maxed-out." He accepted the fact that he did not know what was wrong with the credit card. But, if cash would fix it, he didn't care. "Okay, then?" She nodded. "I am called Hua."

"I'm Carol, this is Jenny."

He was forced to pull out his money and give the flighty woman three hundred and fifty dollars. She could scream for the police at any moment he knew. As she was turning he said, "I very grateful you help me." The instant he said it his dire situation fell upon him. "I in desperate need." The last words tumbled out without him knowing it.

Whatever the woman had planned Chen's expression caused her to pause a long moment studying his face. She then turned. "Come Jenny. Stay close to me."

She went to a different rental counter than the previous one. It worked. She took the rental agreement and collected her bags. Chen fell in behind her after a discreet distance. She turned and motioned him up beside here. "Don't get lost. Here, I didn't need it all." She thrust a small wad of money at him. "Don't put it away, though. We'll have tolls to pay." Chen was familiar with use taxes, so this made sense, though he did not know how or when it would happen.

When the bus from the rental company dropped them off at their car Chen wondered about what crazy mistake there had been. "This right car?" he asked.

"We'll see," she said as she held up the key fob and pressed a button. The trunk lid magically opened. "It's no mistake. I've got the key." He helped lift her luggage in.

"Yeah, we were lucky. They had this Grand Marquis with Minnesota plates they wanted returned to the airport there. We'll work that out as we go."

Chen was aghast at the freeway system around O'Hare Airport. He had no idea how this woman knew which of the twisting ribbons of concrete to take. He happened to see her tense expression in the rearview mirror. That answered his question well enough—she didn't know. They were flying along, and yet other cars were sounding their horns as the angry drivers careened into other lanes and sped past them. Traffic was a jumbled mess in all of China's cities, but it all happened at a fraction of this speed. The size of the cars was another thing. They were all huge and shinny. Semi-trucks virtually unknown in his homeland flowed past them. The huge wheels hummed and thumped on the seams in the roadway as they came past at eye level. The boxy frames or shinny cylinders towered above him as he wondered how he would ever drive.

After an hour and a half the woman pulled off at a place with a restaurant. They sat in separate booths. Chen sat where he could see the car. She had told him to be sure he got some coffee and enough to eat so he was alert. Now he faced the biggest problem. He was forced to use the men's room, and she had the keys to the car. He never urinated so fast in his life. Not stopping to wash his hands, he rushed out. The woman was still there and her look said it all—scared I'd cut out, huh? His look said—can you blame me?

Outside, it was cold. Chen snapped up his light jacket as he watched the woman put gas in the car. He remembered all the movements. "Okay, go pay the man." He stood there uncertainly. "Okay. If it will make you feel better, here're the keys. Your turn to drive, anyway."

Feeling a lot better, he went in to pay. It took a few exchanges to figure out that the cashier was asking for the pump number. Less than twenty dollars. It seemed not too bad to Chen. As he returned to the car, he looked at the pump. His eyes registered on the digital display that had nineteen-fifty on it. Okay, it made sense now.

He put the key in the ignition and turned it a little too long. He was doing everything he had seen the woman do. The shift lever wouldn't move. "Put your foot on the brake or you can't shift it," the woman said from the back seat.

"Never drive car so large," Hua replied. "I drive not so fast at start to feel it, okay?"

"Yeah, yeah, whatever. Just don't take all night. Stick with I-90 West until it goes to 94. Than we want 94, but I'll probably be driving by then. Drive the speed limit, but no more. I don't want any cops on our ass. Now, go already."

Chen had never driven a vehicle with an automatic transmission, but he had carefully observed the woman. She simply put the pointer on the "D" and went. She never shifted. He could not figure out how that worked, so put it off to something about America. Luckily, he did not have to back up to leave. At first he lurched a little, and let off. It really moved quickly. He saw the sign for I-90 West just in time and was on the ramp. Out of the lights of the service area, it was dark. He strained as he followed the white lines painted on the sides of the lane. His speed hit fifty. Cars and trucks were whiffing past on his left as he came to the merge. He was getting the hang of it and feeling better. The side mirror was not aimed right, but he had the inside one which he adjusted. In less than ten minutes, he was up to seventy and under control. He had never heard about speed control so didn't miss not knowing how to use it. In minutes, the two in the back seat were asleep and he was on his own.

There had been a Wisconsin map on the wall where he paid for the gas. Now he went over it in his mind. The car had a clock, as well as everything else. It told him how fast he was going, how many miles per gallon he was getting, even how many miles he could travel on the gas he had left. As he drove, he watched the time it took from one point on the map to the next. At the rate they were going, and allowing for stops, they would get to Hudson about six in the morning.

They were at the woman's house in Hudson at five-forty. She told Chen to drop off the car at the airport planning to give him an hour and then call and check. If it had not been turned in she would report it stolen.

Chen drove away unsure what would happen if the police pulled him over. He stopped and filled up the gas where the woman told him to before he got back on the freeway. The traffic was picking up and it was still dark. However, the well-lighted signs left no question about where to go. Heading south on I-494, he saw signs directing him to the airport. It all worked. At the rental return he was met by a man with a large calculator in his hand who punched in the car plate number, mileage, and how full the tank was, and handed Chen a little slip of paper. That was it.

It was so easy. There was a taxi waiting with the motor running. He hurried over to it. He gave the driver the address and they were off.

It was cold. He could never remember feeling so cold. Along the I-494 belt road in Bloomington, he saw a time and temperature sign. It was five degrees Fahrenheit, and six-fourteen in the morning. The driver connected to I-35W and headed north. Finally, they took the County Road E2 exit. Shortly thereafter they arrived at the apartment building with the street number Chen had given the driver. Chen paid the driver and got out. The building was the right one and he discovered the front door was locked. He walked some distance away to stand near the garages where he was out of the wind. The sky was clear and it was still dark. He hoped Beckon was an early riser. A half dozen people came out as he waited. As time passed, he failed to notice he wasn't feeling so cold any more. Then, he saw him. There were several photos in the file the Chinese had on Beckon. In his late twenties, he had a solid build, stood six feet even, and one-eighty pounds. He had black hair cut short enough to make it easy to handle. His blue eyes set off well-balanced facial features, except for a square jaw.

Chen had no choice but make the direct approach. Stepping into Breckon's path of travel he said, "Mr. Edmund Beckon, may I speak to you? Is much important things I must say to you."

Ed stopped. His shoulders sank. Before he could say anything Chen continued, "I am called Hua Chen. I come from China today. Not true. I escape from China today and come to you. I help you, you help me?" Hua's hands were thrust in the pockets of his light jacket and he was shivering uncontrollably. "Very cold!" Thrusting out his hand, he pointed to the door Breckon had come from moments before. Immediately the hand disappeared into the pocket again. "Might talk where it warm? Cold here!"

Breckon let out a long breath. "Yeah, I guess. In a way, I suppose, I've been expecting you."

Chen was jolted by the unexpected remark. Breckon took his keys in his gloved hand and unlocked the door.

Inside, Chen slumped against Breckon. Snatching off his glove, he lifted Chen's jacket and shirt and felt under his arm. Cold. Instantly Breckon Swung Hua's arm over his shoulder and half carried and half dragged Chen down the half-dozen steps to the bottom floor. Breckon's apartment was partly in the ground with the bottom of the windows six inches above grade. Proceeding down the hall Breckon knew the man was unconscious. He stopped to unlock his door. Limp bodies were hard to handle and he slid to the floor. Grabbing Hua's shirt over his chest, he dragged him between his feet the few steps to the bathroom. Only bumping his head once, he dumped him into the tub. Frantically, Breckon shook off his own coat, and started the shower. They were both in the flow of water. Breckon's shoe caught in the shower curtain ripping it loose. He directed water, just hot enough to stand, at Chen's head. Gradually, Chen began fighting back. Breckon sat him up in the tub kneeling behind him. The tub was filling and Breckon adjusted the water temperature. Chen started coughing and puffing as he said things Breckon did not understand. With the shower off, Breckon slopped to the bathroom door with water squishing out of his shoes. He closed it to build up steam in the room. Breckon started rubbing Chen's head briskly with a towel to get some sensations going. The eyes were still a little wild so he stopped.

"You awake for me?"

Chen was taking in deep breaths. "Better now. You get me warm. I freeze nearly."

"Yeah. You were a few minutes from being dead."

They were both still fully dressed and totally soaked. Breckon took off all but his shorts and dried himself. "Stay there and I will find some dry clothes for you. Do you understand?"

Chen nodded. Twenty minutes later they were both dried off and dressed. Hua sat with a blanket wrapped around him. When Breckon returned from cleaning up the mess in the bathroom, he put two cups of instant coffee in the microwave and they sat at Breckon's kitchen table that also served as his TV stand, computer table, and other assorted uses. Breckon got Hua to tell his hubot story.

After fifteen minutes he was still going. " . . . the magnetic vortex resonator used to make hubots, how you say, connects to the energy in what is called the zero point field, zpf they say, sometimes zpe. These are the forces that give structure to what we call empty space. There is much written about this, but the real meaning of this is expressed using mathematical symbols I do not understand.

"The hubot device only makes the connection of DNA molecules to this zpe and uses small energy. I tell you this, but it is big secret in China. They found what makes differences between live dog and dead dog is live dog has DNA molecules connected to zpe. That is life force. When dead this link is open. When they try to make more hubots, and I feel strange thing. It wants to draw me to it. I want, but don't want. Hard to say to you."

Breckon was fascinated but could see by the time that he'd have to leave for work soon. He asked, "So, how did you escape from the Medical Institute?"

"When hubots fail, do that most times, they have bodies cremated. I hid in cremation box and had myself cremated. See, leave no tracks behind. Good idea, you think?"

"Yeah, I guess so. But, they didn't do a very good job. You're not even charred."

"Not in box when burned!"

Ed chuckled. "I can see that. I made a joke."

Hua thought a second, "You make humor joke. That good. No mirth in Institute. No laughing, all serious, worried. Heavy weight of job to make good hubot. I best one and get away. They in bad luck now."

"Why are they working so hard to make hubots?" Ed asked.

"You do that."

"What! Me! That's impossible."

"It is true. You keep big airplane from blowing up by Dragon Fang. If airplane go boom then no treaty, and scientists have time to make hubots and not need nanotechnology. Now big nano factory being built, China must hurry and have human robots before the rest of world has machine robots."

Breckon sat with his elbows on the table resting his chin in his palms. "Boy, the world is a crazy place. But, I'd think China would want the new nanotechnology."

"Not understand China. All countries make nanotechnology things. This not interest China. China wants to make things like bearings. Sell cheap, so soon only China make bearings. Chinese workers starve with low pay. No matter. If ten million die, no matter. What matters is only China makes bearings. Then same for more things. One day China wants something. Maybe want Taiwan back, or U.S. to take warplanes and war ships from Pacific. You not do, China not sell you bearings, so you do. You look, bearings become weapons."

Breckon got up and told Chen where the food was, that he should try to sleep, and that he'd be back by six. Hua had to be who he said he was. That story was too crazy to expect anybody to believe. Which, he thought, didn't say much for himself.

# — 12 —

When Quan Peng opened his eyes the drape on the window was surrounded with bright light so he assumed it was morning. He was feeling pretty good, though he wasn't in the clear yet by any means. He needed to find a source of income, and, very soon, a new identity. Throwing back the blanket and swinging his feet to the floor, he took the phone book from the small nightstand beside the bed. He glanced at several pages, and looked up. Ah yes, they were all there. He thought of world maps. Those too were clear in his mind. Good. His enhanced mental power was still functioning and he assumed the street smarts were as well. He wondered if he'd do this every time he woke up from a long sleep, sort of a memory-bank test.

Opening the blinds on the window, he shuddered at what he saw. The just risen sun gave a pink tinge to the unkempt towers of steam slowly wafting skyward from every roof. The sky was incredibly clear, something that never happened over the cities of China. It had snowed during the night, and now he remembered how cold it had been walking to and from the restaurant yesterday. The thought of food made his stomach growl and he knew why. It had been fifteen hours since he had eaten.

Putting on the suit coat he had taken off the man in Mumbai, he headed back to Ma's Kitchen. The place was crowded but he managed to get a stool at the counter as a large man got up to leave. As he sat down, he saw salt and pepper shakers as well as bottles of condiments looking back at him. Among them was a small vase containing dusty plastic flowers valiantly trying to do their task of adding a little whimsy to the bleak lives that occupied this little space.

He reached for the menu card safely laminated behind a well-fingered celluloid covering. As if by mechanical linkage, a cup and saucer clanked into position behind the menu. As steaming dark brown fluid flowed into the cup, a surprisingly cheerful voice said, "Coffee," more as a fact than a question.

Peng couldn't help but smile. In heavily accented English he responded, "I come across the world for this cup of coffee. You saved my living." He had always been a smooth talker, but getting the hang of a new language would take time.

The waitress stopped just a moment still holding the spherical coffee-pot. "I saved your life, you mean." She refilled another cup two places down the counter, and then replaced the pot on the hotplate. Returning, and still smiling, she asked, "What'll ya have, cowboy?"

He smiled back. "Two eggs, ham, toast, ah, coffee, too."

"Coffee ya got. Ha-da-ya-want the eggs?"

Peng blinked. "Ah . . . ah, cooked."

"Scrambled it is."

Peng sipped his coffee and inhaled the aroma to invigorate himself. Trying not to be conspicuous, he noted the clientele of the establishment. He was over dressed for the place. These were clearly working class people. His last mark had netted him only businessman clothes. They had been perfect for air travel, but now he had to decide what he wanted to do and dress accordingly.

The food was gone in what seemed a few gulps, and he was still hungry. He had to move, though. He paid in Canadian dollars. As he walked back to his motel, he saw that kitty-corner across the intersection at the end of the block was a large truck fueling and servicing station. That accounted for the patrons in the restaurant.

In his motel room, he thought about his hubot sensation of the previous afternoon. Closing his eyes, he tried to get a fix on the direction. It had only been a vague feeling, but it seemed to have come from the south, or southeast. How far? No way of knowing, not thousands of miles, though. Okay, head south. He pictured a map of North America in his mind. Of course, south. If you wanted to go north, you couldn't get there from here. There was nothing to the east or west, either. Minneapolis was the next large city, and it was to the southeast.

The truck station he had seen meant transportation, so all he had to do was get on a truck headed south. He needed the right clothes, and his money would soon run out. A warm coat would help, too. He knew that killing and taking what he wanted was not the best idea in a place like this. He needed a bigger city. Back to the phone book, he started leafing through the yellow pages. Growing up he had learned how to use charities to get clothing, and now and then a meal. He found what he wanted: St. Vincent de Paul Shelter For The Homeless. He had been living in the same business suit and dress shirt that he had put on in Mumbai. The suit, not being expensive to begin with, looked pretty shabby.

It was too cold to stand out and wait for a taxi so he called one. Twenty minutes later he was let off at the corner a block away from the shelter. He had seen a bank sign that showed -22° C. No wonder his ears were stinging by the time he got to the shelter. As he walked in, he rubbed his hands. A short woman who tended to the portly looked up as he came in and approached him. She wore a floor length gray dress, and a head covering like certain nuns he had seen in China. A white plastic nameplate with black letters was pinned to the upper left of her dress. It said Sister Mary Ann.

"Oh dear, you look cold. The weather has taken a chilly turn, and you're not at all dressed for it. Come in and we'll get you some hot soup." Raising her voice she said, "Samuel, another guest has arrived. Bring a bowl of soup." Then to Peng again. "Now sit down. There is always room at the Lord's table."

Peng tried to object, "But, I have eaten . . . "

The still smiling round face interrupted him. "Yes, yes dear. But, how long ago. It's no disgrace to be down a little. Sometimes the Lord sends us trials so we will forget our little problems and turn to Him for help and forgiveness." Then, "Over here, Samuel."

There were two large tables with all variety of chairs arranged around them. Ten or so were occupied. Some of the collection of motley guests were eating. Others, having finished, perused newspapers with coffee cup rings on them. A man of about sixty and wearing an apron solemnly placed a bowl of steaming soup in front of Peng. Then he carefully placed a paper napkin to the left. Lastly, he laid a spoon on the napkin so gently that it seemed he thought it was made of glass rather than steel.

"Thank you, Samuel. Now please bring the gentleman a cup of coffee."

"Yes, Sister Mary Ann," Samuel said in a slow methodical monotone.

Then turning her attention to Peng again, Sister Mary Ann said, "And, what can we call you?"

"I am Quan," Peng answered.

"Fine, Mr. Quan. You eat your soup, and I will see if we have some warmer clothes that will fit you. You have broad shoulders, but there should be something."

The soup was good; more like the food Peng had eaten most of his life. It was thick with beans, and other vegetables, along with chunks of gristly meat.

No sooner had Peng finished his soup when Sister Mary Ann was back. "Oh, yes, yes. The Lord has blessed us today. As I walked back, I remembered a box of donations from only yesterday. There is a fine coat, and some warm trousers. Oh, I do hope they will fit. Come, come now."

This was not making sense to Peng. Was there such a shortage of poor people in this city that they cherished each one? And, who was this Lord?

In the back room, she thrust a pair of pants into Peng's hands. "Now you try on these trousers first." She tugged at his arm to turn him and pointed to a little dressing room. "Pull the curtain, and I'll see what else I can find."

Peng had his pants off when he heard voices from the dining area. The first was that of Samuel. "Hello, Officer Ricks. Ha are ya?"

"Hi Samuel. The air has a bite to it this morning."

"It's cold today."

"Yeah, Samuel. You ever see the man in this picture? It came off a security camera at the airport in Toronto yesterday. They think he's the one who killed a Canadian man in Mumbai. Stole his credentials and used them to travel to Winnipeg."

"Well, maybe two, three months ago. That's not a very good picture."

"Okay. Thanks Samuel. Where's Sister Mary Ann?"

"In the back room."

Peng stiffened as he pulled up the pants he had been given. He must have dropped something on the ground where he changed clothes with the dead man. Easy enough to do in the dark. Damn! When he talks to that woman, she'll sure as hell identify me. He switched off the light in the fitting room and slid the curtain back a few inches. He'd have to take them silently one at a time so there would be no alarm given. There was nothing in view that might be used for a weapon, only piles and racks of clothing. He heard the police officer muttering to himself as he entered the back room, "Why do I always talk to that Samuel. He's gotta be a lot more than a few bricks short of a load."

Fear and loathing of all members of the human race had been aroused in Peng, especially for the two others in the room with him now. As he peered through the crack beside the curtain, he estimated the distance between himself and the officer as he came though the door to his right.

When the man reached the spot Peng had marked in his mind, he'd move. Three quick steps from behind. A sharp punch to the kidney, then a quick two-handed twist of the head. If the snap from the neck wasn't too loud, the woman wouldn't hear. Then drag him to the dressing room. That'd be one.

Like a cat about to pounce on a bird, Peng measured the movement of his prey with his eyes. A half-second before he would have moved there was a sound from the left. "Officer Ricks. Did you come in to warm yourself, too?" The voice had genuine warmth in it. What's with her, Peng thought? Nobody likes everybody.

As long as the thought took, his opportunity passed. No time to worry about what was gone. Now he'd have to take them both together, and deal with the inevitable commotion in the aftermath. His odds were not looking good. He squinted past the curtain as the officer held up the photo and gave the same explanation as he had to Samuel. The angle wasn't the best, but he could see the two of them with one eye. When the woman identified him, Peng would move low to the floor behind some large boxes to get a better position before he struck. If the policeman heard a movement, he'd have his gun out before Peng could get to him.

A few seconds passed. What's taking her so long? "I can't say that I have. I have a pretty good memory for faces. If he'd been here, I'd remember. The picture is a little fuzzy, but it's a good enough likeness for identification."

Peng had already eased the drape to the side so there would be no movement as he exited the little room. He was crouching near the floor ready to begin his attack. The words he heard hardly made sense. What had she said? That's silly. The officer would not have bothered with a photo that was so indistinct that she could not have identified him.

"Well, okay. It was a try. Keep your eyes open, though. We have to assume this is a dangerous man."

"Okay. Stop by any time."

Then Peng understood. Boy, she was a cagey one. Dealing with all sorts of down and out men, including criminals on the lam, she had to know he was listening. She'd get him out of there, and then call the police.

A few seconds later Peng heard the door to the street open and close. He came out of the dressing room with the heavy corduroy pants on. They fit acceptably well. As Sister Mary Ann walked up to him the expression on her face was just as sweet as it had been before. "Now Mr. Quan, I see the trousers fit well. How do they feel?"

Peng had never been so confused. It was as if the officer had never been there. Was she really that dumb? There was not the slightest bit of tension in her voice. She had to know I might kill her, he thought. That was certainly his plan. Before he could think, she said.

"Good, you keep them. Go get your things out of the pockets of your old trousers and we'll dispose of those rags. I found a coat, it's a little worn, but has a lot of use left in it. In addition, here is a heavy shirt that I think will fit. Well, don't just stand there, go get your things."

As Peng tried the shirt, the coat, and even some boots, Sister Mary Ann kept up an intermittent homily. "Now, Mr. Quan, God created each of us for a purpose. You see, he knew from all eternity that he would create you when he did. With an infinite amount of forethought, he fit you into his plan so you could do good. In fact, you are an integral part of His plan. Since God put so much care into you, he loves you very much. Any time you need help, you must ask God, and He'll help. The evil one, Satan, tries to undo God's plan. You mustn't let evil win out over you, or you will not be able to do the good that you were placed here to do. Remember, the part of you that says 'me' does not die when your body dies. It lives forever. You must make provision for that by doing good."

Some minutes later Sister Mary Ann was showing Peng out the front door. Her parting words were, "Now, Mr. Quan, be nice."

The cold air was a relief. The warm clothing was beginning to make him sweat. The coat was great. It had a sheepskin wool lining with a generous collar that could be turned up to cover his ears. What the collar didn't cover, the wool stocking cap did. In addition to that, he even had fur lined gloves—these people knew how to handle cold weather.

Peng walked a few blocks and finally turned a few feet into an alley. It was a run-down part of town, not unlike those he was familiar with. The lack of activity was striking, though. There were few vehicles on the street, and fewer people. Those people he did see were only out long enough to dash from one place to another. No wonder with the cold. There was a small bush that had grown between the pavement and the building wall. The wind had picked up, and the small branches seemed to shiver. Poor blighter, what a place to try to grow.

In between times, the parting shot of Sister Mary Ann kept coming back. "Now, Mr. Quan, be nice." Be nice! Hey lady, I kill people before lunch every day, and some days continue on into the afternoon and evening. Guess I've been kind of kinking up God's plan, huh? It was hard to shake off, but he had to. His situation was desperate. The police were looking for him, but strangely, he did not think the woman would turn him in. She was daft. Although he had gotten a meal, actually two, and had warm clothes, he would have to get in out of the cold. Even now, he could feel his fingers getting numb.

Peng began to assess his surroundings. Looking to the far end of the alley, he saw only another street bathed in cold sunlight. The alley immediately across the street from where he stood apparently opened into a loading area. It was impossible for Peng to see for sure because of the building facing the street, but it looked like there might be a missing building back there. A dirty white straight-job truck was backed up to a dock. From time to time men came out pushing two-wheel handcarts with cardboard cartons on them, deposited them on the dock by the truck, and hurried back inside. A single man with a heavy coat, mittens, and a cap with flaps to cover his ears, was hefting the boxes into the rear of the truck. Peng could see his breath as he worked. After the last box disappeared into the truck the loader reached up and pulled down the rear door that formed the back of the truck and latched it. A man that was more lightly dressed came out holding some papers in his hand and said, "Thanks, Doug, see ya next time." The cold crisp air transmitted the sounds as if the men were next to him.

The loader raised his mittened hand and replied, "Have a good trip, Harvey." The man called Harvey walked around to the driver's side and Peng heard the door slam. Seconds later the truck started. Without thinking, Peng was moving. Covering his face the best he could he glanced both ways into the street looking for police cars. Seeing none, he crossed, and went to the end of the block and around the corner. Sure enough, there was a wide opening between the buildings. The truck was just emerging. It came to a stop as the driver waited for a car to pass. At that moment Peng opened the passenger side door and got in.

Harvey looked bewildered at first, and then angry. "Hey, what ya doing. This ain't no public bus, buddy."

"Sorry for the inconvenience. It's cold and I need a ride. Start driving."

"I'm not goin' anywhere with you. Beat it, chum."

Peng had taken off his right glove, opened two buttons and fumbled under his coat. Then he poked his index finger against the underside of the coat to look like the barrel of a gun.

"I said, start driving."

Harvey did as he was told. "How do I know ya got a gun under there, let's see it."

"You cannot see it, but you will hear it any time you do not do as you are told. What is your destination?"

"Screw you."

Peng scooped up the papers lying on the seat between them. Keeping an eye on Harvey, he scanned them. "I see, Minneapolis. That is good. Go there."

"You're nuts. You can hold that thing on me until we get to the border, but you'll never pull it off at the crossing. You're history."

Peng understood the warning and was thankful for it, though he said nothing. The border would be a problem. He had seen a map in the motel lobby and now studied it in his mind.

Harvey was nervous, and kept glancing in Peng's direction. In fact, that wasn't exactly right, he seemed to be glancing at the dashboard in front of Peng. They were still in city traffic, and the gnawing feeling crept into Peng that his driver meant to try something soon. He was a big man and in the close confines of the cab, a good first punch could put Peng down. He'd do it at a traffic light, and they were approaching one that would be red by the time they got there. Peng shifted to the right to press his back against the corner formed by the doorjamb and the seat. With his left hand he reached over and opened the glove box.

As Peng's attention was momentarily distracted, Harvey lurched over, but Peng had his foot up and slammed him back to the right. The jerk of the wheel sent the truck to the right augmenting Peng's thrust. Harvey hit his door, and had to correct the steering as a horn blared beside them. In that moment, Peng saw the object of Harvey's interest. The butt of a revolver was visible. Harvey came again. With no longer a need for pretense, Peng had both hands out. With his left he deflected Harvey's right arm down, and with his right landed a fist in the right eye. Harvey recoiled, and they were at the red light. An eighteen-wheeler was coming through the intersection and Harvey planted the brakes. Peng braced himself against the dashboard with his right hand, and grabbed the revolver with the left. Rubber screeched but there was no collision. Peng held the revolver in his left hand down low and aimed it at Harvey.

"Back out of the intersection, now!" Peng barked. Harvey slipped it into reverse and the truck backed. When they were moving again after the light turned green neither man said anything. Peng noticed they had gone off Highway 42 onto 155 to the southwest. The logical route to

Minneapolis was to take 42 which became 75. This led directly south to the border. In North Dakota, it became Interstate 29 at Pembina. They hit the next two lights green, then a red. Peng moved toward Harvey. He pulled the hammer back and stuck the gun under his jawbone.

"You move, I will kill you." Harvey seemed to be a believer as Peng went though his coat and shirt pockets. He found a knife in a scabbard under the left arm, and assorted papers. "You travel well armed for a nice law abiding citizen." Peng backed against the right door. "Now pull out your wallet and be slow and easy about it." Harvey complied.

When they were moving again, Peng put on his seat belt lest Harvey unexpectedly hit the brakes to unbalance him. He started going through the papers. There was a white envelope that was just the right thickness to have payoff money in it, and a note with "Snowflake 11:00 to 11:30" on it. He thought about the map he had seen on the wall in the motel lobby. Mentally he scanned along the border with the United States and Canada for the crossing points. Highway 155 was the route to the crossing near the town of Snowflake.

"What's the note about Snowflake? That's a small town near the border one hundred kilometers to the west from the main route, and very desolate. We are headed that way. Am I right?"

"How da you know so much about this area? I know you're not from around here."

"I saw a map, and took an interest in border crossing places."

Harvey drew in a deep breath through his nose. "There's less hassle at that crossing. There's almost never any problem on this side. The Canadians don't much care what goes *into* the U.S. And we, well, know the guy that'll be there on the U.S. side. Let's say we're old friends."

Peng smiled. "And this envelope," he said holding it up, "contains a token of your friendship. Is that correct?"

"Yeah. Somethin' like that."

# — 13 —

They were at the Snowflake border checkpoint at 11:20. Peng slid down on the floor out of sight as they approached the Canadian side. Harvey lowered his window and handed the load manifest to the official. A few pleasantries later they were on their way. As they approached the U.S. side, Harvey put the envelope under the manifest. As the brakes squeaked the vehicle to a stop he lowered his hand out the window and said, "Morning Bill. Got a little frost last night."

"Hi, Harvey. Yeah. Seems to be hanging on, too. Nearly ten below this morning. Let's see, what ya got here." There was the sound of muttering as he checked the manifest. "Looks like everything's in order. Drive safely. There's icy patches on the road when you get a little farther south." In a little softer voice, "Company today."

"Yeah? Well, see ya when I see ya." With that, the truck lurched and they were on their way.

When they were out of sight of the crossing Peng got up on the seat again. "What was that part about company?"

"Apparently, there was an extra guy who wasn't part of the regular crew in the building. That's unusual. But, it means we'll have to adjust our route a little. Normally I'd head south, catch Highway 2, and go to Grand Forks. Today we'll jog a little west and take 281 south to Jamestown. We'll take I-94 from there all the way to Minneapolis. It'll add an hour, but I don't want to be predictable." Harvey paused. "Why am I telling you this? I don't even like you. Anyway, now that I got your sorry ass into the U.S., what do you plan to do?"

"The border crossing went well. For that, I am grateful. However, I am now certain you are carrying illegal cargo. If the bribe was not enough, the fact that you did not try to give me away proves it." Peng was thinking about what he knew about his trade. Harvey could be hauling anything from untaxed booze to stolen teddy bears. Still, he suspected it was materials for the meth trade. The use of methamphetamine in China was a growing problem. As with everything made in China, they exported far more than they used domestically. This was no different with the precursor chemicals for making meth. One of the largest meth markets in the world was the U.S. He had heard talk that different Chinese suppliers were doing business with Mexico and Canada. From these countries, the chemicals were shipped into the United States. Each side tried to infiltrate the competing organizations that shipped to the U.S. so they could learn of the shipments and tip off the border guards. And, here he was right in the middle of it. With no plans to go back to China any time soon, he might be forced into playing it from this side.

"My plans depend on many things. I need to get to the city of Minneapolis. That is the first thing." Peng let it hang there. After several minutes, he said one word, "Meth!"

Harvey flinched just enough to make Peng certain. "The cargo in the back has to do with meth. No need to deny it. I saw your reaction. We do not want to have a misunderstanding, so listen to what I have to say. I know the, what you call it, plate number, of this truck. Its make, model, color, and size. I know what you look like in detail. If you betray me to the police, I can inform them of this shipment and where it came from. I will not fall asleep before we get to our destination, and you are not strong enough, nor do you have the skill to overpower me. I, on the other hand, could kill you and drive the truck myself. I would still get what I wanted. We do not have to be friends, but hostility is not needed."

Peng saw Harvey's mouth twitch. He didn't like the situation, that was clear, but that was part of the business, and they both knew it. Times like this would come, so roll with it and see what developed. Peng keenly understood this, and now it was somebody else's turn to do the adjusting.

In Fargo, they made a pit stop as both men were about ready to burst a bladder. Though he would have had enough fuel to reach Minneapolis, Harvey filled the gas tank. He did not want to be caught short in case he had to make more detours. After that, they were on the road again.

---

When Breckon returned, Chen was sound asleep on the living room floor. He had found extra blankets and a pillow. Breckon's mind had been working all day on what he was going to do with the guy. During supper, they agreed to snip up the fake passport and flush it. Chen was devastated to learn that Breckon was not working for anybody other than Control Systems Ltd. as an electrical engineer.

"Why do you think it's so important to tell somebody the sensitive information you have?" Ed asked as they were finishing their meal.

In a deadly serious tone, Chen explained. "Goal of hubot experiments is to make human robots like I said in the morning. They always do as told, always. I always do as am told, even this," he said holding out his finger that was nearly healed, though the end was still red. "Told to chop off finger, I chop it off. Told to point gun at head and pull trigger, I do. Might shoot bullet in head, but bullet in gun was empty there."

"They made you play Russian roulette?"

"Yes. Not game. I told not to tell secrets. If I told you who do not understand the meaning, same as telling the wind. Must tell to people where it is important, who want to know very much. I know many secrets."

"If I get this right, you feel a need to deliberately disobey an order. Is that it?"

"Yes. That is it. Maybe then I will know I am not hubot."

Breckon was working on this. It wasn't making much sense. "But, you act, talk, and seem to think just like anybody else. You are just as human as I am. Why does this bother you so much?"

"No, you are wrong. I am not human like you. I have no life in my mind from before experiment. After I wake up that is gone, only see small things of past, this and that. But, I remember everything I see from time I wake up. I look at all the pages of a telephone book, remember everything. I look at all the pages in English dictionary, it is all in my head. You talk words I never hear. Easy. I look at pages in my head, find words, know what you say. Think fast, too. Dr. Mingchang thought I am a real hubot."

"Okay, let's say you're a hubot. You can do things almost nobody else can do. That's not so bad. If you worked at being disobedient, I'd think in time you'd catch on." Ed couldn't help smiling. This was too absurd, he thought. We spend our whole lives trying to be virtuous, at least some of us do. If there began to be more hubots, some university would start offering classes in lying. Then it occurred to him that there were already an awful lot of law schools and journalism departments, but that was another story.

Hua was not smiling. "You do not understand. Hubot has animal soul. You have human soul. They are different. That is true, I think."

Ed saw Hua's dilemma. "Yes, absolutely true. The human soul is a spirit and spirits live forever."

"That is it! Animal soul dies when animal dies. Now you see. If I have human soul, I must find information about that next life. Must know what will happen to me after I am dead."

"But, if you have an animal soul that would mean they killed *you* in the experiment, your human soul left your body, and it is at its final resting place. This means you are, well, not really you, so why worry?"

Chen's face was set like stone. "That is too easy. I am first one like me . . . ever. Never before one like me. Maybe all mixed up. Might have animal soul and man soul, maybe some of each. I want to find someone with deep thinking on what man is."

"I understand. You want to talk with a theologian or maybe a philosopher. Still, I don't see the urgency for it. Why?"

Chen looked away as he spoke. "I think they will guess where I went and send a man to kill me so hubot research is not learned by others. It moves in me to find out about my soul. Must know before I die. You help me. Please?"

Breckon felt forced to say he'd help, but didn't have his heart in it. They cleaned up the kitchen. After that, Breckon took him out to shop for winter clothes. He wanted Chen's money to last as long as it could so they went to a thrift store. Breckon could see he was getting into one of those things again like Iraq and China and he always lost money on them. The idea of an assassin didn't fill him with joy either.

The temperature was already below zero, and as soon as they were in the store Chen demanded they look at coats. "It's always a grab bag at these stores," Ed said. "If a person has time to come often, inevitably the item he wants shows up." They happened to be pretty lucky. There was a heavy almost new green parka that was right except the sleeves were a little too long. It had a generous hood with fur trim and was machine washable. At first, Hua refused to take it off until Ed convinced him it would be safe in the cart as they continued to shop. They also found gloves, jeans, and corduroy pants. There was a flannel shirt of western style, and a heavy woolen one. In the cart they went. Breckon had never seen anyone shop with such determination. There were even some snow boots of a type Breckon had never seen. They fit so into the cart. The bill came to ninety-five dollars, a fraction of what the merchandize would have cost new. As they left the store Hua was wearing the coat, boots, and gloves, tags still attached.

A few miles past Clearwater, Minnesota Harvey said, "Hey stick, I'm due for a stop. There's a rest area a few miles ahead. I'm pulling in."

Peng did not argue. It was after seven and long past dark. Being a Friday evening there was little traffic headed into the city, but a steady stream headed out. An ever increasing number of twin-citians had moved up to year-round cabins in the north country. Many were headed out to snowmobile and do some ice fishing for the weekend. At times, Peng and Harvey had short nearly civilized conversations as Peng asked about this or that. One such was his observation about the unequal flow of traffic. He had never heard about ice fishing other than for Eskimos, and thought it amazing that it would be a recreation.

Pulling into the rest stop, they saw a light tan Crown Vic and a pickup truck. According to the drill Peng had demanded in Fargo, Harvey gave Peng the keys who put the gun under the seat and locked the doors, after which they went in together. Harvey was always to be in Peng's sight. To their dismay, there was a Minnesota Highway Patrol officer talking to a man, who watched them come in. Peng looked at Harvey who gave a slight shrug out of sight of the officer. As they headed for the men's room the other man turned to go out the door they had come in.

Inside Peng checked the stalls. Finding them empty he moved to a urinal next to Harvey and whispered, "Where did he come from?"

"That tan car must be an unmarked patrol car. It wouldn't have mattered, though. If it had been a regular state trooper car, we could not have driven out. That would have been a give-away that we were avoiding the law."

As they were washing their hands, another man came in. He was in his thirties, and of slight build. Immediately he proceeded to use a porcelain appliance. Harvey opened the door and exited the room. Peng was still drying his hands as he tuned his head to watch him. Outside the open door was the officer waiting and was approaching Harvey as the door closed. As soon as the door to the restroom was shut Peng moved up to the other man grabbed his right arm and forced his forehead into the cinder block wall knocking him unconscious. He caught him and rolled him to his stomach on the floor. Instantly, Peng jerked open the door to see the patrolman pointing in the direction of the truck as he spoke to Harvey.

"Officer," Peng said in an emphatic voice, "there is a man in here who went faint and fell on the floor. He hit his head hard, and is not moving. He looks sick."

Immediately the officer responded, though from training he opened the door cautiously suspecting it could be a trick. By that time, a man and a woman had come in. The officer, seeing the man on the floor, held the door open and looked back. Harvey and Peng were gone so he ordered the new arrivals to assist him as he called it in on his radio.

Peng and Harvey ducked out the opposite door from where they had come in. Harvey grabbed Peng's sleeve, "Don't walk too fast or you will draw attention." Peng unlocked the door and got in. He leaned over and opened the driver's side door.

When they were on the road and up to speed Peng asked, "What did the police officer want?"

"He showed interest in the truck, and asked where I had come from and where I was going."

"What did you tell him?"

"I said I had come from Jamestown and was headed for Hastings."

"But the manifest does not say you came from Jamestown! What would have happened if he had asked to see your papers?"

"Don't worry. Nothing would have happened. He would not have asked. You don't need documents to travel in the United States."

"Oh," Peng said slowly. "That is convenient. Why was he interested in this truck? It was that extra man at the crossing, wasn't it?"

"Yeah, I think so. What the heck did you do back in the men's room? I could've handled it! You think that was the first time I ran into a cop? What'd you do?"

"That man that came in looked a little sickly, so I slapped his head into the wall and knocked him unconscious. We needed a diversion. In case you have not figured it out, I cannot have the police inspecting my identification. If they ever ask questions about me, you will be found out. I see to that."

After a few minutes Harvey said, "The way he was talking to that guy when we drove in I don't think he saw our plates. We were too far away and it was dark. From where I parked, there was not enough time for him to go out, look at the plates, and get back while we were taking a piss. I've done this before. Anyway, what's done is done. Maybe he was just guessing. The size and color of this truck are common. That's why it was picked. As a precaution we'll have to take another detour, though."

Monticello was a few miles ahead. There, they took the exit and went east across the Mississippi River to Highway 10. Past Anoka, they took 242 to Lexington Avenue. Here they went south. As he took the entrance ramp from Lexington on to I-35W he said, "I don't know what you plan to do. We're nearly there. My destination is in an old section of Minneapolis not far from the downtown area. So, you wanted a ride, you got it. When I exit the freeway, you get out. If you try something cute like taking over the truck I can have the police on you in five minutes by an anonymous phone call. It won't do me any good, but they'll sure as hell nail you."

Peng was thinking of how quickly he had gotten cold in the alley in Winnipeg. He needed some place to get in out of the cold. He could also imagine Harvey was trying hard to come up with some excuse for having been hijacked. If Harvey could dump him out, Harvey would be in the clear. Peng was working on the idea of linking up with Harvey's organization, if only for a few days. After all, he knew the business. If Harvey was not agreeable he could always kill him and take his chances with the truck. That option had not occurred to Harvey. It would be risky, though. If not the police, the organization would be looking for the truck.

"This is what I will tell you. In China, I was in the same business you are in. There came a difficulty with the police. Someone had to be, what would you say, given up . . . "

"Sacrificed."

"Yes, that is a good word for it. It was me. I found out in time and went into hiding, but picked a bad place. Those I stayed with would have given me to the police. I escaped, and kept going. It takes me two weeks to end in Winnipeg." To this point, everything Peng had said happened to be true, not that it would have mattered. Whatever the goal of the hubot program, *he* had no problem with lying. He'd have to fabricate what came next based on rumors he had heard.

"What happened at the crossing was not an accident. Since the laws in this country have cut off most of your domestic sources of pseudoephedrine, the key ingredient to meth, your organization, as well as others, have been forced to look for other sources of supply. Most of it now comes from Canada and Mexico. You know how easy it is or you wouldn't take the chance. The sources of supply for your two neighboring countries are rivals. The supplier to Mexico, I am guessing, has infiltrated the operations in Canada. Snitches tell border people when and where you come."

"So, are you a snitch?"

"No. It is a thing hard to think that I picked the first truck I saw and it was you with illegal cargo. My luck is not good. You believe, or not believe what I say. I do not know."

Harvey chuckled. "That's sure some story. Can ya prove any of it?"

"Do your people have ways to check police information?"

"Of course. Ya think we're stupid?"

"Alright, I show my identification. You check and find it is from a Canadian business man from Quebec who lost it in Mumbai."

"Suppose we find you're real, ya know any more about how they're trying to mess up our organization?"

Peng readily lied, "Yes. I know more."

Harvey took the exit for University Avenue in Southeast Minneapolis, and turned right. A few blocks later he took a left. He stopped at a vehicle door in an old brick building and sounded the horn. The door opened and he drove in.

# — 14 —

The room was the same, the furniture was the same, and the three people were the same, sitting in the same chairs as if by an assigned seating chart. Only the day was different. Seng Kejian of the MSS glared across the table at the two doctors.

"You finally confirm that a total of two of these experimental, what do you say, hubot beings, have escaped." Kejian used the most officious cutting edge to his voice he could muster, and that was saying something. His normal demeanor was enough to make his own mother cringe, so when he actually tried to debase someone it was savage. Doctors Mingchang and Hongi had known this time would come so were prepared for it. They stoically sat with expressions set. Hongi nodded, confirming this fact.

"If you are to save your careers I expect total cooperation, do you understand?"

Both doctors nodded. The MSS "dirt," as they were almost universally referred to, could easily make any threat into reality.

"These 'things' must be apprehended. We are nearly certain both have fled the country. A minor operation to arrest a couple of petty fugitives has turned into an international operation. I have personally been on this case since reports of a trail of death headed west started coming in. I must have everything you know about where they might have gone."

Hongi chose his words deliberately. "I have dealt only with determining if they were obedient. All of the tests showed they were."

"Well, they escaped didn't they? That was disobedient! You clearly failed in your duty!"

Hongi winced at the accusation. His apparent attempt to distance himself from responsibility had gone awry in Kejian's eyes. This had been planned. Now he would attempt to recover.

"That is not really true," he continued in an even voice. "You see, they were never told *not* to escape." Hongi held up his hand as Kejian prepared to attack and continued before the onslaught could begin. "The hubots of concern have greatly enhanced memory abilities. This is classified information so bear that in mind. For example, they could page through a complete dictionary as fast as they could turn the pages and glance at each one, and remember every word in the book. They were being groomed for very responsible positions with remuneration far exceeding what they had previously managed. It did not seem reasonable they would throw that away. We never suspected this ungrateful, even spiteful response." He made certain not to mention the fact that they were summarily executed if they showed the slightest defect.

Kejian sat back in his chair. The plan, as far as Hongi could see, was working. Even if the MSS officer had commanding authority, he could see these two were not people he would take down without a fight. In addition, the reward for him would be greater if he found the hubots rather than exacting retribution on these careless mind doctors.

With a scowl, Kejian began anew, "Excuses do not bring them back. Where did they go?"

Mingchang sat with unchanging expression beside Hongi. He had blunted the criticism they knew would come from their adversary, and rather adroitly. Now Mingchang could say some things that might meet a more responsive chord.

"As Dr. Hongi mentioned, these hubots were being groomed for tasks in the government where their vast memory powers could be put to good use. As you well know, in counterespionage work there are many small pieces of information that, if all are considered, can solve a case rather quickly. The problem with normal people is they don't remember all the facts. Hubots have that ability.

"We were doing practice sessions on a foreign espionage case. The HB-23 had several sessions using the information from the files. We gave him information a little at a time just as it was actually received. We found he came to the correct solution sooner than happened in the actual case." The "accidental" delivery of the Breckon files to HB-27, as ordered by the general had to be covered too, so Mingchang continued. "To verify the value of enhanced memory on the solution to the problem we were told to have HB-27 work the same case. He had not gotten enough information to draw a conclusion when he escaped."

Kejian was growing impatient. "What are you trying to tell me? You seem to be rambling and wasting my time."

"No, no," Mingchang said. "I am merely telling you background information so you will understand the conclusion I am about to tell you. We think it is likely both hubots have gone by their separate ways to meet the key player in this sample case. It is a rather engaging case with many unexpected twists and turns. Anyone who reads the file says they begin to feel a certain empathy for this foreign agent not unlike one feels for the villain in a well written novel. I began to feel it myself, though I only reviewed parts of it."

It was dangerous to mention the Breckon case in this regard. Both doctors knew what would happen if Kejian told the wrong people. However, they agreed there was a possibility at least one of the hubots had gone to meet Breckon. And, without this background, it was unlikely the MSS would take their assumption seriously.

"We will provide you with all the information you need to follow up this lead. You know, of course, it is to your advantage not to know all the details. What you don't know you cannot be accused of leaking. It is a sensitive case."

There followed the transfer of information about Edmund Breckon. Kejian began to see that someone would have to go to the United States, and if he made the case right, he would likely be the one to go. He had already been on the trail of these hubots for some time, and the fewer people who knew about the hubot research the better.

---

After the warehouse door closed, Harvey killed the truck lights and at the same time overhead lights came on. There was no one to be seen.

Peng spoke, "I will keep the gun. Remember, I can help you." He saw no point in discussing what came next so he flatly stated it as a fact. "I will stay here in this building for a day or two until I make my contacts."

As he spoke, he saw movement from the corner of his eye. A small black man was coming out of an office door to their right. Next to the door was a window that looked from the office into the warehouse bay.

"Here comes Jefferson. He kinda looks after things around here. I'll let you work out your accommodations with him. By the way, don't call him Jeff. He's really sensitive about that."

When Peng opened the truck door the odor of the air was a once familiar, and offensive. He recognized the smell of the gases that were produced when cooking meth. In China, he had been in the part of the business of acquiring the precursor chemicals. All in all, he had spent enough time around the production labs to know what went on. The main gaseous byproducts from the manufacture of meth were ammonia, hydrogen chloride, and phosphine. There was, of course, trace amounts of vaporized meth and other gases. The result was a pungent smell that in small enough concentrations began in time to be taken as normal, almost pleasant. He had attributed this to the small methamphetamine content. This place was another matter.

He could hardly believe any serious producer of meth would allow so many emissions. Anyone walking past when the vehicle door was opened would smell it. A large percentage of meth labs were found by law enforcement when locals complained of bad odors. What must it be like in the room with the vats?

"Hey Jefferson," Harvey said, "smells like you're cooking. The boss around?"

"Nah. Gone for the weekend. Who's the dude?"

Peng did not give Harvey a chance to respond. "Am from China by way of Winnipeg to look at your operation. I associated with your supply of precursor chemicals. Who is in charge of production? Air scrubbers not functioning." Peng could have spoken more perfect English, but chopped up his speech for effect.

"Huh? What's that you're talkin' about? Who's the guy, Harvey?"

As Peng had begun to speak Harvey was about to fumble around with something about needing an extra man in case of trouble with the law, but the words died in his throat. This was better. His eyes darted from one of the men to the other trying to determine if Peng's ruse would gain footing. Now it was his turn. Jefferson was looking at Harvey. His expression portrayed that he only wanted a simple confirmation that the story from this man, who he saw as an intruder, was true.

"Yeah, that's right. What can I say, I'm just the driver. Who's in charge of the cook? Davis?"

"Who else?"

"Okay, we'll find him. Meanwhile, the truck should be unloaded. Can ya get started at it?"

Without waiting for an answer Harvey turned and headed to the office indicating with a slight jerk of his head that Peng was to follow. When they were out of earshot of Jefferson he said, "What do you know about chemicals and scrubbers? You could talk over Jefferson's head, but not with Davis. He's a chemical engineer."

"That is good. He will understand very well. Find him."

They found Davis in the cook room. Its atmosphere made Peng's eyes water. Harvey asked the man in his mid-twenties to go with them into an adjoining room. Jorg Davis was thin with blood-shot eyes in a wan face. He had a chemical engineering degree from the University of Minnesota, Institute of Technology. He thought that was the ticket to the good life. Not so. The only good paying jobs were everywhere else in the world but here. Well, he found a job, and all the meth he could snort to boot. It wasn't supposed to be this way. But, with all the good paying jobs, even complete industries, being out-sourced to countries where environmental laws were much less stringent or nonexistent, what was left? He was an addict. He knew it, and didn't know what to do about it. So, he kept cooking.

With the door closed Davis said, "Who's he?"

"Quan Peng from China," Peng said. "I am associated with your source of pseudoephedrine. I must say, have you no scrubbers operating? The air in here is bad."

"Don't you worry about that. In a few little minutes, it'll be fine. We don't start the fans until after nine when the local foot traffic falls off. Then it'll be better."

Peng feigned a look of incredulity. "You mean to say you simply blow the fumes out without, I think English word is, scrubbing the air? That is how to say it?"

Davis chuckled. "I know what *should* be done. But, I'm only the engineer. Who listens to an engineer these days? The boss wishes I wasn't even here."

His act was important, Peng knew, but he was becoming alarmed that when the fans went on the concentration of fumes outside would cause complaints. Being picked up by police in a meth lab raid was not a good thing for anyone, least of all him.

"So, what ya here for, Quan? Not to sell scrubbers I'll bet." Davis said with another chuckle as he scratched his arm and twitched.

Peng could see Davis was getting high from breathing the fumes. He recognized some to the typical symptoms, euphoria, paranoia, and itching to name a few. He was thin verging on emaciated from loss of appetite and lack of sleep. It wouldn't be hard to handle him.

"Let me ask you this. What would it mean if you could start with pure ephedrine and not have to go through the process of cracking it out of pseudoephedrine?"

"It'd save about half the process. That's good. Ya know where ya can get it? Not in the U.S. I bet. Huh?"

With Davis getting tipsier by the minute, Peng made his case hoping to get a decision in his favor before the man was too drugged to think. "Look at it this way. There are so many pseudoephedrine pills being shipped into North America that every U.S. citizen would have to eat a couple of handfuls a day to use them. The shipments are carefully watched, and a lot of the goods are being confiscated. So, why bother with the subterfuge. We could simply ship ephedrine."

"Why not just ship the finished meth? Huh? Why not?"

Peng shook his head. "It's too messy to make, too much waste. If I may ask, how do you get rid of the five to six kilograms of toxic waste generated to make a kilogram of meth? Seeing you are so careless about the emissions I hope you aren't dumping it down the drain into the sewer."

Davis continually shifted around in the office chair behind the desk using jerky movements and scratching this or that part of his anatomy in random motions. In a quick movement, he waved his index finder in front of him as he spoke. "Don't you worry one little bit about that. The boss was real smart about that part. Ya ever hear about directional bor- ing, also called horizontal directional drilling. That's HDD, ya know. Well, they start drilling a hole into the ground at about thirty degrees from horizontal. From there, they can steer the drilling head any direc- tion they want. Go under buildings, rivers, whatever's in the way. At the other end they steer the drilling head up and, pop, it comes out just where they want it . . . to come out." Davis chuckled a little, feeling good about himself.

"So, they're real smart," he tapped his finger on the side of his head. "They got one of those drilling machines set up in the warehouse and drill a pipe so it comes up in the middle of the river above the dam. Then they drill another one to the middle of the river below the dam at the deepest part with the swiftest current. So, don't ya see? The water flows in from upstream with only a little pump to suck," he made a sucking sound and laughed, "suck it up to us. We mix the crap with it and out it goes to the bottom of the river below the dam." He threw his hands apart and said, "Presto, all gone. Pre-tee smart, huh?"

While this was going on Harvey was wringing his hands wishing Davis would stop. What was the point of telling a new man at the site, no matter who he was, all the secrets? He couldn't say much though, or his failure would come out. But, this was getting out of control.

"Hey Jorg, you sure your process isn't getting out of whack," Harvey interjected in an attempt to get him to stop talking.

"Nah. Just got everything checked when you guys came in. No need to do that for another half-hour. I'll wait 'til the fans go on and clear the air b'fore I have another look. Guy could get a toot on being out there too long." He laughed, and didn't seem to notice that the others failed to grasp the humor.

Quan knew the man's state. He was feeling good but was still mostly lucid. He saw his opening. "Since the boss isn't here I'll have to confide in you, Jorg, since you are the responsible person now, and the one knowledgeable in the process."

Davis leaned forward in his chair and put his forearms on the desk. He hadn't been spoken to with respect for so long he couldn't help but respond to the overture. "So, let's have it."

"We intend to start shipping pure ephedrine. That means a couple of things. The first you grasped immediately; it will make your process simpler. But, you would be able to make twice as much product with the facility you now have. Do you see what that means?"

Davis' face was a vaudeville act of activity. It twitched this way and that expressing astonishment, questioning, doubt, and bewilderment, mixed in with a few minor convulsions to dislodge a pesky fly that errantly picked this day to come out of hibernation. Finally he said, "You're the smart guy, what *does* it mean?"

"It means that half the labs will go out of business. Your lab is well located, its cooking operation is in capable hands . . . " here Davis smiled broadly, " . . . and has the largest problem, that of liquid waste disposal, very cleverly managed. I like this lab except for the gaseous emissions. And, I am prepared to help you solve that problem. With your permission, I will stay here this weekend and develop the plans necessary to install suitable scrubbers. When the boss arrives he will greatly appreciate your good business sense in accepting this offer."

"Yeah. That's good. Offer accepted. Now ya go find a hotel room and see ya in the morning. Yeah. That really sounds good."

"No. You did not hear the exact offer," Peng said very deliberately. "I must stay *here*, on these premises. The emissions are the obvious problem.

I must also see your operation in all its aspects such as security, management of precursor chemicals, personnel comings and goings, all that. We are not going to supply prime chemicals to an unprofessional operation."

Harvey was almost to a point of taking the easy way out and jump off the Third Avenue Bridge. If Peng were from a competing ring, or the law, they were *so* dead. Why wait? The only hope he had was that Peng was really on the lam, and looking for a job. Who knows, he thought, maybe it'll work out. If hope was the only straw he had, and it was, what the heck, grasp at it. He let the scene continue with Peng finding a place to stay, and Davis in no condition to decide anything.

"Yeah, why not. Go with it. I'm in the decision making mode right now. Yeah, do it. You'll have to talk to Jeff," here he chortled conspiratorially, "about where ya might flop your head when ya get tired." After a pause, "Hey, look at that. The ol' clock on the wall," he gestured to an eight inch electric clock, "says time for the ol' fans to start suckin'," here he made the sucking sound again. He got up, walked a little unsteadily to a panel by the side of the door, and pressed a button. "Presto! Snuff out the bad. Snuff in the good," followed by more solitary laughter.

# — 15 —

As Breckon lay awake in his bedroom that night he felt sorry for the guy sleeping on the air mattress in his living room, but he was not going to get mixed up in another one of these things. Twice was enough! Who put me in charge of saving the world, he thought. In the morning we'll have a nice rational discussion and figure out the best thing for Hua to do. What was the last name he gave? It was out there in his neurons some place, but it wouldn't shake loose. After some effort, he thought screw it, think of him as Hua. What did it matter? In a day or so, he'll be gone and he'd never see him again.

He turned over in bed and thoughts of a problem with a control system at work occupied him for awhile. Then thoughts of Iraq and China abused him. Though he was healing from them, there were tough times, thankfully getting further and further apart. Finally sleep came. He woke up and looked at the clock to see it was only three-thirty. He turned over, pulled on another blanket, and was asleep.

The line was getting shorter and he could see the bacon was running out. He could easily calculate in his mind that there would not be enough. These army field mess kitchens were always the same, cold food and always ran out. It came his turn to get a tray. They were serving coffee or Coke to drink. Both were dispensed from large urn-like machines. The GI looked at Breckon, "Coke," Breckon said, "or Pepsi if you have it." This was what he always said in a restaurant, and nine out of ten times settled for Coke. The GI turned without hesitation, bent down, opened what looked like a small refrigerator and pulled out a large glass bottle of Pepsi. He removed the cap with a bottle opener and put it on Breckon's tray without a word.

As he moved along, Breckon saw the last bacon was dumped on the tray just before his. "Be a few minutes," the mess sergeant said. "You're used to waiting." As they waited he and the other eight or ten men milled around in an open area holding their trays. The ground was hard packed yellow clay. Finally, he heard, "Okay, she's done." Breckon had been next in line, but somehow it just turned out the others managed to nudge and tuck in line until he was the last one. He wasn't feeling too well and had almost decided to skip breakfast. Being the last one, the server dumped the last of the bacon, at least a pound, and a dozen biscuits on his tray. The tray almost fell out of his hand.

"I can't eat all of that," Breckon protested.

"You know the rules, take all you want, but eat all you take! You took it, you eat it."

"But, I didn't take it!"

"You calling me a liar?" He was big and he leaned over Breckon. "Hey, sergeant. This here civilian's callin' me a liar."

The next thing Breckon knew he was sitting at a small table with a half dozen big fat men standing close around him. They all wore dirty white aprons, and grimy undershirts. Their hairy bare arms glistened with sweat. "You eat. You eat it all," one said.

Breckon looked up at the ugly unshaven faces glaring down at him. He sprung up and snatched the 9 mm pistol from behind his belt in the small of his back. He shoved it up under the chin of the man who had spoken to him. "Back off all of you or I'll blow this man's head off!" Nobody moved. "Move! Now!" Breckon yelled. Still no movement. Breckon pulled the trigger. Nothing happened. He pulled it again, and again. Big hands grabbed both arms and another gripped his neck. He struggled but couldn't get his breath. Suddenly, Ed was sitting bold upright in bed, eyes wide open, gasping for air.

He swung his feet off the bed and rested them on the floor taking deep breaths as he ran his hand over his face. "Nice going, God! It's back." As his heartbeat returned to normal and he began to dry out, he laid down. The nights were the worst. It got to him during the day sometimes, too, but generally, there were enough things around to get his mind off his tempest.

As he lay in bed the dream played over in his mind again. What was it about the bottle of Pepsi? Oh yes, doing something forbidden. He should have asked for coffee, or at the worst Coke. In some way he crossed the line into forbidden territory, a line known only to others. Still, he didn't have to ask for Pepsi. Whenever he chose to willfully do something he wanted, no matter that there was no obvious harm to others, he got socked.

When the opportunity came to do that robotics project, he wanted it so badly. He did a good job of it, too. And, it landed him as a prisoner in Iraq. Even at his present job, he had made it a condition of his employment that he'd do no international traveling. Yet, when the trip to China came up he grabbed it. He had always wanted to go to a Communist country, and the orient. This was both in one. There he got mixed up in that Dragon Fang thing. To top it off, he didn't have to go to the mountains. But, having been bilked out of his vacation trips so many times, he refused to listen to his inner sense. He knew that if he tried to explain it to others they would never see the connection. Nevertheless, he knew.

"Okay, God. I'll help Hua Chen." Now the name came to him like that of a member of his family. "You win, you always do." After a few minutes he sat up and covered his face with his hands, "But, why me, God. Why me?"

When morning came Breckon got up a little after six and shaved. It was Saturday. He wished he could have slept longer, but there was too much on his mind. He needed time to work things out. While they were eating breakfast Ed said, "You asked me to help you with your quest. I'll help as best I can but you must understand it will be like the blind leading the lame."

Hua brightened up. "You try to make mirth out of somber matter again. Yes?"

Ed had done it without thinking and had to realize it was at least partly so. "Yeah. I guess you're right."

"Ed, tell me a joke, funny story, you might call it, please. I need to laugh now, for once."

Ed thought a minute. "You have to remember that most jokes are a play on the double meaning of words, or subtle cultural nuances so it may not sound funny to you."

"You try one anyhow. Okay for you?"

Breckon nodded and thought. "Well, there was this young man who was reasonably famous for his ability to paint portraits of people. One day a well endowed young woman . . . you know what that means?" Ed made the motions with his hands of outlining a shapely woman, and Hua nodded. "Anyway, she came to him and asked if he would paint her portrait. He said, yes he would. She said, 'But, I have a special request. Will you paint me in the nude?' The man looked a little surprised but said, 'If that's what you want, sure, why not.' Then he said 'That being the case, I have one small request of you.' She said, 'Yes, of course.' He replied,

'Can I wear at least one sock? You see, I need some place to put my brushes.'"

Chen looked deadpan. Finally, he brightened up. "I think I understand your joke. It was good try. Do another one."

"Okay, just one more. I'm not very good at this you know. Now be ready, this is a short one. This is in the form of a riddle. You can't possibly know the answer so you must answer, 'I don't know.' Do you understand?"

Chen nodded enthusiastically. It seemed to Ed that possibly Hua was starting to remember things from before the experiment. 'Okay, what goes . . . no. What makes the sound 'wiffle-snap!'"

"I don't know."

"A dog with laryngitis having his tail broken."

Chen sat for just a moment and then his eyes sparkled and he laughed lightly. "Ed! That was funny. It was dumb, but it was funny."

Ed laughed. "Yeah, it's dumb, and I suppose that's why it's funny."

"Oh Ed, tell me another one, please . . . please?"

They didn't have anything really pressing so Breckon agreed. "This is a saloon joke. You know, a saloon was a place in the old western United States that sold beer and whiskey."

Ed could see Hua looking up the words in the dictionary in his head. He nodded.

"Okay. A skeleton walks into a saloon and puts the bones of his forearms on the bar. The bar tender says, 'What'll it be slim?' And the skeleton says, 'Give me a beer and a mop.'"

Chen chuckled and said, "He drinks the beer, and . . . " and he laughed. Breckon could see he had a good audience so he volunteered one more to Hua's delight.

"Another saloon joke. This duck waddles into a saloon, hops up on a bar stool and the big burley bartender asks, 'What'll it be?' The duck answers, 'Got any grapes?' The bartender snorts back, 'Of course not. This is a saloon. We serve beer and whiskey. Now get out of here,' and he throws the duck out. The next day the duck waddles in again and hops up on the barstool. The bartender looks sort of sideways at him and says, 'Yeah, what?' The duck answers, 'Got any grapes?' The bartender snarls back at him, 'I told you no! If you come in here again, I'll nail your bill to the bar! Now, get out of here!' and he proceeds to throw the duck out. Well, the next day the duck waddles in again, and hops up on a stool. The bartender bends down, and with his face only inches from the duck's bill says through chanced teeth, 'What-do-you-want?' The duck answers, 'Got any nails?' The big bartender snaps back, 'Of course not, stupid!' 'Got any grapes?'"

---

The flight from Dulles airport located between Washington D.C. and Baltimore had left on time. The tattered and tired DC-9 rose above the thin layer of broken clouds to catch the rays of the morning sun. Among the noisiest aircraft still in service, it was a legacy plane from before Northwest Airlines merged with Delta.

A Chinese face turned toward the window. The cold, dark eyes could just make out the dawning landscape below. The ache in his right knee unconsciously drew his hands to gently rub the tendons and muscles. He felt the edges of the mechanical joint beneath the skin.

Muan Yingqu flexed his knee as much as the narrow space between the economy class seats would allow. The knee replacement reminded him of the deadly grudge he felt for *that* man who had taken his real knee from him. The mechanical device was better than being on crutches. However, he had learned that most knee joints were replaced in elderly people, and as such, the mechanical devices were not designed for a man in his twenties to use for a normal life span. At the present level of technology, second replacements didn't work. This state of affairs gave him a span of fifteen years of normal ambulation, some of which had already been consumed. In the time that remained, he intended to exact his revenge. Gritting his teeth, he, for the thousandth time, vowed to succeed.

A posting outside of China had never been in his plans as he applied to the MSS some years before. However, his dreadful meeting with *that* man at the Nanjing airport changed everything. Now it was clear, it had to be this way. He could not exact his vengeance while in China, so here he was working in the United States. A thrill went through him as he pondered his present mission. While *that* man was not the object of this assignment, *that* man was all Yingqu had on his mind. He was being ordered to the city of his nemesis. This would be the time, he knew it in his bones. As the events fell into place the feeling of a manifest destiny filled him.

Yingqu was going to Minneapolis to meet the man coming from China. This was standard operating procedure for important missions. Someone with time in the country and knowledge of the local culture was needed to keep the operation from being exposed. It was also seen as necessary to have an agent direct from the People's Republic of China involved. The lax culture in the U.S. took the edge off the operatives stationed here in a surprisingly short time. He understood this from his mission of some months before when he was direct from China and was assisted by the man from Washington.

His career in Washington was stable as he showed promising results in handling espionage operations out of the PRC embassy. It was a stressful start, as he felt certain the death of his predecessor, Allen Wu, on the mountain top in Montana would be laid at his feet. For once, there had been so much blame to pass around that it largely missed him. The sly plot put together by his superiors to trap *that* man into looking like a rogue CIA agent was doomed to failure, and, predictably, it had failed. Damn, his hide. There is only so much good luck any man had, and yours, Edmond Beckon, was about to run out.

---

They were both still laughing. Hua lightly put a hand on Ed's arm as he wiped a tear from his eye with his other. "Ed, this is merriment. It feels good to laugh."

"Hey, Hua. Only people laugh, animals don't. You must be human!"

Hua was immediately somber again. "I said before, not so simple. I start out as human and they take away some. Maybe they not take this away . . . proves nothing. Maybe it is different for you to laugh than for me. You think of that? Still have problem."

Ed sucked in his breath and said, "Oh boy. A thought occurred to me when we first spoke, then I let it pass. But, now, I really think I may be the first man ever in the history of the world to be faced with the 'Total, Total, Turing Test.'"

"What is this test?"

Breckon chuckled. "This is going to stretch our horizons. To start with, in 1950 Alan Turing published a paper that is now famous titled *Computing Machinery and Intelligence*. He describes a way for humans to test artificial intelligence, AI, programs. In it's most basic form it has a human sitting at a computer terminal interacting with a subject in another room by words only. He must decide based on the responses from the other end of the communication whether or not his 'pen-pal' is a human or an AI program. The idea being that if he could not tell the difference the writer of the program would have made a human intellect.

"Later it was objected that words only were too limited, and the test must include sensory information. For example, I should be able to send some flowers to the test subject and have it respond by telling me about the yellow roses it had received, their delicate petals, the sweet scent, and the sharp thorns on the stems. This is called the Total Turing Test. In this case a room full of sensors could collect all the sense information and feed it into the computer. It was further suggested that this also was inadequate, that it required an android that I could see and converse with, hence the Total, Total, Turing Test, also called the virtual reality or Virtual Turing Test. There was some argument that the Virtual test was unnecessary and that the Total Turing Test would supply all that was needed. In any case, you represent the total-total case. I hope you aren't offended if I look at your situation this way, but you must agree, that appears to be where we are."

Chen did not look at all satisfied. "It is important that *I* find out about *me*, not what other people think of what I am. Can you make that understanding?"

"Yes, I can. As I've said, you have me convinced that you're human. I suppose it's a case of you applying the Turing Test to yourself. Let's try this. Last evening you said it might prove you are human if you could disobey the order not to tell secrets. Maybe, if you practice being disobedient on me it'll start to come easier as time goes on. Come on, tell me a secret."

Chen was withdrawn. Breckon could see he might be offended thinking his comment was cynical, which in part, it was. Chen twitched his mouth and said, "Have one secret you might like to know. When I worked on your file third time my director, that is what man is called who tells me what to find out, said must decide soon if it is possible to make you work for Chinese. If true, must move you so you not die when city falls down. Now you know secret. It has no thinking of importance, do I guess right?"

"Do you know what he meant by saying the city falls down? This city, here?"

"This city, we are here, yes. Falls down, crash. You never know how earth rumble and move?"

Breckon was dumbfounded. "But, we haven't had an earthquake here for hundreds of years, not a big one. Why do they think we'll have one in the near future?"

"Not earthquake, but like one. Director did not say why it happen. Hubot does not ask questions to director."

"Boy, that's odd. Guess you were right, that secret doesn't make any sense to me. Getting back to what we were talking about before, it might be that you have the same quest that all people have. However, since your experiment things have changed that made you aware of something you really had never thought about before."

Chen was intently listening to Breckon not sure where he was going with this.

"We will all live forever, but not as we are now. We know that this life will end. We will die but something, our soul, will go on living. There is at least a moment, now and then, when this comes to mind, though most people immediately shove it from their thoughts because it has such dire consequences for them. If they took it to heart, they would have to change much about their lives. When we die to this life, and start our eternity, God judges us as He finds us. Based on our condition we will spend time without end in either pain or happiness with no chance to change it. The important thing about this is nobody knows for absolute certainty which result they'll get until they're dead. Then it's too late to change things. We can, however, have at least some idea about which it will be based on how we live. Most people have at least a rudimentary idea of this."

"That what you said is what I need. It does not matter what I am if death is the end for humans like animals. How do you know part of us does not die?"

Ed thought for a minute. "I'm far from an expert on this kind of thing. One reason I heard has to do with morality. Some people spend their entire lives doing their duty, helping others, and end up being hurt and finally killed by evil people, while the bad ones live comfortably and die without pain. The argument says that we have a built in sense of fairness that says there must be a life after death where the scales are balanced and good is rewarded while evil is punished. There are other reasons, but I can't remember them."

Chen was pacing the floor listening to Breckon. When Ed stopped speaking he turned and faced him. "My mind fights what you say. Much is good in it, much different. I now have feeling in me, hope, fear. Hope my life too, forever. Fear, yes. How will it be for me? It glimmers dim on the edge. Part wants to be animal. Simple that way. Drawn, though now I am, cannot go back. I must find answers."

"You mentioned hope, that's good. Ah . . . a song of hope."

Hua looked quizzically at Ed. "Song of hope. Hope is a song?"

Ed smiled. "No. I guess not. I was referring to a little poem I ran across some years ago and was taken by it so memorized it. It goes like this.

### A Song Of Hope

When the sun's last ray
Marks the finish of the day
Out beneath the stars I walk.
The tall pines sigh
As I walk by
Me, they seem to mock
'Cause they're among their own
And I'm alone.

My heart cries out
With an unheard shout,
Oh God, this wasn't meant to be.
Guide my life
Through this mortal strife
And end this tragedy
Lest my soul should die
While I stand by.

Hua sat in silence. Then he said, "Even if it is only words, it is like a song. The words make music. What do the tall trees mean?"

"I'm not sure what the author meant but it seems to me they represent the majority of people who lead comfortable lives doing what everybody else is doing. When one tries to break away and truly do the will of God, to love his neighbor, and do good to those that harm him, this causes angst in the looming crowd, the tall trees. This uncomfortable feeling of anxiety and depression causes them to whisper against him, and he finds himself alone. The second part starts out with a silent movement of the will toward God asking not to be allowed to fall back to the mediocrity of the crowd and eternal loss."

"Yes. That could be the way of the meaning. But, there is no word of hope in the lines but hope is in the title."

"I'd say that asking for help, especially help from God, is the same as hope. There's no point in seeking help if there's no possibility of getting any. The words mean more than that, and I'm not very good at figuring these things out. The important thing is, you're looking for help, which means you have hope. I think that shows you're human."

The pain Hua held inside was evident in his expression. To change the subject Ed said, "Guess I'll see what I can do to get you connected with the CIA. How does that sound? From what I've seen of them, though, they won't help at all with your spiritual dilemma."

Hua smiled. "I be grateful. But, what is there?"

"You might be surprised."

With that Breckon turned on his computer and waited for it to boot up. In the aftermath of his last adventure, Breckon preferred to call it "case of mistaken identification," he had met with a Mr. ShuHo Zeng of the CIA. That man headed the Far East Bureau from the headquarters in Langley, Virginia. They had gotten on well. Zeng seemed to have a sense of awe of Breckon's ability to survive some of the most bazaar situations Zeng had ever head of. Even though Breckon protested otherwise, Zeng had insisted they set up a means of communicating that was safe from the prying eyes of the "Snooper State."

With Breckon's phone line in the watch list in the NSA, National Security Agency, every time he used it, it was monitored for flag words. Since the September 11, 2001 attacks on the World Trade Center in New York, the Department of Homeland Security had put the super-giant computers of the NSA to work monitoring the activities of everyone in the U.S. As expected the database was massive, but the data was all there.

Any person in the FBI, CIA, NSA, and alphabet soup without end of agencies, could set up a set of conditions, and be alerted at their computer monitor when a match occurred. If someone decided to check on where Breckon had been, what phone calls he had made, what websites he had visited, when he used his credit card, what books or movies he checked out of the library, when he clocked in and out of work, almost anything, they could find it.

Even the freeway cameras in the larger cities were connected to the database. All vehicle license numbers passing each monitored exit were recorded with the time and date. This meant that the travels of your car could be dredged up out of the data banks.

Beyond this, the Department of Homeland Security was building a digital identification file on everyone in the US, and ultimately everyone in the world. The ID file was more than the person's social security number and driver's license number, though both of those would connect to the rest. There was also a digital photograph, fingerprints, iris scan, and more. There was even a program to put each person's DNA into the ID. When the government got it done, if they were after you, there would be no place to hide, and when caught, there would be no doubt it was you.

What the nine-eleven terrorists could not do to us, we did to ourselves. We went from a largely free society to a slave society. We became a society where the citizens wanted the ultimate freedom, the freedom from responsibility. It had happened many times in the past, even to the ancient city-state of Sparta. We sold our freedom for security, and the security we bought was only a mirage shimmering in the distance, soon to dissipate.

Breckon began by opening a file containing a letter. It was part of the CIA's highly secure messaging system. Its development was a case of necessity being the mother of invention. Come to find out the most secure means of communication in present day America was not through super encryption of data, but through the good old U.S. Postal Service. There was a simple reason for this. All electronic communications could be intercepted, deciphered, read, summarized, sorted, prioritized, and presented to interested people with no human intervention. A letter had to be manually intercepted, carefully opened, and scanned electronically. Then the letter had to be expertly resealed leaving no indication it had been tampered with, and sent on its way. This all consumed vast amounts of real people's time, a commodity that was always in short supply.

The CIA, being what it was, did a decent job of it. Ignoring the use of normal letters, they used first class junk mail. Breckon had some kits in large sealed envelopes that contained regular legal sized envelopes. The file on Breckon's computer contained a form letter from Zeng's U.S. Senator to Zeng soliciting his opinions on issues before the senate. When ready to mail, the envelope would be quite fat since the postage was free to the senator. This made it possible to have a lengthy letter as a lead-in to the survey. Breckon's computer file would print the letter on his laser printer with his message imbedded in it. As part of the kit, there was a return envelope, postage paid, and of course a form to use for a campaign contribution, if Zeng was so inclined.

Breckon opened the file on his computer and found the place to insert his message. The message necessarily had to be short so this particular paragraph did not stand out by being overly long. After some thought Breckon entered his message and the resulting paragraph looked like this.

> While I'm fighting to advance qualified judges to out nation's highest courts, our opponents *presently have hubot house guest from china entered us illegally thurs past ohare has valued info for you needs new identity sought by assassin* stubbornly block, stall, stymie and obstruct their confirmation.

The part Breckon added initially appeared in Italics. When he was satisfied with his message he changed his addition to match the rest of the text.

Breckon took out a box of surgical gloves, put one on each hand. Then he pulled three sheets of paper from the center of a ream of copy paper. After printing both sides of each sheet he matched them up, folded them and put all of the parts into the special envelope being sure Zeng's name and address appeared in the window. He would drop it in the drive-up mailbox outside the post office being sure to leave no fingerprints on it.

Chen watched this project with an amused expression on his face. "If you don't work for the CIA, you fool me," he said at last.

Breckon shrugged and said, "With what I said in the letter we'll get some help for you."

# — 16 —

While Breckon had his computer on, he checked for emails. He had one from a man who owned a small business doing custom machining called Specialty Machining, Inc, or SMI. Ed had worked for Bart, the owner, part time while going to college. After graduation there were occasions when Bart needed some of Breckon's expertise with parts Bart had contracted to make so he called Ed. Through the years, the two had become friends.

The email had a CAD (Computer Aided Design) file attached. As Ed opened the CAD file, Hua looked over his shoulder. "Chinese words on this drawing. You make things for China, or China make them for you?"

Ed shook his head. "We in the U.S. are making them for China. Big surprise, huh? They will be used here in Minneapolis for some experiments. I guess they thought it was cheaper or faster to acquire them locally. The guy who sent this drawing to me is making them. I was at his shop to help figure out the steps needed to machine them most efficiently. He has a big CNC, (Computer Numerical Control) horizontal mill and has a contract to make several of them. Now he wants me to help figure out how to program some tricky machining steps because of some changes the customer wants."

Hua had Ed zoom in on the title block and some comments in Chinese characters. "This is strange," he said thoughtfully. "Many very secret things I saw in the Institute. They test to see if I can do convoluted engineering things. I say that right?"

"Probably 'complicated' engineering would be more commonly used. As you were saying?"

"It is I can remember things. However, engineering takes understanding of things more than what words say. I learn things good. They find it is better to have me draw inference from many facts, and not be engineer. So, I was put back and work on diplomat and espionage things."

"So are you saying this is part of a secret project?"

"Think in my mind it is. You do not know what this says in the Chinese story part of drawing?"

"Heck no. Almost nobody in this county can read that. It's as good as a secret code here."

Chen seemed amused. "You have seen more drawings like this?" he asked.

"I haven't seen any more, but maybe Bart has more. Bart is the owner of SMI, that's Specialty Machining, Inc. He sent this to me. Tell you what, I should stop by to help with this. Let me make a call and see if he's there."

Ed moved some papers to reveal his telephone on the table, picked up the receiver and punched in a number. "Hi Bart. I thought I might find you at the shop—only now opened your drawing." Ed paused and then, "Yeah, I see what they want to do." Pause. "I see your idea, but there might be another way that'd be easier to machine. It shouldn't matter how each part looks just so they lock together with no gaps. Isn't that it? How about I stop over in a bit?" Another pause, "Yeah. See ya."

Ed hung up and turned to Hua. "Let's take a ride and I'll let you see the parts of this thing."

When they arrived at Specialty Machining Ed pulled into the eight-car parking lot. There were parking spaces to the left and the right, but none facing the one story white brick building, "I'm not really supposed to know about this project according to the contract Bart has. I'll have to talk to him for a minute, sort of get him prepared, so you stay in the car, okay?"

Chen nodded. Ed went in the front door and Chen sat thinking about his situation, looking at nothing in particular. Staring out the windshield at the street to the north he absently saw a small black car drive past headed north. Two minutes later he saw a car approaching from the north. A distracted thought tumbled around in his mind that there were many small black cars in this neighborhood. As it got closer electricity shot through Chen's body. It was the same car! Chen bent over out of sight as if looking for something on the car floor. The driver could not help but see him move if he were looking his way. Better for him to see suspicious activity than to make a positively identification. Chen did not have a chance to see the driver, so he was left wondering if he were being silly. It might have been an innocent situation of someone looking for an address.

The car continued on down the street. In the side mirror, Chen watched it until it was hidden by some shrubs. It did not appear to stop. Chen got out and entered the front door of the shop. There was no one behind the receptionist's counter. From the look of the clutter in the area, he assumed there never was a receptionist, and the owner assigned those duties to others. He moved into a room behind the entry that contained a large drafting table, and three computer monitors. Through the door to his right, he heard voices.

Ed and Bart were standing by a large milling machine and discussing the cutting operations. Bart was looking in the direction of the office and Chen's movement caught his eye. "That guy with you, Ed?" he said pointing with a pencil.

Ed turned his head, "Huh, ah . . . yes. Hua, why did you came in?" Then to Bart, "This is a friend of mine . . . " thinking fast. What would Bart say to Hua's coming in unannounced? He had planned to mention Chen to Bart, but had become involved with the machining operations. "He's ah, from . . ." from where? "Ah, China. Remember that job I did on the elevators over there? I mentioned it to you. He's here to discuss some changes and the delivery of final documentation. Bart, this is Hua. Hua, Bart."

"Very much sorry, Ed. It was cold in the car, but I go back if this is not permitted."

"Yeah, I think that would be best. What do you think, Bart? I'm not even supposed to see this stuff."

As Hua turned, Bart said, "Well, just a minute. Do you read Chinese characters?"

Hua stopped and turned looking a little surprised. "Yes. I know Chinese. I am from China."

"Well, wait a minute, then." Bart went to the drafting table and starting peeling back drawings until he found the one he was after and pulled it out. Laying it on the top of the pile he said, "This is the drawing they sent back to me with the request for the changed part. I delivered all the parts exactly as the drawings said. I could see the last one would be hard to get into place since it had to lock in with two neighbors rather than only one for the others. See. All of the parts are placed around what looks like a cylinder. Now they want the last part remade according to this marked up drawing. And, they are blaming me for making the part wrong when they ordered them all to be the same. Is that what these characters in red ink say?"

Chen looked at them for some seconds. "I know what he say, but to make it in your language is hard. First it not written to you, but to some underling by the head of project. See here, this mean 'most top man.' Now here it say any of several, well you see, members of staff, should have been, well, more assertive when they see this might cause a problem before they accept the design." Now Hua softly cleared his throat. "Now, this part instruct underling that no matter, make . . . " Hua stopped.

"Well?" Bart coaxed. "What's next?"

After a hesitation Hua said, "This not nice. He call into question the legitimacy of your birth."

Bart was bristling. "He called me a bastard, is that it?"

Chen cleared his throat a little louder this time. "Yes. He say 'make bastard think it was his fault and get all changes for no extra money.'"

Ed watched the interaction of the two men. Chen almost gagging on the words and Bart getting angrier by the minute. Finally, he burst into laughter.

"Well, what's so funny! The little chinks, didn't call you a bastard!" Then he remembered Chen standing at his elbow and started to apologize.

Ed laughed even harder. "Okay, okay. So, we know the situation. You can make sure those equally illegitimate persons of foreign extraction pay handsomely for the changes. Maybe Hua could look at the other drawings and documents you have and see what we can learn."

"Oh boy. That would be fun. I've been wondering what's really going on all the time I've been working on these things. But, while I'm digging will you do the changes to the machine program we discussed?"

Ed went to work and Bart pulled out several folders for Hua to go through. Bart went to a file cabinet in the next room and brought back a folder. "Here Hua. What do you make of this? They left this drawing here and I made a backup copy like I always do in case I spill oil on it or something. They were back in an hour and took the original saying it was left by mistake. I forgot to mention the copy I made."

In a few minutes, Breckon's concentration was broken by snorts and sighs as Chen was flipping through documents. Finally, he was literally slapping things down.

"Hua, what's the problem?" Ed asked.

"What are you making with this thing? I see the drawing like this at Medical Institute. You make machine for hubots, too! Why you do this!"

Ed was at his side. "I don't understand what you're saying? The parts Bart is making are cooling jackets for magnetic field generators to degauss, that is demagnetize, pieces of steel. At least, that's what they told him."

"Is not! You lie! Used for make hubots . . . I see drawing . . . have perfect memory . . . small changes . . . is it . . . is it." Ed had noticed that Hua had been coming along fast with his English. There were times where his grammar was nearly flawless, though he still had an accent. Now that he was upset he was speaking in partial sentences, and was hardly understandable.

"Hua, slow down. I don't see how this could be used as you described that apparatus to me. You said there was a thing like a dome they . . . " here Ed stopped suddenly aware of Bart, "that was this big." He spread his hands to signify something two feet in diameter, "that had thousands of little things on it. This is as big as this table. It can't be the same. See the dimensions?" Ed pointed to dimensions on the drawing Bart was working from to show what he meant. "These are millimeters. See from here to here is three hundred twenty millimeters, that's this far." Ed held up his hands spaced about a foot apart. "That's one of the parts on the CNC machine now," he said pointing to the other room. "They're machined out of aluminum and will have a sheet of polished stainless steel cladding the outside."

Chen leaned over the table placing his elbows on it and his forehead in the palms of his hands. "They fool you. Draw picture big, but make small so you not know."

Chen started pacing the floor, totally withdrawn. Ed wasn't sure if it was because he had been shown to be wrong, or if this drawing was really disturbing him. He certainly got upset at seeing it. Chen sat down in a swivel office chair nearly in a trance. He poked the index finder of his right hand at the palm of his left hand as if methodically working through some problem.

Bart leaned over and whispered to Ed. "Your friend seems a bit tightly wound, don't you think?"

"Yeah, maybe," Breckon whispered back. "But, he's a very smart guy who's been handed a very difficult project. He mentioned it to me, and said he came on this trip to the U.S. to get out of the office so he could think about it. He said it had something to do with magnetic fields. Maybe there's some connection between what he's doing and these tests at the U of M lab."

Bart nodded accepting Ed's explanation.

Breckon knew that with volumes and volumes of information stuck away in his cranium, it was hard to tell what Chen could put together. It was something many people, especially engineers, dreamed about. There was such an explosion of technical information that it was difficult to keep current on one narrow discipline. This guy could roam over wide fields of study with ease and be assured of not getting facts mixed up or forgetting things.

Several minutes into his self absorbed state Chen looked at Ed. He spoke slowly making a conscious effort to choose the right words. "Ed, there appears to be a use for your," here he paused looking for works, "heat exchangers that makes sense. I must look in your papers for more information. That okay with you, Bart?"

Bart shrugged and said, "Sure, why not if you think it'll help you with whatever you're working on."

Chen leafed through the files carefully looking at each page for about a second. Then he stopped. "This page," he said holding up a sheet with all Chinese characters on it, "I think you were not supposed to get. I think they not worry, not much to say, anyway. It talks of Minneapolis as center of North America, which is . . . " here Hua closed his eyes. Ed suspected he was referring to maps stuck away in his head. "Ah, yes. On flat maps not so true as on globe. Well this is not center, but large city nearest center. Also good feature is no earthquakes here, so test finish easy to know."

Ed broke in, "Could that mean 'test results are easy to interpret?'"

"Yes. That good meaning, too."

"Wonder why they care about earthquakes?" Bart asked. "Maybe they have sensitive instruments that would be affected," he said answering his own question.

"Doubt it," Ed said. "You mentioned they're doing it at the U of M in that building down by the river. The Third Avenue Bridge isn't far away, and trucks crossing it would cause more vibrations than even the tremors in Los Angeles. It has something to do with being the center of the continent."

"What else does it say?" Ed asked.

"Rest about payments for use of Saint Anthony Falls Laboratory, time schedules for making tests, amount of money they spend—no talk about what test is for."

Chen continued looking at the papers in the folder. "Might happen this machine intended to make power from zero point energy, not hubots. You right on that, Ed."

"What's a hubot?" Bart asked.

Hua was about to say something, and Ed interrupted. "It's kind of a long story, and it seems nobody is even sure it can actually be done. It has to do with making better computers."

Bart seemed satisfied, and Ed saw Hua give him an appreciative look.

Breckon spent ten more minutes changing the CNC program and said, "Okay Bart, we'll leave you to cut metal. Be sure to charge 'em blood."

"Don't worry my friend, I will. Oh, remember Hua, not a word about this to anybody."

"I will not tell."

It was nearly noon by the time they left their meeting with Bart, and Hua had forgotten about the small black car.

---

Muan Yingqu's first task after getting off the plane and getting his rental car in Minneapolis was to visit his arms dealer and place an order. He had been directed to provide two silenced pistols, one for the man coming from Beijing, and one for himself. He ordered a 9 mm Glock for the other man. For the task he had assigned himself, he needed something less formidable, one there the bullet would not pass through the victim. A .22 would work, but he wanted something with a little more takedown power. He was pleased that he could get a .32 that accurately shot subsonic rounds and had an integral silencer. That would be perfect for the real mission, too. The short notice, and it being a Saturday, had tripled the price of the items he needed, though the classification of his mission meant money would not be an issue. Items like this could not be taken on the plane so they were always acquired locally. In addition, an order like this was never placed by phone or email.

In the time it would take his supplier to get what he needed Yingqu took a trip to New Brighton to locate Breckon. Luck was with him. He was certain he had identified his mark as he saw him come out of his apartment after only twenty minutes of waiting. This verified he was still living in the same place. The palms of his hands itched. He wished he had been able to pick up the guns at the first visit. Nonetheless, this was a bad place to do it.

Further, Yingqu was unable to identify the man with him due to the generous hood on the coat he wore. If Breckon had picked up a room-mate, it would complicate things. Yingqu followed them to their destination. As he had driven past Specialty Machining, the second man was sitting in the car which seemed a little odd. Reluctantly, he broke off his surveillance to keep his appointment with the arms dealer.

Some minutes after successfully acquiring the weapons, he was taking the County Road E2 exit from I-35W. He knew he could have been in a cozy hotel room had he not been driven by his personal enmity to even the score with Breckon. He arrived at the parking lot of the apartment buildings slightly before six in the evening hoping Breckon would go some place that would offer the opportunity he sought.

———————

Breckon and Chen finished their meal of hotdogs, apples, and potato chips. "The CIA guy will have the letter Monday, and someone will contact us no later than Tuesday, unless I miss my guess," Breckon said. "That gives us a couple of days to lay low."

"Ed," Hua said imploringly, "can we use some of the time to find someone to answer my questions?"

"Yeah. Tomorrow afternoon we might find the right man available. We'll give it a try."

"Why wait for afternoon? Morning would be good, too."

"Good for you maybe, but not him. He's very busy on Sunday morning. You'll see. In the meantime, how about a diversion of another kind. This is the height of the Christmas shopping season, and I could use some socks. How about we go to a shopping center and you can see the culmination of the materialistic mooch."

Breckon could see the questions in Chen's mind so he said, "Come on. It beats sitting around here."

As they approached the intersection of Fairview Avenue and County Road B2 a little before seven, they were in near gridlock. If it had not been for a Roseville police officer directing traffic at the intersection, nobody would have moved. Breckon made a left and then the first right. In spite of the lavish size of the parking lots, there were few places to park. They had to cruise around until they spotted someone leaving and wait to take their spot.

The crisp air had a fresh smell to it. All of December so far had been colder than normal. There were only scattered patches of snow lying around. The merchants wanted snow because it put people in the holiday, that is, spending mood. From the looks of the parking lot, lack of snow wasn't causing much of a problem. They entered the J. C. Penney store on the upper level from the west side of Rosedale. The aisles were crowded and Chen simply followed Breckon as they jostled their way through the women's outerwear department. Racks of leather coats had a placard above them proclaiming 65-70% off. Some poor schlep paid full price, Breckon thought.

They threaded their way around the Customer Service desk, and then dresses on the left. To the left of the escalator island were cosmetics and perfumes. Chen had thrown his hood back and closely followed Breckon. Chen tugged at Breckon's coat. Ed stopped and Hua said, "It would be hard to work here. The air is full of odors."

Breckon smiled and replied, "Yeah. It's a mystery."

From there, it was down the escalator and to the left to the men's furnishings department. There were fewer people in this area. Chen touched Breckon's arm and said, "So many people. All buy many things and carry packages, but nobody smiles. Why they not smiling?"

Breckon laughed. "You're starting to get it. Money can buy comfort, but not happiness. The whole world economy would crash and burn if people figured that out." After making a quick perusal of the sock offerings Breckon said, "They don't have what I want. I guess Fleet Farm's more my kind of store. It's kind of fun to see all of this, though, isn't it? Let's walk out to the central mall. It'll be decked out for the season."

Walking out of Penney's they entered the side mall that ran perpendicular to the main one. Here, both up and down escalators slanted toward them. Beyond the escalators was an assortment of kiosks. One sold hand carved religious articles from the Holy Land. Another sold music CDs and another cell phones. As they walked, Chen stayed behind Breckon most of the time since there was scarcely room for two to walk abreast. People streamed past them each seemingly oblivious to all the others. What a strange society. They would have felt insecure if suddenly they were the only one in the shopping mall, yet if you were to stop one and ask a question they would feel like you were invading their privacy—all alone in a sea of humanity.

The squawking sound of a hand-held radio caught Breckon's attention. He looked in the direction of the sound as best he could determine. Didn't help much, nothing but people and piles of stuff. Then it squawked again and he saw the source, a custodian with a radio clipped to his belt. He had the lid off one of the many honey-pot shaped refuse receptacles. They were about thirty inches high and fit the decor so well they were all but invisible. The man was packing down the contents with his hand. As Breckon passed beyond, he heard plop, plop. Swiveling his head, Ed saw it was the sound of the cover being replaced. No one paid the slightest notice, just one more sound added to the buzz of shoppers discussing where to find what they wanted, the crinkle of packages, and the sound of hurried footfalls that made the decibel level high, just short of painful.

They entered the central vaulted space that was mostly obscured by the crossover walkway of the upper floor. They turned left. It was less crowded here and less noisy as they walked further. Finally, Ed stopped by a round pillar just outside the entrance to Macy's Department Store to get a better look at the gala trappings. What gala trappings? It looked like a Romanesque cathedral to consumerism. The roof was supported by columns spaced about thirty feet that had dark brown marble tiles up to waist height and then just light yellow paint from the tiles to the top. About half of the roof was a skylight with glass panes at a sixty-degree angle like a teepee running the full length, black in the night. There were strings of tinny white lights hanging from the ceiling. There were no Christmas trees, no strings of fake holly with read berries, no colored lights. Only the sound of secular holiday carols playing from unseen speakers.

They took in the sight and Ed commented on the lack of Christmas bunting. Both failed to take note of a free-standing oak hutch ten feet wide and six feet high advertising family portraits, and a particular man partially visible through some glass panels in it. Finally, Breckon said, "Behind us is Macy's, an up-scale store. Let's see what they have." As he turned, there was a sharp ding as paint snapped out of a small divot in the sheet metal that covered the round column.

Instantly, he grabbed Chen and pulled him down. "Duck!" Breckon rudely pulled him around to the far side of the column. "Someone took a shot at one of us. Did you see the bullet hit the column?"

"The sound I heard. Bullet? Can you know? How here?"

"Trust me, I've been shot at enough times to know what happened. From the angle of the bullet he's that way," Breckon said pointing with his thumb, "and probably moving, so let's go. Stay near people and don't stop."

They started running for the entrance to Macy's. Breckon knew that with the first person to be hit, whether one of them or a shopper, there would be pandemonium, and the shooter would have to flee. This meant he would have to be careful with his shots. It happened there was a dearth of shoppers at the moment. Immediately after they passed through the Check Point tag detectors placed at the store entrance to prevent shoplifters from making off with stolen goods, Chen was on Breckon's left. Breckon pushed Chen to the left.

Breckon shoved again and Chen tripped. They both tumbled on the floor into the ladies perfume and cosmetics aisle. Here they were in the odors again.

# — 17 —

Yingqu had taken up his position to wait for Breckon. He discovered there were two separate apartment complexes with Breckon residing in the one further east, while he was parked by the one to the west. With the engine off the windows started to steam up almost immediately. He was also amazed at how fast the car cooled off with no heat. The result was he had to leave the engine running most of the time. A few people came and went in the parking lot, but didn't pay any attention to him. Waiting had always been hard for Yingqu. The thing that took the edge off the distress this caused was his desire to bring the man down.

They appeared as they had in the afternoon, same coats, same relative positions. The man with the large coat was always a step or two behind Breckon. The car backed out of the garage, and was off. Yingqu followed them to the entrance to I-35W at County Road E2. To his surprise, the car passed over the freeway. He had to back off far enough so he could keep track of them, yet not attract their attention. It would have been much easier on a multilane highway with hundreds of cars. Once he lost sight of them and had to guess if Breckon had turned or gone straight. He took a chance on the latter and was rewarded to see them two blocks ahead.

When they entered the glut of vehicles near the mall, he lost them again. He had heard about Christmas shopping but assumed the traffic tie-up was due to an accident never thinking shopping could get so out of hand. He saw Breckon make the left turn and managed to get into the turn lane over the protesting horns of companion vehicles. The officer directing traffic gave credence to his assumption of an accident though he saw no emergency vehicles. He followed them into the huge parking lot by the mall. Yingqu didn't know what to make of it, other than they must be going Christmas shopping. The holiday shopping season was discussed from time to time at the embassy in Washington. In some respects, it made covert activity easier. Nearly everyone was walking with packages or boxes so packing weapons or surveillance gear was never questioned. On the negative side, there were people everywhere.

There was a one-way road at the outer edge of the parking lot going counter clockwise around the complex. On the side of this road furthest from the stores was additional parking. Yingqu saw an empty slot and slipped into it. He grabbed what he needed and put it under his coat. Again, he had lost sight of his quarry. Hurriedly he made his way to a light post. The slender steel column was set on a round concrete base three feet high. He climbed up on the piling and with his arm around the post scanned the sea of cars. He spotted Breckon waiting for someone to back out of a space, and started toward the main mall two rows of cars away. Neither man seemed at all concerned since they never gave a look around to see if they were being followed.

It had not occurred to him to accomplish the deed in a crowded area, though there was precedent for that. With enough people moving about it would mask the sound of the shot. When Breckon went down people would gather about him and cause enough disturbance so Yingqu's presence and departure would be unnoticed. It was risky, though, because someone with a good memory for faces might see him take the shot.

The two men joined the flow of holiday shoppers coming and going as they entered a large store. As soon as they were inside Yingqu ran to the door. He made his way deep into the cavernous woman's apparel department. As he came to an intersection of main aisles, neither man was in sight. His hopes started to fade. What to do? He went ahead and saw the escalators, one coming up from the lower level, and one descending to it. There was no floor above him. Since they were not in sight, they could have gone down. It was a gamble. As he was about to step onto the down escalator, he saw them at the bottom getting off and turning left. While Yingqu was a little above normal height for a Chinese man he was shorter than average here. Even many of the women were taller than he was. It made concealment easy, but pursuit difficult.

Gliding down on the escalator, he was exposed so he rubbed his face in an absentminded sort of way to conceal his features. Given a good look, he had no doubt Breckon would recognize him. As he neared the bottom, he saw them in the men's clothing department. He apologized as he bumped into a woman, and started after them. They left the store and were in a wide corridor with small stores and shops lining the sides, and small sales booths down the center. The noise level was not as high as he would have liked, but good. The tinny music played constantly with a hint of melody recognizable from time to time depending on where he was relative to a speaker.

He was close enough now, but needed a shooting position. The gun with silencer was nine inches long. In fact, he only needed something to mask his upper body as he quickly raised the gun, aimed, and fired. He was fifty feet behind as they entered the main mall. Entering the open space, Yingqu was dismayed at the lack of congestion. They were walking to the left. Masking himself behind a tall oak panel displaying portraits, he closed the distance. The advertisement for Gregory Rademacher Classical Portraits stood on the right of the central space just past a pillar. There was a broad aisle between the row of columns and the shops.

Yingqu found himself in a strangely secluded, yet open space. There was just room to pass easily between the pillar and the right end of the portrait exhibit which was two feet thick with wrap-around glassed-in ends. He could see through the two walls of glass over the portraits within and be unobserved himself. Three feet beyond the glass and sitting next to the pillar was one of the standard honey-pot trash receptacles. His intended victim proceeded across the court and stopped in front of the diagonally opposite pillar. They had stopped to look at the shopping scene. It was perfect. Facing the right and now standing on the end of the glass case he pulled out the gun and raised his left arm resting the silencer on it. The gun was scarcely visible. He had him! With a steady pull, he squeezed off the round. As the pop sounded, he twitched as something bumped his back. Did the shot get off before he was jolted or not?

Instantly he turned to the left so if the shot had gone true people would not see his face. There looking right at him was a woman six feet tall, and two hundred pounds overweight. His gun was fully exposed. She had been passing behind him in the act of throwing a plastic cup into the refuse container when she bumped against him. The scowl on the face peering at him said it all. He was caught in the act. She saw his face up close and the gun. Before he could speak or move she said, "Couldn't wait to get it home, huh? Damn thing will we worn out before the kid gets it on Christmas morning." As she walked away at the only speed her ponderous size would permit he heard her say, "Trouble with men . . . never grow up!"

Instantly the gun was under his coat. Sweat was running down his back under his shirt. Could it be? Yes, it appeared to be so. She thought it was a toy, and no one else gave the slightest notice of him. The silencer was good, and the noise level was high enough so the sound of the shot was not enough to draw attention. Add to that the fact that everyone was totally absorbed in his or her own affairs. There was no disturbance in the direction of the shot so it was a clean miss. The pillar immediately behind Breckon must have absorbed the slug so there was no collateral damage.

"Plop." Yingqu pasted himself against the pillar. Cautiously looking in the direction of the sound, he expected to see someone with a silenced pistol shooting at him. Nothing. Then "plop" again, and he relaxed. It was a custodian having some difficulty replacing the lid on a waste container. He smiled. The sound of his gun and the container lid were strikingly similar.

He started to walk across the mall cautiously looking around. As he neared the far side of the open space, he saw parts of men pressed against the far side of the pillar. This had to be Breckon and the other man. He moved back toward the center of the mall. He started toward them out of their line of sight. They had heard the shot, or more likely seen and heard the bullet hit. Now, they were alerted.

He saw them as they came out of the mask of the column running for the store. Yingqu was peering over some potted poinsettias, but had no chance for another shot. With the gun safely slung under is left arm he cautiously approached the broad entry to Macy's where a trimmed Christmas tree stood at either side. His eyes darted to the left and right and saw nothing out of place. He casually proceeded down the main aisle with both empty hands hanging at his sides. Bearing off to the right he found himself at the down escalators, one coming from the floor above, one going down to the lower level. An elevator was silently ascending and slowed to a stop at his level. It was glassed in on the side facing the escalators and the door was in the rear.

Out of the corner of his eye, Yingqu saw Breckon getting on the up escalator across the way. His first impulse was to run around and get on the escalator behind Breckon, but that would leave him fully exposed as the escalator came to the top. He ran to the elevator. The door was just closing and he thrust his hand between the doors. They paused and bumped his hand again. Then they opened. A woman with a baby stroller glared at him for having interrupted her travels, but he simply smiled at them and kept his back toward the escalators. He raised his hand as if scratching his temple and glanced toward where Breckon should be. He was just stepping off the escalator and turning to his right. The elevator stopped and the door opened. Yingqu stepped off and walked toward a women's apparel department to his right. The clerk was engaged with a customer some feet away.

As unobtrusively as possible he slipped in among the racks of clothing. Breckon and the other man were in another apparel department, party dresses, across the main aisle that led to the escalators. Both had their backs to him. Damn, wish the other man would turn around, need to get a make on him, Yingqu thought. The man tuned his head to Breckon and it was clear he was Asian. Then Breckon turned his head toward his companion and out of the corner of his eye caught Yingqu's movement as he raised his gun. Breckon lunged at his friend. Yingqu squeezed off a shot, and then two more as he tried to compensate for the movement. Both men and the clerk were out of sight among the racks of dresses. There was no way of knowing if he had gotten a hit.

Had to move. The clatter of a falling rack of clothing had caused all eyes to turn in that direction. Yingqu turned around and with a few quick steps was in the short wide aisle headed to the west door. A tall display of luggage in the center of the aisle conveniently provided him with concealment as he made his exit.

---

As Breckon and Chen had gotten off the escalator Ed turned and looked back down to see if they were being followed. Seeing nothing suspicious he glanced at the elevator, but didn't give enough thought to what he had seen. "Stay beside me," he said to Hua as they started forward. Women's clothing on the left, party dresses on the right. An impulse hit Ed. He walked in among the garments and took a dress off a rack. Holding it up as if admiring it as he said, "Keep your eyes open for the shooter." A well turned out young lady with a nametag approached them.

Chen was taken off guard by the idiom and turned his head and said, "What does that mean? My eyes are open."

Ed turned with the start of a smile when the motion caught his eye. Ignoring all else he snapped his head and saw the gun come up. He lunged at Chen, pulling him down. Chen's hand caught on a dress strap and pulled a rack over on him. Rolling back Ed swung his arm at the woman's ankles and swept them from under her. She fell, none too gracefully, on top of Breckon. The ping of bullets, while lost to others among the clatter of the plastic hangers, was all too cogent to Breckon.

"Stay down. Shots were fired," Breckon said in a hushed voice, but with an intensity that left the woman frozen. He was up just in time to see the back of a man making a hasty retreat around a luggage display. He watched for several seconds as the form appeared briefly past the luggage and headed out the door.

Chen was on his feet about to say something. Breckon gave him a firm look and almost imperceptibly shook his head indicating he was to say nothing. "Fumbly, you are like a bull in a china shop. I told you to watch where you were going. You can be such a klutz. See what you can do to get this stuff set up again." Then he turned to the woman and bent with his head just below the tops of the racks and put his index finger to his mouth as he offered his hand to help her up. "My sincere apology for this mess."

The on-lookers that had begun to congregate snickered and gave a few low scoffs. Soon they were drifting off about their own business. Breckon was standing with his back to the checkout station. The woman was now getting her wits about her and with trembling lips was about to go into a tirade. Breckon held up his finger, stepped aside, and used it to point to a small hole in the back of a flat-panel display. The woman bent over the top of the counter and saw a much larger hole in the other side of the blank screen. The hollow-point had mushroomed upon entering the back and done its job.

Then Breckon showed where another had buried itself in the counter, and still another had clipped along a row of hangers on a rack leaving dresses hanging from one strap. She said, "I'm calling the police."

"Wait, a second," Breckon said. "Do you want to close down your department for the rest of the Christmas season, with 'Police Line - Do Not Cross' tape around it? And, what will the management of Macy's say when the talking heads on the morning TV programs are saying this is the place to come if you want to be shot at? By the way, do you have any jealous boy friends?" Ed knew this was uncalled for, but he had to cement the idea that calling the police was not a good idea.

Then she was all business. In a swift motion, the plug was out of the base of the damaged display and it disappeared out of sight below the counter. "It's a strange thing to be stolen, but it doesn't have a tag on it either does it?" meaning the anti-shoplifting tag.

Chen was doing his best with getting the overturned rack back up and the garments back in place.

"Here let me help you with this," she said.

The bullet that had struck the hangers ricocheted and ripped through a row of dresses. They were all the same except for different sizes. Breckon had one off the rack and was looking at it. The clerk came up beside him. "You want to buy something after this?"

"Maybe." Ed pulled aside the last dress so she could see the glob of deformed lead imbedded in the paneling. Then he put his finger though a ragged hole in the dress he was holding. "The bullet glanced off that rack and went through this whole row," he said indicating the rack." Then he said, "She's about your size, maybe a little taller. What do you think, size ten?"

"Better take a twelve." She went to the rack and got the next dress examining it to be sure it also had holes in it before she handed it to him.

Ed looked at the tag and said, "Hmm . . . two hundred forty dollars, give you twenty for it."

"Fifty."

"Thirty."

"Thirty-five."

"Sold."

As she was taking off the anti-shoplifting tag she asked, a quiver in her voice, "Am I in danger?"

Breckon peeled a twenty, a ten, and a five out of his money clip. "No. The guy was after me or the other guy," he said nodding toward Chen. "He's not a suicide assassin or we'd both be dead, so he's long gone, probably to try for us again, but not here. Do you want some advice?"

She nodded.

"Write off these other dresses as moth holes in shipment or something and get on with your life. If you make something of this, you'll be telling your story to the police, the FBI, the Anti-Terrorist Task Force, and organizations you've never heard of. Especially the FBI is bad. They're paranoid as hell, and not very smart. But, they make up for both by being complete jerks. In addition, they have an office downtown. They live here, so you'll never get rid of them.

"This sort of thing has happened to me a couple of times before, just being in the wrong place at the wrong time. I'm guessing that's why this happened. Somebody I don't even know has unfinished business with me. In any case, when they question you, they'll want to know why it was your fault. Simply saying it wasn't won't make them stop. You'll forever be on their list of suspects. I'm sorry this happened, but you're unhurt. Be happy with that. And," he added, "it's almost certain they'll never catch the shooter, anyway. I got a glimpse of him. He wasn't a white male."

She handed the bag with the dress in it to Breckon, and he said, "You're a real stand-up gal." She still had that "deer in the headlights look" as he turned and left with Chen. They walked down the aisle toward the north entrance.

Chen was beside him. "He tried two times. Much afraid he not miss next time."

"Me too," Ed said. "As we get out the door let's run to the right and find some place for cover until we can figure out what to do." The walls of the store angled out away from the doors at forty-five degrees for twenty feet and then bent another forty-five degrees to run east and west. In another hundred feet, the sidewalk to the east ended in a pile of snow under some eight-inch diameter pine trees. Here the wall angled southeast again to a utility area. This is where Ed and Chen stopped after their dash. They bent down under the boughs of the trees getting as much concealment as possible from the snow pile.

"If he had come here to wait for us to leave the store we would be dead now," Hua remarked.

"Yeah, I never thought of that. Ya gotta have a little luck now and then. Any ideas?"

Hua shook his head.

"Okay, how about this. If I go to the car alone, it will look different than if we stay together. When you see me driving in front of the mall entrance to the right you run down that first row of parked cars angled away from here," Ed said pointing, "and I'll pick you up." Ed was about to go when he said, "If you aren't there I'll assume something happened. Try to get back inside the mall and I'll look for you in the area where we first went in. Okay?"

Hua nodded, and Ed was off at a fast walk, his head pivoting in all directions. Chen was at the appointed place, and Ed got out of the parking lot headed toward Snelling Avenue. There was a crinkling noise whenever Chen shifted his position. "Hey Hua. You're setting on my dress. Get off it."

Chen heaved himself toward the door, pulled the crushed Macy's bag from under him, and said, "The color is nice, Ed, but I think it is too small for you."

"Ha, ha. Very funny wise guy. Don't even try to tell me you're not human. I need that dress for bait. In case you haven't figured it out, we have to get you into hiding or you'll be dead in no time, and probably me, too. I didn't realize you were so hot. I know where I want to take you but I have to call ahead. I don't want to call from a pay phone—too exposed. So, I plan to go to the apartment of a friend to make the call. Only problem with that is she's kind of mad at me for not calling more often. I need something to smooth things over."

"But, Ed, that dress has bullet holes in it."

"Yeah. I'm workin' on it."

# — 18 —

Breckon drove south on Snelling Avenue and entered the Har Mar Mall parking lot. Here too, the traffic was heavy, though not as bad as earlier. He exited on County Road B and headed west. They both watched in all directions for a tail, but saw none. A half-mile past Snelling, Breckon turned right and a few turns later stopped by a high rise apartment building.

"Here we go. Watch for anything out of the ordinary." In the entry way with the mail boxes Breckon picked up the telephone and punched in an apartment number. "This is where Cindy Thomas lives. I hope she's in."

"Cindy Thomas. You broke up with her over two years ago," Hua said.

"What did you say?" Breckon asked hardly believing what he had heard.

"It was in your file in China. Do you think Chinese cannot find information?"

Ed shook his head as he waited.

"Who is it?"

"It's Ed, Ed Breckon. I have a little Christmas present for you."

"Suddenly you decide to show up. I'm angry with you, Ed."

"Yeah. You're entitled. Aren't you curious about what I bought you? It's in a Macy's bag."

"Yeah, probably a stale fruitcake you got from a vendor at work that you put in a bag you found in the parking lot."

Ed replied, "No, no. I just bought it at Macy's. Let's see." He pulled part of the dress out to the bag and twisted the label in his fingers. "The label says BCBG Maxazria, and this little tag says two hundred forty dollars."

A pause. Followed by, "Ed, give me a break. You'd never spend that much on me."

"Come on, please . . . give me a chance . . . aren't you a little curious, though?"

Another pretty long pause and they both heard the click as the inner door unlocked. Ed smiled at Hua. "See, I'm not so dumb. We're in, aren't we?" he said as he opened the door.

Inside Breckon said, "You wait here on the first floor. If something happens try to get to the phone at either entrance and call her apartment to alert me. She lives in three-fifteen. Be sure to tell me the entrance where you're located. I hope to be back in fifteen or twenty minutes."

Breckon decided to walk up. The doorbell chime inside the apartment could be heard from the hall where Breckon stood being sure he could be seen through the fish-eye lens of the peephole. It took a full minute before the door opened a crack. Ed held up the bag.

"The bag's all wrinkled. Ed, what's going on?"

Boy, women sure know their merchandise, and they're so suspicious.

"Ya wanna see, huh, huh?"

He could see the start of a grin as the door closed and he heard the door chain come out of the slot. Then the door opened and, as always, he was struck by the beauty of this woman. He had to be mad not to be married to her. A little past her mid-twenties, she had shiny brown hair, and deep-blue eyes that unnerved him when they were smiling. A clear complexion rested on a movie star perfect face. Her figure was stunning by anybody's standard. In addition, she had a nice personality, always understanding and caring about the other person.

The thought struck him hard. This was a big mistake. Getting her involved in another one of these things was unconscionable.

"I got into that dress department and all I could think of was you when I had more important things to think about."

She took the offered bag and frowned, "And what more important things might there be?" She could see from the expression on his face that something was wrong.

Ed walked down the short hall and into her nicely decorated little living room. Why did girls' apartments look so nice while guys' places looked like crap? Another mystery. He sat on the apartment-sized sofa, and she beside him facing him.

"What do you think, I mean, the dress?"

She held it up and a mixture of expressions came across her face, mostly of the variety, what else would you expect from a stupid man. "Well . . . it's cute, and in a hundred years I *might* be invited to a party where I could wear it. You didn't really pay that much for it, did you?"

Ed shook his head looking a little sad.

"You got it at a discount, a big discount, I hope." She noticed one of the bullet holes. "Oh, look. A little snag. It's a second." The sound in her voice was that of disappointment. This Ed understood. You never give a shoddy item as a gift. The gift reflects the giver. If you can't afford a quality big item, give a top quality lesser item.

He shook his head. "No. Not a second. That's the exit wound." He took his finger and put it through the holes front and back. "You see, I got the two-bullet-hole discount." He had thought that statement would somehow sound starkly funny as he was putting together his plan. Now it fell flat.

She might have laughed except Ed's voice sounded so sad. Slipping over next to him she put her arm around his neck and pulled herself against him. "Oh, my guy. Now what happened? It looks like you're not hurt. Can you tell me about it?"

His muscles relaxed as he leaned against her. He guessed this was why the dresses had so attracted him. He needed a little sympathy. What would have been so hard about finding a pay phone at a mall to make the call to hide Hua? Too late now.

"Okay. The short version's all we have time for. I promise you a very long version later." He shifted his body to more directly face her.

"It seems the Chinese are doing experiments on healthy young Chinese men in an attempt to make very smart human animals. You know, perfect soldiers, or for any other expendable use. They aren't doing too well, so they kill all the mistakes. The first successful one was looking pretty good. He has perfect recall, can memorize a whole phone book perfectly. He was being tested on espionage cases. The thinking was to feed all that was known about a case into this guy and he would be able to recall all the facts rather than forgetting most of them like normal people do. Then he could figure out what the other guys were doing. You get the idea. Well, he also figured out that if for any reason they thought he was not perfectly obedient, that is, not an animal, he would be considered a failure and killed. Being smarter than the average cat, he managed to escape."

"Okay, stop. You said he *has* perfect recall. How do you know? And do *I* want to know?"

"I'm not sure, but here goes. One of the case files he was given was mine. They think I'm some sort of a super-spy, but don't know who I work for, and want to turn me to work for them. After he escaped, he came to me because he had so much information on me like my address, where I work, almost everything. I think they want him back very badly, dead or alive. That's what the shooting was about. I need to hide him, and where you sent me a few months ago sounds like a good idea. What do you think?"

Cindy turned away and looked straight ahead still holding Ed's hand. "That's really sadistic, using young men for experiments that way. But, other than degree, not fundamentally different that doing experiments on fertilized human eggs and then killing them, to say nothing of abortions."

"I thought of that, too. Anyway, the good news, if you can call it that, is this won't implicate you because they think we, as having some sort of relationship, are history . . . "

"And do you think it's good news that we're history . . . " she interrupted.

"No. I really do sincerely hope we're not," he said looking at her, a feeling of panic rolling over him fearing she would say she was fed up. "Let me continue. When Hua, Hua Chen, that's his name, saw your name on the mailbox he said we had broken up two years ago. That's how much information they have on me."

"Too fast, Ed. Slow down. He's here?"

"Yeah. He's waiting downstairs. I sent a notification to the CIA using a system they set up with me telling them that I have him. I would guess they should be here Monday or Tuesday. We only have to keep him alive that long. The local police would just laugh. You know that. I'm asking you to call Father Aldrich at St. Isador's and ask if I can drop him off there. Hua's quite a nice guy, and Father Aldrich will have a ball. You see, Hua's trying to figure out if he's human or an animal."

Cindy smiled as she shook her head. "Ed, you have the *weirdest* friends."

"I know, and you're my favorite, 'cause I know you'll help."

In two minutes Cindy was flipping through the phone book saying, "I just don't believe this. Can I meet him?"

"Not a good idea. I may have put you in danger as it is."

Cindy made the arrangements the same as last time and then called a taxi. Ed left, promising to call, *soon*.

---

The three story, hundred year old rectory stood between an equally tall school building—they still had K through twelve grades here—and the huge baroque church. A small parking lot and a garden occupied part of the space between the church and the school. Breckon had the taxi pull into the parking lot and drop them off in the shadows. The driver was told to wait. Ed and Hua got out and headed to the back door of the rectory. Ed had Hua duck behind the five-foot stone wall around the garden as he rang the bell two short times and one long. In seconds the door opened without the light over the door being turned on. That was the plan.

Breckon recognized the man in the dim light. "Father Aldrich, good to see you. Thank you for agreeing to see me on such short notice." He motioned to Hua. "Please, can we come in?"

"Oh, sure. Please do."

Inside Breckon made introductions. "Hua is in danger and must stay out of sight. I have notified my friends at the CIA, and they should be here Monday or Tuesday to collect him. He will tell you his fairly fantastic story. In short, Hua is the result of a DNA experiment aimed at making humans with only an animal soul. He wants to know if they succeeded. I thought you might help."

Father Aldrich chuckled. "What an fascinating life you lead, Mr. Breckon. I'm so glad you picked me."

"I thought you might be interested. Now, as the cliche says, the meter's running so I gotta go. Good night."

---

Father Aldrich, a portly sixty-two year old, led Chen to his study. "What do you think of Ed Breckon?" he asked as they walked.

"He is a nice man. It was a strange thing he said the first time I approached him. He said 'I suppose I've been expecting you.' I was almost frozen then. He saved my life. Later I did not think to ask him why he said that."

"Sounds like what he'd say and do. When he stayed here for a few days a while ago he mentioned that he thought the Dragon Fang business wasn't finished."

They entered a none too tidy room as Chen said, "In some of the time I think I am human, other times only animal. Maybe I have part of each soul."

Father Aldrich had Hua sit in an ornate wooden armchair with upholstered seat and back. He left momentarily to make some coffee. Chen looked about at the shelves of books that covered most of the wall space. His eyes fell on a rather thin book *Theology For Beginners* by F. J. Sheed. There were three new copies lying on the top of the large desk off to the side as if they were give-away books to people with questions. Immediately Chen picked up the top copy and started leafing through it. By the time Father Aldrich returned, he had read and committed to memory half of it.

"Have you always been interested in theology, or is it just since your experiment?" Father Aldrich remarked as he saw Chen return the book to his desk. "I would like if you could tell me your whole story. That is, as much as you feel comfortable relating."

Hua nodded and proceeded. A half-hour later Father Aldrich, though tired after a long day of saying morning Mass, meeting with couples wanting to make wedding arrangements, hearing confessions, saying Saturday evening Mass, and a myriad other interruptions, was paying rapt attention. "And so, Ed brought me to you."

Shifting in his chair Fr. Aldrich picked up the little book. "As I returned from making coffee I saw you were interested in this little book," he said fanning the pages. "Did anything you saw in it help?"

"In my mind I can see the pages I looked at. But, it is not like learning a phone book. Here deep thinking is needed, where I need help."

Father Aldrich nodded. "So it is. To start with, as you came in you asked the question if you might have part of a human soul. I can answer that with certainty. You do not have part of a human soul. The human soul is a spirit, and spirits are simple in that they have no parts. They do not occupy space. That may seem a little odd at first, but we'll spend some time on it. That means, you may have one or not have one, but never part of one."

Hua leaned forward trying to understand the meaning of the words. "The book says that. My question I have is there are many thoughts in my mind, aren't they parts? Why you are sure human soul is a spirit. Maybe it is not a sprit."

"Both are in some respects daunting questions. Plato and Aristotle were the first to go into these questions in depth. We still use much of their thinking in these subjects. They were thinkers of truly staggering proportions. As to the first question, every idea or thought has two *steps* in its formation. It first is a mental picture, called a phantasm, that is in your physical brain. This is what animals do. Then, it becomes a concept which is immaterial and resides in your mind, or soul. As you think thoughts your soul, spirit, actualizes its potency to get to its goal of being wise, or more accurately, finding the truth. This duality is caused by our being creatures with one foot, so to speak, in each of two worlds, the physical and the spiritual. We are rational animals.

"Taking this a step further the true intellectual faculty of the soul is its ability to abstract universals. For example, as a child our parents tell us that a certain thing in the back yard with branches and green leaves is a maple tree. Then we see a sapling that has grown up among the flowers and are told that is a small oak tree. The cone shaped spruce next door is also a tree. In the park you see a huge elm with limbs arching out from the trunk. That is also a tree. Gradually, you abstract the universal concept of treeness. This happens in the soul. At this point, we can organize treeness by going backward, for example from treeness, to coniferous and deciduous, to maple, which we'd call *ad finem species*, or the final end. From here we can only do particular maples, which is where we started."

Chen had followed the reasoning, but was still uncomfortable. "I see what you say follows with no apparent, what do I say . . . "

"Contradiction?"

"Yes, that is it. Tell me now, where do we know the soul has no parts?"

"I have already started into your second question. Here is sort of a formal argument that summarizes the process of getting to the soul with no parts. The image of a tree is received through the senses which is where the sum total of what we call the *accidents* are perceived, such as the image from the eyes, roughness of the bark from the fingers, and the pine smell of an evergreen tree from the nose. These sense images make up the phantasm, the total picture in the brain. Then, what is called the *agent intellect* grabs or abstracts the universal from the phantasm to form the universal concept.

"The universal concept has no parts. It is one thing. Now in common sense, or philosophy, we say that it is unreasonable, indeed it is impossible, that something can make or produce something greater than itself. The effect cannot transcend the cause. If the concept has no parts, the mind, or soul that formed it, has no parts. You would not expect a brain or a computer that is material, that is, has parts, to make something that has no parts. It may take you some time to fully grasp that last statement. All of what we are taking about here are profound concepts. It takes work to fully internalize them. There's no easy way.

"To continue, think of this example. A boulder can be broken down by wind and rain or by a man with a hammer to make pebbles because the two are the same except for one of the accidents, that of size. But, you don't expect to make a boulder to say nothing of a bird out of a small stone. We know this, we really do, and that is the splendor of the human soul. The question you have to ask yourself is, can you form these concepts? If you can, you have a human soul."

Hua was silent for some time before he spoke. "It seems like that happens, but I am not sure. I started out with all the parts, or what you would say are faculties that a human has. Then things were taken away. I can't remember many things from before the experiment. No memory of mother and father, only some memory of houses and streets where I lived. After the experiment, I can remember all of books I read and words I hear. So some is worse, some is better. Much might be mixed up. Might be the treeness you say is left over from before the test."

Father Aldrich was on one hand enjoying himself, but on the other was beginning to wonder if Hua was simply being obstinate. He certainly seemed to be human. "Another way to looking at it is that we say humans are risible beings. What are your thoughts on that?"

Hua nodded. "Ed mentioned that, too. He said I laugh, so that proves I am human. It's not that simple. Maybe I remember how to laugh from before, and can make conclusions of how certain combinations of words would be humorous, like a computer could, so by reflex I laugh. Maybe I do it on the level of phantasms like a pet dog that hears the sound of food being poured into his dish and runs to his place to eat. But, how do you know I feel like you do when you laugh?"

At these remarks, Father Aldrich couldn't help thinking that one who had enough insight to make these objections could possibly be an animal.

Hua continued, "Ed also mentioned this seemed like a case of the Turing Test."

Father Aldrich smiled benignly and slowly shook his head. "No. I'm afraid that does not apply. Ed's an engineer and that would appeal to him, I suppose. You see, engineers and scientists, deal in their work only with what they can measure in the physical world. As I mentioned, these are the accidents of a thing, not the substance. The substance is what the thing *really* is. That can only be known by the intellectual power of a spirit.

"I assume he mentioned the Total, Total, Turing Test which would be your case, a complete mechanism with muscles, neurons, and all the rest. The question remains, are you human, do you have a soul? The Turing Test is meant to determine if the test subject has a mind. There is some debate on the meaning of the word mind, but here we mean it as a faculty of the soul. The Turing Test at any level is fickle. It depends on the tester. Let us assume the test subject is a machine, a very clever one, and a man is trying to determine if it has a mind. That would be a case like you and me sitting here. Let us further assume that I, after diligent testing, and due consideration, proclaim that you are human. Does that proclamation in itself transform you from a machine into a man? Of course not.

"As computers have gotten more and more sophisticated and artificial intelligence has become a household term there has been some serious work on this. Unfortunately, the work has been done mostly by scientists who are constrained by things they can measure. By definition, they do not include man's spiritual soul in their deliberations. It's not that all of them deny its existence, but rather it is something that is beyond their realm of study. They can't *deal* with it since having no parts it has no accidents, and hence nothing to measure. Philosophers, on the other hand, who could add meaningfully to this subject aren't helping much. Either they fall back on stock answers developed before electricity was discovered, or they're off into crazy stuff like new age religions or inventing their own philosophies. Of the former group, they will simply state that humans shouldn't be doing what the scientists in China obviously *are* doing. It's fine to say that it is wrong to do it, but it doesn't help much after the fact as in your case.

"For years we have had computers that can do things, not only as well as humans, but better. They can remember information, and search databases much more efficiently than humans, except maybe for you. Therein lies our problem, doesn't it?"

The priest, seated behind his desk, leaned forward to place his arms on the surface before him. "I still don't quite understand why you find it so important to be convinced you have a human soul? You seem to be as human as anyone else."

"At the Institute I ask myself that, too. I think Ed found out. Human souls do not die, animal souls do. If I am human, I must care about my life after this one here in this world. If I am an animal, no problem with another life."

Father Aldrich smiled. "Now, I see. We'll work on the immortality of the soul tomorrow afternoon because we'll have to stop for now. Sunday mornings are a busy time in my line of work," he said with a wink. "I'll show you to a room where you'll be comfortable for the night."

# — 19 —

Muan Yingqu was upset with himself. He should have wreaked his vengeance upon Breckon by now. Mechanically he guided his rental car to the hotel as the events of the past hour played over in his mind. Twice, he had failed. The first time was dumb bad luck for him, and magically good luck for Breckon. He fought the urge to feel awe for the man. It was like the man was covered with good luck cooties. It wasn't as if the bullet bounced off an invisible shield or anything like that. The fat woman bumped him at the precise moment the bullet sped down the barrel of his gun. What were the chances of that?

The second time was at least a little explainable. Breckon had been alerted. However, the timing of the turn of his head, and the reflexes the man had were nothing but extraordinary. In his mind, more hope than anything, he believed he might have gotten a good hit. The car pulled to a stop in a parking space beside his hotel and the engine stopped running. Yingqu was startled by the change in sound as he realized he couldn't remember getting there. Gotta stop this, he thought. Can't let that man take control of me. Also, I must assume I missed the second time, too. Yingqu was enough of a soldier to accept the conclusion. There would be no finding Breckon for the rest of this weekend. If he were left on his own, he might pick him up again at his place of employment on Monday. By then, though, he'd be occupied with his real mission. He went into the hotel, had room service send up a meal before the kitchen closed, and after eating, went to bed. He'd rest up until his "partner" from China arrived at noon the following day.

---

The taxi dropped Breckon at the apartment building in Roseville. He had half a mind to go up and see Cindy again, but decided better of it. The same thing that had held him back in the past bothered him now. His life was simply not his own, or so it seemed. Having Hua in a safe place was a lot off his mind so he could now rationally consider the information he had received in the last couple of days. The biggest thing that bore down on him was that the Chinese did indeed have a thick file on him. See, he said to himself, I wasn't being paranoid. The world *is* out to get me. If the Chinese were snooping into his life it made sense that the Russians, Israelis, and who knew what other countries had a file on him. This didn't even take into account zillions of U.S. agencies that were assuredly interested in him. Feeling safe now that Chen wasn't with him, he headed back to his apartment.

**Sunday morning, Minneapolis**

Quan Peng left the warehouse by the door on Third Avenue and immediately turned up the collar of his coat to cover his ears and put on his gloves. It seemed to be as cold here as it had been in Winnipeg. He had slept six hours and felt rested. After the exhaust fan started, the air had gotten noticeably better in the entire building. He was headed to that university nearby to find information on scrubbers. Pulling off the little gambit the night before had bought him some time. He had no illusions about this. At most, he could get another couple of days until information was passed around and he was fingered as an imposter, or worse a spy. However, he knew those few days were vital to his getting established in a new life.

He walked down the hill to what the sign said was Main Street. Across the intersection was a small sign next to a paved road leading down hill to a parking lot and building set on earthworks a block out into the river. The sign read: University of Minnesota, St. Anthony Falls Laboratory, Engineering, Environmental and Geophysical Fluid Dynamics. Past that, he could see the river in places. Parts of it were iced over, but large portions were open indicating flowing water. It was no surprise that there were a variety of civil engineering constructs in and around the water. All cities did this to manage floodwaters, allow for river commerce, and if possible extract hydro-electricity.

Crossing Main, he turned left. As he walked, his thoughts returned to his situation. What were the chances that the truck he hijacked would be hauling meth chemicals, he wondered. It was an undisputed fact that meth precursors came from Canada to the U.S. That they would come from Winnipeg to Minneapolis by way of the Snow Flake crossing made sense. Cities traditionally start on the banks of bodies of water, so this was the oldest, most run down part of this city, a logical place to cook meth.

A few blocks south on Main he saw a four-sided information kiosk a half-block to this right. It was located at the start of the Stone Arch Bridge. The bridge was originally built as a railroad river crossing, and now was a foot bridge as part of the local park system. He walked to the kiosk. On one side was a map of the area in a somewhat artistic rendering showing the locks, dams, and islands in the river. He instantly committed it to memory, and started walking south again toward the university. Based on the information from the map, the area was being revitalized. The dilapidated building that contained the meth lab might be demolished soon, though nothing would happen in that regard in the time he expected to be associated with it.

A half-hour later Peng had located the main library of the university and entered. The lack of security was shocking. He simply walked in. It was very large. Immediately he realized he looked out of place without a backpack for books and personal sundries. He should have stolen one before entering. Growing up on the street did not prepare him to use a major library like this. As he walked about trying to orient himself the sound of Mandarin being spoken to his left caused him to stop. A young Asian man was standing beside another seated before a computer monitor as they discussed in hushed voices the party of the night before. There was an unused computer station next to the one the man occupied. Peng sat down and pretended to use it until the standing man left. Then he leaned over to the one sitting at the computer and addressed him in his native tongue. Somewhat surprised the man of about twenty asked him if he could be of assistance.

"Well, actually, yes. You are most gracious to offer. I need to find information on industrial stack or flue scrubbers. How do I go about finding books on that? I was told this was a very complete library. In fact, it is too big for me to know where to start."

The student replied, "You can use computer monitors like those over there," he said pointing, "and type in the thing you want. It will tell you what books there are here on that subject. Then you request the books and someone will retrieve it for you."

Peng nodded.

"But, you might do just as well using a computer like this," he said tapping his finger nail on the flat screen in front of him, "and look on the Internet. It might be faster."

"Show me, please, how I do that."

"Sure." The young Chinese man proceeded to get the Google search engine up and typed "Flue Scrubbers." In a wink, it was finished searching and had ten out of fifty thousand possible websites listed. "Just go down the page and click one that looks like what you want." Peng watched the little hand with an extended index finger appear as the arrow came to the right spot. "If you don't like what you found use this arrow to go back where you were. I'll be here for awhile yet. Ask if you need help."

Peng had heard about the Internet but only had a vague idea about what it meant. This was beyond fantastic. In a half-hour, he had seen enough about scrubbers to talk a good line. He had his newly acquired friend show him how to print selected pages. He would use these to persuade the boss at the meth lab he knew what he was doing.

About to leave, he paused. It almost seemed silly to him, but he decided he might as well try. He typed in St. Anthony Falls Lab. A few clicks later there it was, complete with an aerial photo. He clicked on "Visiting Researchers." There was information about a large project funded by the Chinese, their research on magnetic fields, and the names of scientists. The website managers were even thoughtful enough to put in links to the bios of the main players. From there, he found links to research papers each had written. Much of it was not understandable to him, but he gleaned enough "buzz words" to talk about the subject of zero point energy. It made sense that the source of the hubot feeling in Canada had come from these experiments. If the experiments were much more powerful than the hubot generating machine, he might have sensed it over that distance.

**2:15 p.m., Elgin, Illinois**

"Hello, Finley residence . . . Yes. He's here . . . Is there some problem? Yes. I'll call him."

Holding her hand over the receiver, Mrs. Finley called. "Jason. Phone!"

Jason Finley was glad to be home. His mother had taken vacation, and his father would be home in a few days. They'd all be together for Christmas. He had all of his schoolwork caught up, and was amusing himself with reading and playing computer games. Being a member of a diplomat's family, he was accustomed to being away from home for extended periods of time. In effect, he was an away from home home-schooler. It always surprised him how little time it actually took to do his lessons when all of the overhead time of the classroom was subtracted. Nobody in the educational establishment wanted to admit it, but there were excellent materials available with which someone could get a fine education with no teachers at all. This was the little secret a growing number of parents were learning as they home-schooled their children.

"Coming."

As Jason descended the stairs, his mother said in a hushed voice, "It's the INS from O'Hara. Was there some problem with your flight that you didn't tell me about?"

Jason shook his head as he took the phone. "This is Jason Finley."

"Hello, Mr. Finley. This is Aldon Hartner with the INS at O'Hara. Don't be alarmed, nothing's wrong concerning you or your family. I would like to ask you about the Asian gentleman that came through the diplomatic counter with you last Friday. The agent remembers he seemed to be with you. Can you tell me anything about him?"

Jason was immediately guarded. "He sat by me on the plane. It's a long flight, and we sort of became friends. He seemed a little unsure of himself, like he had never done any international travel."

"That's what the agent said. Yet, he had a U.S. passport."

"Yeah. Now that you mention it, that surprised me, too."

"Anything else you can remember?"

"At first, his English was very bad, and he asked if we could talk so he could practice. I was amazed at how fast he caught on. He used unusual words sometimes, like he had been taught a lot of vocabulary, but little grammar."

"Anything else? Did he talk about his work?"

"Nothing about his work, come to think of it. He seemed a little afraid of flying. Is he in trouble?"

"I'd say so. He used a stolen passport to get into this country. If you remember anything else, or he should contact you, call me. By the way, if you saw him again, do you think you'd recognize him?"

"Yes, of course."

"Good. We may have to call upon you for that. Here's my number."

After Jason copied down the number and said good bye, his mother came from the other room. "Jason, are you in trouble?"

"No, mom, not me. Do you remember that guy I told you about that sat next to me on the plane, that he was nice but kind of odd? Well, it seems there was something wrong with his passport. With everyone's

photo in the database, and the photo on the passport, and the guy standing there, how could there be a problem? If they didn't match, wouldn't
they have noticed it then?"

"I don't know, dear. Do we have to do anything?"

"No. He said he'd call back if he needed anything else."

So, the plot thickens, Jason was thinking as he went up to his room.
Was Hua a fugitive from justice, or a deep cover agent? If so, who was
he working for? In addition, maybe there really wasn't anything wrong
with the passport. Maybe the guy who called wasn't from the INS at all.

### Roseville, Minnesota

Yingqu had slept fitfully the night before which was uncommon for
him. He called room service for breakfast. This was the accepted procedure so he would be seen by as few people as possible. The morning
passed quickly, and now being past noon he was growing apprehensive.
The man from China would rent his own car and take a room in this hotel. They would meet when Yingqu heard a knock on his door.

It was nearly three o'clock before there were three light knocks on the
door. Slowly opening it Yingqu was startled. It took him a few minutes
to collect his thoughts. This man looked at the point of death. The shriveled up face and dark rimmed deep-set eyes looked almost lifeless. If the
man hadn't been squinting so much, he would have seen the whites were
so bloodshot as to be not white at all.

"Yingqu? Let me in!" the man demanded. The voice snapped like a
whip in sharp contrast to the apparition.

Yingqu immediately stepped aside allowing a clear path for the man
to enter. "Mr. Seng Kejian, I presume?"

"Who else!" It was not a question. "I am tired. The many things I had
to do to prepare for this trip meant I got little sleep, but I planned to
make it up on the long flight. An obnoxious woman and two children in
my row made that impossible. Americans are worse than I had ever
imagined. How inconsiderate they are!" He stopped and with obvious
effort collected himself. "That is done. I must rely on you to do some
preliminary work. First I will briefly tell you the reason we are both here.
Two dangerous men have escaped from a mental hospital in Beijing, and
then from China. They are part of an experiment that makes them special. It is thought either or both of them may have come to this city. We
are to find and capture one or preferably both of them. We are not to kill

either of them unless necessary to keep them from the Americans. Once we have at least one in our custody, I am to contact my superior for further instructions."

Yingqu listened attentively and nodded a couple of times. This all made sense from the urgency that seemed to pervade the preparations for the mission.

"Now the part that caused you to be assigned to this operation. Both of our subjects became familiar with information concerning a man who lives in this city. This man is known to you. His name is Edmund Breckon."

At that moment Kejian squeezed his eyes tightly closed and rubbed them with the heals of his hands. It was fortunate for Yingqu because the mention of Breckon's name caused his mouth to drop open. Unable to compose himself in time Kejian saw the remainder of distress on Yingqu's face.

Managing a thin smile he said, "I see you remember him. Very good. I have been told of your animosity toward him. You are not to let that interfere with your assignment. You are included because you will recognize him, and know something of his habits." Pausing for effect, he continued. "We are to insure that he is not harmed. People in Beijing see a use for him, and it would not be in the interest of either one of us to see their plans thwarted. Is that clear!" Once again, not a question.

The palms of Yingqu's hands were slippery with sweat. In the strange alleys of his mind, a thought came in a fraction of a second. He had failed twice to kill Breckon the day before, the first time by sure dumb bad luck. Or, was it bad luck? Maybe some of Breckon's good luck cooties had fallen on him.

Kejian continued. "We were to work together at all times, but I must sleep. I need you to locate Breckon, being most careful not to reveal yourself. Determine if he is alone or has someone with him. I have his most recent address, and I have photos of the two men we seek." Here he fumbled with the combinations on his briefcase, eventually opened it, and produced two photos.

Yingqu nodded and inquired as to their height, weight, and any other characteristics.

"Did you do the shopping you were told to do?"

"Yes," Yingqu replied. He worked the combinations on his case and produced the 9 mm pistol and silencer for Kejian."

"And the other items?"

Yingqu produced a plastic bag from Office Max, and one from Office Depot. Each contained three cell phones that had thirty minutes of call time built into them. That was more time than they would need because each pair would be used for only one call and then another pair would be used. In the extreme case where a fourth call was needed, and there was no time to buy more phones, the first would be used again. This was the most secure means of communication available. The two men carefully recorded the phone numbers of the phones and the sequence in which they would be used.

"Find Breckon. Call me only if you think we can accomplish our mission today. Otherwise I'll see you at six in the morning." With that he tossed his three phones and gun into his valise, closed it, and spun the tumblers. "I am in room 205." He turned and left without another word.

The door automatically swung closed behind him. Yingqu sank down on the edge of the bed feeling a little sick. That was a hard, cruel man, and if it ever came out about the events of the day before, there was no doubt . . . he didn't want to think about it. So, he grabbed his case and slipped phone number one into his jacket pocket. He glanced at the slip of paper. At least they had the address right. Time to go through the motions. He wondered where Breckon really was today.

Yingqu pulled into the parking lot of the adjacent apartment buildings and waited. The apartment was 103 according to Kejian's slip of paper. It was on the lowest level. In this building, that meant it was half in the ground with the bottom of the windows less than knee high above grade. Since Breckon had a garage, there was no point in looking for his car in the lot. He noted that it was not quite as cold today so he could leave the engine off about half the time. About five-thirty, he looked hard straining his eyes. What is this? Yes, the coat was the same. It was Breckon returning . . . alone with two bags of groceries. As soon as he saw his quarry, he backed his car out of the parking space and wheeled up on to the street, and then into Breckon's parking lot between two rows of garages. Slowing down, he watched for lights to come on in one of the unlit ground floor apartments. One lit up, and he saw Breckon come to the large window and close the drape. Okay, that identified his place.

Leaving the lot he drove around the neighborhood a few minutes and returned to the office building parking lot to the west of the apartment buildings. He opened his case and pulled a plastic box from a small pocket. It contained an item that looked like a light-colored lump of dirt. It was a listening device that was meant to be attached to the outside of a window by means of an adhesive with a peal-off paper. There was a remote recorder that could be hidden and left any place within a quarter mile. He placed the recorder among the boughs of a spruce tree a few steps from his car. It was a simple matter to walk along the front of the apartment building where he paused briefly as if lighting a cigarette and stuck the device to the window where it would be covered by the drape even when opened. Besides the recorder in the tree, Yingqu could listen on a receiver in his case.

He waited, watched, and listened, until nine o'clock. Breckon was watching a movie on TV. Early the next morning he'd return to the parking lot and remotely download the recorder. There was no reason not to go back to the hotel and get some sleep. On the way, he stopped at the combination gas station and minimart on County Road E2 and I-35W. He bought some candy bars, doughnuts, and three plastic bottles of soft drinks.

# — 20 —

Fr. Aldrich had talked to Hua Chen for a few minutes here and there during the day, but this was the first opportunity he had to sit down and discuss his situation again.

"Have any of the books I gave you helped?" Fr. Aldrich asked. "I gave you some that discussed the immortality of the soul, though it may be they weren't quite what you needed."

"There were some that helped. The moral proof is what Ed said."

"Yes. That is the easiest to understand, but, in the end, the least satisfying, or so it seems to me. It says that it is in human nature to see that in this life people who do good are rarely rewarded, and those who do evil are seldom punished, certainly not in proportion to their deeds. This argues for there is a life hereafter where things are evened up.

"For most people, the next most difficult to grasp is what are called the psychological arguments. These say that in the human mind there is a craving for truth as well as an insatiable desire for happiness. Neither of these are gratified in this life, and it would be a logical inconsistency that we would be created with desires that had no chance of being satisfied. Thus, a life hereafter is indicated where these longings can be fulfilled."

Hua nodded. "I see this. But, animals show curiosity. And, they want to be well fed, and sheltered from storms."

Father Aldrich nodded. "That's on the instinctual level, though. Humans strive for ultimate truth and goodness which is God. From the books, you know that authors spend many pages saying this in greater detail. Therefore, you'll have to fill in more details from what you've read.

"The metaphysical proof is the most indirect because it depends on the understanding of other things. As we have seen, the soul is simple, or indivisible, and is also a spiritual being, that is independent of matter. Once we have mastered these two concepts, it follows that the soul is, by its nature, incorruptible. From this, we see that God is bound to preserve the soul in possession of its conscious life after death. This last sentence takes more work, not the least of which is, the understanding of what God will and won't do, even though there is nothing he *can't* do."

"Those things you said are in a human soul by its nature. Books tell of the other things put there by God as gifts. Why did God make gifts? It is confusing to me that if we need them, why doesn't he give them to everybody?"

"I can appreciate the problem this is causing you. For now, we must spend time on the human soul in its natural state. Though they are important, the gifts of God will have to wait for a few minutes.

"Let's go over what I talked about last evening. I'll use different words and reasoning, and that may help you understand. When we look at the human soul in what it is, its nature, we see it contains two quite different areas. One area is the sensible order and the other is beyond that called the super-sense, or intellectual order. The first is what we have in common with animals. It includes the external senses, and, in addition, what we call the internal senses. The internal senses are the imagination, sensible memory, and the sensitive appetite. From this appetite comes the emotions and passions, such as sensible love and hatred, desire and aversion, sensible joy and sadness, hope and despair, audacity and fear, and anger. The animal does not pass beyond the sensible. As we have mentioned, animals know items only in their present singularity. The fox knows about the rabbit it is eating, not rabbitness.

"The part that we have that is far above the animals is the intellectual order consisting of the intellect and will. The intellect knows not only universal sensible things like treeness, but also, being and universal truths. An example of a universal truth is 'we must do good and avoid evil.' Since the intellect can know the good in a universal way, it can desire it, that is love it, will it, and make it happen. And, of course, a third faculty of the human soul has to do with the fact that it inhabits and animates a physical body. This faculty is power over material things. It is the soul of man that builds the space ship, and measures the atom."

Hua sat without moving as Fr. Aldrich waited for a response. Finally, He said, "You know what the books say very well. How does this help me? It can be that no person knows if other people are human. Human is assumed because we all got here the same way. Is that wrong? And, how do I know I'm human?"

"That is a very profound concept, and true. When we assume other people are human, we are using a sort of natural faith. For each of us to know for certain that we, individually, are human requires us to use our intellect and will to love God, to have that special faith that He exists and is worthy of our love. That is only possible by one of the gifts that we set aside earlier, the gift called the infused theological virtue of faith. This faith is a supernatural gift from God. But, it isn't like a birthday present in that God, as it were, surprises us with it. We must ask for it, be open to it, and accept it . . . "

Chen shuddered violently stopping Fr. Aldrich in mid-sentence.

"What's wrong, Hua? Did I say something to upset you?"

Hua ignored the question while struggling to compose himself. Finally, he said, "It has come to the time where I must ask for you to help me. At the Medical Institute I was made to wear a thing, what do you say, hanging thing, a pendant I think, on a chain around my neck. Ask doctor why and he did not tell me. Each six hours it did something but I only noticed a little, so I thought it was not needed. Since I arrived in America, I have not worn it. It now comes to me that it is needed to keep me working as a hubot, to stay alive. It is like power to make my muscles do what my brain says. Now gets worse each time it is not there to help me. You must get it for me. Please, help."

"Yes I'll help if I can. Where is this pendant?"

"Boy in Chicago has it. I thought the pendant might be a trick way for them to find where I stay, so on airplane I put it in pocket of boy's bag that sat by me. This I did not tell him, but he has it. His name is Jason Finley. His bag had a tag on it. I will give you information, and you can call on telephone to have him send by quick express to me."

"If it is sent here might they find you? They could be watching this boy."

Chen nodded feeling relaxed again. "Need is past now. Feel better, but must get this. Dr. Hongi at Institute thought it was silly that they could use the perineural system to control the permanency of the cognitive remapping in my brain. Might be the general's scientists know what they are doing."

"I'm sorry. Theology's my line, not physiology. What's the perineural system?"

"I read some about it at the Institute." Hua explained that the nerves transmitted digital signals to the brain. They were either on or off, and communicated only one way. They were the primary way the brain knew about injury to the body. The perineural system was the connective tissue that sheathed nerve fibers. It acted as a conduit for an analog system that could go both to and from the brain. It had been learned that brain waves were not confined to the brain but spread throughout the body by way of the perineural system. It was the main way the brain controlled the healing of injuries. In effect, the combination of the nerves and the perineural cells acted as sort of an antenna by which the brain communicated with all parts of the body through biomagnetic pulsations. This whole area of physiology had been neglected by conventional medical research because it was associated with some of the forms of alternative medicine such as acupuncture, and healers that purportedly used energy from their fingertips to cure certain maladies in their patients.

"As it gets a longer time without it," Chen continued, "something in me wants it to be there each six hours. Please, you go to telephone in store and call Jason. He liked me so will do it. Send to Ed. Ed will send to me. That will keep others away from you. Your help for me must not be known."

Chen wrote the name and information of Jason Finley and Ed Breckon on a slip of paper.

"Will this Jason Finley send it if I call? He might think I am one of your enemies."

Chen told Fr. Aldrich a code that would insure Jason knew it was Hua that was asking. Then he said, "I sleep now. Better at times of pendant when I am quiet, not upset with thoughts." Hua got up and left the room.

Fr. Aldrich was stunned by what had happened. Was it possible that this was actually not a man after all, but a sophisticated robot? One thing was for sure, though. He'd never find out if the guy died, so he had to do what he could for him. Looking at the slip of paper he saw the names, addresses, and phone numbers for the two people. The kid obviously had his phone number on the luggage tag, too. Must be great having perfect recall.

––––––––––––––

At the Finley residence, it was a little before nine and Jason was watching one of his favorite movies on DVD when the phone rang. No one answered and Jason was only half listening as the answering machine kicked in. After the beep the voice said, "I'm calling for Jason Finley with a call from Hua Chen. Could I speak to someone, please?"

With the mention of Hua's name Jason scrambled to the phone and picked it up. "Hello, this is Jason."

"Jason Finley?"

"Yes."

"I am calling on behalf of Hua Chen. He told me something that would let you know you could trust me. There is a word that has two meanings, and said differently. It has to do with Americans not being cannibals. Do you know the last two letters of that word?"

Jason immediately smiled. Hua simply had to be a spy. This was so exciting. He even wondered if all through the flight Hua was cleverly devising a set of codes without Jason having any hint he was doing it. "Yes, I do. They are a and t? And, do you know the other letters?"

"Yes. They are b and r. Is that correct?"

"Yes it is. How is my friend? Is there some way I can help him?"

"As a matter of fact, there is. You have something of his. Did you find it?"

"Yes, I did."

"He asks if you will please send it to the address I will give you. Do you have a pen and paper?"

There was a pad and pen on the table by the phone, and Jason was on one knee as he tried not to drop the phone and got ready to write. "Okay, I'm ready."

Fr. Aldrich read the address as Hua had given it to him. "Can you send it first thing in the morning by Federal Express or Express Mail so he will have it at the latest Tuesday? It seems he is in rather dire need of it."

"Yes, I'll do it first thing in the morning."

"I thank you on his behalf. God bless you, and good night."

*God bless you!* Jason thought with surprise. That guy moves with a strange bunch of spies.

The movie was completely forgotten as Jason tore the top five sheets off the pad of paper. He couldn't let anyone else learn the secret address by looking at the imprint of his pen on the page below.

In his room, Jason opened the bottom dresser drawer where he kept his treasures. He dug to the bottom of his stamp collection box, a collection that had not gotten very far, and pulled out a small brown envelope. He took the bead chain out and let the pendant dangle in front of his face.

It was the one he had seen Hua wearing on the plane, and had found tucked in a side pocket of his carry-on bag when he got home. It had such a strange shape and little gold tabs of the edges. He could only wonder what it was for, and the reason for the urgent call late at night to return it.

**5:45 a.m., Monday, Hotel, Roseville, Minnesota**

Muan Yingqu was eating doughnuts, the kind with white powdered sugar on them, and sipping a cup of instant coffee that came with the room. This was interrupted by three light knocks on the door. He had no doubt the throbbing drum beats, as his mind interpreted the sounds, were made by the master of charm, his superior, Seng Kejian, summoning him to be let in. Springing across the room, lest he be accused of not being up and ready for work at this hour, he twisted the doorknob and jerked the door open. Before him was the same figure of fifteen hours before. No change.

"Please, come in," was all Yingqu could manage to say.

The instant the door clicked shut the visitor spoke. "What did you learn yesterday!" Not a question. The attitude hadn't changed, either.

Yingqu could only think that this was one man who could not tolerate jetlag. Anybody who looked like this all the time would be dead within a year. There were two chairs by the small round table where Yingqu had his coffee and doughnuts laid out. "I can make you a cup of instant coffee if you like. And, help yourself to some doughnuts."

"Yuck! You'll be dead within a year if you keep eating like this. I had some food sent up. It was bad, but not like this."

Yingqu fought the urge to laugh at the realization that each was thinking the same about the other. He clenched his teeth and absorbed the energy in tightened stomach muscles and pressure behind his eyes. The mirth passed.

"To business. Did you locate Breckon and either of our men?"

"I observed Breckon return to his apartment building at five-thirty carrying groceries. When he went to his apartment, I observed which apartment was his as he turned on the lights. Luckily, it faces the parking lot. I am sure it was his because the drapes were open and I saw him come to the window and close them. Then . . . "

"Enough chatter! Was anyone with him? Did you observe anyone else in the room?"

"He was alone when he arrived. The apartment was dark when he entered it. As I was about to say, I placed a listening device on his window with a remote recorder. I stayed and listened until nine o'clock. He hummed a little, talked to himself a few times, and then watched a movie. There was no indication of another person."

"Return now and download the recording. Follow him. I assume he will be going to his work, but this will verify that. I received a message that there is another matter that requires my attention for a few hours. I will see you back here at noon."

---

Kejian's other business took him south on I-35W toward the center of Minneapolis. He had been alerted to this situation shortly before he left Beijing. The half-hour briefing was not nearly enough for him to understand what was involved. He was told he might have to make a stop and interview two people, each separately. His pre-departure briefing had included directions to the site. The message on his email this morning said simply to investigate and report on the Falls Project. The only other information in today's message instructed him to drive into the parking lot of the site at exactly six-thirty.

The traffic was getting heavier on the freeway as rush hour picked up, but still ran at the posted speed limit. By six-twenty-two, Kejian pulled to a stop where he saw a small sign that read St. Anthony Falls Laboratory. This was the place. Traffic on Main Street that ran through the trendy partially restored river-front district was getting heavy so he was forced to move on. He drove around a few blocks and parked on a steeply inclined street across Main from the lab. At six-twenty-nine he pulled away from the side of the street, crossed Main Street, and drove into the parking lot. He parked up against a four-foot stone wall. To his right was an unmanned wrought iron gate standing open. As he got out of his car, an Asian man approached through the gate from the inside.

"Seng Kejian?" the man inquired.

"Yes," was the only reply.

"I am Ju Feng, technician on the Falls Project. We were alerted minutes ago that you would pay us a visit. Please, follow me."

Kejian spent the next several hours interviewing members of the project. It rankled him that none of the people would spell out exactly what this "conjecture" was really about. As he was interviewing Heng Lu for the second time, as usual alone, it occurred to him there was something sinister going on here. He was deliberately not being told the full extent of what was involved. He began to wonder if even they knew the full story. One thing was obvious, though. The current management structure of the project was not working. The man in charge was also one of the protagonists. After the interviews, he demanded and got the private use of the team's office for a few minutes. Using Jian Niu's established secure connection to Beijing, he sent a message saying there had to be a neutral leader with each of the opposing scientists having exactly equal status under him.

When he saw there was little more he could do, he asked to be escorted to the gate and went on his way. This had been a distraction from his main mission. However, he was able to come up with a conclusive, easy remedy to the lack of progress on the project. In spite of the inconvenience, it would show he could competently handle an unexpected assignment in addition to his main mission. This always went far when promotions were being considered.

## 8:20 a.m., Southeast Minneapolis

Quan Peng had slept well for the second night in a row. He thought it was partially because of the bad air caused by cooking meth. Everyone in the place was a little high on meth at least part of the day. He was having coffee with the man they called the boss. No one had previously mentioned the man's name and this morning the boss did not offered it. They sat in strained silence. The boss's demeanor was just short of hostile toward Peng. Harvey left in the truck before the boss arrived, so it seemed doubtful they had spoken except on the phone.

Peng sat motionless and when the man across from him didn't say anything, he began. "Whatever you may think of me, you must acknowledge that the gaseous emissions from the cook will soon cause your operation to be discovered. It is ingenious how you have managed to dispose of you liquid waste. Why lose it all because of the gases? You need scrubbers on the exhaust stack, and I can provide them for you."

The fiftyish man, with black eyes squinting out of a pudgy face, leaned back in his chair and crossed his legs. He knew he needed scrubbers. It was the next thing on his list of improvements. If demand for product hadn't taken a slight up-tick, he might have had Davis working on them now—and then again, maybe not.

Like any businessman, he followed trends in the sale of his merchandise. As it was, the overall use of meth was in a slight decline. That was good and bad. It was good because it took the pressure of the media and law enforcement off the drug. Everyone could take credit for making progress in getting the use of the substance under control, even though meth use was down only four percent in three years. But, it did mean the demand for his product was falling. An additional favorable statistic related to meth was the dramatic drop in the number of meth labs seized. This, of course, was due to the startup of professional operations as the amateurs were weeded out. Meth had a built in drawback, too. Of the major illegal drugs, the time from first use to rehab was the shortest for meth which meant there was constant pressure to get new customers. None of this explained the presence of the guy across the desk from him.

"I find it strange that you show up at this precise time with the suggestion that we need what we already knew we needed. We aren't stupid. Scrubbers are the next thing on our list of improvements. And, your story about getting precursor direct from China is exactly what we need. With ready to sell meth coming across the border from Mexico, we need the precursor to stay competitive. You will pardon me if I am skeptical about these coincidences. It sounds too good to be true, and that always makes me cautious.

"Harvey's out on another run. Before I make any decision about you, I'll have a sit-down with him. I know he can be a klutz at times, but I don't know what you could have told him to get in here."

Peng knew all along this would be a hard sell. He had thought about the possibility of torturing this man to tell all he knew about the operation, killing him, and taking over. From his point of view it was a good plan, except he really didn't want to be in this business.

Peng nodded accepting the situation, then said, "In the meantime, I could make a list of needed equipment, and draw up preliminary plans. Nothing need be changed until you are ready."

The black eyes were like drills boring into Peng. The man's distrust of this situation was obvious. "Can't be any harm in that. They foolishly let you see the entire operation anyway." Then with a snort he continued. "Davis might be getting a little too immersed in his job, if you get my drift, to do any serious engineering anyway. Stay out of sight, and no calling suppliers, or any of that until I say to go ahead. Now, I've got some stuff to do, if you don't mind."

Peng rose and left the small room.

**10:45 a.m., Elgin, Illinois**

Jason answered the door in response to the door chime. "Hello. I'm Aldon Hartner from the INS. I'm looking for Jason Finley."

"That's me."

"I talked to you on the phone yesterday, remember?"

"Yeah, sure. Now what's happening?"

"Jason, who's at the door?" called his mother from back in the house.

"Can I come in and talk to you for a few minutes?"

Jason shrugged. "Sure. Why not?"

"It's the guy from the INS, mom. The one that called me yesterday."

Hartner stepped into the entry and stuffed his brown gloves into the pocket of his light brown coat. Jason offered to take his coat, scarf, and brown hat that matched his brown eyes. His brown and tan glen-plaid sports coat was rumpled. Here was a flabby middle aged man who was clearly ill at ease. The deep vertical creases in his cheeks on either side of his mouth accentuated his longer than normal face.

"Hello. I'm Mrs. Finley, Jason's mother."

Hartner introduced himself, produced an identification, and offered a business card. He was ushered into the living room. Jason's mother, always one to be on guard lest anything happen to impugn her husband's reputation was the first to speak.

"Jason told me about that odd man that sat beside him on the plane. Is this about him? We'll help if we can."

"Yes. I'm sure you will. From the point of view of the INS, this is a little embarrassing. You see, we have many safeguards to prevent from happening precisely what did happen. The man that sat beside your son on the plane, and sort of befriended him, had stolen the passport he used from another man in China. He then had an extremely professional counterfeit made of it with his picture on it. However, it wasn't really his picture, sort of a composite of the rightful owner and that of someone we assume is the imposter. Added to this, the photo that is taken of everyone who enters the country as their passport is being checked was smeared in some way."

"What?" Jason asked. "You mean they take my picture every time I come home? I've never seen them do that."

"Yes. It's rather surreptitiously done because it unnerves some people. However, Congress passed a law directing that it must be done, so it is. We are left with the fact that we really don't have a good idea of what this man looks like. Of course, we assume that anyone that goes to so much trouble to enter our country illegally is a potential threat. I need to ask you, Jason, if there is anything else about this man that you can tell me. Please, don't think this is all in good fun. That man is a serious criminal who will use anyone in any way to achieve his ends. Now, think hard. Is there anything you haven't told me." The muscles in Hartner's face were as hard as his voice.

Jason looked away and fidgeted a little.

"Jason!" his mother snapped. "I know that look. You're hiding something, aren't you? You must tell everything you know. Your father has a very sensitive position, and you will do nothing to jeopardize it. Now, tell the man what you know!"

The fidgeting did not stop as Jason looked at Hartner. "He is not a criminal, I'm sure of that. And, I think he is in trouble. I think he's a spy of some sort, but on our side. Check with the CIA. He said he had urgent information for them. Didn't the agent checking the passports tell you that?"

Hartner almost sneered. "What a clever idea. If he were working for the CIA, wouldn't they have had someone there to meet him? Ever think of that, eh?"

"It's not like that. He seemed to be coming of his own accord. They didn't know he was coming, at least not on that day."

"Jason," his mother said. "You know something you aren't telling. What is it?"

"Well, when I got home from my flight and started unpacking, I discovered a thing, a bauble of sorts, that I had seen him wearing on a chain around his neck. He obviously had taken it off and put it in a pouch of my carry-on bag. I don't know what it was, or why he did that."

Hartner interrupted. "What do you mean, was? Where is it now?"

"I was getting to that," Jason continued. "Last evening I got a call asking to have it sent to him, which I did this morning. That's all. Why is that so important?"

"It's very important, because you have an address where he'll receive the thing you sent. I must require you to give me this address. How did you send it, and when will it be delivered?"

Jason gave a half frown, ignoring his mother's intense gaze. "I sent it priority mail. It should be delivered tomorrow morning." Jason was becoming increasingly ill at ease, as things seemed to be getting far too serious. He thought of mentioning that Hua was not the one who called, but decided he wouldn't. Let Hartner find out.

After Jason returned from his room with the address, Hartner sat back on the sofa looking at it and thinking. Then he addressed Jason's mother. "This address is in the Minneapolis area. Would it be possible for me to fly up there in the morning with your son so he could make a positive identification of this guy when we pick him up? It would make things go a whole lot easier. He said he'd have no problem recognizing him again."

Giving information that could potentially harm a perfect stranger was one thing. Now it was hitting closer to home, and a different set of rules applied. "I don't see why that should be necessary. You have what you need. Bring him back here and I'll bring Jason in and he can identify him."

Hartner twisted his mouth around, his eyes getting like steel rivets. "There is likely to be a problem there. Without your son's ID, we will encounter delays in bringing him back. If, after all of that, he is the wrong man, the real criminal will have had time to disappear completely. Time is extremely important in cases like this." Hartner paused letting Mrs. Finley think about the situation. Then he began again. "Where can I reach your husband? Maybe he'll see it differently." To the normal hardness in his voice, he had added a threat.

Working at sensitive levels of international politics was not without its hazards. Mrs. Finley and her husband had encountered similar situations before. It was obvious, she as well as Hartner had said too much. She should not have mentioned that her husband was in a sensitive position. It would be easy enough for an agency like the INS to find out, though. Mr. Hartner clearly revealed too much of what was really behind his visit here this morning. The part of government he worked for had made a huge blunder in letting that man into the country. Now, they were in a near state of panic to rectify their error. Expecting them to contact the CIA, FBI or any other branch of government that would be able to help find this man was unlikely to happen. Mrs. Finley saw it was now necessary to get Hartner out of her house without either of them revealing just how panicked they both were. At the same time she must leave the door open for further assistance, and above all, keep things on a professional, civilized level.

Mrs. Finley forced a relaxed expression and replied. "Mr. Hartner, it would be difficult to reach my husband at this time seeing as he is in transit." After a pause, "My son is twelve years old. You can't expect me to turn him over to a perfect stranger to travel to another city. May I suggest this? You apprehend the suspect in Minneapolis. When you have him in custody, let us know. Then you provide plane tickets for Jason and myself. We will meet you there. It should only take a few minutes for Jason to verify the man you have as his seating companion, so book a return flight a few hours later. Since it's the height of the holiday travel season, any plane tickets still available will be expensive. You provide them on your account. How does that sound?"

Hartner had met his match. The offer was too reasonable to argue with. After a few stiff pleasantries, he took his leave.

As soon as the man was gone Jason's mother turned to him and said, "Jason, pack an over night carry-on bag so we're ready to go. We haven't seen that last of that man. Be sure to put in a change of underwear, a warm sweater, stocking cap, and gloves. The forecast says snow's coming. Put in a pair of boots, too. Plan to take a warm coat."

"Ah, mom. I won't need all of that for a few hours trip."

"Son, trust your mother. We're going to Minnesota in the winter. They probably don't even have central heating there."

———————————

As Hartner was driving away, he had already decided he'd make reservations to go to Minneapolis for himself in the afternoon, and the two Finleys for tomorrow morning. This was going to be handled swiftly and right.

# — 21 —

Muan Yingqu was online in his hotel room getting caught up on messages from the Embassy in Washington when he heard the three light raps on the door. It had been less than twenty-four hours since he had first heard that rapping and he was already sick of what was causing them. His desire to hunt down Edmund Breckon was becoming secondary to finding a way to guillotine that ornery, officious, maggot. He opened the door and there stood a young man in uniform from room service with his lunch. Rapidly changing his state of mind and accompanying expression he smiled and bid the man enter. Not knowing what to do, he had ordered two lunches in case Kejian should arrive while he was eating.

Minutes after Yingqu started into his club sandwich there were three light raps on his door—again. This time he was not disappointed. The nightmarish specter appeared as the edge of the door passed his eyes. Kejian strode in without a word, pulled up a chair by the small table, and began to eat the other sandwich. Yingqu sat down and said to himself, you're welcome.

After finishing his meal, Kejian went to the bathroom to wash his hands. He returned and refilled his cup with coffee from the carafe. Finally, he spoke the first words since entering the room. "Where did Breckon go from his apartment this morning?"

"To his job at Control Systems, Ltd. It's the place given in the information you had when you arrived."

Without acknowledging the response Kejian said, "This morning I visited a lab where the Chinese government is conducting some sort of experiment. There are five Chinese scientists and technicians there. A dispute had arisen about authority between the two senior members of the team so I was ordered there to see what could be done. I tell you this in strictest confidence because I need your input about this country. You understand!" It was not a question.

Yingqu nodded saying nothing.

"I had been told I might be called upon to make this visit before I left Beijing. In my briefing, they were circumspect about the reason for the test. At the lab, they would not tell me the purpose of the experiment, either. They wouldn't even let me see the apparatus. It must be very secret. If I'm correct in this, it's odd that they would do it here. What could cause them to do that?"

This was like asking why the dinosaurs went extinct, but Yingqu knew he had to give it a try. "In spite of what we are told about the Americans, they still do more scientific research than any other country in the world. My guess is there are some facilities in this city, at that lab in fact, that would be hard to duplicate in China. What is the name of the place?"

"Saint Anthony Falls Laboratory."

Yingqu lifted his laptop computer off the bed onto the table. It was still connected to the Internet so he invoked his search engine and entered the name. Immediately he had what he needed. "See here. That lab has an international reputation for the modeling it does of rivers, canals, dams, and associated structures for countries around the world. That is likely the answer," but you won't agree, went unsaid.

He didn't disagree. He didn't say anything. After an entire minute of silence Kejian said, "Maybe." Then, as if saying it to himself he continued, "Something isn't right here." Looking at Yingqu he said, "You go to Breckon's place of employment and follow him if he leaves. I have other things to do."

When Kejian left the room he was eager to begin the other things he had to do, only one actually—get more sleep.

## 12:20 p.m., Monday, Langley, Virginia

The brown envelope was handed to ShuHo Zeng just as he was about to leave his office for lunch. "Sign please," the messenger said. Zeng did as requested, though it sounded more like an order, but in fact, it was neither. It was simply two employees of the CIA doing their jobs.

The envelope was brown, but it had those blasted diagonal red stripes on it. He took the letter opener from his desk, slit the end, and dumped

the contents out. Nothing but a four-and-a-half by nine-and-a-half white
envelope with his address in the window. Damn, one of those. It was important. When his housekeeper had brought in the mail as she was instructed to do each day as soon as it arrived, this piece of junk mail met
the specification she had been given. She had placed a call to the number
as required by the situation. Someone from the agency had made a special trip out to his house to get the letter. That was all very expensive, so,
as the receiving party, he was obliged to act on it immediately.

Normally these were from sleeper agents, but not all. He lowered his
slight frame into his chair. His quick black eyes had a look of anticipa-
tion in them as he slit the letter open. Pulling out a file folder, he checked
the code on the bottom of the first page against a list. Well, that's interesting, he thought. From Edmund Breckon. He recognized the format
and went to the fourth paragraph on page two. The imbedded message
didn't mean much to him. If it had been anybody else, it would have
been handled by an established procedure. Breckon was different. Zeng
had met him and knew he was an enigma, but not frivolous. That noted,
he was crushed with work with a full afternoon. Since Breckon had become friends with Greg Daley at the NSA, and since the term "hubot"
meant nothing to Zeng he send a short email over the secure lines to
Daley including the verbatim message. Now, he'd have to eat fast.

———————

When Greg Daley returned from lunch, his monitor showed two
emails had arrived. The one marked "urgent" was first. Well, hi Ed, he
thought. What's been going on? Wow! If that doesn't beat all! Half the
world is looking for that hubot, and guess who just happens to have him.
Damn it all, he must not know! Wonder if he's still alive?

———————

Zeng's phone was ringing as he returned with a cup of coffee in his
hand. Stabbing the hands free button he said, "Yeah, Zeng here."

"ShuHo, this is Daley. Got your email. We must meet, today!"

"Got a full afternoon. What ya got?"

"This could be real big. I'd like to brief you in person seeing as we
both know the guy. It simply can't wait. How about I drive over to your
place and we meet at two-thirty?"

"Can't. How about three? It is all right if I bring Sam Li to the meting?"

"Yeah, he'd be good. But, nobody else until we sort this out. Okay? See you at three."

Daley hung up and ShuHo reached over and pressed the disconnect button. He sat thinking. Damn that Breckon, how does he do it? What was in that message? He could tell by the urgency in Daley's voice that it was not going to be a put-me-to-sleep meeting. He made a quick call to Sam, his right hand lieutenant, and made sure he shook loose some time at three.

———————

Greg Daley had on occasion visited the headquarters building of his best customer. He showed his badge to the uniformed guard at the gate to the CIA compound in Langley, Virginia. The drive from Fort Mead, the home of the National Security Agency, had taken forty minutes. Knowing how things worked, and where to go, got him to ShuHo Zeng's office a little before three. Zeng was the Far East bureau chief, a busy and important man though his status did not get him preferential seating at restaurants.

Greg was shown in and ShuHo greeted him warmly. Daley was a little over six feet tall and average build. His dark eyes and pointed nose were the features that made his otherwise average looking Anglo-Saxon face memorable. Pressing the intercom button Zeng said, "Sam. Daley's here. Can you join us?"

Seconds later Sam Li appeared and took a seat. Li was taller than average for a Chinese, though his features left no doubt he was of that race. He was strong and in superb shape.

Zeng and Li had worked with Daley less than six months before on a case involving Breckon. If the three of them hadn't closed ranks and put up a phalanx around Breckon, he would have been convicted of high treason as had been the plan of the Chinese government. He was finally proven innocent, but it left some ruffled feathers, as was the norm in this business. Zeng had a sense about Breckon going into that thing in August that he couldn't rightly explain. In hindsight, he was glad he had stood up for him. Now it appeared something had flared up about it so he was eager to hear what Daley had to say.

"Okay, your meeting, Greg. Let's hear it," Zeng opened.

"Hubot," Greg said, letting it hang for a moment. "Either of you ever hear the word before you saw it in Breckon's message?"

Both men shook their heads.

"Over the past few weeks the Chinese have been frantically trying to apprehend one. Seems it or him, we assume it's a man, what else we have no idea because we've tentatively ruled out a space alien, has escaped. They have, as we can piece together, issued orders to bring him back dead or alive. We've tracked him from Beijing all the way through China to Urumqi in the western most province. From there, he went to Mumbai, then Cairo, and ended in Winnipeg. I got involved in Cairo, as you might suspect, that being my territory. They lost him in Canada. Minneapolis is the large city closest to Winnipeg."

ShuHo and Sam had used the results of the NSA's global listening capability many times. The two agencies worked together a lot, sometimes not as smoothly as one would guess, but a lot. The NSA scooped up all of the electronic communications on the planet. This included radar signals and any other emissions. They had breakout boxes in nearly all fiber optic cables. All the phone calls between microwave towers were monitored, including all cell phone calls. They heard calls from air traffic controllers, to aircraft, and electronic money transfers between banks. They had it all. This massive amount of information was fed into the largest computer bank in the world. Not only did they measure their computers by the acre, but they were the fastest, ten to a hundred times faster than the fastest commercially available super-computers.

Added to that they had the best algorithms for breaking codes, and some of the smartest code breaking scientists in the world. Their programs could listen to a foreign language conversation, translate and print an English transcript of it in real time, noting each speaker as it went. They could pick out a single conversation from a room full of people all talking at once far better than the human ear.

Into these computers, qualified people and agencies put "flag words." This could be a phone number, name of a ship, or a person's name. Of course, "hubot" qualified. Once it became something of interest, and was put in as a flag word, any communication anywhere on the planet using it was automatically sorted out, translated, and forwarded to the computer monitor of the requestor. Greg was up to speed on this because it had been a topic of discussion at a recent meeting.

Greg paused collecting himself for what he had to say next. "Needless to say, some people in my shop would like to get their hands on this hubot at almost any cost. That is the reason I'm here. This thing has left a trail of bodies behind him. Six at least in China, and one in Mumbai. He seems to operate without remorse. If he needs money, he doesn't just rob someone, he kills them and than robs them. He also appears to be smart, or at least cunning. They thought they had him contained a couple of times and he slipped out."

ShuHo and Sam were listened intently. All three were silent after Greg stopped. "Wait a minute, Greg," Zeng said. "You said the hubot got to Winnipeg. Breckon's message said he come through O'Hare. You sure you got that right?"

"So he flew from Winnipeg to Chicago." Even as he said it, Greg was having his doubts.

"If the Chinese tracked him all the way to Canada, how did they miss the trip to O'Hare?" Sam asked. He followed with, "Did you manage to intercept a picture of the guy?"

Daley shook his head.

ShuHo drew himself up and said, "Something's wrong. And seeing it's Breckon, I know," he paused for emphasis, "I just know it's not going to be simple."

"My feelings exactly," Daley said. "The fact that Breckon's still alive is in itself a mystery."

"Oh, oh," Li said rubbing his hand over his mouth. "Just thought of something. I got a routine notice this morning that one Muan Yingqu arrived in Minneapolis Saturday and rented a car."

Greg and Sam looked at each other. ShuHo said, "See, I told you. It's starting to come apart before we even get out of the meeting."

Swallowing hard Greg added, "Maybe they're both dead already."

Zeng give a faint smile, "No. At least Breckon's still alive. I'd bet on that."

"So, what do we do?" Sam asked.

"Not we, Sam, you. You get on the first plane to Minneapolis. I'll cover for you here. Greg, stay handy. We'll be needing you and your forest of computers, I'm sure of that. When you get there, Sam, absolutely first thing find out if Breckon is still among the living. If not, it goes standard. We've got out backsides hanging out as it is. If he's alive—like I said, I'm pretty sure he is—link up with the local CIA guys, Breckon's old pals, Mel and Burl. Breckon'll love that. We can keep it quiet for a couple of days at most so work fast. Greg, do the database check on arrivals of any out of place Chinese in Minneapolis, will ya? This'll take a few funny twists, you know it."

It was after dark when Quan Peng slipped out of the historic but run-down building on Second Street. He had to get some fresh air. Even though they weren't cooking at the time, the odors hung in the air no matter where he went in the building. This gig couldn't last long, he knew, or he'd be an addict, too. He also knew it wouldn't last long from the way the boss had been making calls and coming and going all day. He was clearly pulling out all the stops to learn more about a man called Quan Peng. He pulled his coat collar up around his ears as he walked down the hill toward Main Street and turned right. There was a combination pub and eatery a half block ahead. He could use a good meal and a beer. Peng had arrived in Minneapolis with money from the man he killed in Mumbai. Since Harvey made regular trips to Canada, he asked him to exchange his Canadian dollars to U.S. currency. This he did at a hefty exchange fee.

Entering the establishment he was met with a different, much more agreeable aroma, that of fried food and beer. If it had been China, there would also be cigarette smoke in the mixture. No wonder these people are dying, he thought. They've made everything enjoyable in life illegal. He took a chair at a small table near the back of the room. A small blond woman of about twenty came to take his order. She was chewing gum, a habit he could not even remotely understand. He ordered number five, fish sandwich, off the menu not knowing exactly what he'd get, and was met with, "Sorry. Ran short of the walleye. Can't get ya that. Too much breading so not that good anyway."

"Well than, number two, and a good local beer."

"That'll do."

Having never heard of walleye, he accessed the English vocabulary he had soaked up at the Medical Institute. The definition for "walleye" mentioned the type of eye in a horse or certain kinds of fish. He had never eaten eyeballs before so saw it as no loss. It made him wonder about the California Berger he had ordered, though. His beer arrived at the hand of the same female. It occurred to him she was a student at the university working to help pay expenses.

The first deep draw on the brew was the best thing he had tasted in a long while. As he was savoring it a few words of Mandarin fell on his consciousness. Ever so slightly, he turned his head to the left. There were two Chinese men in a booth one leaning halfway over the table speaking in hushed but emphatic tones to the other. The general buzz of a dozen conversations made it impossible to make out what they were saying.

But, he thought he heard mention of *falls* or *falls project*. Falls Project was what the Chinese thing at the lab across the street had been called on the website. After several minutes the man leaning on the table got up and said. "Don't worry so much, Heng. It'll work out. I'm leaving. Don't stay here all night. We need you alert tomorrow." With that, he left. The blond women returned hurriedly to the booth with the bill lest the remaining man should leave without paying. He waved it away and ordered another beer.

After it arrived Peng got up, and acting somewhat intoxicated, approached the booth. Speaking in Mandarin he asked, "Do you mind if I join you for a few minutes? I don't think the crazy language these barbarians speak will ever catch on."

The man perked up and motioned to the opposite seat. Peng continued, "I couldn't help hearing a few words of a proper language as the other man left. By the way, I'm Quan Peng, came from Beijing a few days ago. May I ask your name? Been here long?"

The man was guarded in his answer, but not as much as he would have been sober. "Oh, yes. I'm Heng Lu. I've been here some weeks. It was good at first being away from the watching eyes. Now, things are different. I fear I am about to fail. Then my career is over. Advanced pretty far, though, for a simple country boy. I'm one of the best theoretical physicists in China. The worst part is I know the conjecture is true, and the big reputation of the senior man will say it is false. That'll be bad for the future of China." He took another sip of beer, and took out a pack of cigarettes, then slapped them on the table in disgust. "These crazy people and their damned laws. They deserve everything they'd get if it were a fair test!"

Peng recognized the name of the man across from him as one of the principals associated with the Chinese project at the St. Anthony Falls Lab. His survival instincts, honed from youth, grasped about for a way to become associated with the project. He wasn't looking for a lifetime career, just another week or two to stay alive. The meth lab thing wouldn't last long.

With his total recall, Peng accessed the research papers that he had called up on the computer. He found "conjecture" mentioned a few times, but never a definition of what it meant. He had to assume this was something internal to the scientific community in China. For this and other obvious reasons, he had to keep from getting into a technical discussion about it.

It helped his purposes that this man was fairly well inebriated and despondent about his pending failure to prove his side of the issue. That must be what the Falls Project was supposed to accomplish. All Peng needed was a way to extend him a ray of hope. "I represent financial interests from China, and we don't want anything to damage China's reputation. Could I ask what you are concerned about?"

Out of his foggy mind, Lu was trying to ward off what sounded like an attempt to get him to tell classified information. This was done all the time. In fact, to get a promotion in some of the security agencies the candidate was required to get someone to reveal classified information. This demonstrated the competency of the candidate, and unfortunately destroyed the person who divulged it, usually resulting in a long prison sentence. His resistance was offset by his desire to bring harm to Jian Niu. That pompous slob had thrown his weight around to the point where he'd kill him himself if he could summon the courage to do it.

"I won't say what my work is about, but Jian Niu must be stopped. We thought we had a plan to get things going again, when this morning an MSS agent shows up with ten minutes warning. All the way from Beijing. Can you imagine that? He talked to each of us, always alone. Niu lied about everything. I know he did. He always lies. He will be believed because he is the *respected one*, comes from the *upper* class" he said, hate lacing his words and at the same time pushing the end of his nose up with his finger for emphasis.

He took another sip of beer. "Boy, I could use a cigarette." Then continuing, "The piece of MSS crap got his report in quick too. Few hours ago we got a message that the way-up pigs in Beijing are delegating a new leader to come here. Be here day after tomorrow. Supposedly he will be in charge, sort of an umpire, and we will both report directly to him with equal status." With a snort he said, "Nothing will change."

Peng was curious. "Do you say that because you know the man who is coming?"

"That's the problem. None of us have ever heard of Shan Jin. He can't be anything in the theoretical physics community or at least one of us would know him. That means he's a dum-dum bureaucrat. Niu has the big name and party connections, so Jin will listen to him. See, no change."

Now, it was Lu's turn to ask questions. "What kind of financial interests do you represent?"

Peng leaned back and took a drink of beer. "I am here to search of ways to invest money. Most people are not aware of how international finance works. China has a huge trade imbalance with the U.S. They buy much more from us than we buy from them. When we sell them goods, we get their dollars. Simply having numbers on a balance sheet saying we have dollars does us no good. In some way, those dollars must make their way back to the U.S. That is, we must spend them. Even if we buy something from another country using these dollars, raw materials from Brazil for example, they now have to buy something from the U.S. It works that way with all international trade."

Lu took another sip of beer fidgeting with his cigarette pack. He nodded and said, "Continue."

"In effect, we are buying the U.S. one piece at a time. Most people in this very city with mortgages on their houses are unaware that Chinese interests hold a growing percentage of those finical instruments. We buy office buildings, hotels, even certain government facilities." He didn't know if the statement about the government property was commonly true. In a few cases it was, and China frequently bought property that the U.S. government leased or rented. The simple statement of it was enough to produce the idea Peng had been searching for, a way to connect to the St. Anthony Falls Lab. After a pause to let the idea gestate, Peng continued, "One of the pieces of property I am investigating on this trip is the St. Anthony Falls Laboratory. It is not such a large facility, but its international reputation would be beneficial to the People's Republic of China if we owned it."

With a look of surprise Lu said, "That is where I am working."

"Ah, that is where I recognize your name," Peng said in feigned surprise. "You are associated with the Falls Project. In fact, it is that project that drew the attention of the investors I represent."

Lu was guarded again. "I find it hard to believe that the Americans would sell such a facility, one owned by the government."

Peng smiled. "Under President Clinton, British Petroleum bought controlling interest in the Alaskan North Slope oil field. That company is sixty percent owned by the British Government so the British control all that oil. You see, the Americans don't mind selling their national assets to foreigners."

Peng's idea was coming along and Lu seemed to be accepting it. Now he needed a reason for Lu to help him. "I came into this pub to get a couple of beers and a meal. Please understand that I did not come here to meet you. But, our meeting may have been fortunate. You mentioned that it would be bad for China if this conjecture were true and this test incorrectly demonstrated that it was false. I am not a scientist and don't want to get into any classified areas that could harm you. However, there are strong financial interests in China with connections around the globe that do not want to see China embarrassed. Maybe we can help each other, and in the process help China in more than one way."

Lu shook his head. "I see no way you could help me. You have no idea how complicated my situation is. There is no way I could help you. I know nothing about money matters."

Peng immediately said, "And, you have no idea how much influence extreme amounts of money can have. I can think of a way I can help you, if you can help me. I need to get an unbiased opinion of what that lab across the street can do, and why other labs around the world cannot do it. That is the only way I can establish a price for it. And, don't you see, you could help me do that."

# — 22 —

**6:30 a.m., Tuesday, New Brighton, Minnesota**

Muan Yingqu was in the driver's seat, and Seng Kejian occupied the passenger seat of the rental car. Each was looking out the windshield at the dark, cold, December morning trying to pretend the other wasn't there. It has snowed a couple of inches over night, and a few lazy, late in getting out of bed, snowflakes continued to land on the glass. It was not enough snow to warrant plowing the streets, but the crews were out covering the freeways and streets with a lavish coating of salt. That was the only way the modern American economic machine continued to function in winter. No salt, streets too slippery for travel. No travel, nobody at work. No work, no revenue to companies, no income to employees. No taxes. No taxes, no salting crews. Every last resident in a fit of rage. Ergo, lotsa salt.

Yingqu sincerely hoped Breckon would do something, anything, to get this assignment moving. He thought he would go ballistic if he had to continue keeping company with the sour excuse of a man in the next seat. They were parked in the lot of the apartment complex next to Breckon's. When they arrived an hour before they had downloaded the apartment sounds of the previous evening and night. The bug on the window and the remote recorder in the spruce tree had dutifully done their jobs. Since it only recorded when there was sound, there was less than an hour of material, most of which was him humming to himself and the clatter of dishes and pans. The guy seemed to lead a boring life, though Yingqu knew that their lack of results was due to his having tried to kill him on Saturday.

Kejian had wanted to accost the man and force him to tell what he knew. Yingqu had a hard time convincing him they were not in China, and they were not dealing with Chinese who were intimidated by the

MSS. Beyond that, if neither hubot had contacted Breckon, they could beat him all day, get nothing, and in the end lose their most likely point of intercepting their targets.

They were listening to the apartment in real time, now. Breckon was up and making breakfast. From time to time there were beeps and buzzes from what sounded like a microwave oven interspersed by a grunt or word as the food preparation process went well or ill. They noticed the car pull into a parking place. A man got out and went into the entry of Breckon's apartment building at a time when most people were leaving. It could have been someone stopping to give a friend a ride to work. A second later, the phone rang in Breckon's apartment.

---

The phone rang as Ed Breckon was taking a bowl of oatmeal out of the microwave. That indicated someone was at the front door. He had a sinking feeling he knew who it was. He hadn't been sleeping well since the shooting and was out of sorts. Setting the bowl on the table he walked the few steps and picked up the phone.

"Yeah."

"Is this Ed Breckon?"

"Who's this?"

"Sam Li. I'm from Virginia. I met you with ShuHo some months ago. You sent a message to him last Saturday. Please let me in."

Ed sighed in resignation as he punched the button to unlock the front door. Now, it would start in earnest, as if being shot at a couple of times hadn't started it. He wished it had been ShuHo who had come, though he knew the man's position put him above fieldwork. It had seemed so straight forward when he sent the coded letter to Zeng. Now it was a mess. Why did things always have to get into such a turmoil?

The two light knocks at the door startled Ed. He opened it and vaguely recognized the man. He motioned him in, looked into the hallway to see if there were anyone else out there, and closed it.

In a subdued voice Ed said, "ID please."

Li appeared somewhat taken aback as he produced it.

"Hmm. Sam Li. Guess it matches. Just about to start breakfast. Hope you don't mind if I eat before it gets cold. Got to be at work a little early today for a conference call."

Sitting on the only other kitchen chair Li said, "You sent a message that you had a rather special house guest. I come here on a last minute rush trip and you act like this. Excuse me. What's going on? You're not the only person in the world."

"*Had* a house guest is correct," Ed said as he finished the oatmeal. He started popping walnuts into his mouth as he put the dishes in the sink. "Things are never as they seem, are they? You must be accustomed to that. Give me a number where I can reach you and I'll be in contact. Got some stuff to figure out."

Li knew Breckon could be a difficult man, and saw he was in no mood to be pushed. He took out a business card and wrote his cell phone number on it. Breckon took it and said. "Sorry, but I must be leaving. Can't be late for the call."

―――――――――――

The atmosphere in the little car became electric, if for no other reason than something was happening. Yingqu who understood English better than Kejian was getting the full meaning of what was happening. Kejian started to say something a couple of times and was immediately hushed. By the time both men had gone their separate ways, Kejian was reduced to a black ball of fidgets. "We can't let them all get away. Follow somebody!"

"No! We know where Breckon's going. He's going to work. As for the other man, I think he's out of the Washington office of the CIA. Breckon asked for his ID so the man is an official of some kind. With the name, I can call our embassy and verify it. If we followed either one we might be spotted. Our best approach is to keep them from knowing we are here at all.

"Here's what's happening," Yingqu continued trying to keep Kejian from ordering something rash. "Breckon had a visitor. We can assume it was a hubot. He contacted the CIA. By the time the CIA got to him, his guest was gone. Don't you remember he emphasized that he *had* a house guest." Yingqu hoped he did not break out in a sweat on a cold morning like this. It would give away that something was wrong. The *had* part of it was clearly due to Yingqu's attempt on Saturday evening. He continued with his analysis. "For some reason, he's had a change of heart. He's not sure he can trust anyone. Remember, he said he had some stuff to figure out."

"Yeah, it all fits. He decided the hubot was too hot to keep around so he hid him. That means he knows where he is. We grab Breckon and make him talk. Don't worry, I can do that! He'll talk for me!"

"Don't get ahead of what we know. We only have one chance at this. If we make our move and are wrong, we fail in our mission. What you said is too simple. Breckon's smarter than that. He may have brought him to someone who brought him some place else, so he doesn't know where he is. We can't start leaving a trail of bodies around this city. Besides, you said we are not to kill Breckon because someone sees a future use for him. If we tortured him until he talked, even if we didn't kill him, what good would he be?"

Kejian sat silently for awhile. Finally, "Breckon sure was cagey with his visitor. Maybe he knows about your bug. He asked for the guy's phone number. He'll call him later and tell where the hubot is."

Yingqu was more worried that Kejian would figure out about Saturday night than finding the hubot. He had to get away from him lest he slip and say something. "I don't think he knows about the bug. That's the way Breckon is. He's notional. How about we do this. I'll drop you at the hotel so you can check with Beijing. They might have come up with more information. We're assuming Breckon is still in the game, but maybe this is all a dead end. I'll check that he went to work. Then I'll come back to the hotel and verify that Sam Li is CIA."

---

Standing by his rental car in the parking lot, Li watched Breckon drive away. A few minutes later as Li got on to I-35W going south, he finished a call to ShuHo Zeng, leaving him a message about what had happened. He drove to downtown Minneapolis and entered the building that housed the FBI, and assorted agencies. There he'd meet with Mel Winger and Burl Carlson. They were CIA employees attached to the local FBI as part of the Joint Terrorism Taskforce. After going through security and getting to the right suite of offices, he saw the names on the door. To his surprise, both men were already at work.

Burl's name fit. He was a large burly man with a thick neck and big hands. His face was unspectacular with large brown eyes the main attracting feature. Maybe it was his relaxed, casual expression and movements that made him rather unnoticeable in spite of his size.

Mel Winger was another matter. He was small and slim with quick, almost startling movements. His dark gray eyes darted about and only maintained eye contact for brief seconds. His nose was too long, ears a tad oversized, and lips too thin.

After introductions, Sam began. "There is a man in this town I believe both of you are familiar with. His name is Edmund Breckon."

Winger let out a sharp breath. "Not again. I thought, or rather hoped, I guess, we were through with him. That guy is a real disaster. And, since you're here in person, it must be sorta serious."

Carlson was more circumspect. "He almost killed me the first time I met him, and saved my life the second time, so what's cookin' now?"

"It's serious," Li said. "He mailed an urgent coded message to Zeng last Saturday, and it arrived yesterday, Monday. I rushed here on a late night flight hours after the message was received. I met him before he went to work this morning, and got a complete brush-off. He's scared. I'm aware of the fact that you two have a history with the man, but don't let it get in the way. What I'm about to tell you is so classified, we don't know what to call it. Understood?"

They both nodded and Li briefed them on what he knew. "We've got to get him to open up, otherwise we're running blind. Got any ideas?"

Carlson nodded. "He knows where the guy is, that's for sure. However, as you guessed, something happened from the time he sent the message and today. I suggest this. You and I go to visit him at work, and Mel, you check around the apartment. Don't get upset. I'd suggest the opposite for us, but you know he hates your guts."

Mel pursed his lips, but nodded in agreement.

---

The white cube truck pulled up to the Second Street entrance and the tired driver beeped the horn twice. A minute later the door opened and Harvey drove in. He had started out in the early hours of the morning hoping to stay ahead of the snow, but it had overtaken him. After hours of nursing the truck along the snow packed interstate, he was beat.

"Hi Jefferson," he said as he alighted from the truck. "See ya only got a couple inches here. Boy, coming through the Red River Valley I really got socked. Kept on truckin', though. Gradually pulled out of most of it. Roads were slippery most of the way. Almost lost it once. Not a good idea with a load like this."

"Glad ya made it. According To Jorg, we need the stuff ya brought. Boss told me to tell you to find him as soon as ya got in. He's jivin' an' swearin' about the chink ya brought us. Keep yo head down."

Harvey dreaded the wrath of the boss as much as any bad thing he could think of. It seemed there was always some infraction he was being clobbered with, and this was not a small problem. Luckily, he had plenty of time to figure on it. He found the boss with the Chinese guy discussing scrubbers on the floor above the cook room.

"Ya lookin' for me, boss?" Harvey said as he walked over to where they stood.

"Yeah, Harv. Gotta talk ta ya." Then to Peng, "Keep figuring the duct runs like we've been doing. Plan to connect to the exhaust duct we're using now to go through the roof."

Then he directed his attention to Harvey. "Now you. Come with me."

When they were seated in the little office off the warehouse bay where the truck was gradually shedding its layer of ice and snow, the boss looked at Harvey with a long cold stare. "Alright. Let's have it. Why'd you haul that chink dude in here? And no bullshit."

Using his contrite demeanor, which he always did in these situations, Harvey began. "I was leaving the warehouse in Winnipeg. Had to stop at the street for a car to pass and he hops into the passenger side. One of the guys from the loading dock must have opened the door and forgot ta lock it. He pretends to have this gun under his coat, but after awhile I gets to thinking it's just a bluff. While I'm in traffic he pops the glove box and finds my gun. Then he's got me. Rode like that the whole way. When we stop for a piss he takes the keys and stays behind me. Not chance to ditch him. Tried to grab the gun once when he was distracted. He's quick and strong. Thought he'd kill me. He's still got the gun in case you didn't know." Here Harvey stopped, hoping this would be enough.

"Okay. Lotsa screw ups. Did he talk? What's he want?"

"He's running, all the way from China, can ya believe? Seems he was in our business over there and they needed a scapegoat. He found out and went into hiding. Those hiding him snitched, an' he got away and kept goin'. Even said that he grabbed the first truck he saw and couldn't believe we were doin' the same thing he was runnin' from. Said it was like he couldn't shake it off."

The cold eyes were still on Harvey as they sat in silence. Then, "Yeah. Pretty fantastic story. Might be some truth in it, though. Seems to know his way around a meth lab. And, I been doin' some checking, just quiet around the edges so's not to draw attention. He's here to get inside so the chinks can take over. But, first he wants to get the operation cleaned up. I figure he wants us to keep running it for now so if the emissions get us caught, we'll be the ones to go down. After it's all up to snuff, they'll take over."

More silence. Harvey got the impression the boss was talking to him as if he were mistaking him for the reflection he saw in the bathroom mirror, letting the words roll out to help himself think. "Can't bring in any heavy mob heat 'cause we ain't exactly playing by the rules all the time. Got to find out where he goes, who he meets." Then looking at Harvey as if he hadn't been talking to him, he said. "Don't need another run for a couple of days, and could delay that if we had to. I want you to stay with him as much as you can. Ya can't just hang on him, ya know. When he leaves, try to follow him the best ya can. See where he goes. Find something for me and I'll tend to overlook the mess ya made. Okay?"

Harvey couldn't believe how easily he could get out of this. "Absolutely, boss. I'll get somethin' for ya. I'll show ya."

# — 23 —

**8:20 a.m., Control Systems, Ltd.**

The phone on Breckon's desk made its funny little sound. Why couldn't phones just ring like the used to. "This is Ed."

It was the receptionist. "Ed. Two guys are here from Reliance Electric, you know, Rockwell. They say they don't have an appointment, but it's important they speak with you about an order."

Ed hated it when peddlers came in unannounced. If there was a problem, why didn't they handle it by email? "Yeah, yeah. They'll only get two minutes though."

As Breckon entered the lobby, he immediately recognized both men. "Oh, you!"

Carson spoke, "Is there some place we can talk?"

Breckon led the way to one of the vendors' conference rooms. When the door was closed and they were seated Breckon asked, "Is Carson cleared for this?"

Li answered in a way that made it clear he was not speaking in jest. "He is," he said looking at Burl. "If he leaks he'll be found floating in the river within twenty-four hours."

Carson's eyes got wide.

"What's the problem? You contacted us?" Li asked turning to Breckon.

"I'm sick to death of being shot at, that's the problem! This guy and I went to the shopping mall Saturday evening to get out of the house and watch the Christmas shoppers. How he missed both times is a miracle. At the time, we both thought he was after Chen. Then, I got to thinking about it. I glimpsed the shooter the second time. Now I'm thinking he was after me. Why? Got any ideas?"

Li nodded as a look of understanding came over his face. "We're pretty sure who the shooter was. I'll tell you if you agree to talk to us. Agreed?"

"Okay. You first."

"I got a routine notice that Muan Yingqu from the Chinese embassy in Washington came to Minneapolis and rented a car last Saturday morning. He was working for the MSS in China when you, shall we say, ran into him. Now he's attached to the embassy in D.C. Remember who he is?"

"Not likely I'd forget. So, he knew Hua Chen was coming to see me. That figures. There's more to it than that, though, isn't there? Why are you personally here? Why didn't you simply have Burl and Mel come out to talk to me?"

"You mentioned in you message you had the hubot. That's the magic word. The whole world is looking for him. In addition, he's extremely dangerous. Killed a half dozen people, maybe more, getting to you. By the way, did he say how he got from Winnipeg to O'Hare in Chicago?"

"Stop right there. Something's mixed up. This guy wouldn't hurt a fly. Besides, he said he came on a direct flight from Beijing to O'Hare."

They were all starting to think the same thing, but Burl said it first. "Two."

Sam pulled out his cell phone and as he did it started to "ring."

"Yeah." He listened for thirty seconds and then said, "Good work. Go back to your office and call my office. See what they found from the data base." He hung up.

Li looked a little bewildered as he addressed Breckon. "Ed, you apartment is bugged. It's stuck on the outside of your living room window so it will be behind the drape even when it's open. Mel Winger went over to check out the area." He held up his hands, palms toward Ed. "Don't worry. He didn't go in. The bug! Is that why you were so short with me this morning? Why didn't you say something now?"

Ed could feel himself getting angry. "I didn't know about the damned bug! Okay?" Once again, he felt like a pawn being sucked deeper and deeper into a sinister plot. He cast his eyes down and putting his hands over his face lethargically said, "Why me God? Why me?"

"Before we can get any place you have to tell us about the hubot. Wait. First, I've got to make a short call." Li punched a speed dial on his cell phone. Someone answered immediately. "ShuHo's not there, huh? As soon as you can find him, tell him we're almost certain there are two. He'll know who to call. Yeah, thanks. Bye."

"Okay, Ed. The NSA is really interested in the hubot thing. We had Greg Daley over and the three of us, ShuHo, Greg, and me, decided to see what was happening here in Minneapolis before everybody went nuts. We can't sit on this for long, so tell us about the hubot, and where he is."

"Where he is will wait until I decide. That's my insurance. Plus, he's a nice guy. I don't want him killed any more than I want me killed. I'm a nice guy, too. Here goes. You may wish you weren't part of this Burl."

Breckon proceeded to tell all he knew about Hua. He even told about the strange secret he told him, and about the Chinese project Bart was working on for the St. Anthony Falls Lab. The enormity of the situation was settling into both of the CIA agents as Breckon talked. When Breckon was done, they agreed with Ed to keep Chen stashed away.

When Breckon was back in his cubical the thought came to him. If his apartment had been bugged when Li visited this morning, whoever else was looking for Chen now knew that a man named Sam Li had visited him at a strange hour. Ed had to assume that if Li knew who Yingqu was, then Yingqu would know that Sam was with the CIA. This would mean that Yingqu now knows, or strongly suspects, that Ed had their hubot and hid him, and that the CIA was also trying to find the hubot.

He was worried on two accounts. First, the Chinese would have no qualms about kidnapping him and beating out of him where he had put Hua. The other bothersome thing was how easily the CIA guys let him get away without telling them where their man was.

Fifteen minutes later Breckon had another call from the receptionist. An Express Mail envelope had just arrived for him. He knew if he didn't get it immediately, he'd forget about it, and then she'd call again later with a sharp edge to her voice.

Back in his cubicle, he wondered about it. It was fun to get express packages until they were opened. Most commonly, packages coming to the front desk were documentation he had requested which was anything but exciting. However, that sort of thing was not sent at overnight rates. More likely, it was a failed part from a customer that required a fast analysis, and response. He found it was a little strange that there was no return address on it, though. In fact, the address was odd. It had his name, followed by his apartment number, and then the complete correct address of the plant. Strangely, his company's name was not given. He flipped the glossy cardboard envelope over in his hands and finally decided he might as well get it over with. Pulling the tab on the opening

strip, he emptied the contents. A folded note and a small brown envelope
fell on his desk. The note read: "Please deliver the enclosed item to Hua
Chen. He needs it urgently." That was it.

The brown envelope was not sealed so Breckon slid the contents out
into his hand. The octagonal pendant, twice the size of a silver dollar,
appeared to be made of a tough engineered plastic an eighth inch thick
with gold plated tabs on each flat edge. A small hoop at one of the corners held the bead chain. There were two Chinese characters on the face
of one side. A small readout gave the incorrect time for Minneapolis.

Breckon looked around and it seemed none of his colleagues were
taking any interest in him. He went to the copy machine, laid the octagon
on the glass, closed the cover, and made a copy. The page was mostly
black, but the shape was clear as well as the characters. He slipped the
pendant back into the small envelope and put it into his shirt pocket.
Back at his desk he pulled some electrical drawings over and pretended
to be studying them. What should he do? He wanted to deliver it personally to learn what it was about. However, if he were being watched, he'd
lead someone to Hua.

After a moment, the thought occurred to him that he wasn't at all sure
if he cared if someone found Chen. This was starting to wear on him.
Would these episodes of horror ever stop? He was almost ready to sell all
he owned, not that much, and become a monk. This was now the fourth
day since the guy showed up at his apartment. He was worn out. Sleeping was hard as he tried to figure out what was happening, to say nothing
about trying to stay alive. When does a person say enough is enough?

Oh piss on it. I'll send the damned thing to him and call it good.
Breckon grabbed a small box from under his work surface, poked the
small brown envelope among the packing worms, and taped it shut. From
a phone book, he found the address for St. Isador's. He wrote a hand address label to Father Adrian Aldrich, not using his title nor the church's
name, and struck it on the box. It looked like any other package going to
a customer. After that he filled out a form on his computer and emailed it
to the shipping department as was the procedure. He'd have it sent by a
courier, Quick Silver, Road Runner, or something similar, and charge it
to one of his projects. Since he was sure he was saving the world again,
his company should not complain about fifty bucks. He walked the box
back to the department where they shipped the spare parts orders and told
them it was urgent. He was promised it would be delivered in less than
two hours.

---

Aldon Hartner pulled into the dead end street as directed by the Magellan GPS system in his rental car. That was the only way to travel in a strange city. After picking up his rental car, he simply put the address where Jason Finley had sent the pendant into the little device and the voice told him every turn to make. But . . . this didn't look right. These were all businesses, and the address contained an apartment number. He made the final right turn and was informed by his electronic guide that he was at his destination. The sign on the building proclaimed Control Engineering, Ltd. The building number was right. He must have put in the wrong street, maybe north instead of south. Going back to the last turn, he pulled over and checked the street. It was right. "That stinking kid gave me the wrong address!" he said half aloud.

Opening his briefcase on the seat beside him, he found the number of the Finleys. After punching it into his cell phone, he let it ring until the recorder picked up. Glancing at his wristwatch, he hung up. Having been so sure of himself, he had made reservations for Jason and his mother to come to Minneapolis. They were on their way. He had her cell phone number and called that. No answer. He called the local information number and got the number for Control Engineering. After giving the number the automated voice said, "For ninety cents, I will connect you to that number. Press two if you accept." He pressed two.

"Control Engineering. How may I direct your call?"

"Ed Breckon, please."

"Just a moment."

On the first ring he heard, "Ed."

All Breckon heard was, "Click."

---

"What was that all about," Breckon mumbled as he slammed the phone receiver down. Something was funny here. He grabbed the Express Mail envelope, stuffed the note in it, and got up to go to the men's room. On the way he stopped in the print room and threw the envelope into the gaping maw of the super-mondo shredder. It chompped it up and didn't even burp.

Going back to his cubicle, he heard the PA system. "Ed Breckon. Please come to the reception desk." As he walked into the spacious entry, he saw Trudy from accounting who was sitting in for the receptionist who was on coffee break. She pointed to a man in a brown coat.

"This gentleman from the INS is here to see you."

Hartner glared at Trudy, and walked toward Breckon. Without offering his hand he said, "Is there some place we can talk in private?"

Ed nodded and said, "I suppose. Let's see if one of the vendor conference rooms is available. We'll have to leave if someone who has reserved it arrives."

"This won't take long."

They entered the same room where he had met with the CIA less than an hour before. "Got a business card, and some sort of ID?" Ed asked.

Hartner snapped a card on the table and flashed a badge. Breckon didn't make an issue of the fact that it could have been from a toy detective set. The guy was obviously not in a good mood. Ed sat waiting.

"You are Ed Breckon?"

"Yeah. And you're Aldon Hartner of the Immigration and Naturalization Service," Ed said looking at the business card.

"Yes. I'll make this quick as I am quite busy. Did you get an Express Mail envelope this morning?"

Ed was reeling. Now what? "The morning mail hasn't been distributed yet. Should I be getting one?"

"Yes, I believe so."

"Should I call you if one shows up? I have your card. Is there anything else?" Ed said getting up. "You're busy, and so am I."

Ed walked to the door and held it open.

Hartner sat thinking for a moment. Then he got up. The muscle on the side of his chin twitched as if he were clenching his teeth. "Be sure you do call. You could be an accessory to a federal crime." He walked past Breckon and headed for the door.

Trudy said, "Sir, you have to sign out." Hartner ignored the request as he opened the door and left.

Trudy looked at Ed. "What was that all about?"

"Can't say I know," Ed replied in a flat voice.

Aldon Hartner was rushed because he had to get to the airport and meet the plane the Finleys would be on. Somebody wasn't telling the truth.

---

As Jason and his mother settled in their seats, he said. "What kind of plane is this? Everything looks worn out." He pulled the card out to the pocket of the seat in front of them. "Hmm . . . a DC-9. Must be old. Bet it was made before I was born."

Jason's mother let out a sigh. "Jason, this plane was built before *I* was born. This is one of the old Northwest Airlines planes. Northwest was based in Minneapolis and probably didn't know there were any newer planes on the market."

Her cell phone played its little tune to announce a call. She opened it just as the attendant announced that all electronic devices had to be turned off lest they interfere with navigational equipment. She saw the number of the caller and recognized it as Hartner. Too late now. It would have to wait.

Snow was falling in earnest as the plane pulled on to the runway and the pilot applied full power. On the taxiway, he had informed them over the speaker system that it was good old-fashioned snow with no rain mixed in. That meant there would be no delay for the plane to be deiced.

The flight to Minneapolis took a little more than an hour, and they arrived at their gate only a few minutes late. As they exited the Jetway, Jason's mother looked for Hartner. "Where is he?" she said in an agitated voice.

"Mom, I think you need a ticket to get past security. He'll probably be waiting for us as we exit the controlled area, or he'll page us."

"Come on Jason. He's with the INS. He could've been waiting for us at the gate. I don't like this. I wish you had minded your own business on the flight from Beijing."

Jason hated it when his mother got this way. He knew she had a lot of work to do preparing for the obligatory holiday entertaining when his dad got home. This wasn't his fault. A guy had to do something with fourteen hours to kill. Besides, he had come to like Hua. He hoped he wasn't in trouble.

When they got beyond the security gates and arrived at the main ticketing space there was still no Hartner. Large groups of passengers stood looking at flight arrival and departure monitors. Their departing flight left at three-thirty. They stopped at the Northwest Airlines bank of monitors and saw a lot of departing flights were blinking. The blinking ones all involved O'Hare in Chicago. Theirs was delayed with no departure time shown.

"Quick, Jason. Where's the down escalator. We've got to get to the baggage claim area."

Getting off the escalator his mother spotted the courtesy phones for the hotels near the airport. She grabbed the one for the Marriott, one of the few not in use at the moment. In a few minutes, they had a room and none too soon. They were filling up fast as the weather worsened to the east. As they waited for the courtesy bus to take them to the hotel, Mrs. Finley called Hartner. He answered, apologizing for being caught in traffic. He was told to meet them at the hotel.

On the bus, she pressed the speed dial for Northwest Airlines reservations. After pressing a few numbers and then their flight number she was informed the flight was canceled. This happened routinely enough in good weather, that's why she took the chance of getting a hotel room while she could.

---

Quan Peng was noticeably annoyed when the boss told him that Harvey would stay with him and be his helper. If he needed anything, he was to ask Harvey. The boss made it clear that getting the scrubbers installed was a high priority. It came as no surprise to Harvey that some time later Peng told him to get some sheet metal screws and duct tape to join the pieces of duct for the scrubbers. He was sent off to find a hardware store and acquire these supplies. Harvey knew these would not be needed for some days so understood it was a ploy to get him out of the way. He took the cube truck and left the building as if going on his errand. However, he circled the block to the east and coming back in sight of the lab saw Peng walking down the hill toward the river. He parked the truck and followed on foot on the other side of the street staying a block behind.

---

Seng Kejian had spent the past three hours watching the entrance to the St. Anthony Falls Lab. Cars came in now and then, and others left. Some people were on foot. It seemed that most of them were students. Finally, he knew he had to get back to he hotel and contact Beijing before it got too late. As he drove away he noticed a taxi turn into the drive down to the lab, but thought nothing more of it.

---

With Harvey out of the way, Peng knew he had his appointment to keep. He grabbed his coat and gloves. As he stepped out of the building, he pulled the sheepskin collar up over his ears and started down the hill toward the river. He glimpsed a taxi driving into the St. Anthony Falls Laboratory parking lot. He needed a taxi, and if this was a drop off, he could hale it as it left and be gone before anyone saw him. As he crossed Main Street, the taxi was still stopped by some parked cars. There seemed to be a disagreement between the driver and the rider. Perhaps some misunderstanding about the fare, thought Peng. He used the delay to walk down the drive toward the lab buildings. The faint humming of the Excel Energy substation on his right made him turn his head. It occurred to him this was the ideal place for high energy experiments. He was nearly at the taxi when the driver got in and slammed the door. Peng motioned with his hand that he wanted a ride. Suspecting a payment problem with the previous rider he opened the rear door and immediately handed two twenty-dollar bills over the seat to the driver and said they'd settle up at the airport. The driver smiled and they drove away.

———————————

Harvey hadn't seen the taxi drive into the parking lot, but did see Peng walking down the drive toward the lab. When he got to Main Street, he saw Peng getting into the cab. He turned as it approached so as not to be recognized. The vehicle took a right and headed south on Main Street. He knew the truck was too far away for any chance of pursuit. He wondered what it was about this lab that Peng would choose to meet a cab here. He must know this place, maybe even called a taxi to be picked up here. It had been a standing rule not to become known in the immediate vicinity of the meth lab, so Harvey was unaware of the facilities and infrastructure in the area. Out of curiosity, he continued down to the parking area. Walking between two parked cars, he looked over a pile of snow and a stone wall. He saw black water flowing through a forty-foot wide channel and disappearing into a red brick building. The chain-link fence on top on the wall made it certain no one would fall into the swirling, angry looking water. He shivered at the thought of toppling into the torrent and being sucked into the maw to a frigid suffocating death.

He slowly ambled away in the direction he had come. His attention was drawn to the sound of chattering on his left. Glancing in that direction, he saw Chinese men and a woman get into a van and drive off as if headed out for lunch. He unconsciously nodded his head. Of course. This is where Chinese were working. These were Peng's contacts. He already had information for the boss.

# — 24 —

Quan Peng arrived at the airport a little before eleven hoping Shan Jin had not yet arrived. Having traveled from China to Winnipeg he had been in several airports so knew where to start. Immediately scanning monitors, he found those displaying arrivals. There seemed to be no flights coming directly from Beijing to Minneapolis. Northwest Airlines had the most counters in the ticketing concourse but there were long lines by each of them. He recognized United Airlines as another major U.S. carrier. It had only a few counters. He spotted an attendant with no one waiting, so he hurried over and inquired about his man. He wasn't even sure of the spelling of the name or if he would use that name while traveling. They had nothing. A United flight would have come directly from Beijing to Chicago, with a connecting flight to Minneapolis.

It seemed Northwest was his best bet. There was one counter for first class check in with one party by it. He went to it. When his turn came he looked the woman in the eyes and said, "I am here to get with someone coming from Beijing today. Do not have flight number. You find, please, if he already arrive? It is important that I am here for him." The last sentence added nothing to the request, but he knew that sometimes a note of urgency and helplessness got a better response from people, especially women.

"I can tell you that if he came by the most direct route, he has not arrived. That flight goes to Tokyo, and connects with a flight to Minneapolis. It arrives at four-fifty this afternoon."

"Good. Good. Then I haven't missed him. Can you tell me if he is on that flight? Name is Shan Jin."

The woman tapped on the keyboard a few times and nodded. Shan Jin is on the flight. Presently it is on schedule. Could be a little early."

"Thank you. Thank you." Peng said vigorously nodding his head. All he had to do was identify his quarry as he got off the plane. It didn't take long to discover that he wouldn't be doing that. With no ticket, he was not allowed thought security to get to the arrival gate. At the information kiosk he learned he could wait for him in the baggage claim area. He expected that it might be hard to pick out Jin since there'd be a lot of Chinese men on that flight. With time to spare, he went to the baggage claim and noticed some people holding signs with a name on it. Clearly, it was common for people to meet passengers they had never met.

---

After the guy from the INS left, Ed returned to his cubicle and sat looking at the business card. He had given up all hope of concentrating on his work. What a morning it had been. First, the meeting in his apartment with Li. Then the CIA dudes coming here. Then the pendant, followed immediately by the visit from Hartner. Somehow, the INS had traced Hua Chen to him through the pendant. What was that thing all about? He was wondering if it would be safe for him to make a visit to the rectory at St. Isador's. With all the interest, he had to assume he was being watched. When his phone rang again, he knew it had nothing to do with his job.

"Hello. This is Ed."

"Ed. This is Sam Li. We'd like you to come in to the FBI offices in downtown Minneapolis for a secure telephone call. I'll send someone out to get you if that'll help."

Ed thought for a minute. It was already nearly eleven o'clock. Maybe he could use this.

"Ed, are you still there?"

"Yeah. Excuse me, but I do have a job and I'm trying to figure out how to fit this in. And, no. It will not help if you call my boss. Stay out of my real life, okay?"

"Yes," Li answered in his heavy Asian accent.

"How about I leave at eleven-thirty in my car and you have some sandwiches ready. We'll make the call at about noon. Tell me where I can park without too much hassle and not be towed away. Think you can do that?"

"Sure. Here's Mel. He'll give you directions."

### Hotel, Roseville, Minnesota

Yingqu got back to his hotel room and immediately connected his computer to the Internet in an attempt to find out about Sam Li. Again, the three light knocks on his door. He jumped up and was not surprised it was Kejian. The door wasn't even closed when he started to talk.

"Did you learn anything?"

"Nothing other than Breckon went to work as usual." Looking at his computer screen he said, "I've got a reply from an email I sent a few minutes ago." Tapping a few keys he said, "Sam Li is with the CIA, Far East division."

Kejian nodded. "I contacted Beijing and got very little. I am sure there is a lot about this mission I have not been told. Yesterday you suggested they might be doing some testing at that Falls Lab prior to building a new dam or something. I don't think so. The men we seek are associated with that test, and it has nothing to do with erosion or the like. When I met with the team at that lab they asked if I had brought a certain device with me that is needed for the experiment. When I told them I had no knowledge of it, they were perplexed since they were in need of it. One of the technicians thinking I must be the courier and had misunderstood showed me a picture of the device. He was reprimanded there on the spot for having done that. In Beijing, I interviewed one of our men. He was wearing a device on a chain around his neck. It matched the picture of the device they need."

Yingqu started slowly. "Are you certain our men escaped from China? It sounds to me like they were brought here to help with the experiment and escaped in this city. We are supposed to find them. Then what? We'll probably be told to bring them to that lab with, of course, that device."

"No. The man we seek that I did not interview was the first to escape and left a trail of bodies as he traveled. There were many eye witnesses that confirmed he was the one."

Kejian sat with his elbow on the table and his hand supporting his chin as he thought. It occurred to Yingqu that the man's demeanor was at least partly due to over work. Although he himself put in many hours at the embassy, he had forgotten the intense pressure in China. In his home country there was always a thousand people lined up to take a man's job if he failed in any way, especially a good paying government job.

"There was something said when I interviewed that man. It was about an energy field, something to do with him personally."

Yingqu called up his search engine again and typed personal energy field. "Would it be human energy field?"

"Yes. That's it."

"There are many entries about that." After a pause Yingqu turned the computer so the other man could read the article on the screen.

Kejian slowly nodded his head. "Either or both of these men might have come to see Breckon, maybe for food and a place to get out of the cold. However, that's not why they came here. They came to be part of that test as if they were drawn to it, perhaps without them even knowing it. The man I interviewed did act sort of like a zombie. The first one to escape sure was intent on getting out of China. But, that's not really the point. He wasn't escaping China as much as he was coming here. I think they were both coming here. If we watch that lab, either or both of them will show up."

"If they'll eventually show up at the lab, why did they send us?"

"I'm not certain they know they'll show, at least not for sure. This thing with the hubots is new. They were messing with their heads. Maybe they're working on a way to program someone's mind using electronics. If we watch the lab and see one coming we can grab him, take him away, and call our superiors and say we were successful in our hunt. They will probably say to deliver him to the lab. So what? The important thing is for us to be successful."

"What about Breckon? He knows where one of them is."

Kejian didn't answer immediately as he pondered the situation. Yingqu was somewhat amused to see his nemesis, the snap-quick autocrat, in a quandary. "Yes, Breckon. You stay with him, and I'll watch the lab. If either of us spots one of the hubots, he'll immediately call the other. Take what action is necessary to apprehend the target. We'll assume a hubot can perform his function it he's wounded a little. I'll give you exact directions to the lab at the falls."

**12:05 p.m., Minneapolis FBI offices**

Burl Carson was watching Ed Breckon's movements with amusement. Breckon's eyes darted from here to there, with occasional quick glances behind him. He even hesitated to sit down in the conference room where they'd set up the secure call to Greg Daley at the NSA. An urn of coffee sat on the table, as well as a large plate of sandwiches, and a fruit plate. Burl filled a Styrofoam cup with coffee and passed it to Breckon as he eased a tray of sugar and creamers in his direction. With the cup setting on the table Ed put both hands around it, and stared at it.

"Go ahead, Ed. It's not poisoned," Burl said.

Without cracking a smile he replied, "I'm at a point where I'm not sure I'd care if it was." He took a sip of coffee. "Just getting into this building took it out of me. I'm ready for a nap." Looking around he continued, "You're all the same aren't you. You all got finger printed, took lie detector tests, had deep background checks made on you, and who knows what else. And, you all passed. Anybody that clean has to be empty. Did any of you ever do anything in real life?" Before anyone could retort he continued, "Let's get on with it. Who are we calling?"

"Your friend at the NSA, Greg Daley," Winger answered. He had the connection made in less than fifteen seconds. "Greg, this is Mel. We're all here. Are you ready to go secure?"

"Let's go." With that, the line took on the characteristic faint hiss. The encoding system encoded the transmission at all times even when no one was talking. "Okay, we're on," Greg said. I have my supervisor, Al Lindstrom, here with me. Also, Markus Mueller, a staff physicist, is with us. Who's on your end?"

"I've got Sam Li, Burl Carson, Ed Breckon, and myself Mel Winger."

"Hi Ed. It's been a few months. You said you'd stay in touch, but you never write, you never call. I'm hurt." There was unmistakable whimsy in the voice.

Ed perked up a little. "I've been busy planning a trip to the mountains. I know this great place. It even has a place to land a V-22. Are we on for this summer?"

"Better stop there, Ed. Not everyone is cleared for that job. To business, though. Burl and Sam have relayed to me the comments you made when they talked to you this morning. I've done some mining of our data bases and some disturbing things are coming out."

"Just a minute," Lindstrom broke in. "Before we get into this too far I have a comment to make to you, Mr. Breckon. We really want to get your hubot in to debrief him. There are things here that may go far beyond what you think. If we had him, we could leave you out of the loop. I hate to say it, but what you're about to get into is mostly of your own making. So don't get upset if the going gets tough."

Ed was starting to bristle. "Lindstrom! The guy came to me for protection as much as anything. I know how you guys manipulate people. You look at it as your job, but people have a habit of ending up dead when your ilk gets involved. Tell me that isn't true! I'm so far out on borrowed time already, what's the difference if you waste me? Hua's a sensitive, scared man who has been used by his people just like you Feds prey on U.S. citizens. I don't want him to be treated by us as badly as his people have abused him. Understand! So, cut the crap! Have you ever had your ass out there being shot at?"

Breckon's face had gotten red, and he was up pacing behind the chairs. Sam started to get up to face him.

"Sit!"

The tone of Breckon's voice was such that Sam fell back into his chair.

"What was that all about?" It was Lindstrom again.

Mel spoke. "Lindstrom, you really got Breckon riled up. He was walking it off behind the chairs and Li got up. Li is now sitting down. Surprisingly, Li is still conscious." In a soft warning voice Mel said, "Sam, don't do that again." Then to the speaker box, "Both Burl and I know firsthand what happens when employees of the Federal Government push Breckon too far."

Lindstrom spoke again. "I am under the impression there are some personal things here that I'm not up to speed on. What I said was obviously inappropriate. Please accept my apology."

They could hear some whispered comments on the NSA end, after which Greg spoke. "Ed, we need to ask you some questions, or get some clarifications of what you told Sam and Burl. You know, there's always something lost in the retelling. Are you with us on this?"

Ed had returned to his chair and gulped down his coffee. "Yeah, I'm here. Shoot."

"With your history, we can understand the Chinese thinking you are an agent, and wanting you to be a double agent for them. But, the part about needing to get you out of Minneapolis before an earthquake destroyed it is puzzling. We've done a number of seismic analyses, and the probability of a severe earthquake happening there in the next hundred years is remote, to say nothing of one happening within a month or two. Are you sure that's right?"

"That's what he said. No, not exactly. Let me explain. I prodded him to tell me a secret because he let on as he had several secrets for the CIA. For me, he said it would be 'like telling the wind.' Those were his words. That was because I wasn't in the CIA. It was as if he thought you guys would know what it meant. However, he didn't call it an earthquake. He said the city would 'all fall down.' I said, you mean an earthquake. He said, 'No, but something like that.'"

"Are you sure he distinguished it from an earthquake?"

"Absolutely."

"Okay, the next item. You mentioned your friend, or business acquaintance, Bart, who is making heat exchangers for a project at the University of Minnesota. You consult for him, is that correct?"

"Yes."

"When you and Mr. Chen were at Bart's place of business, one thing led to another until you were having Chen translating the Chinese characters on the drawings. He even read and translated some of the other papers associated with the project. Is the true?"

"Yes, it is."

"You said one of the documents mentioned the project was being conducted at Minneapolis because it was the center of North America, and there were no earthquakes there. Is that correct?"

"Yes. It said it was good there were no earthquakes because that would make the test results easy to interpret. There's another thing I forgot to mention to Sam and Burl. One of the drawings showed the complete apparatus and this upset Hua. He said it was a machine for making more hubots. From what he said the evening before, I gather hubots are made by connecting the DNA molecules in the brain cells to the zero point force. According to the theory, this connection is the difference between a live cell and a dead one. I said the machine on the drawing he was looking at couldn't be used that way because it was so large. Then he went into one of his little trances as he accessed all the stuff packed away in his head. Finally, he said, I was probably right. It was not for hubots, but to make energy from the zero point field."

"Can we get a copy of that drawing?" It was Markus almost hyperventilating.

"Sorry, can't," Burl interjected. "We thought about talking to Bart so we called him a bit ago. He said he delivered the last of his parts earlier today. When he got back to his shop, it was on fire. The fire department was there, but not before it was a total loss, burned to the ground. Arson. Professional. He's all right, Ed."

They were all silent. Then Ed said, "They must have had someone waiting to burn him out as soon as they were satisfied the parts were good. I called Bart from work after you guys left this morning to check on how things were going. I got him on his cell phone as he was returning from the lab. He had just delivered the last of the heat exchanger parts. They are having a dispute over payment because they insist one of the first units was made wrong and it was Bart's fault. As a result, he demanded to be let in to make sure this last part fit, or he'd refuse to let them have it. He had learned before that they were on a tight schedule so knew he could push them. After a lot of wrangling, they agreed. As he related it, the place in the St. Anthony Falls Lab where they have their experiment set up has been walled off from the rest of the facility. It was awesome, like a combination of Star Gate and Space Odyssey." After a pause Ed continued. "Would it make sense to get some protection for Bart? What if they think he saw too much?"

Burl said, "We could consider it, but he's not talking. He's scared."

Daley continued "Out of the blue, you were visited by a hubot. You've been shot at, and now your associate was burned out. We're working hard to figure it out, and solve this mess. What's the chance we could talk to the hubot?"

"I doubt he'd be interested in that now. Another thing that happened was that when he arrived at my apartment he was nearly frozen to death, literally. I dragged him in and put him in my hot shower saving him from dying of hypothermia by minutes. He was grateful to say the least. We got along, even told some jokes. He had been though something terrible with the hubot thing. I got the feeling he thought there was a chance he might actually be human, again I mean literally. He talked to me because he trusted me. I doubt he trusts anyone now."

Mueller spoke up. "If you could communicate with Hua, can you ask him it he knows anything about a term called 'the conjecture?' This comes up in intercepted communications we get from the Chinese. It's an internal code phrase used in their theoretical physics community. There's a hint that it's in some way related to something that's going on in the U.S. Whatever is happening at that U of M lab is a likely project. By the way, Ed, do you have a copy of the drawing for the heat exchangers Bart made, and how many they will use? If we had the drawing, we could do some calculations on how much heat they are expecting to exchange. It might lead somewhere."

"Yeah. I have one. Guess there's no reason for you not to have it. I'll see somebody here gets it and they can pass it along." Ed paused for a long moment. The others could see he was pondering, wondering if he should tell something. So, they waited. Then he said, "You might as well know. The INS out of Chicago is also looking for Chen. It makes sense because he used a fake passport to get here. The real owner must have shown up, or they were tipped off some way. One more guy to mess things up."

Mel nodded. "We'll look into it and see if we can get him backed off. Got any information on who he is?"

Breckon handed him the card. Mel had a copy made of it and gave it back.

They closed the call and Ed got up to leave.

"Just a minute," Mel said. "We've talked this over and decided we'd like you to take a secure phone with you in case we need to make another call on short notice. The guy getting his building burned down has gotten more people interested in this. I have a briefing to give in an hour. I may have to call you."

"What if I don't want it."

"Don't start that." He slipped a form out of a folder on the desk. "Here's the receipt form. Sign it."

Breckon looked at the form then looked up and said, "How about a deal? I'll take the phone if you put speed dial numbers in it for you and Daley. Something might come up. The way things are going everybody wants me, and I don't have a cell phone."

There were scrunched up faces all around. Li was beginning to see why Winger and Carson didn't get along with Breckon. He was hard to get along with. However, it made too much sense to simply brush it off. He agreed. "Okay. Mel, put the numbers in and then notify Daley that Breckon has his number on a secure phone." Then to Breckon, "You be sure you use that thing judiciously. No playing games with us. Got it?"

"I promise. So, if it sounds like I'm playing games, know that I'm not. Got it? The damnedest things seem to happen to me."

Li nodded.

Breckon signed the form, and was given a phone about three times the size of a normal cell phone. It was still small enough to put in his coat pocket, which he did. He took a sandwich and a can of soda with him as he left.

# — 25 —

Several minutes later Breckon was wondering what he should do as he ate his lunch seated in his car in the parking ramp. Finishing the last of the ham salad between two doughy pieces of bread, he started the engine. Putting on his seat belt, he felt the secure phone in his pocket. He pulled it out and looked at it. Then it hit him. Yes, it was a phone, but it was also a tracking device. From what he had learned from his last meetings with the CIA he was sure it had a GPS transponder in it. That's why they wanted him to have it, not for a call from some meeting. And that's why they had such consternation on their faces when he said he wanted it set up so he could actually use it.

As he drove out of the parking garage, it was snowing lightly again. The streets were wet because of the salt laid down earlier in the morning. As he approached the tangle of freeways south of the downtown area, he was stopped at a red light before he could get on I-94 East. Immediately he took the lane to I-35W North. In Roseville, where Control Systems was located, he took Highway 36. He walked to his desk, put the phone in his file cabinet and locked it. Then he left. He had to talk to Hua.

As he drove, he tried to tell if anyone was following him. He didn't see anyone obvious, but if they could bug his apartment, they could have stuck a tracking device on his car. No matter. He turned south on Dale Street, and soon entered the part of St. Paul that was known as Frog Town. It had gotten this distinguished title because before the city built up it was a low lying swampy area. The parking spaces in front of the rectory were all taken. The west half of the parking lot across the street to the north was filled with cars since it was a school day. Children out on recess used the east half. He could hear the screeching of small girls. What was it about small girls and the need to screech?

He had taken a roll of drawings with him as he left the office. He'd walk up to the front door of the rectory with the drawings as if his firm were involved with some renovation project of the old buildings. It would be a plausible cover except there were a lot of people expecting him to show up some place like this with a plausible cover. The Chinese guy, Yingqu, would still be after the hubot, as was the INS guy. That was to say nothing of the CIA. He left his car in one of the empty spaces and walked across the street with his drawings. The slate gray sky maintained its steady yield of lazy snowflakes.

The door was answered by a priest he had never met. Breckon said, "I'm here to see Fr. Aldrich. May I come in?" Without asking for a reply he stepped in and closed the door.

Somewhat taken aback the middle-aged priest said, "Excuse me sir. Is he expecting you?"

Ed could see the man's discomfort. "No. I must say he is not. However, he knows me and we have a common acquaintance. You have a houseguest, who I hope has not been any trouble for you. I brought him to you. Actually it is that man that I must see."

"Oh," the man said in recognition. "The gentleman with the unique problem. We have enjoyed our conversations with him around the dinner table. You must be, let me see, Mr. Breckon?"

"Yes. Is Hua here? May I see him?"

"I suppose you can. And this," he said pointing to the roll of drawings, "is this for him?"

"Oh, no. I work for Control Engineering, Ltd. We do all types of electrical and control system projects. These are my cover. I would appreciate it if anyone calls asking if my company is doing work for you to tell them that you have contacted us to look at renovating some of the old wiring in one of your buildings. It's possible I've been followed. There are several people who would like to talk to your guest. Some of them might be rather unfriendly."

"I'm Fr. Kemper, the pastor here. I thought the CIA would be here to get him by now. I don't want to seem rude, but this is getting beyond the scope of what we do. When will he be leaving?"

Breckon could see this could get antagonistic. "Tomorrow morning at the latest. Maybe yet today. It is important that I talk to him. Is that possible?"

Fr. Kemper nodded and turned. They walked up to the third floor. He stopped and knocked twice on a door. Without waiting for a reply he opened it and entered. It was a small room with a bed, writing table, and similar furnishings. Hua looked up and smiled as he saw Ed.

"Hi, Ed. You come to get me?"

Breckon smiled and turned to Fr. Kemper. "Shall I stop to see you before I leave?"

"Yes. Please." The tone was not hostile, but firm.

When the door was shut, Ed sat on the only other chair by the table ninety degrees from Chen. "I'm not here to get you just yet, but soon. A Chinese man from the embassy in Washington, D.C., is in town. He was probably the one who shot at us. Do you know Muan Yingqu?"

Chen nodded. "His name was in your file. You broke his knee at the Nanjing airport. He is unhappy about you."

"Yeah, I know. Who else might be here?"

"MSS agent talked to me at the Institute. Name Seng Kejian. Small man, dark eyes, mean. They might send him to find me."

"Got a few more questions. Did you get that thing I sent you this morning? What is that all about?"

"Yes, yes. It came to me okay. Next time to come on is two in afternoon. Told at Institute I need waves from thing on chain each six hours on time."

"You mean every six hours it comes on and does something to you?"

"Yes. Not so sure at first if it is true. Afraid it might be thing to tell them where I am, so put in boy's bag but he did not know. Then needed and had him send it fast." He pulled on the chain and it appeared from under his shirt. "They at Medical Institute, how you say, circumspect, yes I think that is it. They not want to say anything about it. In reading, I found it augments my energy field. Don't know why I need it, but it must be that I do."

Chen turned it over in his hand a few times and then dropped it behind his shirt again. In something of a reticent tone he said, "At times when it would have come on, I learned new thing. I feel other hubot like at Institute in Beijing. He has one, too. Maybe he has come to this city.

"Yeah. The guys at the CIA sort of expected that. By the way, they asked about something called 'the conjecture.' Ever hear about that?"

Chen nodded. "It is related to zero point energy work. Maybe cause like earthquake, maybe not. This is the secret you asked for, and I told you."

"That's it? You know nothing more about it?" Hua shook his head.

Breckon knew he had to get back to work so he stood up to leave. As he put his hand on the doorknob, he paused. He remembered what had been nagging him. He turned around.

"Hua, what happened in China that they have all this interest in zero point energy? In some fashion, they're using it to make hubots, and that experiment at the U of M seems to involve it, too. Did I understand you correctly?"

Chen gave a faint smile. "Chinese look for new ways but in old places. Look to past for ways to answer problems of today. They studied ancient writings that were found many years ago, but nobody could read. Worked hard at it. Then solved. Found surprise that very old people, long before Chinese, had better machines than today. They used what is called zero point energy. Chinese learned how from writings."

Breckon stopped to see Fr. Kemper and assured him Chen would be out of there by the end of the next day. He almost ran to his car. He had a phone call to make.

---

Muan Yingqu was delighted that his erstwhile, at least he thought of him that way, boss had come up with the conclusion that the hubots would head for that lab at the falls, and that he should keep an eye on Breckon.

Knowing for sure where the sunken-eyed piece of crap from China would be keeping vigil, he was free to pursue his nemesis. If he could take out Breckon he might even make a visit to that lab and do the same for Kejian and consummate the erstwhileness of their relationship. It was a little surprising to him to realize how he had already come to think in terms of them, in China, and us, here in the U.S. What wasn't to like about this country?

Shortly before noon, Breckon left his pace of employment. Yingqu followed him until he turned off the freeway in downtown Minneapolis. There, due to traffic, he lost him. He returned to Roseville and bought lunch at a fast food place near Control Systems Ltd. Returning to his observation point he parked on the street and settled down to wait. The snow piled between the street and the sidewalk conveniently hid the bulk of his car while allowing him to see the parking lot. About one o'clock Breckon returned. Yingqu was deciding whether or not to give it up and go back to the hotel for a few hours when Breckon came out again. He followed him to inner St. Paul. Breckon parked in the west end of the lot across the street from a huge church, and took a roll of drawings to a smaller building beside the church. He had him fooled at first. Then he realized this must be where the hubot was hidden. With the children playing in the east end of the parking lot, he knew he couldn't do Breckon here.

He was parked on the street at the west end of the church parking lot, and a hundred feet back from the entrance to it. With his engine still running, he looked about at the neighborhood. It was old inner city with the houses in various states of repair. He wondered if it was a good idea to stay where he was. As he considered his options, he heard a thump on the trunk of the car. Immediately there were large black men around him. One of them knocked on the driver's window. The man standing near the front fender brushed the accumulated snow off the windshield with his gloved left hand and tapped the glass with an iron club.

Having left it in drive as he pulled to the side of the street, he pushed the accelerator. The car lurched enough to cause the men to step back, but the front wheels spun on the snow. A star appeared high up on the windshield. He slipped it into reverse and jabbed his foot on the gas. He backed, again discouragingly slowly, until he was jolted to a stop by the front bumper of the car behind. Into drive again, he floored it. This time the wheels gained purchase and he managed to speed away. Speed on the snow was a relative term. It was faster than the men could run. At the first intersection, the cross street had the stop sign so he went another block. Here he had the stop sign. He slowed, and seeing it was clear, sped through the intersection. In his side mirror, he saw no pursuit. At the next street he slid around the corner to the left and down the length of the block, and left again. Slowing at the intersection two blocks later he looked left and saw the children running across the street from the parking lot to the school. Making a left, he immediately pulled to the side of the street watching in all directions for the thugs. There was no movement save the lazily falling snow.

He pondered what had happened. It was unlikely Breckon or anyone connected with law enforcement could have predicted exactly where he would stop, and the tactics were clearly those of toughs. Those men were expecting someone, and it wasn't for a social visit. It had to be a case of bad luck that he showed up at that exact minute. Probably something to do with a drug deal gone bad. But, in exchange for a slightly damaged vehicle, he had learned the probable location of the hubot. Looking at all the imposing structures, he realized the down side of his discovery. The hubot could be stashed in any one of those buildings that collectively covered an entire city block.

Several minutes later Breckon came out of the building, sans drawings, and drove away in his car. Maybe it was a business call after all, Yingqu thought. Yingqu followed him back to Control Systems, Ltd. where Breckon parked and went in.

---

Jason Finley and his mother were settled in their hotel room when the phone ran. It was Hartner. "I'm sorry for all the inconvenience I've caused you Mrs. Finley. I see that all the flights back to Chicago have been canceled. Thankfully, you managed to get a hotel room."

"The apology is nice," she said tersely. "I have a lot of arrangements to make for the holidays. Now what happens? Have you found the man that has caused us all this bother?"

"That's the difficult part. It seems that what we in the INS thought was a relatively simple matter of a stolen passport and illegal entry, was part of a CIA operation. Now I have been warned to stay away from the case, and like you I am stuck in this city until tomorrow."

"So, that's it? I'll still be expecting you to pay for the plane tickets, the hotel, and expenses. Is that agreed?"

"Yes, of course."

"Will the CIA be wanting Jason to identify the man? Do you have a contact?"

"I don't know the answer to that. A Mel Winger talked to me. Here's his number."

When she hung up, she sat thinking. Then, turning to Jason said, "Well, son, you sure can pick 'em. You are right in the middle of a CIA operation, though I doubt it will amount to much."

"I told you mom, I didn't pick him. He just sat beside me. Did he say if they found Hua?"

"He wouldn't say. Why don't you go down and buy a book? I have a lot of calls to make, and I don't want the TV on."

---

When Breckon got back to his cubicle he unlocked his file cabinet, took out the CIA phone, and put it under some drawings. His desk phone was blinking so he listened to his messages. He was beginning to wonder if there was any point in trying to hold down a normal job. His "hobbies" seemed to demand all his time. As pressing as some of his duties were, he had to contact Daley. Maybe, after that, the CIA, NSA, and the rest of the denizens of spookdom tasked with keeping us safe, could handle it. On the other hand, nah, they'd flub it."

He had thrown his coat over the back of the chair so he slipped it on again. He grabbed the drawings and folded the phone in them. Leaving by the side door, the outdoor route to the shop used on nice days, he went to his car.

He pressed the speed dial for Daley and waited. To his surprise, it was answered. After a minute, he had Daley.

"Where are you?" Daley asked.

"In my car in the parking lot. It's the best I can do. I have some information for you. Want it?"

"Sure do. Try not to be too specific, though. We have no idea who could be listening in on your end."

"Okay. Our friend said the "blank" you asked about has to do with the experiment going on at the lab that Bart helped with. It will either cause the event our friend told me about, the secret, or won't. That's probably the purpose of what's going on. It makes sense. If it does, they wouldn't want it to happen back home. Right?"

"Yeah, I think I got all of that. This call is being recorded, as you might expect, so I can go over it and be sure I understand. I'll call you back if I need clarification."

Breckon continued, "The thing that was sent to me and I sent to our friend comes on every six hours and interacts with his personal energy field or something like that. Sorry, had not choice but to say that because it's new. He also thinks, or senses, another one like himself is in town. I think that confirms something.

"Here's a strange lead that may help you, maybe not. I've noticed that the object of the test at the lab, and that which gave our friend his, shall we say, unique condition, is the same. So, I asked our friend why all the interest in that where he comes from. He said they were looking to the past to help find answers for the present. There are some ancient writings that have been known for a long time, but have never been deciphered. With tenacity, they did it. From these, they learned that an old civilization from way before that of his homeland was more advanced than we are and used this thing. And, those writings apparently told his people how to do it."

"Anything else?"

"No. That's about it for now."

"Okay. Anybody else know about this?"

"Nope. I'll leave that up to you to tell as many or as few as you want. If certain others contact me, I'll tell at least some of it. Now, I've got a real job. See ya."

---

When the arrival of the Tokyo flight was announced on the public address system, Peng was ready. He had prepared a sign with Shan Jin's name on it. Underneath it in Chinese characters, he wrote "Falls Project." This would be sure to alert the man that this was the correct person to meet him. He was in position as the flood of passengers descended on the luggage carrousels. The people stood around and waited, but no one acknowledged him as they did others holding signs. Finally, as luggage began to appear he saw various parties leave that had gotten together during the wait. Still, he stood alone. One man, Asian, nearly stopped in front of him and then brushed past. The area was clearing out. He glanced over his shoulder as the man stopped at a car rental counter. There were two others, one of which was also Asian, waiting for a car at that counter. A few stragglers were left at the luggage carrousel, but none were Asian. Was his man the one who had paused by him? Decision time. He went with his instincts.

As he walked up behind the man who had looked so intently at his sign, he heard him say with a heavy accent, "Car for Shan Jin." He handed his reservation slip to the attendant.

"Sorry sir. We don't have a midsize as you requested. You can have either a compact, or an SUV."

Peng said over his shoulder, "Better get the SUV. It is snowing. You will need a bigger car."

The eyes covered with thick glasses snapped around to Peng. In Mandarin he said, "Who are you? You are not from the project. I was not to be met at the airport."

Peng replied. "Your office called after you were in transit to tell us who to expect. With the weather getting bad, you will have a difficult time finding your way alone. It was decided someone should meet you. Please accept my assistance."

Shan was flustered. Being tired from the long flight, in a strange country, strange city, he was not making sound decisions. Peng had been planning on this. "I will see you safely to your hotel. If you don't want any further assistance that will be your decision. In that case, I will see you at the lab in the morning. Your presence is desperately needed there.

That is one reason I was sent to help you. We wanted to be sure you would be rested."

The crowd had thinned out and Peng could see there was no one within earshot who could understand them. Shan Jin seemed to accept that, too. Finally, the fatigue won out and he nodded. He looked at the attendant and said. "I take the SUV."

When they found their vehicle, Peng drove. During the day, with time to kill, he had called the hotels in downtown Minneapolis and found where Shan Jin was registered, and what parking ramp to use. "You are staying in the center of Minneapolis at the Radisson Plaza Hotel. Is that correct?"

Shan, having given in to what would happen replied, "You seem to know everything. Go there."

When they were parked, Peng was out of clever ploys. He reverted to his old self and accosted the man in the passenger seat at which Shan Jin produced his wallet. Flipping it open, Peng found the thing he most needed, Jin's credit card, an American Express, of all things. After breaking only one hand, Jin answered all the questions Peng could think of, including the PIN, Personal Identification Number, to get cash with the credit card. Then he strangled him.

Getting out he looked about for people. There was a man walking toward the elevators. Peng busied himself as if organizing some papers until there was no one in sight. He went to the passenger side. Opening the door, he found the lever to make the seatback fall back until it was nearly horizontal. Rifling the pockets, Peng found the rest of the man's personal effects. Pushing the body into the back, he returned the seat back to the normal position. He slipped Jin's coat off. With the knees forced up against the chest, the coat easily covered him. The light was dim, so if someone took a special interest in the car it would look like the owner was covering some possessions so as not to invite thieves. It was cold enough so Jin would soon freeze. After practicing Jin's signature a few times, he went in and registered.

In his room, he discovered none of the man's clothes fit. They would be expecting someone in a business suit to arrive at the lab. He knew it was possible that someone had emailed a picture of Jin to the lab, but decided to deal with that if and when questions came up. He still had Harvey's gun if it came to that. Most pressing, though, he needed clothes.

At the front desk of the hotel, he inquired where he could buy a suit and was directed to a store called Macy's. He was given a map showing a series of glass enclosed bridges connecting all of the stores, hotels, and office buildings in the downtown area. He stopped over a street and watched in amazement as the traffic passed thirty feet beneath him. Then he moved on.

In the men's apparel department of Macys, a young woman approached him. "Hello. My name is Sherri. Can I assist you."

Peng wasn't pleased. "Find the man in charge for me. Need many clothes for meeting in morning. Find now." His voice was elevated enough to carry some distance

The woman, somewhat indignantly, replied that she was perfectly qualified to give him any assistance he needed. At that moment, a slender, partially bald, man of about fifty came over.

"I'm the department manager. What is it you need?"

"Good. Fine. Luggage lost. Need suit of clothes for important meeting in morning. Need tonight."

"That might be difficult because we close in less than a half hour."

Peng grabbed the sleeve of a suit on the rack. "Suit cost seventeen-hundred-dollars. I pay two times that much. You have tonight. Need shoes, coat, tie, shirts. All two times price. You can do?"

The man made a thin smile and said. "And, the means of payment would be?"

Peng pulled out the American Express card. "You check. It good, okay?"

The man held out his hand and said, "If you please," as he took the card. Turning he handed it to the young woman, and nodded to her. Then he said to Peng, "Sir, let me help you off with your heavy coat and we'll get started. Peng picked a dark blue suit. Along the way he looked at a mannequin and pointed to the tie, belt, and socks. The manager nodded. He understood. He needed the works.

They had the suit size established when the woman returned. "Credit line of fifty thousand. Only five thousand used."

"Fine. Sherri, tell Frank to stick around. We'll need him to make some alterations before he leaves for the day."

# — 26 —

Quan Peng was up at five-forty-five. He couldn't remember ever having slept so well. After he had settled in his room the night before he had called room service and ordered a steak dinner. They asked if he wanted a bottle of wine with it. He said yes. When asked what he wanted he realized that with all of the facts he had tucked away there was nothing about wines. He said they should surprise him with something that went with the meal he had ordered. There was some hemming and hawing around until he got the message. He said, anything up to two hundred dollars a bottle. He wasn't sure why it was selected, but it was good. As he was finishing the meal, his suit and accessories were delivered from the clothing store. Man, this was the way to live.

He now went through the packages that had arrived the evening before. In one was a small case containing an electric razor, a toothbrush, a bottle of expensive cologne, hairbrush, shoe polish and shoe brush, along with several other items. There was a note suggesting that since his luggage had been lost, he might need these items as well, and that they were provided as a token of appreciation at no charge. It was something of a shock until he realized he had left them over three thousand dollars as a gratuity.

As he started to dress, he found that the new shirts had been taken out of the packages, pressed, and hung on hangers. The suit fit perfectly and looked good. Looking at himself in the full-length mirror, for the first time in his life he felt like somebody. Too bad it wouldn't last.

*Wouldn't last!* What was he thinking? It would never start, and why should it? For some odd reason, the night before his only thoughts were of taking the umpire's place, going to that lab, and putting down a certain member of the upper class. Why do that at all? With the credit card and the PIN number he had taken from Shan Jin, he could get plenty of money. He had a good vehicle with a tank full of gas. He ought to get in the SUV and hit the road for a large city. Yes. That was exactly what he'd do. His planning was interrupted by a complaint from his stomach. About to order breakfast from room service, he changed his mind. He'd go to the dining room for breakfast. He had to let people see him in his fine suit.

---

Three light raps on the door! Muan Yingqu's back stiffened at the sound. He opened the door and the apparition from the netherworld greeted him. He was no longer the erstwhile boss of his fantasies from the day before. He was, in his demonic reality, here. No amount of imagining had been able to make the creature disappear. What was it about that man that so controlled him?

They had discussed the events of the previous day over a meal in Yingqu's room the evening before. It was odd how he never got into Seng Kejian's room. He probably had bats flying around in it or similar sinister rodents skittering about. Kejian had reported that he had seen neither hubot, though there were comings and goings of Asians at the lab, as well as someone from a building up the hill to the east of Main Street. Yingqu told of his experience at the church. It was all inconclusive.

As Kejian entered the room he began as the door clicked shut, "I have decided . . . "

Not if I cut your throat you right now, Yingqu thought as he turned to face him.

" . . . that you should stay with Breckon as least for the start of the day. Get to his apartment—you should be early enough for that—and stay with him. I'll go immediately to the lab and see who shows up there. From what I gathered on my visit to the place, they are close to starting the test they are so intent upon. If anything happens with Breckon call me on phone number one."

Yingqu agreed. What else was there other than what he was inclined to do? He had to stop thinking that way. Maybe another time. With that, they left on their respective missions.

---

Heng Lu was desperate. The umpire was due to arrive this morning and he knew the first man he'd talk to was the senior man on the project, Jian Niu. After that, he'd have no chance. The experiment would be tilted in such a way as to disprove the conjecture, something that would be easy enough to do. The previous evening he had called around and located Shan Jin's hotel. At first, he had thought to call him in his room then decided against it. It would be too easy for the man to brush Lu off at the impersonal distance of a phone call. He decided he must see him in person. The only way to do that was to meet him in the hotel lobby before he left for the St. Anthony Falls Laboratory in the morning. There was one problem with that plan, he didn't know what Shan Jin looked like.

It was convenient that Jin's hotel was downtown the same as Lu's so he had only to use the skyways to get to the right hotel. Arriving at his destination, he descended on the escalator to the ground floor where he stood a moment to orient himself. People were already up and getting ready for the day. There was a small counter that was doing brisk business selling over-priced and over-caffeinated Starbucks Coffee, brewed fresh right here. Nice. However, having no desire to bounce off the walls from a caffeine induced high, he passed it by. Wondering among the one-meter square posts with floor to ceiling mirrors set in dark stained wood, he searched for the checkout desk. There it was. A counter five meters long with only one person behind it. Such a big hotel at such a busy time. Why such a small staff? Then he saw them. Two gray out of place robots standing off to the side. Each was a Cyclops with a five centimeter square flat eye perched on its shrunken head. Above them, a sign proclaimed "Automatic Check-in and Check-out." Patrons walked up choosing the queue their cognitive powers determined would present the least delay to the start of their busy days. In turn, they bent and did homage to the selected god of efficiency as they inserted magnetic room keycards followed by credit cards.

Lu stepped to the counter and asked if Shan Jin had checked out, though he doubted he would have. He was told that he had not. Stepping away, he glanced at the robots again. He had never thought of himself as an art critic, but they were garishly out of place. The whole entry and eight-meter high foyer was tastefully done in dark reddish mahogany trim, lavishly so, and complementary lighter walls with coordinated granite and marble floors. Here stood two battleship gray appendages to the scene like insects off a manure pile that had slipped into the rural home of his youth. He felt the impulse to reach for a flyswatter.

The momentary mental digression to his home brought to mind the feeling he always had in this city. Here in the downtown area it seemed like he was not wanted. It went beyond being unwelcome. He had long understood you didn't have to like someone to do business with them. If there were some mutual gain to be had even people who held each other in contempt could maintain a civilized relationship long enough to conclude a deal. Getting his degree had been such a situation. His advisor had nothing but disdain for the rural peasants from which Lu had sprung. But, Lu's exceptionally high class standing made the advisor and the whole department look good. So, the man begrudgingly set aside his prejudice in exchange for the chit of having another outstanding student in the graduating class.

Lu wasn't sure if others shared his feeling here in the heart of the metropolis. It seemed the people doing obeisance to the machines would rather have been dealing with another person, then again, maybe not. Was it the city's way of saying, "I don't want you," or was the feeling mutual? Was it a case of dead people coming from afar to commune with the inhabitants of a city of the dead?

In Beijing, many of the residents were people from the rural areas like himself. They possessed a greater sense of the living having eked out their sustenance from the seasonal ebb and flow of life. When a society was entirely made up of second, third, and beyond generations of city born people that disappeared. Adding the crass money driven mentality of the present culture, it produced a numbness that disliked, even feared, living things.

Suddenly realizing his mind was far away, he hoped he had not missed his man. Seeing no new addition to the people milling about that could possibly match the object of his mission, he looked diagonally through the small forest of mirrored pillars and spotted the informal dining area. He made his way in that direction. Thought a square patterned trellis, he saw silver chafing dishes containing hot food. People were walking by in disciplined order religiously taking a portion of scrambled eggs, bacon, and other articles of bodily nourishment from the sterile repositories.

He surveyed the tables in the area with his eyes. There was only one Asian man he could spot. He was reading a newspaper as he sipped his coffee. From the linen protruding from the sleeves of his expensive suit, he looked like a high rolling businessman. Even his bearing, the way he sat and turned the newspaper seemed to set him apart. The accoutrements almost made Lu forget to look at his face. When he did, he was astonished that he recognized him. It had been dark in the pub, and the man was wearing an old sheep lined coat. He even had a smell about him as if he didn't bathe regularly. For his part, Lu had had more than enough beer, but he had been only centimeters from the man. That was the same man, he was sure.

Looking back in the direction of the registration desk, he saw no other Asian men. Proceeding into the coffee shop, he approached the man. "Hello, sir. Do you remember me from the pub the night before last?"

---

Peng discovered it was easy to match his bearing to the clothing. He was enjoying himself as he turned the pages of his newspaper. The presence of the man standing before him, and the sound of someone addressing him gave him a start. He made the connection immediately, but before he could say anything Lu continued.

"You said you were considering purchasing the St. Anthony Falls Lab. Do you remember our meeting?"

Having total recall didn't necessarily mean one always knew the proper response to a question. Peng remembered every word of the meeting. Should he admit he remembered? What harm could it do? "Yes, of course, I remember. You are the man who is waiting for someone from Beijing to oversee your experiments in an impartial manner. Ah, please, won't you sit down and have a cup of coffee?"

"Sir, I would like nothing better, but I am here to meet the man from Beijing, and I don't want to miss him."

"Yes, of course."

"If I may, quickly. You mentioned that you might be able to intervene in some way to make the tests fair. Have you been able to do that?"

Peng saw he had to get out of this situation before he revealed his true identity. The check had been placed on a tray on the table shortly after he had seated himself with his breakfast. This was the norm so patrons didn't have to ask for the check if they were pressed for time. Peng signed the check using Shan Jin's name, wrote his room number on it, and slid the tray to the aisle side of the table.

He saw Heng Lu glance at the signature and then quickly back at Peng with a look of surprise. Peng uneasily questioned him, "Is something wrong?"

Incredulously Lu said, "You are Shan Jin, the man I have come to meet!"

Peng was stung with the feeling of failure. Why hadn't he simply flipped a couple of twenties on the tray? Now he was caught. His mind raced through his options. The first was obvious. He could offer to drive this man over to the lab, and on the way kill him, and leave town as he was considering doing anyway. The other option was bold and dangerous. He could go to the lab and actually take Shan Jin's place. Having had a taste of what the Chinese insiders enjoyed, he was envious. If he proceeded according to the first plan, he'd be back on the street starving like he had been all his life. What was the point of that? At least if he went to the lab he could muck with the lives of some of the privileged few that had stomped on him for so long. Having taken out Shan Jin was a start. Why stop there? Besides, he continued to feel at times what he had first sensed in Winnipeg. From what he had learned, he was certain it came from that lab. Without being conscious of it, the feeling had grown until he seemed drawn there.

In an instant, his mind was made up. Smiling at Lu he said, "So, I am."

Realization showed on Lu's face. "You were already working on your business here when they called you. That's how you got here so fast."

"Most perceptive of you. Now, you see, I am admitted to the lab and will be given every courtesy as I personally appraise its worth."

Lu sunk dejectedly into the chair on the opposite side of the table. "Does that mean you care nothing about the tests?"

Peng was struck with empathy toward the man, something he could not remember having felt before. He saw his plight as not that different from most of the Chinese people. It was true that a free market system had emerged in China, but there was a distinct level above which the average man did not rise. The upper positions were for the party elite and their families who just happened to be from the clans of the old ruling class. This appeared to be a case of a competent man born at the bottom.

"Don't sell me short. I too have come from humble beginnings. Briefly, again, tell me the situation at the lab."

Lu looked up defiantly. "What is this you are saying? Look at you in the expensive suit, living the good life. You know nothing about the real people of China."

Just as defiantly, Peng shot back. "You think a suit makes the difference. This is the sum total of what I have. It is necessary for me to look important so I am accepted by those I must deal with. I have nothing more. In addition, why do you suppose I met you in that pub? Have you considered that? I was out fishing for some way to learn about the laboratory. If I were lucky, I hoped to find someone who was employed there, or a student helping with research. Do you in your wildest dreams think any of China's fine elite would stoop to that?"

"You then thought I was a graduate student?"

Peng had never heard of a graduate student but the term came up in the dictionary so he could reply. "I talked to you because you were speaking Mandarin, no other reason. But, yes, I had hoped that some graduate students from the lab would be in the pub. I was under pressure to determine a fair price for that laboratory. The people I work for understood the difficulty, and upon hearing of the situation at the lab they intervened and got me assigned as the umpire. Now, please tell me more about your situation."

Lu began enthusiastically about how the project had started out okay, and then how the pressure to keep the schedule had resulted in the defective heat exchanger. This caused further delays which created more pressure, and eventually more mistakes. He mentioned that Jian Niu had reported to Beijing that the delays were Lu's fault, and had asked to have him replaced. Instead, the MSS agent arrived at the lab resulting in the delegation of an umpire. Heng Lu suddenly stopped his little soliloquy.

After a pause Quan Peng prompted, "Yes. I understand that. You look as if you are uncertain about something. Please go on."

"Something is odd here. The original plan was to have a scientist come here for the start of the final test, which we are now ready to begin. That was changed in favor of sending an umpire." His face was distorted in a scowl as he continued. "I suppose this was because, given the situation, it was thought a diplomat was more useful than a scientist. That aside, whoever came was to bring the keystone device that is needed to start the final experiment. Since you were already here, how could you have it? Answer that for me if you can. I am beginning to think you are not who you say you are."

Peng had been in tight places before, and never liked it. His mind raced. What had he overlooked in Shan Jin's effects that could be this keystone device? He needed time to adjust to the situation. "Tell me, if you will, what the keystone device looks like."

Lu fidgeted even more than he was normally given to. Finally, he said. "I see no harm in telling you its general appearance. We only have the receptacle into which it fits, and I have seen a picture of it. It has an octagonal periphery with electrical contacts on each of the eight sides."

It occurred to Peng with considerable relief. Lu meant the pendant he had taken off Jin. Smiling, he reached into the breast pocket of his suit coat and pulled out the device keeping it shielded with his hand so only Lu could see it. "Would this be the item to which you refer? I have never heard it called a keystone device."

"Yes . . . that is it." Lu's eyes were wide. "How did they get it to you so fast if you were already here? And . . . the keystone device is supposed to be matched to the person who carries it."

Here, Peng played the aloof card. "There are things that it is best that I do not tell you. The test will proceed. That is enough."

Lu's expression looked as if he were trying to decide if he would accept that as an explanation. "It seems to me," Peng said, "that all that is necessary is to keep Jian Niu out of your way while you do your job. If the conjecture is false, Niu needs to do nothing other than be sure you got a chance to give it your best try. The proof is on your shoulders."

Lu brightened. "Yes. That is exactly the case. All I need is a fair chance."

"Then," Peng replied, "I'll see that you get a honest chance. Do you wish to drive to the lab with me?"

"No. That would not be good. It must not appear I have influenced you."

As Lu got up Peng said, "I assure you, you have not influenced me. You will get a fair test." On an impulse, Peng thought of something else. "If you see some things that do not appear quite right, do not react strongly. There are reasons. Be assured, things will work out."

With that, Heng Lu made his way back to his hotel to meet with the other members of the team before they left for the lab.

Peng ordered another cup of coffee as he pondered his situation. His day as the replacement umpire at the lab was not on his mind as much as it should have been. He should have been worrying about what special instructions that man might have received. What concerned him most was the pendant. The evening before he had carefully compared his pendant with that of Shan Jin. From all outward appearances, they were identical. Neither had a serial number or marking of any kind that was different. It had bothered him a little then, though he had simply thought that Jin must have been a hubot too. Now he had learned that the device was needed to start the experiment. What was about to happen at the lab that required a device identical to the one he needed, as a hubot, to remain normal? And, what was this growing desire that had arisen in him to be there?

———————————————

At the same time in the meth lab, Harvey sat in the boss's office facing him across the desk. He appeared nervous though he wasn't. It was the pose that always worked best in a bad news situation. The boss lifted his cup of coffee to his lips. If Harvey had wanted some coffee, and if he were willing to have it served in a second hand Styrofoam cup, it would have been offered with no complaint. However, this not being a social occasion, the boss felt no promptings to courteously make the overture.

"So, what's our big shot chink doing now? You've been watching him, haven't you?"

Harvey shifted in his chair as he shook his head. "After he got in the taxi down the hill at that lab place he hasn't been back." He shrugged. "Maybe he was on the lam like he said, and just wanted to get to a city like this and disappear."

"Yeah. Maybe. Maybe not. Wonder what's going on at that place in the river down there. The Chinese guys you saw there bother me. Tell you what. It's early enough. Go down there—stay out of sight—and watch as they come to work. Find out how many there are and see if they look this way or give any sign of interest in what's up the hill here."

Harvey nodded his head. "Sure." It was cold to be standing around outside, but it wasn't as if he had a choice.

He put on boots and as many warm stinky sweaters and other garments as he could find lying about. He had a dark gray coat, a stocking cap, and some lightweight chore gloves. He'd have his hands in his coat pockets most of the time, so that didn't matter.

# — 27 —

Kejian parked on the hill looking west toward the river on Third Avenue. He was at the first parking meter back from Main Street. This is where he had been the day before. It was not a good spot. He could see vehicles coming and going from the lab parking lot but he was too far away to make out faces as people parked and went into the lab. A person entering on foot from the street would be easy to recognize, but in this weather few used that means of arrival. He hesitated to use the lot because parking seemed to be at a premium at the lab during the day as cars were parked in every possible nook. Even at this early hour, the lot was a quarter full. Then it occurred to him he could park down there since if anyone checked parking stickers, or something like that, he could leave. Starting the engine, he proceeded across Main Street and down the ramp to the lot. Of course, it would be down, because the lab offices were only a foot or two above the dam's headwaters. Halfway down the ramp he saw an extended parking area lower down on his left. That would be perfect. At the bottom of the incline, he made a hairpin turn and backed into a parking position a short distance from the foot of the ramp.

He watched as three cars arrived. The occupants all walked away from Kejian, through a wrought iron gate standing open, up an incline and then turned left across a bridge to the office building. He saw the minivan next. He counted five get out. His position was perfect allowing him to identify them as Asian. Two of them he positively recognized as being from the project.

———————————

It was cloudy with a chill wind as Harvey walked the block down the hill. Crossing Main Street, he turned to the left thirty steps. Descending some wooden steps covered with snow into the park, he encountered a trail. From there he slid down an eight foot bank, crossed some rocks, and then climbed a steep slope until he come to the south side of the parking area. It was a bosky area which in summer would have provided many places to conceal himself. At this time of year with the leaves off the trees and brush, and with snow on the ground, it would be harder to remain unseen. He decided that if he stood motionless among the trunks of a close set clump of trees it was unlikely that those who arrived would notice him.

There were already a number of cars in the parking area most of them clustered as close to the gate as possible to minimize walking distance. A few had been there all night, and one was backed in slightly to his left that had come this morning since the snow was melting on its hood. If he had missed the Chinese men, he had missed them. Why worry? In a relatively short time, other cars arrived. None contained Asians. Then a minivan pulled to a stop against the stone wall that stood as a barrier to the flowing pool of water that ran between the parking lot and the offices. Five people got out. Some wore caps and others had coat collars pulled up around their ears, but they were Asian in appearance. In the clear cold air he heard them talking, and not English. They were the Asians that concerned the boss, no doubt about it. They stopped at the gate and proceeded to have a short discussion. Finally, there were short words from several as if they had either understood instructions or given assent to a plan. Three of them proceeded away from him up the incline between tall chain link fences, then across the bridge, and disappeared from view behind the corner of the building. Looking across the water Harvey saw what was a two-story office building with room air conditioners sticking out of every third window. This was at the height of the headwaters of the falls, so there were likely more levels below the offices.

The two men left behind immediately pulled out cigarettes and lit them. They walked around stomping their feet to keep warm occasionally passing a few words between them. Off to his right Harvey saw another car, actually an SUV, stop half turned into the driveway down to the lot. It came slowly and stopped at the bottom of the ramp, then proceeded until the driver parked on the south side of the lot some fifteen feet to Harvey's left with no other vehicles near it. There were several security lights high up on poles so the parking area was well lit with the yellow sodium vapor light. The headlights of the SUV went out, then the motor stopped. Nothing more. Finally, the door opened and the driver go out. What do you know about this? went though Harvey's mind. The Chinese guy. And, look at the duds. The suit coat, tie, and white shirt were visible beyond the lapels of the topcoat. The black shoes glistened even in the artificial light.

Harvey watched Peng as he stepped from one vehicle track to another trying not to get snow in his shoes. The two men by the gate flipped their half-finished cigarettes in the snow and proceeded to meet Peng as soon as they recognized he was Asian. There were hands offered in welcome and the warm sounds of greeting in Chinese. One man gestured in the direction the others had gone and the three proceeded until they, too, crossed the bridge to disappear beyond the corner of the building.

Harvey waited another few minutes not expecting anything more to happen. His feet were getting cold so he stepped over the pile of snow marking the limits of the parking lot. He glanced at the backed in gray Ford and noticed someone sitting in the drivers seat, but thought nothing of it as he started up the ramp to the east. His mind was entirely fixed on what he had seen moments before. That was the same man who had ridden with him from Winnipeg. It was! But, it couldn't be.

———————

Kejian also saw the SUV arrive. He recognized Quan Peng as he got out. His first thought was that he had his man. Not so fast. Peng was immediately met by the two members of the team and soon all three were walking into the lab. It wouldn't do to kill two of the technicians just to deliver his man to the team. Damn the luck. He had succeeded in finding his man, but too late. He could report that he had spotted his man going into such-and-such building and not mention that he recognized the other two. It wouldn't answer why he had failed to apprehend him, though.

A few minutes later a man came over the pile of snow the plows had pushed off the parking area and walked in front of his car. It seemed unlikely someone would do that in this place at this time of day especially as cold as it was. He could be an indigent, but the man walked with purpose as he made his way up the ramp. Realizing his mission had been thwarted for the moment, Kejian waited a minute and then on a whim started his engine and followed after the man who by now was crossing Main Street. As Kejian got up the ramp and stopped at Main Street, he saw the man enter the door of an old building on Third Avenue. Kejian made a right, proceeded a couple of blocks, and pulled to a stop by parking meters. What could that have been all about? Someone else was waiting to see Peng arrive exactly as he had been. He made no attempt to intervene, and left as soon as he had the information.

He got out phone number one and called Yingqu. It was answered almost immediately. Without preliminaries, Kejian began. "I waited at the lab. First, I saw the five member team arrive. They left two at the gate. Then the first of our two men arrived. He met the two team members and immediately went into the lab with them. I had no chance to apprehend him. That means, to be successful, we need the other one, so don't lose track of Breckon. I'll stay here unless you call. There may yet be a chance to get the first one. Our superiors don't know we know about the connection of our men with the test. Any questions?" Two seconds later the call was terminated.

———————————

Five minutes later Harvey was seated across the same desk from the boss. After relating the story, he didn't even stop to wait for the question he knew was coming. "It was him! I am not mistaken. I spent eight hours in that truck cab with him coming down here. The parking lot was well lit. He didn't have a cap or hat on. I was twenty feet from him this morning and, even though he spoke in Chinese, I recognized the voice. It can't be, but it was."

The boss leaned back in his chair. "Okay, okay. It was him." He repeatedly rapped his knuckles on the desk as he thought. "While you were gone I got Jorg Davis on the Internet and he checked out that lab. Would you guess it? That place has an international reputation for its studies of water flow problems. People even come here to model huge dams before they build them. And, the Chinese are presently doing some big project there. That explains the Chinese guys going in there. So, how does a high roller from a super-power country doing big time research in a world class lab get into the underworld activities of cooking meth? It doesn't figure, no way you cut it."

They sat is silence. Harvey had never seen the boss with a lack of direction. He didn't like it. Not knowing what to say he blurted out, "Do you suppose he's told anyone?"

"Wa-da-ya-mean?"

"About us."

"How'd I know."

"Is it possible that someone is leading two lives?"

"Doubt it. From what I know about that place, I mean China, is that all the people at the top are from the old ruling class, sort of all in the family. They take money from government jobs, from owning companies, and then probably also control the underworld and take money from there, too. Why not? If ya have the power and control everything, why not?"

"Nope," Harvey relied. "Not a chance that guy's from the ruling class. When he got in my truck in Winnipeg he was cold, lost, an' outta luck. He put on a good show of it, but now that I think of it, he was like a puppy dropped out of a car along the road."

"That's not helping, Harvey. Everything you say makes it worse. All we know is the same man is working them and us . . . wait. Maybe he doesn't belong either place. He sure worked his way in here. Suppose he did the same there? Could be he's the only problem. We get rid if him, we're cool again. Might help them, too, not that I'd care."

"So, what ya gonna do?"

"Don't know for sure. He'll be hard ta get. What we need is a big ass accident that makes that whole place down there go floating down the Mississippi with all them in it."

———

Quan Peng was led down flights of stairs, through a test area, down more stirs, and into the space walled off for the test control room. The entire Chinese staff was there. Peng made a point of not looking at Heng Lu. This was not hard because Jian Niu took over making introductions of the others and finally himself as leader of the project. Peng immediately understood Lu's concern. The man was overbearing and arrogant. Immediately Niu began what was almost an interrogation of Peng wanting to know how he was connected to the ruling class.

Peng looked at him with a deadpan expression and said nothing. He didn't know how much of the man he could stand before he killed him. He was suddenly glad he had decided to be the umpire. This was going to be sweet. First, they had to conduct this test, whatever it was. Niu had to give his approval that it had been a fair test, and then, well . . . he'd have some time to think about the most painful way to dispatch him.

As though Jian Niu had said nothing at all Peng asked, "When will you be ready to proceed with the test?"

Niu made a double take. "You have not answered my questions."

Peng looked at him, peering into his eyes as he leaned slightly toward him. "I have not come all the way from Beijing to answer your questions. I have come to ask you questions. I have asked you one. Answer it!"

Blinking and stepping back a pace, he answered. "We are ready to proceed at once."

"And, what does the other half of the team have to say about that?" he said looking at Lu.

"He is not the other half of the team. He is simply a member of my technical staff," Niu retorted.

Peng snapped his attention to Niu. "I did not speak to you. In the future, you will not speak unless spoken to. Is that clear?"

Turning again to Lu, he asked in a conversational voice, "Are you ready?" The amusement in Lu's eyes was worth it to Peng whatever else happened.

"The first operational window will be at eight o'clock. That is only minutes away. We will not be ready then. I suggest we set up to run at the next window, at two p.m. with the provision that if there are any of the symmetry parameters less than nominal, even though technically within specification, we be given the chance to stop, realign, and run at eight p.m."

"That is not . . . " Niu began, but Peng held up his hand to silence him.

Peng turned to Niu and said, "We will proceed as Lu has suggested. No objections. You stay out of the team's way. Clear?" Then in a more conciliatory tone he said to Niu, "You will now, please, give me a tour of this entire facility? We'll let them do their work."

---

When they reached the top floor, Niu had to excuse himself to use a men's room. He was so angry he was ready to beat a hole in the wall with his fists. He splashed cold water on his face as his emotional state made him shake uncontrollably. Finally, he composed himself resolving to get to the bottom of the situation. The exchange in the control room might have seemed rude to westerners, but for the reserved Chinese it was way beyond the range of acceptable behavior. No one acted like that unless he had nothing to lose and was intent on destroying someone with his last breath. Even then, it would be doubtful anyone would act like that. In the desk in his office was a small digital camera. He would get it and surreptitiously get a photo of this guy and verify his authenticity. What was going on he could not guess, but he *would* be vindicated.

For the next two hours, Quan Peng was constantly at Jian Niu's side. He always had another question, another thing to see. When shown the small cement block building to the north of the offices that controlled the inlet of water to two levels to the test facility, Peng insisted Niu get a key for the door so he could see what was in the building. Niu was frustrated by the time this took, but had to be careful in case he was overlooking something that made sense of Shan Jin's requests. Beyond that, he had no intention of responding in kind to the boorish behavior that had been visited upon him.

From Peng's point of view the whole facility seemed, what would he say, well, messy. He had imagined a well lit, clean shinny place on the par with a clinical lab. Here, of course, they were dealing with nature at its most basic level, and nature tended to be untidy. The labs went down four stories below the headwaters of the dam. At many places, the naked sandstone of the river bluffs formed the walls. There were experiments half constructed or half decommissioned with the pipes, boards, instruments, and whatnot lying everywhere. When the test demanded a pipe cross an inconvenient place, no problem. Everybody simply worked around it. To prolong the tour Peng had stopped to talk to some of the scientists. It was clear that they hardly saw the disorder. It was the heart of the experiment that mattered. The challenge was prying earth's secrets from its breast while the earth seemed to resent having its hidden life bared. The data being generated was the stuff of life to those people.

Finally, at ten-fifteen Peng excused himself to use the men's room. Niu immediately went to his office, slipped the camera in his pocket, and quickly sent an email to Beijing requesting that a photo of the umpire be sent to him. He gave no explanation, only marking it as urgent. After the message was sent he looked at the clock and realized it was after midnight in China. Nobody would be at work to act on his request until later in the afternoon in Minneapolis. It could be a coincidence, but Niu doubted it. Something was wrong with this man who had presented himself as the umpire.

---

Peng had known Niu would try to verify his credentials so the monopolization of his time for a couple of hours was no accident. It was now the wee hours of the morning in Beijing so he felt safe from that quarter until later in the afternoon. He hated to duck out on Heng Lu and his team before the critical test. It was against his nature to let Niu win by default. Such was the enmity between the casts in China. However, self-preservation had won the mental discussion. As he emerged from the men's room, he had decided to make it to his vehicle and be long gone by the time two o'clock rolled around.

To his consternation, he was met by Jianli Huang patiently waiting for him in the hallway.

"Please, you will come with me to the test area? Heng Lu urgently requires your assistance on a matter concerning the test. Please, you come now?"

If it had been one of the men, Peng might have blustered his way through some excuse to make a quick trip to attend to other business. However, he was disarmed by the petite woman with something between pleading in her voice, and fear in her eyes. Was this test so important to these people? Every instinct said to be quit of this place, yet he followed with not a word.

He guessed that Heng Lu had called an impromptu meeting of the team as soon as Peng and Niu had left on their tour. He would have related the strange circumstances of his two meetings with Peng, and expressed his concern that Peng would leave at his earliest chance, hence his guide.

As Peng came down the steps from the offices to the level of the test, he was met with the sound of rushing water. It was the main test flume of the lab. The walls of the water passage had been adjusted to direct the entire water flow though the test apparatus. Clear polycarbonate panels formed the side of the flume which also served as the wall of the control room providing a direct view of the test. Bright lights both above and below the water lit the apparatus so the polished stainless steel heat exchanger glistened in the slightly turbid water.

The team members were engrossed in their work. Flat but firm comments were exchanged continually. It seemed they were having difficulty arriving at the exact setting of a certain parameter. As they neared the required precision, one or the other would remark that some other variable was slipping away from nominal. With the sound of the door closing Lu glanced up and said, "Good, you found him. Please have a seat for a moment." Then to the woman, "Jianli, we are closing in on system optimization. Please see what the field symmetry coefficients are doing. If they can be held within limits while the thermo transfer increases, we can increase the field strength and frequency to the point of positive power without anomalies."

This was beyond what Peng had ever imagined as they had discussed the test over breakfast. His earlier visit was so personality charged that he hardly noticed the apparatus. Here, in this out of the way place, some truly world class research was being conducted, possibly even historically significant research. He began to understand the intensity of the team's desire to succeed.

Peng watched with fixed interest for the next half-hour. Finally, Lu pushed back his chair and said, "Let's let it hold there for awhile. Everything is steady just below positive power." Turning to Peng he continued, "We would like to see the keystone device and make sure it will fit the receptacle. As we have been putting the equipment together, we've found places where parts didn't fit. There's no point in taking a chance."

Peng shrugged and took the pendant out of his suit coat pocket and handed it to Lu.

Using a dial caliper Lu carefully measured the appliance as he referred to a drawing. Peng observed closely as Lu next took it to a chest high solid black pedestal set by the transparent wall. Gripping it between thumb and forefinger on two opposing corners, he held it slightly away from a recess of similar shape. Moving the device first close to the receptacle and then pulling it back as he moved his head from side to side, he was satisfied it would fit its intended place.

Returning it to Peng he said, "Everything looks fine. I hope you don't mind that we ordered lunch to be brought in. We want to stay close and be sure the system remains stable." Nodding, Peng took his chair again.

Niu had arrived a few minutes before and taken a seat at the far side of the room all the while eyeing Peng like a cat contemplating a mouse. During the time Peng was watching Lu match the fit of the pendant Niu managed to get several pictures of Peng without others noticing. After a suitable time he excused himself, went to his office, and sent the photos to Beijing.

It was now nearly noon and all could see it would be a tense two hours running up to the start of the test. Not only that, Peng had no chance to escape without significant violence.

# — 28 —

As two o'clock approached, everyone in the lab was on edge. Everyone except Jian Niu. He was seething. Never in his life had he expected to receive such treatment from a peasant as he quickly categorized their lauded umpire. But, that roach of a man had the pendant. Even Niu had not been trusted to bring it to the site for the final test. He had not liked this, but had put it off as a largely ceremonial function that would be given to someone his senior. That's how the game was played. Everyone stayed in his place, deferring to those above him, and receiving deference from those lower. The whole system rested, of course, on knowing the order of things. It was clear, this ruffian was *not* in the order of things anywhere except the unwashed underclass.

Peng, for his part, had taken to wearing the pendant he'd taken off Shan Jin's dead body hanging from the chain around his neck. It dangled out in the open for all to see as if daring Niu to question his right to be there. During the hours of waiting, Niu would from time to time ask Peng a leading question in an attempt to learn his background, and specifically why he, of all people, had been sent with the keystone device. Peng answered obliquely and immediately responded with questions into Niu's life and position. Getting nowhere, Niu reverted to prodding him for information about the true nature of the test. The rest of the team remained silent as they watched the thrust and parry of the two combatants.

Lunch was delivered to the lab. They each selected a sandwich plate covered with clear plastic wrap and a soda. Returning to their places, they ate in silence. Peng pulled his chair up beside Lu and questioned him about the exact part he was to play in the test. He was told he was to insert the device into the keystone socket during the one minute time period starting at two o'clock. A large round clock hung above the place where the keystone device was to be inserted. It had a bight red sweep second hand so there could be no question of the time.

Peng knew from his own pendant that would be the time both devices would be active. He wasn't sure what would happen since he intended to use Shan Jin's keystone device for the test and it had likely been tuned to that man's energy field. The thought came to him that it would interact with his pendant, and both would interact with his energy field. In this, he was left with only speculation so he dismissed it.

The technical team had the day before, and again in the morning, repeated the first test and found the replacement heat exchanger segment had corrected the thermal transfer instability. With all variables holding steady through the morning, they were expecting a clean start to the test. If everything went as expected and the power became stable and self-sustaining between fifty and one hundred megawatts, they would lock the doors to the chamber containing the experiment and leave town. Each had a bag in the back of the minivan. The experiment would automatically stop at six p.m. on Sunday after one hundred hours of running. If they started at eight this evening, the following opportunity, it would stop at midnight Sunday. They would monitor the condition of key data sets during the hundred hours via cell phone. Other cell phones would transmit the output of seismic sensors in the lab as well as a dozen others they had surreptitiously placed at increasingly greater distances from the lab. The seismic sensors would also transmit directly to satellites in geosynchronous orbit for the benefit of those in Beijing.

The stress had reached a numbing level as, at last, Lu gave the one-minute warning. Peng stepped to the position where the keystone device was to be inserted into its receptacle. The socket was conveniently located at chest level making it possible to leave the bead chain around his neck as Lu had instructed. Peng had been told nothing about what to expect as he found himself standing less than an arm's length from the strange pedestal. He inquiringly touched it in an action reminiscent of the scene from the movie *2001 Space Odyssey* where the primates curiously approached the black monolith. Above the pedestal, he could see the flow of water in the flume by means of bits of debris that had passed through the screen up-stream. Glancing up he could see the underside of the surface thrashing about by the unseen turbulence immediately beneath it. The cylinder remained motionless with the gleaming segments of the heat exchangers interlocked around it. It occurred to him that if something went wrong and the wall burst, the room would flood in seconds and he would be the first to meet the torrent. He also noticed for the first time that the rest of the team sat behind consoles as far back in the room as possible. He alone was at ground zero.

"Thirty seconds," Lu said in a clear, but noticeably tense voice.

Finally the clear female voice of Jianli Huang started counting backwards from ten. Peng followed the movement of the second hand on the clock with his eyes.

"Insert the keystone," Lu instructed as the second hand passed the twelve on the clock.

Peng did as he was told. Peng felt his pendant come on as usual giving him the positive reinforcement he had come to expect. In fact, it was back to the level it had been in the Medical Institute. It was clear; this was the right place for him to be. Maybe this machine would recharge his pendant that had been falling further and further below expectation with each activation.

"Thermo transfer coefficients solidly symmetrical," Huang sang out, pleasure in her voice.

"Moving toward positive power generation," Ju Feng said.

Lu was intent on his monitor. Now was the time for the via to zero point to begin opening. "Via located," Lu said. "Via opening to base line positive power generation." This was normal and was as far as they could go without the keystone device. It was time for the keystone to engage. To get into positive power generation was one thing, to make it self-sustaining was another.

At the boundary between our world and that of zero point sub-space, quantum mechanical events were constantly and everywhere occurring with a net zero interaction with our world. The goal was to use the unique structure of the ceramic cylinder to destabilize this demarcation line by feeding back some subatomic particles in a lower quantum state than when they appeared in our world. This would cause a net gain of energy on our side of the margin. The keystone device with its connection to the human energy field, and hence the DNA molecules, was to be the means of initiating self-perpetuation of positive energy.

"Moment of truth," Lu said his voice laced with anxiety. "At keystone threshold. Opening, opening . . ."

———

Peng was following the chatter of the technical people behind him still wondering what would happen. Suddenly, he sensed his pendant was varying. Increasingly it drew on him like the device needed him more than he needed it. He leaned forward placing the palms of his hands on the smooth black surface either side of the keystone device. His peripheral vision darkened and his fingers trembled. He heard the technicians as through a long tunnel.

"Via opening to ten percent," Lu intoned.

Peng's knees started to shake. He was becoming disoriented, vertigo was taking over.

"Via becoming unstable . . . interference with keystone device indicated . . ."

Peng had taken all he could tolerate. As he twisted to the side he managed to grasp the bead chain, and falling to his knees, he jerked it out of its socket. Like a switch being snapped off, the physiological effects ceased. The normal effects of his pendant were felt again. Not knowing why, he felt that the disturbing effects were the result of having two pendants. Slowly coming to his feet, he made eye contact with Lu who was on his feet with a look of betrayal on his face.

As Lu was about to say something, Peng slowly shook his head as a reminder of the warning he had given Lu earlier in the coffee shop. Lu sat down again. "Review the data," he commanded, a little too harshly.

Jian Niu was immediately behind Lu. "You failed again! Not only is the conjecture not true, but you are too incompetent to even get the test started properly. I will see to having you replaced by someone who is at least marginally competent."

Peng had no way of knowing what Lu was thinking, but he surmised it was something to the effect that his career was sliding away, that he'd be lucky to find work in a toy factory after Niu finished with him. Of course, the enigma of Peng, the umpire, would be a point of growing hostility with him. He clearly had doubts as they discussed the situation earlier that morning, and now he'd want answers

As Lu's mind was thus engaged with a tangle of conflicting thoughts, Peng approached his console unsure of his next move, other than getting the attention off him. He was tempted to make an excuse to leave the room, make a dash for the SUV, and start driving. However, the state of his pendant was not at all agreeable to him after such a chaotic episode. It irritated him that he felt forced to be present for the next test. Wearing only one pendant would likely change things a lot. The question he couldn't sort out for certain was which pendant to use.

Wu Zheng, the engineer on the project, was the most reserved of the team. As the others called out the readings of the parameters under their

control he quietly, but intently went about his work which was to measure and record the magnetic vortex parameters that opened the via.
Heretofore, he had not had a chance to make good measurements since
the test vias had always been too small and short-lived. Niu continued to
make sharp disparaging remarks about Lu. He stopped, unsure of what
more to say, since no one had acknowledged his remarks.

Zheng used the pause to interject in his unassuming way, "More
analysis will be needed. It may not be the keystone device that caused the
problem. This was our first use of the device, and the first step toward
self-sustaining positive power. The data suggests that our assumptions
about the magnetic vortex parameters may need some adjustment."
Looking directly at Niu, he continued in his voice devoid of inflection.
"Please, don't be too anxious for immediate results. If we run only a few
minutes and then stop, it will produce only a small unnoticeable anomaly
if the conjecture is true. We may have to start several more times until
we get our hands around the exact settings required. The basic physics
won't change, but the realization of any theory in the practical would is
in the engineering details."

Niu gave a snort and turned. "I'll be in my office upstairs." After the
door to the chamber closed everyone relaxed. Lu looked at Peng and then
locked his eyes on Zheng as if asking if he were serious or just getting
rid of Niu.

"Okay. We do need to review the data and adjust the magnetic vortex
settings. But, there was clearly something wrong with the pendant," he
said looking intently at Peng.

Peng was feeling caught again. How much did these guys really know
about what the pendant should do? What could he get away with? Whatever the case, he saw had to take the initiative. "If I had not pulled the
keystone device out of the socket would the test have started successfully?" The question was to put the staring eyes on the defensive. At least
for the time being it appeared to work.

Zheng twisted his mouth. "I'm not sure. The vortex parameters were
not quite right."

Lu broke in. "The via was opening as planned for a few seconds, but
then became unstable. It seemed like the keystone device was in some
way under powered. I'm not even sure that's the right way to describe it.
Even if the vortex were not perfect it should have opened the via further
in the fifteen seconds we operated. I think the vortex was stable enough
to have gone a lot further. And, what about the physical effects you

encountered?" he said his eyes boring in to Peng. "There was no mention of that, ever."

The other three technical people were now standing around Lu as they looked at Peng who stood with the console between himself and the others. Peng's head was swimming. How did a street kid from Shanghai get himself into a situation like this? To add to his discomfort, his new expensive shoes were beginning to chafe at his toes. In time, he'd break them in, but he'd likely be dead before that happened. Unless, of course, he killed all of these people first. He knew he'd have no problem doing it with his speed and strength. After that what? Kill Niu, too? The urge came back to leave this place, get in his SUV, and drive. To where? Besides, he still felt a need to resolve the uncertainty with his pendant. For the moment he decided to stay which meant he had to get things back on track so these people had something to do besides accuse him.

Nodding his head Peng began yet another stratagem. "You would not have been informed of such effects because they would never happen to you. Only the keystone carrier needed to know that. And, it is possible even I have not been told the whole truth." Grabbing on to the remarks of Zheng, he continued. "You are not certain of the exact settings for this complex machine," he said waving his hand in an arc to include the contents of the room and the cylinder and heat exchanger in the flume. "In the matter of the keystone device there is uncertainty, also."

None of them was saying anything, though their expressions gave away a lot. They had suspected the physicists in China were not as certain about whether the system would operate as they were told. Heng Lu knew the theory of how the energy would be generated well enough. The discovery of the keystone device was literally the key to getting the process running independently. Without it in place and functioning properly, the whole exercise was for naught. To his chagrin, his confrere, Dr. Anfa Lung, was not sharing the secret of the keystone with anyone.

His voice devoid of inflection, Lu said, "Continue."

Peng didn't want to go too far but knew he couldn't stop now. His condition as a hubot had something to do with the human energy field. The pendant, he knew from what he had heard and read at the Medical Institute, interacted with his human energy field. This field obviously had something to do with the test here or there would be no need for the pendant, and it appeared, the person wearing it. "I do not understand what is involved being nothing more than the delivery mechanism," he said as he took the pendant off and laid it on top of the console. He loosened his necktie, opened the top two buttons of his shirt, and pulled out his own pendant.

There were looks of astonishment all around. "What is the meaning of this?" Zheng blurted contrary to his normal demeanor.

Peng lifted an eyebrow. "Simply, two keystone devices as is obvious. Low power . . . high power," he said pointing at them in turn. "It appears they forgot to tell me that I could not be wearing both of them when the test started, though they suggested I might experience some, how did they say, 'some mild discomfort.' Or, they didn't know what to expect." Not knowing why he said it, he added in confirmation to what Wu Zheng had said before, "When you set out to revolutionize science, don't expect anyone to have all the answers."

It seemed to have the desired effect since they returned to their places. Seated, they continued to look at Peng, with mixed expressions. Zheng appeared the most positive. "With an analysis of the data I'll be able to optimize the magnetic vortex. With the high power keystone, and the other out of the way to prevent interference, we'll have a perfect start."

They started conferring with one another. Screens of data were scrutinized. A printer spat out pages at regular intervals. Peng was largely forgotten. His mind reverted to the dilemma of whether to stay around and see what happened the next time his pendant was due to energize or make a hasty retreat to parts unknown. He wished he could experience that time without having to be connected to that ugly machine. If his pendant had been recharged, he'd have no need for any of this. If he stayed for the next test, it was possible the master plan was that his entire energy field would be consumed by the cursed machine as it seemed it was trying to do during those few seconds of the test just past. If that happened, it would be the end of him. Yet, the deleterious effects could have been due to his having two pendants. With things done properly, his pendant might be supercharged. He'd be a god. Was it worth the risk to find out?

---

Hua Chen had been waiting all day for Ed Breckon to come for him at the rectory. It was a pleasant enough place to be if the pastor wouldn't ask him when he was leaving every time they met. Since the last time his pendant activated at eight a.m., he decided he needed to see Breckon to discuss his condition. When he had received the pendant from Jason Finley the day before, the first time it came on was at two p.m. It seemed entirely normal at that time. When it came on at eight p.m. the boost he had come to expect was less than needed. At that time, he considered the possibility that it had been designed to decay in power until he didn't need it any more. It might be expected that discomfort would accompany this weaning process. The ensuing times his thinking changed. His need for it increased even as the effects became weaker. It was his hope Breckon could connect him to the CIA and from there to someone doing research in this field to get relief from his increasing pain.

It was now nearly two in the afternoon. He had forgone the studies that he hoped could shed light on his ontological state. He could no longer concentrate as he watched the hands of the clock on the wall creep toward two o'clock. As the last minutes approached he pulled the pendant out of his shirt and watched the digital display methodically work its way to the engagement time. With five seconds left, he pressed the pendant to his chest with his hands. The sensation started the way it should have. It built better than the previous time. He relaxed as he sensed it was back to its normal capacity. Suddenly, there was a disturbance in his energy field. He went from tranquility to turmoil, from pleasure to pain and all other imaginable states in seconds. Springing to his feet, he paced about the room unable to understand what was happening or what to do. As he turned about, he determined the intensity varied. He had the presence of mind to locate the approximate orientation of the strongest effects. As suddenly as the torment started, it stopped. He looked at the face of the pendant. It was sixteen seconds after two. For the remainder of the minute the device stayed active and he felt okay. Not great, not as good as he had at the Medical Institute, but okay.

For a half-hour, he puzzled about what had happened. He kept coming back to the drawing he had seen at Bart's machine shop. He had immediately thought it was for making hubots. Then Ed had convinced him it was for something else. He had even worked out that it was likely for generating power. This was being done at that place near the university, the St. Anthony Falls Laboratory. The sensations he had felt at two o'clock were of the hubot kind, and, though chaotic, must have emanated from that lab. Whatever that lab was doing, hubots were involved. That's where he must go.

Besides the declining effect of the pendant, he was becoming concerned about Breckon. He had said he'd come for him today. The day was wearing on and he had not come. Remembering the shots fired at them in the shopping place, he assumed the worst. The assassin had been successful. Ed would not be coming. He was on his own, and it was clear he could not stay here, nor did he see any benefit in doing so. Having never seen a street map of the city, it would be hard to find the lab. With Ed gone, there was only one other person in this whole city he had any connection with, Cindy Thomas.

Remembering the apartment building where she lived, he followed in his mind the sights of the streets, intersections, and buildings, as the taxi took them from there to here. It could not be more than ten kilometers. It was two-forty now and it would take two to three hours to walk there. He assumed she had a normal job, so would be getting home about the time he arrived. He was wearing his warm coat, gloves, and boots when he arrived so would not get cold.

After suiting up in his cold weather apparel, he cautiously opened the door to the third floor hallway. Not a sound. Descending the steps to the second floor, there was still no movement. No sound. Down to the first floor, he heard the voice of a man coming from an office engaged in a phone conversation. Seeing no reason to disturb anyone with his departure, he went to the back door and left. The path led to the right. There he took the main walk between the rectory and the church to his right. Passing under huge pine boughs just above his head, he came to the street that ran in front of the church. It was snowing steadily and the freshly fallen snow crunched under his feet. The city seemed serene with its harsh sounds muffled by the snow suspended about him.

Heading west one full block he recognized where he was. If he turned right on this main thoroughfare he would go north several kilometers and then head west on County Road B. It was easy because other than a block or two of travel on either end they had used only those two streets to get to the church.

# — 29 —

**3:00 p.m., Roseville, MN**

Yingqu was tiring of the game of being what amounted to a private investigator. Sitting in a car for hours and waiting for someone to do something was boring. Worst of all, it seemed to be working on his mind. His disdain for Kejian was gradually being replaced by pity. The sunken eyes and drawn complexion were bringing back memories of what he had seen in his instructors at the MSS. His job at the embassy in Washington was trying at times, at most times, in fact. It offered the advantage, though, that when he left the place, even after a long day, he could live in another world. That was easy to do because this really was another world. If his living quarters had been in the embassy, it would be like living in China.

Having observed Kejian now for a few days, Yingqu could see his own life in the MSS in China had ended before he achieved a responsible position. The incredible stress to get results took its toll. Even now, he felt it by association. Here he was, doing nothing, but nonetheless apprehensive lest he not be able to deliver some useful information about Breckon. That, even though, he had no control over what Breckon did.

He had, if only for the time being, given up his passion of exacting revenge upon Breckon. Was it because of the empathy he felt for Kejian? If it was, it could only mean he was losing his edge. Or, was it because he was beginning to see a bigger picture. Killing Breckon might, in the end, be a favor to the man. Better to make him suffer, perhaps kill those he cared about. No! No! He shifted in his seat and ran his hand across his face. That was silly. The real reason for these thoughts was his failure on so many occasions to kill Breckon. Be weak, and go for softer targets. Was that it? For now, he had to be careful about not killing Breckon too soon. If he could kill the hubot and Breckon at the same time, that would work to everyone's benefit. If only something would happen.

It was cold and the snow was still filtering down. Every twenty minutes Yingqu started the engine to run the heater to clear the fog from the windows on the inside. He also ran the passenger side window down and up to wipe off the accumulated snow. People came and went from Control Engineering every few minutes, so there was little exceptional about the appearance of yet another man coming out of the door. This one did not turn to the visitor parking area as he had expected. Then it registered. It was Breckon. Yingqu immediately started his car and ran the wipers to clear the windshield of snow.

Breckon got on Highway 36 heading west. This time Yingqu resolved to stay closer and not lose him. Highway 36 joined I-35W and they headed toward downtown Minneapolis. Breckon took the Washington Avenue exit. By now, Yingqu was immediately behind Breckon. The previous time he had been three cars back and lost him when the car in front of him stopped for a red light. Not this time. Sure enough, he turned into a parking ramp near a large government building. Yingqu continued past the entrance, around the block, and then entered the same place Breckon had. He'd search until he found the car, and then park and wait. On his first pass through he spotted Breckon's car. He parked a few cars past it on the opposite side. Adjusting his rear view mirror, he could see Breckon's car without looking around. He waited.

### 3:30 p.m., CIA offices, downtown Minneapolis

Mrs. Finley and Jason had been picked up at their hotel and brought in after being told they would only be needed a short time while Jason identified the man he had sat beside on the plane from Beijing. The CIA was still in a quandary about whether or not there were really two hubots. If Hua Chen could be identified by Jason, it would mean there were two. The security analysts had been amazed at how all of the camera images were hazy where they thought they had him spotted. Some of the scientists offered the explanation that he had an extremely strong aura, or human energy field. This, predictably, led to bickering that it couldn't possibly be that, so it was dropped in favor of simply accepting the fact that the images were not conclusive.

When Winger called Breckon, he tried to extract a promise that he'd bring in the hubot. Breckon was evasive, but left the impression that he'd do it. Breckon arrived as promised, but without Hua Chen. There was a display of anger by Mel Winger, though he was not really surprised that Breckon didn't have him. When it came time to inform Mrs. Finley of the situation, the honor fell to Winger. Mrs. Finley gave a display of outrage in her turn. Finally the two Finleys, Breckon, and the two CIA agents were seated in the conference room. After introductions, Winger began.

"I'm sorry for having put you out this way, Mrs. Finley. Really I am. But, this is a situation that goes a bit beyond inconvenience."

"Why is it my problem if you consistently can't deliver your man? Look at the time," she retorted.

"We thought Mr. Breckon here was going to bring him in, but he didn't." Winger replied.

Mrs. Finley glared at Breckon. "What kind of an outfit is this if your people won't follow orders?"

"He isn't one of our people," Winger said almost gritting his teeth. "If he were, you can be assured he would have brought him in." In exasperation he added, "If he were one of our people he would have been fired long ago . . . " He trailed off.

"It's a very complicated situation," Breckon said defensibly. "Not the least of which is my job. I have a real job in which I must absolutely deliver results or I *will* be fired. That's the way it is in the private sector. Everyone else in this room lives off the government where results are the least of anyone's worries."

Mrs. Finley bristled and was about to let go at the disgusting man for the disparaging comment.

Carson leaned forward looking right at Mrs. Finley. "I think you deserve to know a little about what's involved."

Winger was about to break in. Carson held up his hand to stop him. "Know this. There is the real possibility of something happening that could be called an extreme terrorist attack."

"You mean like 911?"

"Much worse."

"Oh."

"Mr. Breckon is what might be called an average citizen. Except that he is not at all average. He has become involved in a couple of high profile international incidents, as far as anyone can tell, by accident. They seem to be attracted to him. The man we want your son to identify escaped from China and did not come to us, but sought out Breckon. We believe the Chinese man is in some way programmed to be part of the major terrorist disaster I mentioned."

"That's simple!" Mrs. Finley snapped. "Force him to bring the man in. The public good certainly over rules this man's personal fetishes."

"It's not so simple," Carson continued. "If we had done that the other times the disaster would have happened. Breckon alone caused them *not* to happen. We are very much afraid to force the situation. I know it doesn't exactly make sense, but we here have kinda gotten used to the idea that we have to let things proceed unhindered."

Mrs. Finley was aghast, looking at Carson as if he was crazy.

Breckon was becoming uneasy with Carson's chatter. "Maybe I could take Jason to see Hua, and identify him. How would that be?" he offered.

"I don't know you. Can this man be trusted?" she asked looking at the two CIA men.

Carson blew out a breath. "If he promises to keep you son safe, he will be safe even if the world should end along the way." He held up his index finger. "Not that Breckon wouldn't be the one causing the end of the world, mind you."

The phone on the table beeped.

"That must be our call from Fort Meade," Mel said. "This is a classified call, Mrs. Finley. If you stay, you will have to be extensively debriefed afterwards. That could take hours. We would like Jason to stay since he might be able to add information from his seating companion on the plane. What do you say?"

"I'll step outside. Only information from my son. Nothing more."

When the call was completed, Daley came on. "It's just me and Markus Mueller on this end. Who do we have in Minneapolis?"

Ed started. "Hi, Greg. How ya doing?"

"Been better. My wife is ready to leave me. Every time I get mixed up with you, I'm never home. Been working my ass off on this hubot thing. Who else is on your end?"

When they mentioned Finley there was murmuring heard on the other end. Mel spoke up. "We think it's important because he might remember something from on the plane."

Mueller broke in. "Hold old is he?"

"Twelve," Finley answered.

"Know much about theoretical physics?" Mueller asked with a chuckle.

"Nothing."

"Well, I doubt there's much problem with him. You'll have to debrief him, though. We'll be talking in little more than platitudes anyway. No offense, but none of you would understand the mathematics of what we'll discuss either."

"Okay. Your show. Tell us what you've found," Mel said.

"With the information you gave us from the hubot we've made some rather startling discoveries. The part about China using ancient writings was most helpful, as was the idea that the human energy field was involved.

"Let's go back a little. There are some ancient writings that have never been deciphered, such as Linear A. There are others. The NSA is in the business of breaking codes and from time to time we give things like that a try. The important thing about breaking a code is to have some idea about what has been encoded like key words or whether it's a poem or a shipping manifest. Once things like that are known, the computers at the NSA can hit the code with a million-billion possible solutions a second. We had some of Linear A figured out, and the information you gave was the key to finish it.

"The Linear A tablets did not seem to be nearly old enough to be what the Chinese were talking about. However, we found that they are a transcription of much older tablets that were eroding away and were close to becoming unreadable. Apparently, the originals were not fired properly as if the writer were in a hurry. This comes from an introduction the transcriber left. In the rewriting process, some of the then current symbols were used making it even more confusing. The good thing is we got valuable information on how ceramic cylinders were used to draw energy from zero point, which leads us to believe that's what helped the Chinese. With this knowledge, we could fill in some of the empty places using other old writings, many of which are decoded like the Vedas of ancient India. The Vedas describe many things including airplanes, space ships, nuclear weapons, and zero point energy. One place they even mention how to avoid bird strikes on airplanes. Are you with me?"

There were a few nods and a yeah because nobody know where he was going with this, though Mueller's speech was quite animated.

"Now, to the present and zero point energy. There is supposed to be ten raised to the hundred-and-eighth power Joules of energy in a cubic millimeter of space. A Joule is three-fourths of a foot-pound for those of you who like to think in that system of units. That is a number that is so large it is beyond comprehension. To bring it into focus, that is enough energy to create another entire universe. By inference, if there were ever to be an *empty* cubic millimeter, our entire universe could disappear into it. It is speculated that the zpe would be infinite if it were not for the Planck cut-off frequency, which is used to arrive at that large number.

"I'm going to tell you a new theory we've come up with. In the theoretical physics business, somebody comes up with a new theory every day to explain this or that. Virtually all are eventually discarded. However, they are needed to keep the thought process going. With that disclaimer, I'll make my case.

"As a starting point, one physicist has come to our rescue to help understand zero point energy in common terms. He suggested that it really doesn't matter how much there is because we are unaware of it. He gave the analogy of a boat floating on water. If the boat has a draft of one foot, then any depth of water from two feet to twenty miles doesn't matter. The boat floats on it unawares.

"It's an interesting analogy that can be taken further, even though all analogies break down at some point. The first apparent breaking point of this one is that it assumes our world is two-dimensional, the surface of the water, and that the zpe extends in a third dimension, its depth. It also implies that the boat and any occupants extend up into this additional dimension, too, only in the opposite direction of the water.

"Where does this leave us since we already live in a three dimensional world? If zpe is an underlying sea of energy, it would extend into an additional dimension, a fourth dimension. Here surely the analogy breaks down because we have no understanding of a fourth spatial dimension. We are stuck unless we assume time is that additional dimension. As you know, time is commonly referred to as the fourth dimension.

"To follow the analogy we would have to assume time *is* the sea of zpe that our world floats on like the water in lake on which the boat floats. This would make time identically equal to zpe, or zero point energy an attribute of time, or time an attribute of zpe. We don't have to sort that out now. If time is the zpe under our three-dimensional space, then like the boat and its occupants, we are protruding up into this dimension in the opposite direction of the zpe side. That is to say, we poke up into, or you might say, move forward in time because there is this sea of time/zpe, identified with the past, which would seem to be pushing us on.

"The Planck cut-off frequency says time/zpe does not extend back to infinity, it had a beginning. 'In the beginning God created . . . the Planck cut-off frequency.' That's not blasphemy. If God created the universe and everything in it, He certainly created the Planck cut-off frequency. Without this cut-off frequency, there would be no beginning, no creation, no big bang as scientists would rather say. Is everybody with me?"

"You were right," Jason said. "It doesn't matter that I'm here. You left me back at Linear A."

"Don't feel bad," Burl said. "I'm back there some place too."

"That's okay because that was only background. The real question is what happens when we draw energy out of zpe to use in our world? It would clearly affect time in some way if this particular model is correct. In fact, rather than converting mass into energy we might be converting time into energy. Maybe as we draw out zpe it would gradually draw the machine back in time, that is, into the sea of zpe, under water so to speak, by stretching the space/time fabric. When the machine was stopped, it would want to pop back to the surface, that is, become synchronized with the time of its surroundings. It might be that the gravity wells created by massive objects are such a stretching. Only here, turning off the machine would be like having a chunk of mass suddenly disappear."

When Mueller stopped to take a breath, Breckon broke in. "Wait a minute. If what you say is true, as time moves on, zero point energy must be increasing. Where is that energy coming from?"

"Our idea is it's wrapped up with entropy and the second law of thermodynamics. We've known for centuries that the universe is winding down, the result of all natural processes being irreversible. This means that after an action is completed, the energy consumed is no longer accessible and ends up by increasing this unusable reservoir of energy called entropy. According to our theory, the energy goes into the past, that is, into zpe. This is a somewhat odd way to look at time. It says that what we call the future is potential energy. This means, the present is that cusp where available energy, potential energy, at a measured pace, becomes kinetic energy on its way into entropy, the past. That is, the act of energy changing from one state to the other produces the present. For now, we don't know what it is that regulates this flow of energy from the future to the past, or how long the "present" really is.

"As an aside, this isn't just theoretical. The food we eat contains chemicals with stored energy. When they are combined with other chemicals they release the 'potential energy' they contain and this fuels our metabolism. We can think about the future and remember the past, but we only live in the present that, if you will, moves along as the energy in and around us changes state."

"Are you saying the pool of zpe would want all of its energy back?"

"According to our theory, yes. It seems that if someone did manage to draw out zero point energy, when the machine stopped it would all have to be paid back, so to speak. It seems likely there would be a disturbance when that happened. It would not be 'free energy' as some think."

"If the Chinese experiment were to be successful, how big a chunk of matter, or is it a chunk of time, are we talking about?" Carson asked.

"If they ran at fifty megawatts for a hundred hours that would be five thousand megawatt hours. That amount of energy converted to mass is two tenths of a gram. I haven't had time to think of this in terms of time."

"You can't be serious," Winger said. "Two-tenths of a gram is nothing."

"You have to consider what you're talking about," Mueller replied. "A little matter goes a long way when converting mass to energy. The atomic bomb that was dropped on Hiroshima at the end of World War II was equivalent to fifteen thousand tons of TNT. That bomb converted seven-tenths of a gram into energy. The one dropped on Nagasaki was somewhat larger and converted a whole gram."

"If zpe and the past are basically the same and you drew some out, how far back in time would it go?" Breckon asked.

"That's a tough one. We don't know enough about this time-energy equivalence yet to say. For all we know, it could be quite noticeable."

Mel was getting fidgety. "All of that is fine. We need something to act on, and all of what you have said is way too thin to justify action. Give me some real world facts to work with."

"Well, how about this. Breckon sent me the drawings of the heat exchangers his friend Bart made. They could accommodate the entire three-hundred cubic feet per second of water that can be ported through the St. Anthony Falls Laboratory."

"Where'd you get that number?"

"They post it on their website."

"Oh. Okay."

"Then, think of this. If they generated thirty-five megawatts of energy, it would heat that flow of water only one degree Centigrade. If you get out your freshmen physics book you can verify that. They could be planning to produce a hundred megawatts of energy and nobody would be the wiser. If they ran that for a few hours, to say nothing of several days, it could possibly make enough disturbance to make Minneapolis 'all fall down' as that guy purportedly said."

"I've been thinking, that's probably the meaning of the conjecture," Breckon said. "Will it or won't it?"

"Dammit, you guys!" Mel said. "I can't go to a judge and get a search warrant on evidence like this. Imagine the peals of laughter if I told him we're afraid the city will be destroyed if a certain machine goes back in time a fraction of a second. Come on. I need something to work with. Where's the hubot, Breckon? We need him."

"He told me all he knows. With what Mueller said, we now know more than he does. I say we leave him where he is. Maybe something will happen or he'll remember something. Pressuring him won't help. You'll just rattle him." After a pause, Breckon continued, "My offer still stands. I could take Jason to see him where he is now. In a non-threatening environment, he might think of something. What do you say, Jason?"

"I guess, if it's all right with mom, it's okay with me. What Mr. Breckon said is true. Hua appeared very unsure of himself. Maybe it's an act, but I don't think so. From what I remember of him, pressuring him would make him fall apart."

Mel glowered. "See what you can do."

# — 30 —

Muan Yingqu was pleased with himself when he saw Breckon appear. Who was the kid with him, though? That was an odd turn of events. As they went down the ramps to the exit, Yingqu stayed close enough to keep the car in sight. He pulled up to the pay booth immediately after Breckon and flipped out a twenty dollar bill. At the reply to keep the change and raise the barricade there was a moment of hesitation, after which the bar lifted. On the street, the snow had been piling up. Where the streets had been wet and slushy when he had entered the ramp, they were now showing distinct tracks with snow forming rows between the lanes.

---

It took some convincing, but finally, Mrs. Finley agreed to let Jason go with Breckon and identify Hua Chen. They were leaving the parking garage at ten minutes after four.

"It'll be slow going," Breckon commented as they entered the flow of traffic. He got onto Third Avenue and, once over the Mississippi River, took East Hennepin. The plowing crews were making a valiant effort to keep up with the winter whims of mother nature by continuously clearing the streets and then doing it again, all the time leaving patches of salt mixed with sand at the intersections.

Jason sat in the passenger seat looking at his boots. "Mom said I had to bring boots, a heavy coat, cap, and mittens. She said she wasn't sure the people in Minneapolis had ever heard of central heating or snow-plows. She thinks this is really cow country. But, I'm glad I've got 'em."

"It could be you'll need them more than you imagine before the day's out. Did she also tell you to pack your forty-five automatic?"

Jason looked at Breckon not sure if he was joking. "I don't have . . ." Then he got it. "Well, no. Didn't bring any rocket propelled grenades either."

"Bummer."

Jason laughed. Then more seriously, "What did Carson mean about all the international incidents you've been involved in?"

"As they say, they're so classified that if I told you I'd have to kill you to keep you from leaking the information."

"Is this really another one?"

"Yeah. Guess it is."

"Why didn't you bring Hua Chen in to them? It seems that would have been the sensible thing to do."

"I guess your dad is part of the—what—the embassy staff in Beijing?"

"Assistant ambassador. The second man."

"So, he works for the government. That means any and all means will be used to keep him and by association you and your mom safe. That's where it ends. I don't work for the government and neither does Hua. If we end up dead that isn't at all high on their list of concerns. When the CIA gets involved, people die. I've seen it, so don't blubber on about how it isn't so."

"What did you mean I'd need my boots more than I imagine?"

"I'm not sure. It just seems like something is unraveling here, and it'll be a long day."

"Why did they refer to Hua as a hubot? He never mentioned anything to me about that."

"You've got a lot of questions, haven't you? I guess I could tell you about that without getting into trouble. Hua was the subject of an experiment in China where they are trying to make men into smart animals with no free will. This would make them perfect soldiers or something like that. If I get it right, they think the difference between a live animal and a dead one is that the live one has the DNA in each cell attached to the zero point field. You know, nobody has ever figured out what it is that makes a living thing alive. Anyway, the idea is to kill the brain and keep the man alive on life support so his human soul leaves the body. Then, they try to reconnect the brain cells to zpe in hopes of getting an animal. In the process, they turn on all the brain cells so he's really smart. Scientists think that normal people only use a small fraction of their brain cells. Hua does have total recall so it seems they got part of what they were after.

"He's trying to figure out if he's a man or an animal. I told him I was pretty sure he was a man. Now that I think about it, I'm certain he's human because he's asking questions. No animal ever asked a question."

"How do you know animals don't ask questions? Maybe they do, but we can't understand them."

"Animals don't ask questions because they aren't rational. They don't have intellects. They don't have spiritual souls. From that point of view, there's no difference between a mosquito and a grizzly bear. Neither of them ever looked with wonderment at a beautiful spring morning or was troubled by thoughts of what was right or wrong. You see, in this world of ours, man is totally unique. I think that's the reason why the environmentalists look at people as a pestilence on the earth. Unconsciously, they recognize that we are completely different from anything else on the planet, a foreign interloper, so to speak. The idea that we are the next step up from an ape is ridiculous."

"You mean to say, you think that we didn't get here by evolution?"

Ed chuckled. "Yeah, that's what I'm saying. We're not going very fast, and we have time to kill, so let's discuss it. Have you ever planted a garden?"

"I helped mom plant the flower beds a couple of times."

"Did flowers grow?"

"Of course."

"Would you ever think of planting small pebbles and expect flowers to grow?"

"That's silly. Of course not."

"That's right. It is silly. But, that's exactly what you are saying when you believe in evolution."

"Nah. Evolution takes millions or even billions of years."

"Aha. What you are saying is that something that is manifestly absurd in a short time is not only possible, but entirely expected in a very long time. This means that you believe in God and you believe in creation, only, what I call God, you call time."

"Ed, that's not fair. I'm only a kid. I can't answer an argument like that."

"Yeah. You're right. It is unfair. However, if you were a fifty-year-old scientist your response would be to say how stupid I was, and stalk off guffawing about the dumb ideas people have nowadays. There's nothing wrong with the logic of my argument. In addition, there's a philosophical principle that says the greater does not come from the lesser. Flowers don't come from pebbles. Life doesn't come from non-life, rational beings don't come from irrational ones.

"In this country, we have the strange debate about whether or not creationism, now called intelligent design, should be taught in our schools. To look at human beings with their complicated personalities of hopes, fears, loves, hates, ability to use a cell phone and all the rest, you must admit it is not reasonable that this all evolved from, that is, was created by, a muck pond. It is cleverly presented as possible if it took a long time and was accomplished in many small steps. The muck pond cannot make something greater than itself. We know this, we really do.

"Scientists say it all started with the big bang. In the ensuing fifteen billion years or so after the big bang, the energy sorted itself out into energy and matter and formed stars, galaxies, and all the rest that we see through telescopes. Then, very recently, recent relative to the fifteen billion years, that is, life sort of stumbled into existence by accident. It was simple at first, but evolved until it arrived at humans.

"However, the evidence shows that the entire universe was designed from the beginning *for* life. And, not just any life, but life as we know it. The chemical and physical properties of the carbon atom and the water molecule are so unique among all the other elements and molecules that there is no hope of there being life as we don't know it.

"This is all kind of beside the point, though. Instead of asking how it got here we should ask *why* is it here?"

Jason smiled. "You sound like a politician when you get going. This is fun, though. You know a lot of stuff. I think the reason it's all here is that we like looking at sunsets, walking in forests, and watching butterflies suck nectar from flowers. We have warm feelings for members of our family and friends. And, all of this makes us happy."

"It's more fundamental than that. What are your thoughts about French fries and cheeseburgers? Without plants and animals, we wouldn't have anything to eat. The final answer to the *why* is that everything exists for us. In other words, 'Why did God create the universe? Because He thought we might like it, not to ignore the fact that we also need it.' Think of it this way. If the universe started fifteen billion years ago, or was created complete with galaxies and fossil record one second before the first rational man came into existence doesn't matter because prior to the first rational mind, there was no *reason* for it to exist."

"Well, okay. Then, why does everybody believe in evolution? Why have I been taught that with such certainty all my life?"

"Keep asking the questions. That's the only way you'll learn. But, watch out. You're on your way to becoming a dangerous man."

"I don't care. I still wanna know."

"Good enough. In a sentence, the answer to why you are taught evolution with such tyrannical insistence is that it chops away religion and replaces it with atheism.

"Let me give you a brief outline of where that thinking comes from. Most people know that the idea of evolution caught on when Charles Darwin published a book titled *The Origin of Species*. They wouldn't know when it was published, but for the record, it was 1859. He didn't come up with the idea, but his book popularized it. What most people don't know is that Darwin and Karl Marx were contemporaries. Marx published the *Communist Manifesto* in 1848. Some years later in 1867 he published his work *Das Kapitol* that went into the economic aspects of communism. Besides the books, both men published tracts and articles in that period. These two men knew one another and corresponded. The reason these men with theses from seemingly dissimilar fields of study got together was that their ideas fit together like a hand in a glove. Communism is a totally atheistic system and people, if they were to adopt it, would still ask the question of where they came from. Darwin provided the answer, even if an unsatisfactory one. Marx desperately needed evolution."

"Okay. But, we're not communists. This isn't a communist country."

"Darwin helped the western societies, too, especially America. From the beginning of our country the reason people came here was to be free, free in many ways. Perhaps the freedom most of them wanted was the ability to keep the fruits of their labors. They wanted the chance to have a better material life for themselves and their families. Evolution relieves us of that twang of conscious that says we're greedy. With it, people can say that they're simply more fit, higher on the evolutionary scale, if you will, than those they take their money from. This leads to atheism and inextricably to communism. Of course, when it comes here it won't be called communism. They'll use some meaningless term like 'new beginning' or simply a common word like 'change.'"

"What got you working through all of this stuff? Almost nobody else knows it."

Breckon adjusted the heat control, and changed the intermittent period of the windshield wipers as if avoiding the question. Then he answered. "It's a funny thing about life. A few months ago after one of those ordeals

Carson mentioned, I had to get out of circulation for awhile. I was also kind of messed up because once again people had died, and while I might have been killed, I wasn't. By the way, people always seem to die in these things, so don't think this is some sort of game. My girl friend took me to a place to hole up. I discussed a lot of stuff with a man there. It has changed a lot of the way I look at life."

After awhile Jason said, "Getting back to Hua, I'd think he, of all people, would know if he were human. He can't be all that smart if he can't figure that out."

Ed nodded. "Remember that he went through the experiment and came out changed—a lot. This got him asking some fundamental questions about what it means to be human. This was especially so because he had surreptitiously learned that the purpose of the test was to make him *not* human.

"In a society like that in China, religion is not only suppressed, but the communist leaders find it necessary to actively murder God. Under those circumstances, people find life is easiest if they simply put all thoughts about the transcendent, life after death, etc., out of their minds. Hua had done that all of his life. After the test, he was forced to consider them. I don't doubt that at first he was trying to decide if he was an animal or a man. After awhile, though, his inquiry subtly changed from man or not man to what does it mean to be a man at all. That is, if I am human, what am I made of, does it matter if I'm honest? What happens when I die? Not too many people any place in the world spend much time thinking about these things."

By this time, they were turning into the Rosedale Shopping Center where Ed and Hua had been shot at a few evenings before. "You have him stashed at a shopping center?" Jason asked in surprise. "Bet he's got a lot of packages by now."

"I like the sense of humor," Ed replied.

Breckon drove into the huge parking lot, and stopped at a drop-off zone at one of the mall entrances. He motioned for Jason to get out as he did the same. At the rear of the car Breckon said, "This is only part way. We have to get a taxi here because I'm almost certain they put a tracking device on my car. It might be bugged too, that's why we're talking out here. I'll have to find a place to park. If you see a taxi drop off a shopper, grab it. Got any money?"

"Yeah. Mom gave me fifty dollars when we left home, just in case. Still have most of it."

"Okay. If the taxi driver won't wait give him a twenty until I get there."

Breckon found a place to park on the fringes of the silent herd of cars. On a hunch he opened his trunk, put on his boots, and traded his light coat for a parka. Walking toward the mall entrance, he saw a small hand waving over a taxi. When they were on their way Jason asked, "When do I get my money back?"

"Never. That's another thing about dealing with the CIA. They don't pay your expenses."

Breckon leaned over toward Jason and in a low voice said, "I have Hua staying at the same place I stayed. It's the rectory at a Catholic Church. The priest I talked to during my stay is really something else. I can only wonder what he and Hua have been discussing."

They made good time because they were going into the city and the evening rush-hour traffic was mostly headed out. Breckon had the taxi stop in the small parking lot between the church and the school. He told the cab driver to wait for them and the two of them trudged to the back door of the rectory.

As it happened, Fr. Aldrich answered the door. The two stepped in. Before they could say anything the priest said, "He's gone. Left this afternoon without saying a word. The last we saw him was at the noon meal."

"Had he said anything that might indicate where he was going?"

"No. He gave no indication he might leave. Come to think of it, after lunch when we were alone he said he was grateful I had gotten that thing he wore around his neck with the digital clock in it. But, he mentioned it wasn't working too well."

"You're absolutely sure he's gone."

"We searched rather thoroughly. Of course, this is a big plant and we didn't look in every possible place. His coat, boots, and gloves are gone, so we assume he left."

"Okay. I'll get back to you about paying for his keep. We have more important things to do now."

As they walked to the taxi Jason said. "On the plane he said the pendant that he wore came on every six hours. He said it measured something about his health, and that it made him feel good. He assumed that was so he would continue to wear it. If I remember the time right, it would have come on at two o'clock. If it stopped working, maybe he left to find help."

They got back in the cab and the driver was surprised to be told to return them to the point where he had picked them up. The fee was building up so Breckon let him swipe his credit card for payment.

———————

Yingqu was even more pleased with himself as he watched Breckon park his car and take a taxi at the shopping center. He was covering his trail, which meant he was headed to get the hubot. Leaving the parking lot, they took the same streets as the day before. It was falling into place. The hubot was at the church. He had to be.

Eventually the taxi pulled into a parking area between two large buildings. Yingqu pulled to the side of the street and eased forward so he could see the two figures get out of the taxi and go to the rear entrance to the rectory. The taxi remained. Surely, they were here to collect the hubot. He had his cell phone with the number two on it in his hand ready to call Kejian as soon as he saw them come out. Five minutes later both Breckon and the kid came out and got into the taxi. Nobody else. This had to be the place. What was wrong? He was tempted to rush into the building and demand the hubot at gunpoint. That would never work, though. He couldn't possibly get control of everyone in a three-story building before an alarm was sent to the police. There was nothing to do but stay on the tail of Breckon.

———————

On their way again, Breckon and Finley found the going was slow partly because the snow had started to build up, and partly because they were going the direction of the heavy traffic flow. The snow kept coming. "If that pendant he wore wasn't working, where would he go?" Jason asked.

Breckon leaned back in the seat and closed his eyes. "You're going to be glad you brought your boots."

"What does that mean?"

Breckon shook his head and pointed at the driver. "Later. By the way, you wouldn't have a cell phone, would you?"

"Of course. I should be calling my mom about now. She worries about me all the time."

"Yeah. I gathered that. But then, what mother doesn't? Okay. Call her and tell her we're caught in traffic and haven't gotten to the place where Hua is yet. Tell her you'll call again in a half hour."

"But, that's not honest. You expecting me to lie?"

Breckon shrugged. "You don't want her to worry, do you? And, this could turn nasty. Think I'll leave you at the shopping center where I left my car."

"No you don't. You're not going to abandon me. If you did you wouldn't have to worry about the CIA or any bad guys, my mom would kill you first."

"Yeah, suppose she would."

# — 31 —

It was the middle of the night in China. General Dong and Dr. Luan were conferring on the outcome of the recent test in Minneapolis. Both men were tired, but neither gave it a thought as history making events were in the offing in that far away backwater. Their mental picture of the location of St. Anthony Falls was similar to that of a small mining town in the far northern steppes of Siberia, located in the center of a vast lightly populated continent, hardly accessible.

General Dong had received the picture of Quan Peng as soon as Jian Niu had sent it. Niu was getting no response from China, not because everyone was sleeping, but because they were ignoring him. "He's a crafty one to have gotten that far," Gen. Dong was saying. "That he managed to identify Shan Jin and assume his identity is nothing short of phenomenal. We'll have to be careful of that hubot program. No telling what could happen if a few of them got loose in China."

"Yes," Dr. Luan broke in. "About the test. If HB-23 were the hubot on site, we'd know exactly what to expect because I had the opportunity to download his pendant many times. HB-27 is more of an unknown. I'm concerned that he, being brought up on the streets, had the ability to survive by improvisation before we did anything to him, and that none of those skills were lost in the experiment. The cognitive remapping did not affect him as much as it did twenty-three. This means he might be hard to control."

"Are you saying he won't produce a good test?"

"He'll do at least as well as Shan Jin would have done. It's too bad we can't cut off a finger a few seconds before the test. That would prove the conjecture in short order."

"How about if he's angry or upset? That would elevate his level of monoamine oxidase, wouldn't it? We've discussed that effect on hubots several times."

"Yes. If he were angry, it would definitely help. The few times I had a chance to download data from HB-27s pendant, it had much more variation than the other one, though on average it was lower. Dr. Hongi, especially, seemed to elevate his energy field." Dr. Lung scoffed. "Anybody getting near Hongi would have his energy field, to say nothing of his blood pressure, elevated. He's such an ass."

With that, General Dong left Dr. Lung to his work. The mention of monoamine oxidase reminded Luan of what he had learned from watching the levels of that chemical in the hubots. Monoamine oxidase caused the release of dopamine and norepinephrine. These drugs were secreted into the blood stream when a person experienced fear or terror. This fear was not to be confused with the jitters a person experienced before giving a presentation in front of a room full of people. It was the rush experienced when confronted with the sudden threat of immediate death. This was the body's response to pending damage to make it ready to promote healing. It was the fight-flight response—do you stay and fight the danger, or fly from it. During the testing of the hubots, Luan knew the sadistic bent of Dr. Fei Hongi, and that he was trying to terrorize his subjects into revealing they were not obedient. Obedience was not important to Luan, rather their response to terror. Unintentionally, Hongi's methods served the ends of both men.

His studies had shown that the human aura was immensely strengthened when dopamine and norepinephrine were released into the system in large amounts. The response measured by the pendants proved this to be even more intense in hubots.

Dr. Lung set these thoughts aside as he continued analyzing the data from the two o'clock test. The team in Minneapolis knew there was a satellite link from the control room to China. When each test was completed, the team encoded and transmitted the data to the lab of Dr. Luan. This would insure no data was lost in the event of a disaster on the premises of the test. The team did not know that the data transmission would happen with or without their intervention. More to the point, all of their activities dealing with the adjustment and alignment of parameters and preparation for tests were constantly being monitored to Luan.

Luan saw that after the aborted two o'clock test, the team readjusted the variables as needed and left the system running slightly below the point of positive power generation the same as they had done in the morning. The system remained steady.

Shortly thereafter, Lu received a call from Dr. Luan who inquired as to the status of the tests. Lu gave a commentary to complement the data files sent to China including details about how Jian Niu was being most difficult in dealing with the umpire. Nothing was mentioned about the two keystone devices, even though Luan could tell from the data that Peng had used the other man's pendant. This small act of deceit did not surprise Luan because he suspected Lu was thinking it was a case of a theorist back in an office not having all the answers.

Lu informed Luan that after a thorough review of the two o'clock test data, they expected to have a clean start of the test at eight o'clock. Luan suggested that Lu might try advancing the settings slightly over the edge to positive power generation. If it stabilized there, it would be proof of a successful start at the next opportunity. They had done this for brief periods before, but were concerned about causing electrical disturbances in other areas of the building. Considering the hour, it was an acceptable risk.

After the call terminated, Luan observed that Lu did as he had suggested. After the adjustment, it was putting out a small steady amount of positive power. Lu was a good man, Luan thought, though a little egotistical. He knew that about this time Lu was begrudgingly admitting it had been a good idea.

---

After the two o'clock test, Peng was never alone. Even when going to the men's room one of the others happened to need the use of the facility at the same time. Jian Niu was seldom around the lab. It was as if Niu were leaving the control of Peng to the team since he was more important to their purposes than Niu's.

Niu spent most of the time in his office with the door closed. Repeatedly he called Beijing trying every number he had. To his consternation, everybody seemed to have taken this night to leave work early and come in late in the morning. He had just hung up the phone after another frustrating attempt to make contact with the project when a notice appeared on his computer screen announcing that he had received an email. Immediately opening it, he saw it was from the Falls Project office. In Beijing, the tests were known by this name. Clicking on the attachment, he had a photograph of Shan Jin, the umpire, on the screen. It was decidedly *not* a photo of the man presenting himself as same.

Vindication! He now had proof the man calling himself Shan Jin was an imposter. What action could he take, though? It would not do to call the local police and have the man arrested. That could lead to all kinds of entanglements. The matter had to be handled among themselves. More importantly, the imposter knew about the test so who could he be? Heng Lu wouldn't care who the man was as long as he had the keystone that would make the test proceed.

Now that he thought of it, what did it mean that an imposter had the keystone device, in fact two of them? It was simple. He'd bring his evidence to Heng Lu and the three of them would have a sit-down in this office while the man presenting himself as the umpire explained who he was. Then, he sat back in his chair. It wouldn't work. Lu would suspect it was a trick, a real nasty act-of-last-resort trick, to derail the test by the faction that sought to prove the conjecture was false. The explanation of why the two o'clock test failed, and his possession of the keystone devices was physical evidence that was almost impossible to overcome.

At a light knock on his door he said, "Yes."

It was opened and Wu Zheng stuck his head in. "We ordered some food for before the eight o'clock test. It has arrived if you wish to join us."

"Where is our umpire now?"

"Don't worry. He's in the restroom, and I've checked. There's only one way out, and that's the door to this hall." Niu's office was ten feet down the hall and across from the men's room.

Niu nodded and said, "Give me a second. Before you go back down notify me and I'll go with you." The door closed and immediately Niu began printing a color copy of the photo.

The phone rang. Niu snatched it up before the first ring ended.

"Yes," he said a little too tersely.

"Is this Jian Niu?"

"Yes, it is." Niu thought he recognized the voice.

"This is General Dong. The messages you sent to the Falls Project office have been forwarded to me including the photo of the man you attached. This leaves us in a unique position to . . . "

There was a knock at the door. "I don't know what you are saying. For the moment, I have to contend with the situation here. The umpire has not one, but two, keystone devices. How do you explain that?"

"Yes. I would guess he would have two devices. That is what I must talk to you about . . . " Another more determined knock at the door.

"General," he said the title with anything but respect, "I have other things to tend to. I will call you back shortly."

"Be careful of that man . . . "

"Yes. Yes. Back to you in a few minutes."

The photo had finished printing when there was a third summons from the door. Niu grabbed the sheet of paper from the printer and went to the door. They were both standing there when he opened it. Niu let the page with the photo bend over his hand so part of a man's face was visible. Looking right at Peng he said with a hint of humor in his voice, "Now, Mr. ah . . . Shan Jin, is it? Come into my office and let us discuss . . ."

---

Peng was drying his hands in the men's room and was well aware of the time in Beijing. At any moment, he was expecting to have Niu challenge his identity. He gave a quick glance around the room and saw there was no other exit. As he stepped into the hallway, he was relieved to see only Zheng. They started down the hallway, and stopped partway where Zheng knocked on an office door. It was fitted with a lock like those on the control room. He knocked again. This must be Niu's office. A third time he knocked. The door opened. He saw the man and the photo in his hand. The sneer in the voice as Niu spoke settled it. Peng lunged out and connected his fist with the man's face who fell back into the office. Next, he swung a left to Zheng's abdomen followed with a right to the jaw. Zheng bounced off the wall and with a grasp on the upper arm Peng threw that man into the office, too. Glancing both ways, the hall was deserted. Peng stepped over the unconscious men into the office. He grabbed a heavy stapler from the desk, and with a solid blow, he struck the knob on the special door lock used to open it from the inside. In the hall again, looking for anyone who might be about, he found himself alone. He eased the door closed, but it refused to move the final inch to latch. Bracing his knee against the doorjamb immediately beside the knob, he forced it. A test revealed it was solidly jammed.

Fifteen feet down the hall to the right he was in a large room with a dozen desks in it. One against the windows on the left was occupied. He walked to it. The young man turned at the sound of his approach. Peng smiled and a second later smashed him in the face with his fist. He rolled the limp unconscious man under the desk and moved the chair up against him. At the next desk, he examined the window. It was not the type one could open. With his elbow, he broke the lower pane. With a heavy coffee mug from the desk, he broke the shards of glass still adhering to the frame. Sticking his head out he saw a four-foot wide passage between the building and a low stone wall. It was six feet down to the snow accumulated behind the wall. Immediately past the wall was the forty-foot wide channel of water flowing to his right into the power plant. Beyond the channel in front of him was the parking lot.

Putting the palm of one hand on the desk, he grasped the bottom of the window frame with the other and worked himself out. He dropped into a foot of snow. He instantly felt the cold on his shins. To the north, the space between the building and the wall where he stood led to the end of the bridge that crossed the water channel. That was the direct way out. He had taken two steps in that direction when he caught sight of someone leaving the building. Peng stopped in mid-stride to avoid having his movement attract attention. Slowly he lowered himself below the margin of the wall to the level of his eyes. He watched as the individual walked to a car in the lot. Peng reversed his direction not wanting to be seen by someone who could summon the police before he could reach and silence him.

The place where he had broken the window was only twenty feet from the southeast corner of the building. Once there, the four-foot wall made a right angle to join the building. It was constructed of rough slabs of stone. The wall was thicker at the bottom so he could climb with some ease by stepping from one protruding slab to another. On top, he had to duck under an electrical cable as he came to a railing. To his left was the maw where the torrent of water fell into the power generating turbines deep within the building. Over the railing, he could discern a walkway behind a five-foot high steel beam with a maintenance trolley on it that ran along the inlet to the power plant.

The pathway was on the roof of the power plant building. The entire area was flooded with security lights which was good and bad. It was light enough for him to see where he should go, but likewise he might be seen by anyone who happened to glance his way. At the east side of the power plant inlet he paused not knowing how to proceed. After a moment, he saw a short stair covered with snow going to the left. Everything he touched was iron covered with snow and by now his fingers were getting numb. He thought of the warm clothing in his SUV and resolved to get there as fast as he could.

Part way down the steps he caught the heel of the left shoe on the step. It didn't register at first, but the next time he put his weight on that foot it did. The shoe had slipped off his numb foot. He had no choice but to sit in the snow on a step, tap the shoe on the railing to dislodge the packed in snow, replace it and redo the lace. This was difficult since his fingers were not working as well as they should. Trying the lace for the third time with fingers lacking feeling, he caught the sight of flashing lights out of the corner of his eye. A police car was coming down the driveway to the lab. Someone from inside the building had heard him break the window or otherwise discover his point of egress and called in the alarm.

Finally, managing some knots in the shoe lace he looked up and surveyed the area. In the direction of the parking lot was an eight-foot high chain-link fence. The fence proceeded to some trees to his right and made a corner. Keeping low, he moved to his right as he examined the fence. Most of it had three strands of barbed wire along the top. However, a short distance after the fence made the jog to the south there was no barbed wire, and snow had been pushed up against it to clear a road into the area behind the power plant. In addition, to add reinforcement to the corner, an extra horizontal galvanized pipe was inserted half way up. Since the fence was intended to keep people out, the extra pipe was on his side. It would make a convenient step. If that weren't enough, the fence in this short area was covered with vines.

As the police car was pulling to a stop by the gate into the lab, Peng was launching himself over the fence. In his good physical condition, the eight-foot drop on the far side was done with ease, though the loss of most of the feeling in his feet caused him to roll in the snow. From there, he scrambled down a steep wooded and brushy slope to the bottom of a draw. Picking himself up he made his way across a small steam strewn with rocks. The stones were slippery due to the snow and his leather soled shoes. He nearly fell twice. Across, he climbed an eight-foot bank and was at a pathway. To his left, this led to steps which brought him up to Main Street a hundred feet from the driveway to the St. Anthony Falls Lab.

Walking to the corner, he looked in the direction of his vehicle to see a second police car stopping not ten feet from it. That avenue of escape was blocked. He considered going to the tavern a half block away, then discarded the idea. If the police talked to the man he had knocked unconscious, and he described him, they'd soon connect him to the test project. Niu would be all too happy to provide a description of him, maybe even a picture. With that information, the police would scour the nearby establishments. If someone thought to mention his SUV, they'd also find Shan Jin's body. All of this went through his mind in a flash.

Though feeling the cold, the adrenaline flow was making him less encumbered by it than he had been. As he was brushing himself off, he looked up the hill. With much foreboding, he realized it would have to be the meth lab, no other way about it.

---

Seng Kejian had left his post in the parking lot twenty minutes before. He hoped he had not missed anything, but there was nothing he could do about it. He had to use a men's room and get something to eat. He had gone to Aster's café on Main Street. It was only a couple of blocks from the lab. Upon his return, he slowed as he approached the drive into the parking lot. A figure was standing on the opposite corner in the falling snow brushing snow off himself. What was the point of that, he thought. Then it occurred to him. The size was right, and he was wearing a suit. Kejian was guarding against seeing what he wanted to see. The mind could play tricks after a whole day of watching and waiting and not finding his man. That, and looking through a wet windshield with the wipers swishing back and forth, made him cautious. The black hair, shape of the head, and finally the face made his recognition of Quan Peng almost certain.

Without realizing it, he had come to a stop. Peng had turned as if to proceed down the drive to the parking lot, but remained where he was. Kejian saw this as his chance, so why not get out and force him at gunpoint into the car. Peng remained motionless as if undecided what to do. Glancing the direction Peng was looking, Kejian saw the flashing police car lights and understood the cause of Peng's uncertainty. At that moment the sound of a car's horn behind him cause him to jerk spastically so intent was he on the situation. The realization dawned on Kejian that he was blocking traffic.

Suddenly, as if decided on a course of action, Peng looked across Main Street and started in that direction. Kejian lowered the driver's side window to get an unobstructed view. A second sustained beep from the car behind Kejian caused Peng to stop halfway across the street and look in the direction of the sound. Kejian knew Peng had never met him so he would make no connection even if he had clearly seen his face, though, with the open window he had gotten a good look at him.

Kejian sped away as fast as he could. At the first opening between oncoming cars, he cramped the steering wheel to the left bringing him crosswise in the opposite lane. Backing, he managed to turn around. He ran the two windows down on the passenger side since they were covered with melting snow, too. As he came to the intersection he slowed and could see the dark figure of Peng going up the hill. Pulling a hard right he started up the hill in the oncoming traffic lane that was, at that moment, thankfully, free of traffic. His front driving wheels lost traction so he proceeded no further. It was far enough, though, because he saw Peng enter a building two-thirds of the way to the next street. Having spent a lot of time watching people as part of his job, Kejian noted that he did it with purpose. There was no hesitation as he seemed to know the door would be unlocked. That was strange, he thought. When Peng left the street corner, he knew where he was going.

His traffic situation was precarious and the visibility was bad. With police cars only a block away down the hill, even the slightest accident would have them on the scene in seconds. Carefully he backed and turned until he was headed down hill toward Main Street. He stopped at the stop sign at Main. He went left and at the first chance left again. At Second Street he took another left to circle around and see what type of establishment Peng had entered. Coming to where the building fronted on Second Street, he was surprised to see it was an old run down structure with a "For Lease" sign on the front. For whatever reason, Peng knew that was a place where he could get out of the cold, and out of sight. Maneuvering around, Kejian parked in a position where he could see both the side of the building where Peng entered and that on Second Street.

He picked up the phone labeled number two and punched the speed dial for Yingqu. It was answered almost immediately with, "Yeah."

"I know where our first man is, but I'll need your help. You know where I am. How long for you to get here?"

---

Yingqu, still following the taxi with Breckon in it, had taken the Fairview exit from Highway 36. "I don't know. I'll have to look at a map. I'm following my charge who went to that same place again. This time he left his car in a shopping center parking lot and took a taxi. Still no sign of man number two. We are now back at the place where he left his car."

"This is certain. We must concentrate our efforts here. I am one block up the hill opposite the entrance to the place we know about. Look at that map I gave you and you'll see what I mean."

"It may take me awhile because traffic is slow and congested in the snow."

"If I'm not where I said, it means I had to do something on my own. I'll call you on three if I have to move."

The call ended with no courtesies, but that was to be expected in this business. Yet, Yingqu was taken again by the change in demeanor of the man. Could being out of China such a short time bring about the noticeable transformation? He knew it had been surprisingly easy for him to make the adjustment. Kejian was acting almost like a human being. It was unsettling.

---

Quan Peng turned his head in response to the blaring of a car horn on his right as he crossed Main Street. The sound was in response to a car blocking traffic on Main Street at the driveway entrance to the lab on the river. He saw the driver of the offending car. The face did not register as belonging to anyone he knew. It was Asian, most likely Chinese, with deep-set dark eyes. Continuing across, his thoughts raced to connect the situation. It was not expected that a car with a Chinese driver would be stopped with his window open holding up traffic at that exact spot. He thought he might be over reacting, but the man seemed intent on him. What could be the reason for that? As far as he could tell, he had been informed of all of the members of the team working on the experiment. Looking to his right the car was now continuing down Main to the south.

Walking up the hill his mind reverted to the situation he'd face in the meth lab. This was definitely not to his liking, other than his options were severely limited inasmuch as he was freezing to death. The story he had arranged in his mind seemed plausible enough to anyone interested in a plausible explanation. It was impossible to know what they could have learned about him in his absence. And worse than that, the workings of minds without information could result in conclusions far worse than the facts, if known, would warrant.

Peng would enter the meth lab by the door on Third Avenue that he knew was rarely locked. He put his hand on the latch of the door that opened inward. Turning his body slightly as he entered he looked back the way he had come without making it obvious that was what he was doing. He was not being followed by anyone on foot, but there was that same car from the intersection caught in snow in the wrong lane. It had not been his imagination, the driver had been intent on him.

Once inside the odors hit him. If he hadn't been so cold, he would have gone any place but here. Here it was warm, even overly warm, but it felt good since his clothing was soaked. The melting snow had scavenged his body heat faster than he had thought possible. There was no one in sight, though he heard rustling and scraping noises from the shadows deeper in the building. It was either rats or more likely Jorg Davis rooting through his inventory collecting up chemicals for the evening's cook. A short distance in from the street Davis's office was on the left. The door was ajar. Pushing it open revealed the room lacked the presence of anything human, or partially so, had it been Jorg. Alone, he wiped his head, face, and hands on a jacket he found hanging on a nail.

He was startled by the voice behind him, though he thought he didn't show it. "Well, look what the cat dragged in?" Peng turned to face Davis. "And look at the gentlemanly attire. Been out rubbing elbows with the finer set, I see. The boss is in a snit looking for you. You had better have a good story to account for why you just up and vanished. In fact, an extremely good one, because he's getting together a hit team to take you out."

Peng knew his disappearance would cause some dissatisfaction, but this level of ire was not expected, even in a sordid business like this.

"Why's he so upset? I've been out getting information on what's going on with the Chinese in that place down the hill."

"That's what you say. He sees it differently. Doesn't matter much to me who you are or what you've been doing. Stay put and I'll let him know you're here." Jorg grabbed an old wrench and banged twice on a pipe. "That tells him I've got something to tell him. If I hit it three times, it means it's an emergency. I saved you from the emergency response. You owe me."

The desk was up against the wall on the left as one entered the office leaving a space between it and the far wall so the occupant of the swivel chair faced the door. Peng plunked down in the desk chair and Davis left the room to go about his business. How ever they got the heat for the building, it must have been included with the rent because they didn't spare it. He adjusted his position so the blast from a heater up in the corner of the room was aimed directly on him. By the time he dried out he'd be suffocating, but for the moment, it was pure heaven. He took off his shoes and socks wringing the water out of the latter.

From Jorg's remark, it seemed that in some way they knew he had met with the people working on the test. Was the Chinese man in the car working for this bunch of rabble? Somehow, that didn't fit. Putting those thoughts aside, he worked on his options. It would be easy to kill Jorg. From there, he might find a weapon and if he were lucky, and there weren't too many of them, he could kill them all. A hit team would have guns though, and finding one lying about for himself was unlikely. All in all, this wouldn't be a bad place to stay out of sight for awhile. He knew they had food around since, it being an illegal operation, they couldn't be seen coming and going for meals three times a day. Setting back, he put his cold feet up on the desk in the stream of warm air, and feeling comfortable, dosed off.

# — 32 —

Jian Niu was the first to regain consciousness. As he did, his first sensation was a throbbing pain in his left cheek. Cautiously opening his eyes, the scene was unintelligible. Why was he looking at the underside of a small desk drawer that jerked as it tried unsuccessfully to rotate? He closed his eyes as his hand, of its own accord, touched his cheek. Ouch! That sent a rush of adrenaline into his blood stream. His thoughts collected and he remembered being punched by Quan Peng. Anger rose as he determined to settle the score with that disgusting peon. Thus energized, he began to sit up. His head met the underside of the work surface causing him to fall back with yet another score to settle. More cautiously, he tried again and managed to get into a sitting position. His surroundings slowly relented in their persistent effort to rotate.

Beside him, Wu Zheng moaned. Niu reached up to the work surface for a half cup of cold coffee and threw it in Zheng's face. Zheng jerked, rolled over, and got up on his hands and knees swinging his head from side to side. "Stay away from that guy's fists. Boy, he can hit hard." Zheng got up far enough to slump into the desk chair. As his head cleared, the situation began to fall into place. "Your abusive attitude toward Shan Jin finally caused him to lash out. You are doing everything you can to cause the test to fail! If he isn't the umpire, why did he have the keystone device, in fact two of them?"

"General Jia Dong has the answer to that," Niu retorted. "He called as you were waiting for me in the hall. He said to be careful of the man. But, I had only seconds before received information proving the man was an impostor. I was intent on confronting him with it and ignored the warning." Niu still sitting on the floor looked around the room. "I had that photo in my hand as I opened the door," he said pointed to a slightly crumpled paper near the wall. "He must have seen it and realized I was on to him."

Zheng, still seated, rolled the chair over toward the wall and picked up the picture.

"You agree, that's not the man here as the umpire," Niu said.

"I agree, this is not a picture of the man calling himself Shan Jin. So what? You contacted Beijing requesting a photo of the umpire, didn't you? One of your comrades sent you this as a diversion, as a trick. You want to twist things to say Shan Jin is an impostor. If he is not who he says he is, why is he here, and most of all, why does he have the keystone devices?"

Niu pulled himself to his feet and with a snap of his hand ordered Zheng out of his chair. Zheng moved and went to the door. It wouldn't open. "Our friend jammed the door."

"Find something to pound on the lock. Do something while I make a call to the General." The haughty attitude, hardly beneath the surface, was evident in Niu's voice.

"First, call the control room and have someone come up to help with the door. We must locate Shan Jin. We will need him and the keystone device."

Niu made the call to the test room and then made the call to Beijing. A minute later, "Dong? Jian Niu here. I am ready to discuss the imposter you sent us."

There was an audible rush of air as a breath quickly being drawn in. General Dong was clearly irritated by Niu's refusal to use his rank when addressing him. This gave Niu satisfaction since Dong was also from the lower classes who had worked himself up to a position which, in Niu's opinion, he was ill suited to handle.

"Where is the man now?"

Niu pursed his lips. He would have to ask that one question. "Ah, we don't know." Immediately, Niu realized he had left hesitation in his voice.

General Dong noticed it immediately. "Do I sense you ignored my warning? What happened? Don't hold out on me. Not only are you in danger, but you could smear the reputation of all of China if you are not forthcoming with the real situation. There are things about your present situation that are unknown to you. What happened?"

Regardless of his contempt for the people with which he had to deal, Niu knew he had to safeguard the reputation of China or he would be made a pariah. "Obviously, he learned, or possibly only suspected, that his real identity had become known. From his clearly rough demeanor," he restrained himself from using the word underclass to describe the man, "he had to suspect that someone would notice and want to verify his identity. A few minuets ago when Wu Zheng and I were talking to him at the door of my office, he suddenly took it into his head to knock us both unconscious. We have just now sufficiently recovered to the point of making this call. I am waiting for an explanation."

---

If expressions could be seen over the phone, Niu would have seen a smile on the general's face, though his voice did not portray it. "As I was about to say before you terminated our last call, that man, as you have surmised, is not the umpire that was delegated to you. I understand the project transmitted a photo of the real umpire to you, though at this time it would seem to be a moot point. That man is undoubtedly dead. The gentleman posing as the umpire leaves us in a unique situation."

General Jia Dong had fought his way through the superior attitudes of the ruling class his entire professional life. The elite cared little about the Chinese people knowing there would always be more than enough slaves to provide them with wealth and power. However, with the present situation, he felt he had the means to deal a blow to them at their own hand. In the long run it wouldn't change anything, but it would cause some immediate pain while putting into his possession the tool he sought for his own ambitions.

In this strange world, opportunities came in many forms. In fact, the Chinese had a proverb that said there were no such things as crises, only difficult opportunities. He knew going into this project there was a chance of the conjecture being false, though, Dr. Luan seemed totally convinced it was true. After all, the tests now of concern were half funded by military budgets because they were betting the conjecture was true and it could be used as a weapon. The other half was financed by the civilian bureaucrats who expected the conjecture to be false and they could proceed to build power plants. Whatever the case, the important thing was who would be in charge of zero point development from the beginning. That meant it was vital for him to at least make it appear the conjecture was true. Moreover, the more incontrovertible the proof the better it would be for him.

He knew that Niu was too conceited to think he could be wrong, so a decisive test was unimportant to him as long as those opposing his view could be silenced. That Niu thought it would take days of running before the result would be conclusively shown, was to Dong's advantage. Dr. Luan had come up with theoretical proof that it would be possible to get the desired result in only minutes of running if the test were handled somewhat differently than originally planned. In that case, the ruling class would be short one member, namely this scumbag, Jian Niu.

For the present, Niu had to be placated. General Dong began, "At the same time pioneering work was being done on the extraction of zero point energy for useful purposes, work was progressing on understanding what it was that caused a living thing to be alive. The latter work led to the study of what is called the human energy field. Are you familiar with that?"

"Yes. I keep up with the work of my fellow scientists."

"Very well. A breakthrough was made by a clever scientist that permitted the human energy field to be used to assist in the zpe endeavor. This was so unexpected that it was covered with a heavy blanket to security. Passing over a lot of details, let me say that the keystone device substantially magnifies the energy field of the wearer, to whom it is specially tuned. This is used to push the ceramic cylinder into self-sustaining positive power generation. The point that concerns us now is controversial, and therefore the most classified. Is that understood?"

Niu suspected he already knew what Dong was about to say. This was another case of someone from the lower class wanting to make himself look important. However, he decided to hear him out. "Yes, I understand."

"Good. In the first place, it is almost certain that the man posing as Shan Jin, whose name, by the way, is Quan Peng, killed Jin and took his keystone. However, it probably doesn't matter because Shan Jin was not, as we might say, completely tuned to the device he carried. His device would have been able to make the cylinder produce power as planned. However, it may not have been at a level high enough to prove or disprove the conjecture. When someone is properly and completely tuned to his device it affects him in other ways. One thing we have learned is they become highly resourceful. We expected to deliver Peng to the site for the test. Before we could do that, he escaped from us, and completely on his own, traveled halfway around the world to show up at the site of the test. He can handle almost any difficulty he encounters. Another one escaped, too, and may show up. That gives you a redundancy, so to speak, because you only need one.

"It is important for you to know that we suspect that it will cost Peng his life to start the test. Some people might get a little squeamish about that so if he dies, it must be handled as an unfortunate accident. Don't forget, though, you absolutely need Quan Peng and his keystone device to properly conduct the test. Is all of this clear?"

There was a pause. Niu began to realize how little he knew about what was really going on. It angered him, but he knew this was not the time nor the place to handle that issue. He answered, "Yes."

"Also, there is no need to go looking for him. If he wants to stay hidden, you won't find him." Dong gritted his teeth, as he dearly wanted to say Niu would not be smart enough to find him. "Don't worry, though. He will be drawn to the apparatus as the time of the next test approaches. His keystone works on his energy field to cause him to have a need to be there."

Now, General Dong took a measured risk to get payback on Niu. He knew how Quan Peng could not tolerate being belittled or put down. A few days of that from Dr. Hongi at the Medical Institute and he escaped leaving a trail of wrath in his wake. "When he shows up at the test be certain that you handle him firmly. He may be in something of an agitated state, or possibly elated, that the test is about to start. Either way, he must not be allowed to take the initiative in the slightest thing. Understood?"

"Yes."

"If these few things are observed, I'm sure the test will start without incident, the conjecture will be settled, and you can get back to Beijing, to civilization." General Dong ended the call.

During Niu's call, Ju Feng came up from the control room. With him in the hallway and Zheng inside, they worked at the door latch. Finally with their combined strength, they managed to break the strike of the lock out of the doorjamb. At the sound of the crash, Niu saw the door open. To the men he said, "See if you can find our umpire."

When he was alone he chanced to glance out the window to see flashing police car lights in the parking lot. That man, what had the general called him, Quan Peng, had likely hit someone else in his escape which led to having the police summoned. As head of the project, he had to go out there and try to settle things down. A promise to compensate for injury or damage usually handled situations like this.

Hua Chen remembered the route to Cindy Thomas's apartment building and had no trouble finding his way to it. He made good time being glad to be out and getting exercise. Arriving a little after five o'clock, he called her apartment from the entry the way he had seen Breckon do it. After the second attempt with no answer, he went outside again. In China, there were always so many people about that he would have had no problem standing in the entry, not so here. He walked away from the building not wanting to be seen as loitering.

It was a little after six o'clock before Chen saw someone get out of a car that looked like it might be the right woman. Walking fast, he was a hundred feet away by the time she reached the door.

"Cindy Thomas," he called.

She immediately stopped and turned satisfying him he had been correct. "I am Hua Chen, friend for Ed Breckon, who you know, yes?" As he got closer he said, "Ed said you are pretty. He is right. I need from you some help. Time is short until maybe I will die. You looking cold. We go into entry where it is warm. Okay?"

Cindy nodded. She knew she should have been expecting something like this. When they were inside she asked, "Where is Ed? Why didn't you call him? Why come to me?"

Hua had not thought that he might have to tell this woman that Breckon could be dead. He sensed more than having a conscious thought that it would be counter to his mission to say anything about that.

"Ed said he would come to get me at the church place today. At two o'clock, it was time for my pendant to come on. Here, I show you." He pulled on the bead chain and fished out the device. "This comes on to help me out, every six hours. At two, no help. Ed lives that way," he said pointing. "You are closer. I walked to here. There is a place I must go to get help with this," he said holding up the chain with the pendant swinging on it. "Must be there at eight o'clock. You help me find where place is. I go there alone. You don't come. You help me, please?"

It had all come so suddenly Cindy didn't know what to do but knew she had do decide. "Aren't you the guy who doesn't know if he's human or not?"

"Ed told you of me. I see that is true. Time to search for answer is soon gone. I must get to the place. You help. Please?"

She knew it was something she shouldn't do but gave in against her best instincts. "Come on. I have a street map in my apartment."

Cindy opened her cell phone and pressed a speed dial number while Hua, seated at the little dinning table, scanned every inch of the map committing it to memory. "Must go to St. Anthony Falls Laboratory. Your map does not list it. Bart said the lab was part of the University of Minnesota."

When Ed didn't answer, she put some water on to heat for tea.

"You have book of telephone numbers, and addresses?"

"Sure." She pulled the phone book out of a small closet in the kitchen. "Look for government offices, and State of Minnesota, University of Minnesota."

Seconds later, "Not have laboratory shown there. Not University, too."

Cindy came over and flipped to the business listings. "That's strange. The U of M is listed under businesses. For all the tax money it gets, you'd think it would be part of the government. Let's see." She started to methodically look down the full page listing of departments."

"No lab in list," Hua said as he turned the page for the rest of the U of M numbers. "Not here either."

"What? You read all of that as fast as you can turn the page?"

"Yes. Of course. I am a hubot. Remember it too. Ed didn't say?"

"Wait a minute? Let me see." She pulled the book away and turned back to the full page of listings. "What's the address and phone number of the Financial Aid Office."

Instantly the correct response.

"That's amazing."

"Must find lab." He buried his head in his hands. "What to do?"

"Let's try the computer." Cindy went to the corner of the living room where she had her office and booted it up. The kettle on the stove started to whistle. "You want some tea?"

"Yes. That is good. Thank you."

With a cup of tea served she went on line and entered the lab in the search engine. "Here it is."

Hua was behind her in a second. "I see address now, and how it is on a small island in a river. From map you have, I can find it. Memorized map too, you understand?"

"Yeah. I guess. Suppose if you can glance at a phone book page and memorize it, you can do the same with a street map."

"I go now. Must get there before time gets to eight o'clock." Suddenly he stopped still, almost like being frozen in place. When he moved again, it was to slowly slump down in a living room chair.

Cindy was alarmed that he might be dying sooner than he had expected. "Hua. What's wrong? Are you dying?"

He shook his head slowly. "It is seven kilometers to the lab, same about as to here from the church building. Even if I am running it is too far." Pausing his complexion turned ashen. "Very afraid now. Expect dying will come and not know if hubot has soul. From what Father Aldrich said, and reading his books, it is important more than before to know."

"Why? What happened at the rectory?"

"Must know. Must know."

"Okay. I'll take you. My car isn't very big, but it has all-wheel drive. No arguments. Let's go." She put on her coat and flipped the scarf around her collar. Hua was still sitting. "Come on! Do you want me to go to the lab without you? I am going, so you might as well come along."

Hua got up. "You are woman, what is word . . . disputatious, irascible, captious, pugnacious, truculent. No. I think I use feisty. Yes. That is it. That is why Ed likes you so much, I think."

"You might as well leave Ed out of this. He could be dead for all I know."

Hua stared at Cindy wondering if she knew or only suspected. "What are you looking at? He never calls me unless he needs something. Come on. Let's go."

She knew if they could get on Highway 36 headed west, traffic would be moving so which street should she take to get to it, Snelling, or Fairview? She decided on Fairview. Not good. It was moving but at a snail's pace. The clock on the dashboard showed seven-eighteen.

---

Ed Breckon and Jason Finley rode in silence. The traffic actually moved better than one would have expected. On Highway 36, they headed west. Going toward the city, traffic was relatively light and moving at close to the posted speed limit.

They took the exit for Fairview Avenue and went right. It was getting harder to get around. Traffic was heavy and the snow was coming in earnest. The snowplows were mixed in with the traffic and could only plod along with everyone else. When they went through an intersection they left the road just ploughed clear, but it left a windrow of snow across the streets that ran at right angles to it. Most drivers were not smart enough to leave some space between where they stopped for the traffic light and the row of snow so they could not get up speed before they hit it when it was their turn to go. This caused much spinning of wheels, which melted snow on the pavement, which in turn immediately froze leaving an icy spot. Frequently, only one or two cars made it through the intersection for each cycle of the lights producing near gridlock.

In the area where Breckon had left his car there were two police cars with lights flashing so he had the driver make a left on County Road B2. Breckon made an excuse that he had to pick up something in the shopping center across Fairview from the mall and it would save some steps to be dropped off there.

After the taxi was gone Jason asked, "Did you forget where you left your car?"

"No. Did you see those flashing lights in the parking lot across the street? That's where I parked. As I suspected, those CIA guys tracked my car and when it stopped at the mall they had the local police try to find me and, of course, Hua Chen."

"I guess this is why I'll need my boots, huh?"

"Yeah. If you intend to tag along with me, you're going to need them a lot more. Let's go. We have to find another vehicle, something that'll get around in the snow."

As they walked Jason asked, "You know where Hua went?"

"Yeah. I think so. He's a hubot, and he needs a shot of zero point energy. Far as I know, there's only one place in town to get that."

"Zero point energy. That's what that phone call was all about. Where's Fort Meade?"

"In Maryland. We were talking to the NSA. In case you didn't know, this is the big time. Hua is headed to that place where the Chinese are doing the experiment with zpe to see if the city falls down. That's where I have to go, and since you're so insistent, *we* have to go."

# — 33 —

The snow crunched under their boots as they walked. It fell all around them swirling into little blizzards as the wind gusted across open areas.

"So, you know there's a car rental place near here, right?" Jason asked.

"No. A Cadillac dealership."

"Ed, a Cadillac isn't going to get around in the snow any better than your car."

"I know. They sell something else that interests me. It'll work better if you help. Here's what I want you to do."

In less than a half-mile, they were in view of the Cadillac-Hummer dealership. They trudged up to a shinny dark gray Hummer with a small open bed in back. Jason said, "Are you ready for sticker shock? This goes for sixty-three thousand dollars."

Breckon was on his knees looking under it checking the ground clearance as a salesman walked up behind him. "Interested in one of these bad boys, are you?"

Breckon got up and looked at him. "Might be. Need something with good ground clearance. Up at the cabin, they rarely plough my road. Since I'm the only one that goes in there in the winter guess they don't feel it's worth it."

Jason came around the back of the vehicle and said, "The one we tested at the Ford place didn't have tires as big as these. Bet this one would make it though."

Breckon nodded as he opened the door and got into the driver's seat. "Mind if I start it?"

"Oh, sure. Here's a key."

It came to life with a roar. Mainly he wanted to see the fuel status. The needle was pegged on empty.

Jason had gotten up and was standing on the step in the open door. Ed had told Jason what he thought the problem would be so he said into his ear so the salesman couldn't hear, "This one's empty." Dealerships never left cars on the lot with more than enough gas to get out for a short test drive. That was done to discourage thieves.

A light blue one with an enclosed back like an SUV sat away from the rest. "That blue one might be used by someone here," Ed indicated. "Watch for my sign."

Breckon turned it off and got out. "Nice sound to it. How about that blue one over there?"

"Ah, that's the one the sales manager drives."

"Is it for sale?"

"Sure. Everything here's for sale."

"Mind if I take a look at it?"

"How about all of these?" he said waving his hand at the dozen or so Hummers in the lot.

"Like the color," Breckon said as he was already walking that way.

Breckon opened the door and got in. "Is there a key?"

The salesman was fumbling for the key with something approaching a scowl on his face, but he came up with the right one. After it was running Breckon turned, made eye contact with Finley, and nodded slightly as he said to the salesman. "I like it."

Finley started. "If you hope to sell mom on a Hummer this is exactly her favorite color. It's perfect. And the enclosed back looks like an SUV rather than a pickup truck."

"Since the sales manager's been driving it I could even say I got a good deal on it as a 'slightly used' one, is that right?" he asked looking at the salesman.

"Yeah. I guess we could do a little something in that department," was the reply.

"You're going to need all the ammunition you can get," Jason added.

"Tell me about it. But, I like it. Heavy, good ground clearance, and listen to that engine—lots of power. This is it!" Turning directly to the salesman he said, "Mind if I take it around the block?"

"Not at all. You'll have to give me your driver's license, though."

Breckon got out the license and motioned to Jason to get in.

The salesman said, "I really should go with you."

"Can't go far," Breckon replied. "Look at how the traffic's backed up all over. First, tell me how you do four wheel drive in this thing, just in case."

The salesman leaned in and pointed out the control with a short explanation of the various modes. Breckon thanked him and slowly started out.

"This is like driving an eighteen wheeler," he said. "Got your seat belt on?"

"Yes, of course. Mom always makes me wear it. You were right, though. Traffic's just about stopped on all the streets. We aren't going far."

"We have to get onto 35W headed south. That should be going pretty good since that's into the city, and that's where Hua had to go."

Breckon drove on the shoulder and every other place as soon as they were out of sight of the dealership. He came to County B2 again where it went west over 35W. "I'm pretty sure B2 won't do. The bridge doesn't have an access to the freeway. Guess we'll have to go to County Road C." Once through the light on B2, traffic was full in all lanes and hardly moving. Blowing his horn wouldn't help and there was no way to get around on the shoulder. They had no choice but to creep along with the rest of the vehicles.

"Okay, Jason. Call your mom. I'm assuming she's still downtown."

Jason made the call saying he was all right, and that they were now en route to downtown, but the going was slow. At Breckon's instructions, he got the number of the conference room. He would call in a few minutes because Breckon wanted to talk to all of them. After what seemed like enough time for them to get together, Jason made the call. When he had them on speakerphone, Jason handed the phone to Ed.

"Mel. When we got to the place where I had Chen, he was gone. But, I'm pretty sure he went to that U of M lab where the Chinese are doing that zero point energy test."

"How'd you put that together?"

"They use zpe to make those hubot guys and zpe is what they're doing at the lab. It's just a hunch, but a good one. I'm going to stop by there and have a look on my way downtown. This is what I want you all to hear. Is Jason's mother there?"

"Yes. I'm here. Is my son all right?"

"Yes. As he told you, he's fine. I need your help with something, Mel. I dropped my car at the Roseville shopping center and took a taxi to go to Chen suspecting you might have put a tracking device on my car. That's exactly what you did, because when we got back to the shopping center you had my car surrounded by police cars. I'm responsible for Jason, but that doesn't bother you at all, does it? How was I supposed to talk my way out of that mess and get my car to return Jason? At best, we'd have spent the whole night in the Roseville police station, mug shots, fingerprints, the whole bit. Jason's just a kid. What a thing to hang on him." Breckon thought he was over-playing the dire consequences of the police cars in hopes of getting the proper response from a certain person.

Jason was leaning across the center console as close to Breckon as possible so he could hear both sides of the conversation, too.

"What!" It was Mrs. Finley.

"Yeah, yeah." Mel sounded ever so meek. "What do you need?"

"Well, we went to the Roseville Cadillac-Hummer dealership a couple of blocks away and took this Hummer for a test drive. I need you to call the dealership and convince the salesman that this is a national emergency or something, and commit to paying any rental charges. And, in the very remote possibility there are any damages on the vehicle, you'll pay them, too. Okay?"

"Breckon. I never authorized you to take that big thing. You got any idea how much they cost?"

"Yeah. Sticker price sixty-three big ones."

"No way, Breckon . . . "

"Yes you will!" It was Mrs. Finley again. "Or I'll have your head on a platter!"

"Okay. Okay. I'll handle it. Watch that you don't scratch that thing!"

"Thanks. See you soon. Bye."

Jason was laughing. "You're good, Ed. Really good. I was wondering how you'd get away with stealing this thing. Very clever."

"Hey. Just using the resources available. I'm beginning to like your mother."

---

At last, Cindy was making her way up the loop of the on-ramp to Highway 36. When she was into traffic, it was moving slower than she had hoped. There were cars in the median and cars off the road on the right. There had been fender bender crashes that were abandoned. The snow was still coming and the wind was fierce in the open areas. At last, they were in the open and Cindy could increase her speed.

"You are good lady to help me," Chen said hoping to break the tension. "Wish something I could do."

"There is. You can say a prayer that we don't get stuck. I have it in all-wheel drive so we can keep going, but that means it's easy to lose control."

"I never prayed. How is that done?"

"Just ask God to help you, and if you are of a mind, end with amen."

No sooner had she said it when the left wheels caught a ridge of snow and the car skidded. She let up on the gas and the wheels slid up against the deeper snow thrown to the side by other vehicles. Before they were completely stopped she hit the gas again and fishtailed back into the traffic lane.

Hua Chen stared out the windshield with his teeth clenched and eyes bulging. "God help me that this crazy woman does not kill me . . . and her, too . . . Amen.

Cindy was over driving the conditions with the reduced visibility and accumulated snow as they came upon an accident with cars blocking the way. She hit the brakes and started to skid. As they were about to take the impact, it was clear the cars on the left were closer than those on the right. Veering to the right, she cut immediately to the left. The little SUV spun completely around and was clear of the vehicles headed almost in the direction they wanted to go.

"See? You pray very well."

"God is fast, too."

"He tends to do that for beginners. Wants to keep you praying. So, keep at it. Meanwhile, watch the signs. We have to take the off-ramp for Fourth Street. That's a ways yet but watch for it."

---

As they waited in traffic, hardly moving, Breckon said. "Got a hunch. Get out your cell phone and put in this number then give me the phone." Ed listened to the phone ring until all at once his eyes lit up. "Hi. How are you . . . well, yeah. I'm not at home or at work. It's been sort of a busy day. I was wondering, Hua Chen, you know, the Chinese guy we put in the rectory at St. Isador's . . . "

"He's with you? Where are you?" After a long pause Breckon said, "Are you sure you're okay? We're on our way. We'll call you every few minutes to see how you're doing. Bye."

Handing the phone back to Jason he said, "That does it. We've got to get out of this traffic jamb." They could see the traffic moving north on 35W and, across the median, the southbound lanes. "There's a service road on the other side of the freeway that has an entrance, I think. Oh, yes. If I remember right we can pass under the freeway just a little south of County Road C."

"Yeah. But, that doesn't matter. We're hardly moving."

"It's only half a block ahead to where that street comes on. The light's red on County C and the oncoming lane is open. Here we go."

Breckon drove over the center curb and into the oncoming lane. A car had made a right turn on red without stopping and was headed right for them. Breckon swerved to the right on to the median which consisted of curbs with bricks between them piled with snow. He took out a couple of traffic signs as snow flew onto the windshield. Past the car, he got back into the oncoming lane. The light had changed to green and he slid onto Rosegate Lane to the right just in time and gunned it.

"Ed! Sharp curve! Fifteen miles an hour."

"Oops. You're right." He hit the brakes and they hardly slowed until they pounded sideways into the reflective echelon signs marking the sharp curve. This road was virtually free of traffic.

"Where's that darned on-ramp?" They drove a half-mile and rounded a bend. Visibility was not good, but he could see far enough to know there was no on-ramp, and the road across the freeway fence on his left was, by now, Highway 280. In frustration he pulled into a parking lot and turned around.

"Call that number again," he said to Jason.

"Cindy. Where are you now? We're trying to get onto 35W heading south."

"Ed. Thank goodness you called. There are several stalled cars on the off-ramp going up to Fourth Street. And that's where we got stuck."

"I'll be there in a few minutes, just hang on."

"But Ed, you'll never make it. I didn't make it and I have all-wheel drive."

"Hey my little sugar-pie, don't worry. We'll make it. See you in a few minutes."

In the background, he could hear her talking. "Hua! What are you doing? . . . Stop! Hey. Stop!"

"What's going on there? Is the guy going crazy? Cindy! Are you all right?

There was noise and talking in the background as if there were a struggle. Then the call was terminated.

Breckon handed the phone to Jason. "Damn! What do you suppose Chen did? There's no way of knowing what those lousy Chinese scientists programmed into him."

By this time they had backtracked around the curve and were beside the southbound 35W lanes—so near and yet so far. Breckon dove into the parking lot of the Beltman Group building turned around and said, "Jason, hang on. We're getting onto that freeway right now." He switched to four-wheel drive and punched it down.

"Ed, you're crazy!" Finley yelled as the freeway fence bore down on them.

He took the chain-link fence head on. Luckily, it was old and in poor repair in this area. The vehicle pitched up as they hit the snow. All four tires had aggressive tread and they dug in. They bore through the snow with only thirty feet to the shoulder of the freeway. For a time, it seemed like they would become hopelessly bogged down, but they maintained their forward progress. Finally, coming free of the snow the Hummer sprang forward into the traffic lanes.

Breckon wrenched the wheel to the right as they careened across three traffic lanes narrowly missing another vehicle, and slamming sideways into the guardrail. Flipping it into rear wheel drive only, they were off again.

"There ya go. We're on the freeway headed south. No problem."

Jason was wide-eyed not sure he had really seen what had just happened. It was snowing and the wipers were slopping from side to side. "Ed! Watch out! There's an accident up ahead . . ."

They skidded to the right around the first cars on the left, and then bounced and slid off the cars on the right.

After they were clear of the mess Ed said, "I'm getting to like your mother more all the time."

"Maybe you should slow down. We can't save the world if we're dead."

"Screw saving the world. I've got to get to Cindy. Watch for the Fourth Street exit."

Visibility forced him to slow down because he couldn't afford to miss the exit. If there were any stalled cars directly in their path, he'd still have a hard time avoiding them.

"There!" Jason shouted. That's the exit."

Snow flew as Ed gave it gas swinging around stalled cars. Almost too late, he recognized the little SUV. He lurched to a stop beside it and hit the horn. It was loud. He threw the door open and jumped out. Cindy was opening the driver's door as he got to it. He threw his arms around her and said. "Are you all right?"

"I'm fine. This is nice. You big handsome stranger come to rescue little ol' me?"

"Don't joke. What did Hua Chen do?"

"He got out and started walking. He's going the rest of the way on foot. He has boots and a good coat and gloves. I suppose it's not so far any more."

"Oh . . . sure. Come on. Get in." She got in the back seat behind Ed. Ed got behind the wheel and swung his door closed with a squeak and clunk having to bang it twice to get it to latch.

"Buckle up!"

Ed backed to get a running start and gave it all it had. He slid left and then right until finally he broke through the snow barrier left from plowing Fourth Street. Fourth was one-way to the right and that's the way they went.

"Where'd you get this piece of junk?"

"He stole it, and I helped," Jason replied. "It was new when we got it."

"Okay. Who's the little criminal? Seems like I know the big one."

"Glad I found you, sweetheart. This is Jason Finley. Jason this is Cindy Thomas. Jason's dad is the ambassador to China. And his mother is a truly great lady, very special."

"What's this?"

"Mom got the CIA to agree to pay in the unlikely event anything happened to the Hummer. Actually Ed said 'very remote possibility of any damage,'" Jason chortled.

"I see. That explains it. As I was getting in it looked like you had been in a demolition derby. Now what?"

"Now that we've settled the love angle of our adventure," Finley said, "it's off to the St. Anthony Falls Lab. Time we got back to saving the world."

Cindy loosened her seatbelt and leaned forwarded and nuzzled Ed's ear. "And what love angle might that be? Hmm . . .?"

# — 34 —

It was seven-fifteen and snow was coming in earnest. Seng Kejian had seen no activity at the old building, so he decided to drive around on the chance he might be missing something. In the traffic lanes, the snow was packed and slippery. Driving the fifty feet to the corner, he turned down the hill past the old building. There were no cars parked on the street which made sense because parking meters lined both sides. He had checked the day before and the found the meters were enforced round the clock. Down the drive to the lab, he noticed the Chinese team's vehicle was still there along with a few others. He recalled that during his visit, they had mentioned they could start tests only four times during a twenty-four hour period, at two and eight, morning and afternoon. He assumed they were planning a test at eight this evening and thought nothing more of it.

It was slow going up the drive from the lab, but he managed. He swung to the left and stopped at the pub for candy bars and to use the men's room. Back in his car, he continued north, took a right, and a right again. He drove south on Second Street stopping at his former observation point.

---

Jorg Davis was busying himself getting ready for the evening's cook when the boss walked up to him. "Ya have something to tell me?"

"Yeah. The chink's back. Asleep over there in the office," he said with a twitch of his head.

"Well, doesn't that just about do it. Don't disturb him until I get back . . . going to get some of the boys."

Minutes later the boss with three men including Harvey came down the steps from the top floor and went immediately to the small office.

Peng was jarred awake by his feet being shoved off the desk. Instantly alert, he took in the situation. The men standing around him could see what must be going through his mind. He was trapped, and they knew he knew.

"How about you explain a few things before we sort of take you apart," the boss said with malice.

Peng fixed eyes with the man who had spoken. "This is some thanks I get. I almost got myself killed finding out if there was a threat from that place down the hill. For your information, you can forget about them. The Chinese government is doing a secret test using that facility. It seems that place has unique capabilities not available in China."

"Yeah, says you. What's with the fancy clothes and you meeting them like you was down home buddies. Seems like you got friendly with 'em awful fast."

Peng shrugged. "I suppose it might have looked that way. Not surprised you had somebody watching. Couple of nights ago, by accident, I heard two guys in the pub down on Main Street speaking Mandarin. Few others in this town would have understood. I did. They were discussing the project down there. One of the guys left, and I started a conversation with the one remaining. He was sort of drunk, and I got useful information out of him." As he spoke, he put on his still wet socks, and then his right shoe. There was no telling when things would break down. He was working on the knot in the left shoelace as he went on. "It wasn't too hard to make up a story based on what the guy said. When I showed up, they thought I was someone sent from China to review their progress."

"Nice story. Where'd you come up with the clothes? Seems like you were pretty down on your luck when you showed up here. I doubt the guy in the pub had anything to do with that."

"I'm used to getting by, making do with the situation, as you might say. I found a Chinese tourist and lifted his wallet. His credit card provided that I needed."

One of the toughs, a head shorter than the others, said. "So, smart guy. Let's see the credit card."

By this time Peng had the other shoe on and the lace tied. He pulled the card out of the breast pocket of his suit coat and flipped it on the desk. The man, whom they referred to as Shorty, snatched it up. "Shan Jin. Sure that's not who you really are, and you've been lying to us?"

Peng smirked. "I couldn't very well roll Fred Olson, could I? I hardly look like someone with a name like that. And I doubt that Fred Olson would have a Chinese accent."

It was crowded in the small room, and Peng was the only one seated. Those standing were shifting from foot to foot as if they needed something to do like smash up a man. Then he thought of the Asian man who had been watching him. "Where'd you come up with a Chinese man to keep tabs on me. Pretty good for an outfit like this."

They looked at one another. "No Chinese working for me," the boss blustered. "You can bet on that. He must be from that secret test. Somebody you missed."

Peng shook his head. "I met everyone on that team. He's not with them. If he's not with you, there's somebody else. Maybe the cops, maybe one of your rivals. I suggest you ask him in and have a talk with him. He's in a gray Ford car, small man with dark, deep-set eyes. Sometimes he's in the parking lot at that lab, sometimes at other places up and down the street outside of here."

"Yeah," Harvey said. "I've seen him a couple of times, too."

There was a moment of hesitation, and then the boss pointed to Harvey and another man. "Harvey, you and Bruno take a sweep around the area. See if this guy's blowing smoke. If you spot him, like the man said, ask him in for a chat."

———————————

At seven-twenty-five, Seng Kejian was having a hard time keeping the car windows clear enough to see out. He was running the engine most of the time leaving the windshield defroster on high and the wipers on intermittent. The rear window defroster was falling behind. Every few minutes he lowered the side windows to wipe them clear. When the driver's side window was down he reached out and cleared the snow from the outside rearview mirror. If he saw anyone, he was prepared to stop the engine immediately so as not to look suspicious.

He was beginning to think he would lose out to the snow and be forced to go back to the hotel. There. Two dark figures came out of the old building and walked down the hill toward that laboratory. He couldn't tell for sure, but neither one looked like Peng. When they had gone a hundred feet, they were lost from sight. He sat back undecided as to what to do. The snow was now deep enough so it would be easy to get stuck if he drove around. He pushed the speed dial on the third phone. It was immediately answered.

"Where are you?"

"I'm on East Hennepin Avenue behind a snow plow. I missed my turn to get on the freeway, but this goes well. It is probably as fast as any other way. I should be there in twenty minutes if the plow doesn't get stuck."

"Okay. Two men left the building and walked in the direction of that lab. Nothing I can do until you get here. Use number one next time." Kejian punched the button to end the call and then turned off the phone. His thoughts turned to the two men. How ever many there were in the building, it meant there were now two fewer. If he could apprehend Peng, it would only take minutes for him to deliver his man to the lab. If his assumptions were wrong about the purpose of his mission, it wouldn't matter. Since he had been there, the test team would recognize him. Moreover, being in a foreign country, they would be obliged to assist him. If nothing else, he had the credentials to force their help.

After a few minutes of mulling over his options, he reached over and found the plastic bag with the phones in it. Fumbling around he was unable to discern the number in the dim light. He had to use the dome light to be sure he had number one. Finding it, he set the power switch to on.

---

Harvey and Bruno walked partway down the drive to the lab parking lot and could see the small gray Ford wasn't there. They walked back and turned left. A half-block later they took a right through an alley north of the pub. Emerging on Second Street, they immediately saw a car parked to their right.

"That could be it," Harvey said. "With all the snow on it, though, it's hard to tell."

"Funny thing," Bruno said. "Looks like the motor's running. And, it's parked where he could see the door we came out of. Bet it's him."

"So, how do we get him? Count on it, he's got the doors locked. If we pound on the windows he'll just drive away."

Bruno replied, "Best thing is to act like we're cops. I could flash my wallet at him. In the dim light and wet windows he'd never know."

"What if he is a cop?" At that moment there was a dim glow through the partially melted snow on the rear window as Kejian turned on the dome light.

"Doubt he's a cop. A cop would've never done that. Here goes."

They moved up quickly behind the car. Harvey stood at the left rear corner while Bruno approached on the driver's side. Before he could rap on the window, it came down. A hand reached out to clear the snow off the mirror. The arm was grabbed as a fist landed on Kejian's face. With the door open, Harvey and his accomplice had the man by the arms, one on each side. In his struggles, Kejian tried to trip one of his captors. This resulted in his being lifted until his feet were off the ground.

Entering the old building from the same door they had left, the two men presented their prize to the boss. "Here's the guy been watching the place. Better we tie 'em up. He's pretty wiggly."

The boss nodded and Harvey stepped out and a moment later returned with a length of cord. With his hands and feet tied and two men holding Kejian up, the boss went through his pockets. Then he was dropped in a straight back chair.

Peng used the commotion of the two men bringing Kejian into the office to get up and step around the desk. As Kejian accessed his situation, he spotted Peng. He knew Peng wouldn't recognize him other than possibly from the street corner. But, his look of recognition registered with Peng. Kejian knew the man was dangerous, and Peng would assume Kejian was from the Chinese police here to bring him back.

All of this was lost on the other men in the room. Peng's vacating the swivel chair behind the desk was seen as little more than a sign of respect to the boss who now sat down in it. Due to the small space, two of the thugs stood just beyond the door. One exchanged a comment now and then with Davis. The boss went through Kejian's personal effects. They had failed to find his MSS identification which he kept under the insole of his left shoe. Unfortunately, he had his nine-millimeter gun in his shoulder holster when he was grabbed. This was now on the desk along with his wallet containing his Chinese driver's license, passport, credit card, and some cash.

The boss tossed the wallet on the desk and said, "If you know English might as well talk or we'll beat you until you do. If you don't speak English, we'll beat you until you die. Talk!"

---

Kejian had expected it would come to this. Being bound he would have no chance to defend himself from them, or worse, Peng. Even if the others managed to take down Peng before he killed them all, he was still tied up. His only hope was to separate himself from Peng.

"Okay. I'll talk," Kejian began in his heavy accent looking the boss squarely in the eyes. "I have information it is best only you hear first. If you want to tell them later, that'll be up to you. If they all hear now, you lose the chance to decide. I'm tied up. You have nothing to fear from me."

The boss leaned back, and thought. "Okay. I'll play the game. You guys go outside and close the door. If you hear a ruckus in here, don't wait. Watch Peng. Don't let him leave."

With the room cleared and the door closed Kejian began to make his case. "If you will take off my left shoe and look under the insole you'll find something. Please, do it. I can't hurt you."

Cautiously, the boss did it. Upon retrieving the MSS credential, he pursed his lips. "What's this?"

"It's an MSS identification. That's like the FBI is here. I've been sent to apprehend the Chinese man standing outside the door. His name is Quan Peng."

"Seems kind o' odd. Why didn't you go to the FBI and have 'em help you?"

"The whole story is this. In China, some part of the military is trying to make the perfect soldier. They want him strong, smart, resourceful, and completely obedient. In the case of Peng, they succeeded in the first three, but utterly failed in the last. He is strong, smart, and vicious. He killed seven people that we know of getting out of China and to this city. That, with no money or credentials."

"I ask again, why not have the FBI help you?"

"Peng is a foreign national. Your FBI would have to be careful not to mistreat him lest perhaps there was a mistake and they picked up the wrong man. They would treat him with too much deference, and this would lead to any number of your FBI agents being killed. Dead federal agents would cause an international incident. Neither country wants that. My advice is to kill him, now."

"Yeah. Nice try. What if you're working for the FBI and this is a sting operation?"

Kejian sneered, "Even we don't go to the extreme of getting someone killed as a means of entrapment." He made a futile attempt to adjust his uncomfortable position and continued. "Okay, try this. You have two of your men hold guns on him while the others tie him up. I'm sure you have guns. Maybe, it would be best to knock him on the head before you try to tie him. I stress, he *is* dangerous."

———————————————

Having been on the wrong side of the law most his life, the man behind the desk had become respected as the boss of the largest meth operation in the Midwest. Along the way, he had received an advanced degree in the school of hard knocks. Experience had taught him how to handle the law, suppliers, distributors, competition, and a raft of similar "managerial" duties. The necessary juggling of his class schedule meant that international relations was one of those subjects that had fallen through the cracks. This left him with what he viewed as a simple problem. Two members of the Chinese race must cease to exist. He didn't like killing people, took no joy in it—normally. Nevertheless, business was business.

The boss sat without looking at Kejian for a minute. If that guy, Peng, was smart and dangerous, he was the immediate threat. His guys were dangerous enough. It was the other category that bothered him. It was necessary to inform them about what they had to do without alerting the Chinese guy any more than he already was. Looking at Kejian he asked, "Does this guy, Peng, know you and that you're with your MSS?"

"I know him from pictures, but had never met him until a few minutes ago. I don't think he would know me, but that's impossible to say. My feeling is, he suspects I'm was here to capture or kill him."

The boss nodded. That meant it all had to be done in one action. He couldn't bring in one or two of his guys and instruct them as to what to do. It would be too obvious a plot was being hatched. To make matters worse, he didn't want any shooting in the cooking room. No telling what a bullet might hit.

Kejian was sitting in a chair to the right of the desk as seen when entering the room. The door hinged on the right. "Tell ya what," the boss said as he pulled the bottom desk drawer all the way out and palmed a .38 stub nose. "I'll untie your right arm and let you have your gun. I'll call Peng in here and you kill him. If you're FBI and this is a sting, well, you do the killing. As he enters, I'll stand partially behind the door with my gun on you. If you even twitch like that gun barrel's coming my way, I'll blow your head off. After you've shot Peng, you drop your gun. Then you get untied, take your stuff, less gun, and leave. You've accomplished your mission. Leave the country or you'll be shot on sight. What do ya say?" With this plan, the boss figured that all the bullets would be headed toward the outside wall rather than toward the cooking equipment. He knew Jorg was far enough along with the evening's activities to have sufficient volatile chemicals collected around him to destroy the place if they were ignited.

---

Kejian saw no alternative but to acquiesce to the offer of the man they called the boss. It was in his jurisdiction to terminate either or both of the hubots if there were no other way to stop them. His biggest concern was the part of the deal where they let him go. Still, bodies were uncommonly hard to dispose of, and one unarmed Chinese man walking away might be seen as an acceptable alternative.

Kejian nodded. "I accept your offer."

The boss took the nine-millimeter pistol and made sure there was a round chambered. With the gun out of Kejian's reach, he cut a cord that freed Kejian's right wrist.

"Here's the way it'll be. I crack the door enough to stick my head out and call in Peng on the excuse of translating. He's a lot better at English than you are so it'll seem reasonable. When I see him come this way I hand your gun to you barrel first. You grab the barrel, lay it on your thighs, and grab the butt, swinging it behind you out of sight. As he enters, I swing the door part way between him and me while I have my gun on you. Any mistake, your mistake, my mistake, anything goes wrong, and I kill you, then him. Any questions?"

Going through Kejian's mind was the thought that this guy had street smarts. He had been burned a few times and lived to tell about it. The only problem with the plan was that, while it would all happen in less than a half a minute, it was too complicated. Elaborate plans never worked. Yet, having no alternatives, he nodded his approval.

The boss had his gun behind his belt buckle, and the nine-millimeter in his right hand. Opening the door with his left hand, he looked to the left expecting the men to be in that direction. Instead, they were to the right standing near the street door. This upset the thought process a little, but the proper adjustment was made. He spotted Peng among the other three.

"You. Peng. Come here. This guy's not too good at English. I need some help with translation. You others, go over and see if Jorg needs any help. Make yourselves useful." He had to give this last order because any nine-millimeter bullets that did not land solidly in Peng would go through the wall and hit his men.

---

When Hua Chen left Cindy Thomas stranded on the off-ramp, he was torn for a minute, but this was quickly overcome by his need to get to the place where the energy seemed to originate. If it had come from the Falls Lab, he knew from the map where to go. It was three blocks in the direction of the off-ramp past Fourth Street and six blocks to the right. With this in mind, he went right on Fourth Street a block, then left a block. Continuing this pattern until he was on Main Street, he walked on the sidewalk at a good pace and was getting warm with his heavy coat. He zipped it open letting the snow fall on his head and shirt. Without realizing it, he went past the driveway to the parking lot. Suddenly, it didn't seem right. Reversing direction, the small sign soon alerted him to the place. About to start down the drive, the flashing lights of a police car caught his attention. It wouldn't do to be stopped for questioning by the police. Walking across the drive again, a sign that said "Park Trail" was posted a short distance ahead. He proceeded along the sidewalk and saw steps that descended into a wooded area. He went down the snow covered steps to the level of the parking lot and walked toward an electrical switch and transformer the size of a garage. With his boots, the knee deep snow gave him no trouble. Coming to the edge of the plowed area, he climbed over the pile of snow and onto the parking area beside the driveway. The new snow had accumulated to more than six inches.

He stopped and waited knowing the time was growing short. To his relief, the lights stopped flashing and the police car drove up the driveway. At this, Chen wondered how he would gain entrance to the lab at this late hour.

---

Breckon turned left on Third Avenue and after two blocks drove past the old building used as the meth lab. He stopped at Main Street and the headlights illuminated the sign announcing the St. Anthony Falls Laboratory.

"There's the sign," Jason said. "It must be just ahead down the hill." A car was coming up the one lane drive at the moment Breckon started across Main. He stopped to let the police car turn to the left. It didn't stop at the stop sign, but who'd give him a ticket?

"Wonder if there's already been trouble down there?" Cindy remarked.

At the parking lot, Breckon pulled to the left and parked beside a snow covered SUV. The front bumper crunched against the pile of snow left from previous plowings. Ed got out at once as did Jason. Ed saw a dark shape motionless fifty feet away. He called out, "That you Hua?"

The figure moved. "Ed! You are here. I was worried a lot that the man had finally shot you. You come fast. Did you find Cindy Thomas not moving in the snow?"

By this time, Cindy was out of the Hummer, too.

Hua expressed his relief that all were accounted for, and immediately was intent on his problem. "I must get into that building. The feeling is strong that I go there before the eight o'clock time." He moved toward the building as the spoke. In a few steps he was through the pile of snow, and up on the stone wall looking over the fence at the flume directing water into the power plant on his left. "There is a river here. How do I get in the building?" The draw of the power being generated and the state of his pendant controlled him to the point where his normal logical thought processes were not functioning.

Breckon bounded after him and was up on the wall just as it looked like Hua might jump into the water and attempt to swim across. Firmly grabbing his arm, and pointing to the right, he said, "There's an open gate that leads to what looks like a bridge across the water. Come down off the wall. We'll find a way in." Stepping off the wall they were immediately in the snow pushed against it by plows, and then on the parking area.

---

Quan Peng was fully aware that the two men in the office were preparing a plan to, as Jorg had said, take him out. He surmised that they hadn't made a move on him yet because they didn't want shooting with all the chemicals around. He saw five-gallon plastic containers of acetone setting near Davis ready for use. That stuff was even more volatile than gasoline. In some way, their reticence to shoot might give him a slight advantage, though there were plenty of guns around. There was for certain a nine-millimeter in the office that they had taken off the Chinese guy. The boss probably had one, too. He had seen the man they called Bruno flash one behind his front waistband. The other man, a head shorter than Bruno, had one behind his belt in the small of his back.

From the man's natural movements, he occasionally pulled his jacket tight and the lump was unmistakable. Harvey was another matter. He wore a bulky coat that he never took off. Even now, with it hanging loose with the zipper open, it was impossible to tell if he was packing. Peng assumed he was.

This unhappy analysis revealed everybody had a weapon but him which was why he was still casually mulling around with the other men. If he started anything, even if he were quick, one of the men would get a bullet into him. It was reasonable that Jorg and Harvey would understand the danger of the chemicals. The other two were new as evidenced by their aversion to the odors. They had been standing with the door partially open. Jorg came over and slammed it shut at one point telling them the fumes on the street would reveal the plant.

Peng knew that whatever was likely to happen would occur soon. The boss's head appearing in the office doorway meant it had started. At the remark to be useful, Bruno moved over by Jorg. Harvey went a couple of steps past the office door. The smaller man hung back. Peng moved as quickly as possible sensing it was the only unpredictable thing he could do to set a plan off its timing. Sure enough, the Chinese man's right arm was still moving back as he appeared in the doorway. Immediately, it reversed and started to come forward. That it was not tethered meant only one thing. Peng bent his knees as he grasped the doorframe with his right hand. With a thrust of his arm, he landed on the floor to the right as bullets splintered wood where his head had been. There were more shots in the office, but since there was no evidence any of them had stuck him, he completed his roll coming up clipping Harvey from behind. Harvey had his gun out of the holster under his arm as he fell to his knees. Peng grasped the barrel with his right hand and sent his left fist into the temple. Harvey fell on his face, limp.

Bruno was drawing a gun coming from behind his belt. Peng snapped a quick shot catching Bruno in the leg as Peng fell and rolled again. Two shots came over him from behind. The sound of a bullet hitting a container filled with liquid was unmistakable and ominous. Peng shot again at Bruno and missed. Looking around he brought Harvey's gun up and back for a shot at the short man. The door stood open and he was gone.

Peng sprang low toward the door shooting wildly twice in the direction of Bruno hoping to keep him from getting a well aimed shot. Scrambling and slithering to keep a small, moving target, Peng was at the door. With his last glance, he saw Bruno rise up with his gun pointed his way.

He was beside the split open acetone can. The shot went high, but Peng didn't hear it as the flame front of the conflagration threw him out in the snow. He thrashed about in the snow to make sure he wasn't burning, then managed to get his feet under him and ran across the street. More and more of the plastic cans of light hydrocarbons: paint thinner, camping fuel, toluene, acetone, xylene, and who knew what else, succumbed to the increasing heat.

Peng shoved the gun in his belt and swatted some of the snow off. He was cold and wet again. Running down the hill toward the parking lot where Shan Jin's vehicle awaited him, he felt and heard the continuing muffled explosions. There was still a chance he could get away.

# — 35 —

Fire Station 11 was four blocks from the old building that was enveloped in flames. The explosions and flames drew a lot of attention even on this snowy evening. Calls to 911 gave the alarm seconds after the first flair of burning fuel lit up the landscape. The first truck was on its way little more than a minute after Peng had been unceremoniously thrown into the street.

Muan Yingqu skidded to a stop as an engine sped across University Avenue in front of him. About to proceed, the wail of another siren heralded a second engine approaching the intersection. Looking at the street sign, he realized this was Third Avenue where he had intended to turn right. With the rapidly accumulating snow he pulled in behind the second fire truck where the huge tires left a hard packed track. A block later as he approached Second Street he was surprised to see he had come upon the scene of the inferno which had caused the engines to stir from their station on such a night. A man in black clothing with green reflective bands jumped off the engine and directed him to take a right. This he did and saw Kejian's gray car parked across the street with the window down and the interior light on.

He proceeded a couple of hundred feet and pulled to the curb. The firemen were about their business and ignored Yingqu as he approached Kejian's car. It was empty, the dome light was on, and the engine was running. He slipped into the driver's seat and looked around. There were soft drink cans and food wrappers on the floor. The three phones were on the front passenger seat. Someone had taken him, and the burning building across the street to the front was the likely place. He turned off the light and the engine, put the keys on the floor, and the phones in his coat pocket. Back in his car, he had to back up and make a track in the snow before he got enough speed to move away from the curb. At the corner, he turned left and on Main Street left again. Police cars and more fire trucks were arriving all the time so he pulled to the side. Consulting the hand drawn map he had gotten from Kejian it was clear that a half block ahead, at the bottom of the hill from the fire, was where that laboratory was located. Leaving his car, he jogged along hoping to get into the lab grounds before the police cordoned off the area.

---

The flair of orange light from up the hill drew the attention of everyone in the parking lot. A moment later the thud of the explosion reached them. Then the tongue of flame from the door was joined by others from windows as the flames pulsed further into the air with the ignition of each additional barrel of flammable liquid. A figure, silhouetted by the flames, appeared crossing Main Street coming in the direction of the lab.

---

Quan Peng reached Main when a shout from his left made him slip his hand on the butt of the gun in his belt.

"Hey! Chinese man!"

It was the voice of the short man from the meth lab. Peng knew he had two shots left. If the man had not reloaded, Shorty had four. He doubted he had reloaded. Without slacking his pace Peng turned and identified the man's position not twenty feet away. He shot once. He took another roll in the snow as two shots returned his one. Both men missed. Peng was up and running fast. As he neared the bottom of the drive he pressed his pants pocket and noted the car key was still there. He approached his SUV oblivious to the Hummer on its left. Harvey's gun, fully loaded, was under the front seat. He had the key in the lock when another shot sent a shower of glass on him as it passed though the Hummer missing his head by an inch. The key turned as Peng looked up. The short thug had gotten into a position where he could clearly see Peng and was holding the revolver with two hands.

Peng had put his gun in his left hand as he worked with the car key. This meant his opponent could not see his movement as he leveled it at him and fired. The man took the bullet in the chest and crumpled to the ground before he had a chance to shoot. Dropping the empty gun Peng swung the door open and scooped up Harvey's.

Hua took a step toward Peng as Peng aggressively moved from between the vehicles toward him. "Why are you here? I feel you are a hubot." A look of recognition came between the two men. "They were about to terminate you. You are twenty-seven, the failure!" Hua howled.

Peng spat back, "You must be twenty-three, the darling. You let them work on you for weeks. I, at least, was smart enough to escape. What'd they do, give you a first-class ticket to come here and find me? You re-volting morsel of humanity."

Hua softened. "You have said it. I may be human. You are the one who certainly is not. That is what drives you to kill. You resent people their humanity. You are intent on getting onto the lab as the time grows short. You want your humanity back."

Quan, stunned, looked glassy-eyed at Hua.

With the shooting, the others had fallen on the ground. The untram-pled snow was now up to eight inches so they were not particularly obvi-ous. Besides, the two hubots were so intent on one another the others were forgotten. The conversation beyond Hua identifying the other man as a hubot was in Mandarin. Breckon, not knowing what was being said, noted that the conversation had grown less heated. He slowly crawled on all fours hoping to come up behind Peng. He was surprised that the hubot with the gun was not pointing it at Hua as if he didn't care, or more likely, saw no need for it.

With ten feet to go, Breckon sprang up, lunged forward, and caught Peng from behind at the knees wrapping his arms around them. Peng taken by surprise was enraged as he fell. He flung off Breckon's grip as if he were a child, got to his feet, and leveled his gun at him.

"Not Ed!" Hua yelled charging at Peng. As Hua connected with Quan's shoulder pushing him back, a shot sounded from the left. Shorty was up on one elbow aiming at Peng. The bullet hit Hua in the side coming from the back. Peng's shot went wild. The chest-shot man slumped back into the snow.

After the unexpected shot, Peng lay with the other hubot on top of him like a dead weight. He rolled him off and sat up expecting to have pains shoot through him. No pain. The shot had struck the other one. The sound of the shot was from the direction of the man he'd shot. The call of twenty-three came from that side. His peripheral vision had caught the movement. Yes, the geometry was right. HB-23 had shoved Peng out of the line of fire and taken the hit in his stead.

That pleased him. It was only right. With his gun in his hand he got up, and swung it around. Everyone lay still in the snow. It was right that they should. He had the gun, and what's more, they owed him the respect even without the gun. He was cold, wet. The snow filled the air. The gossamer flakes fell on his eyelashes distracting him. Oh, yes. The vehicle. Escape. He glanced up the hill. The fire was out of control. No. The way was blocked. The cold. Yes, the cold. Not that. Not cold only. Anxiety, pulling, yearning. The pendant! The energy was drawing him. Time was short. He ran toward the black wrought-iron gate—standing open. Of course, it had to be open—for him. He didn't want to escape. He wanted to go to the energy.

---

As soon as Peng was gone, Jason, Cindy, and Ed were kneeling beside Hua looking at him with worry and pain. "Hua, how bad are you?" Cindy asked. "We'll call an ambulance."

The eyes opened. "Not an ambulance. Not hurt bad. You help me get to the place they make the energy. It is working now. Must get there by eight o'clock. Need that more than doctor." He struggled and sat up. With Ed to help, they got him standing. He held his side. The four of them were about to make their way to the wrought-iron gate when the other man laying in the snow groaned.

"Cindy, can you and Jason help Hua to the inside of the building? I'll see if there's anything I can do for the man over there. He intended to help us, even if Hua took the shot meant for that other hubot. That one's strong as an ox. Stay away from him."

Cindy answered, "Ed, don't be long. I'm not sure how far we can get with Hua." The three started out and Breckon knelt in the snow by the man who groaned from time to time. He turned him over, pried his fingers off the gun, and let it fall in the snow beside him. Ed saw his chest heave up and fall. Then he was silent, dead. Breckon rubbed the palms of his hands on his thighs as he sat back on his heels. It was happening again. Dead people. The exploding building surely meant more dead people. Now, this one taking his last breath as he knelt helplessly beside him. Although Hua made a good show of it, he didn't look like he'd make it either way—with medical care or the energy thing.

Lost in his thoughts Breckon failed to see the man walk up holding a pistol aimed at him.

---

Muan Yingqu had heard the shooting in the parking lot because he had been expecting it. The emergency vehicle sirens, and the rest of the commotion caused by the spectacular fire was the center of attention for the emergency workers. He was stopped by a policeman. When he said he had work to do at the lab down the hill, he was immediately forgotten. It was too open and obvious to saunter down the drive. He walked to where the trail started and descended the snow encrusted stairs which only minutes before Hua Chen had taken. He put his feet in the same steps in the snow that Hua's passage had left. He observed the final shooting. When Cindy mentioned Ed's name, he put it together. Now, at last, he had him.

Stopping a short distance away Yingqu said, "Breckon! At last, I've got you."

Breckon looked up and said, "Now what!" He didn't recognize the man, only that he had an Asian accent, and was pointing a gun at him. In addition, it was one more of those things that kept happening. "Well, shoot, asshole! There're dead people all over here. One more won't matter. You think I care!"

Yingqu was taken aback. After all the times he had failed to kill Breckon, it seemed like the man was disappointed. "You don't know who I am, do you?"

"How the hell should I? You think I know all one-point-two-billion Chinese personally? Oh, excuse me. Since you are obviously male, that would only be point-six-billion Chinese men. That should be a piece of cake. But, call me a dummy. I still don't know!"

Revenge was supposed to be sweeter than this. He was supposed to be afraid, begging for mercy. He could kill him and the man wouldn't even care, wouldn't even know who had done it. This wasn't right at all. "You really don't know me? I'm Muan Yingqu. The man whose knee you broke in the Nanjing Airport."

Ed couldn't help laughing. "Oh, this has been a day. Okay, slime-ball. Listen to this. Some of your countrymen are about to start an experiment in that building over there." He pointed with his outstretched hand without turning his head from Yingqu. "The object, of which, is to use zero point energy to destroy this entire city with a massive earthquake. It is set to start at eight o'clock. I'm going to look at my watch, okay? Don't go getting twitchy on me. Okay?"

Yingqu nodded.

"That's fourteen minutes from now. There are two hubots in there. One's monstrously strong, the other's wounded. Exactly how they fit into it I'm not sure, except that they have these things they wear on a chain around their necks. So, stud, you can kill me and die yourself in the earthquake, or you can help me stop this thing. Can't say I care all that much either way."

Yingqu hardly knew what to think so he asked, "Why are you so hard to kill?"

"Divine providence is the only answer I can give. That means that God allows evil to happen, but also causes good to come from it. Don't have time for the long answer. There's a gun here beside this dead man. I'm going to pick it up and go into that building. I won't shoot you with it. What do you say? Want to help me save the stinking world that doesn't deserve being saved?"

This was deplorable. The guy was almost likeable in his brash, agitated way. How could life do this to him? After all the months of getting by on the cursed mechanical knee, all the nights he had lain awake thinking of the satisfaction of revenge. This was unfair. His next thought was even more unsettling. Maybe that's why he hadn't managed to kill him, he was needed for something. He had to do some last deed in a way that was, what, mystical? What was he saying about providence and good from evil that was so confusing? Oh, damn his hide. Shoot him and have it done.

# — 36 —

After crossing the bridge, Peng ran between the buildings. At the office sign, he entered the door opposite the one with the sign. He knew the way. A few steps inside, he opened the hall door on the right and was on the top landing of the stairs. He was close now. This was the right thing to do. Down the stairs, across the floor, down again. As he descended his eyes came below the level of the floor and the new walls of the control room met his gaze. It was satisfying, like coming home after a long absence. At the door, now. It wouldn't open. Couldn't be locked, not for him. Stuck. He braced his knee against the wall and pulled with both hands. Metal screeched, wood snapped and splintered. The door opened out. Stepping inside he felt refreshed. Why were the people staring at him, mouths agape.

---

Jason and Cindy helped Hua as much as they could. Every time he stepped on his left foot he winced and sometimes let out a short grunt. Once across the bridge, the path in the snow made the route obvious. There was a long gap between two office buildings forming a dead end alley. Moving forward Cindy pointed to the small sign that said "Office."

"Let's go in there. Maybe we can get directions to the Chinese experiment," Cindy said.

Fifteen feet inside the door, there was a room to the right with the door open and lights on, but no sign of life. "Must stop, rest a time," Hua gasped. Looking back, they could see blood on the floor each place where Hua's left foot had landed.

"We're going to have to look at that wound," Cindy said. They opened Hua's coat, dropped it to the floor, and then pulled out his blood soaked shirt. Cindy drew in a quick breath. Having had nothing to do with medicine, wounds, or injuries her entire life left her unprepared for what she saw. A few inches above his belt was the exit wound. The bullet had turned sideways going through and left a ragged gash in the skin. Tissue from internal organs hung out with blood dripping from it. Somewhere the admonition about not letting the person know how badly he was hurt came to her.

"Well . . . it's not too bad, not good, but we need to get the bleeding stopped. There," she said pointing to a shirt hanging over a chair. "Jason, grab that." He did, and the two of them got it placed over the two bullet holes. Cindy wrapped her scarf around his waist to pull the bandage tight and knotted it. "You shouldn't be moving, Hua. Are you sure you don't want to lie down and let me call for medical help?"

Between short, halting breaths, Hua responded, "Need to get to the place of the energy." He pointed out of the room down the corridor. "That way first, then down and to the left. I feel it is almost strong enough to help. Must get closer."

---

Breckon didn't want to be shot as he knelt in the snow with the out stretched pistol aimed at him from ten feet away. He was out of options, though, and time. He had to go after the others and help them with Hua. Slowly picking up the gun he didn't even look at the man who had called himself Muan Yingqu. He had only glimpsed the man who had tried to steal his suitcase at the Nanjing airport. Add to that the fact that now he was wearing a coat and stocking cap. Besides, those guys all looked alike.

The gun was cold in his hand. He knew he should check the load as he thrust it behind his belt. If he was shot dead in the next few seconds it wouldn't matter, so what was the point? The point was, he should be trying some last ditch attempt to take out the Chinese man so his back trail would be clear. This way, even if he wasn't stopped here, the threat would remain. The mood that had befallen him was discomfiting. It was as if his life were on autopilot and it didn't matter what he did other than move ahead on the most obvious course. As he walked he glance at his watch, eleven minutes to go. He started to run.

---

Jian Niu was seated in the only comfortable chair in the control room tapping his fingers on the top of a work surface. The minutes ticked away until now there were only nine left until eight o'clock. They were as ready as they could be, but without the pendant and the right person wearing it, the test could not begin. That crazy man, Quan Peng, was long gone, probably dead by now the way he was last seen jumping out of windows. That was one dude with serious issues. Without him and the keystone device, or devices, he corrected himself, too bad. That was another thing that didn't add up. In fact, the only thing that did add up was that this was a sham. It was all about little people wanting to make big names for themselves.

Well, it wouldn't be long. No test, no proof of the conjecture. As soon as the hour came and went, they could relax. He would positively reject any suggestion that they be ready to run the test at two in the morning on the off chance Peng would show up in the intervening time. The message he would send to Beijing was already formed in his mind. He might even copy that general if the mood struck him. When they were all back in China, the accounting would be made. It always was. The ruling class was simply never, ever, challenged.

---

Heng Lu was as certain as he could be that the man with the keystone device would not arrive in time for the test. This, in turn, would leave the way open for Niu and his crowd to assume the conjecture was false. Not only would this destroy his career, but if it were true, as he was certain it was, China would be on its way to an international embarrassment.

The wrenching sound of the door being forced caused all heads to turn. Lu was the closest to the door. With nerves taught as banjo strings, he was instantly on his feet. The appearance of Quan Peng left him befuddled. It was good he had returned so the test could start. But, the door.

"Sorry. The door was a little stuck," Peng said. "I am here for the start of the eight o'clock test." He smiled. "This time it will be successful because I have discarded the keystone device of this afternoon, and I will use this one." He pulled his pendant out from his shirt. "The feeling is on me that you already have the experiment started at low power awaiting me as the hour approaches. You need me, and of course, my keystone."

Peng's exuberant expression faded slightly. "Why are you all looking at me that way. I am here and have my high power keystone device. I will make the test go as planned in a few short minutes. I am the reason you did all of this, is it not?" He swept his hand around the room. "Now that it is ready for me, I am here. It is something I am waiting for with great expectations."

The look on Peng's face, especially the wild eyes, disturbed Lu. Megalomania had taken control of the man. He had never heard anyone use the personal pronouns so many times in so few sentences. This, to say nothing of having the strong door ripped open as if it were made of Styrofoam. A normal knock on the door and Lu would have admitted him immediately. The whole plan was to start the test, lock the doors, and leave word they were taking a long weekend to go to Chicago to visit friends.

A short time before, that grad student had called the police. He told the police, and anyone else who would listen, that the perpetrator had been a Chinese man. Upon seeing the damaged door, the U of M staff would assume the intruder's objective had been the work spaces of their prized client. This could lead to complications none of them could anticipate.

The fact that Peng seemed oblivious to the damage to the door, in fact, to his own strength, wasn't lost on anyone in the room. Lu glanced around at the others. They looked as horrified as he felt. At least, the man with the keystone was in a good mood. The only thing Lu could think of was to keep him that way for the next few minutes so the test could start. Maybe the physical effects on him would be as bad or worse than they had been earlier in the day. That would give them with a chance to subdue him. Peng, for his part, looked intently at the large round clock above the pendant station as if assuring himself that he was not too late.

Lu leaned over to Wu Zheng, the engineer. "Will you see if you can find a way to secure the door so we aren't disturbed as we start the test?" Wu nodded and went to the door. He examined it and went on his mission.

Peng was at the pedestal that contained the socket for the keystone device. Looking in amazement at the whole apparatus, it seemed as if he were seeing it in detail for the first time. In his state of mind, he appeared to be imagining that it had all been built just for him.

Off to the side was the large differential temperature readout, Delta-T. It showed the difference in temperature of the water upstream and downstream from the ceramic cylinder. Since it would take thirty-five megawatts to heat the flow of water one degree, a thousandth of a degree represented thirty-five kilowatts. The digital meter now rested at all zeros except the least significant digit displayed a one. It occasionally changed to two, and at times, zero. Forty kilowatts was the output of the ceramic cylinder operating in its present quiescent state.

A minute later Zheng was back with a length of plastic rope. He looped it around the doorknob on the outside and pulled the two strands in. He removed a fire extinguisher from its holder bolted to the wall beside the door. After tying the rope to the holder, he tried the door. It was tight. He shrugged as he looked at Lu. It wasn't the best, but time was short.

---

Jian Niu was in a funk since Peng had arrived. He could not see how he could affect what was to happen. The gutted latch of the door, and the man's casual ignorance of anything abnormal, made him realize that the situation was now out of the control of anyone except Peng, maybe out of his control, too. Whether the others realized that or not, he at least, knew this for a fact. Wait! Maybe not. He remembered what the general had said about the hubots being drawn back to the control room in time for the test. What had that low-life said? "He can handle almost any difficulty he encounters," like tearing open a locked door. The beast was incredibly strong. There was the other instruction, too. Oh, yes. He would be agitated or elated so it would be important to handle him with a stern hand. It seemed his state of mind was one of euphoria. In that state, he doubted Peng would follow anyone's instructions, let alone his. Still, with the start of the test so near, he needed to distract him, cause a disturbance, so the critical time would pass without him placing his keystone in the receptacle.

"Quan Peng!" Niu's command cracked like a whip. Peng looked at Niu. "I know you are not Shan Jin. In fact you killed him and took his keystone. That is why you had two. With Shan Jin dead, we are unfortunately forced to have one as unsuitable as you take his place. However, you will do only what I order you to do, and when I so order. Is that quite clear!" The denigration in Niu's voice was more pronounced even than the words.

Peng's gaze became hard as it bore into Niu. The others froze remembering this man's belligerent attitude toward Niu earlier in the day. They knew Peng was hyped-up about the approaching test, not to mention the physical strength he had so recently demonstrated. It seemed suicidal to confront him in such a caustic manner. Niu was obviously trying to derail the test again to say nothing of getting them all killed.

---

Hua Chen looked like he'd die any minute, but he was insistent that they keep going. "Okay. Lean on Jason and me," Cindy said. "We'll do the best we can." They shambled down the hallway to the door at the end where the passage turned to the right. Jason looked inquiringly at Hua. "This door?" he asked.

Hua nodded. His complexion was like that of a cadaver; even his lips were without color. "You don't look so good," Jason said as he pulled the door toward him.

"Don't feel good either," was the weak reply.

Past the door was a small room that was really a large landing at the top of a stairway. The center of the landing was open with a railing around it. Beyond the rail, one could see four floors down to the bottom of the lab spaces. Large pipes and other utilities ran vertically in the well. Past the open space they turned left, descended a few steps, and then turned right. There was only one way to go. From there, it was down a long steel staircase. On the left was the bare limestone bedrock that formed the Mississippi bluffs, on the right was a steel pipe handrail. "Sort of like the Bat Cave," Jason remarked.

They proceeded down, came to a landing, and turned. Hua was making a hard time of it, but was driven to keep going. Then down more steps and turned again at the next landing. "That way," he said turning into a poorly lit space. "Now on the right level. Not far." Everywhere, there was evidence of experiments being set up, and those that must have been completed, but not yet taken down to make room for the next. Lumber, pipes, bricks, and tools were scattered about. Along the dark walls, pipes and utility cables followed the aisles and stairs. So far, they had not seen another person. No one to question who they were and their reason for prowling about at this hour.

Hua stopped. Though labored breathing he said, "Behind that new wall is the place."

They approached the door and tried it. Locked. Jason beat on it with his fist. No response. He picked up a piece of two-by-four and pounded on it. The latch turned, and the door was cautiously opened a few inches. Hua fumbled with the top buttons of his shirt as Cindy stood beside him holding his upper arm. Before the eyes that appeared in the crack of the door, Hua dangled the pendant. He uttered, "I have come with this."

---

The distraction caused by the persistent banging jangled nerves already on edge. There were looks from one to the other. The new ruckus had the unintended consequence of ending the dual of contemptuous stares between Niu and Peng.

"Well. See who it is!" Niu snapped.

Jianli Huang's workstation was closest to the second door. She unlocked and opened it enough to see out. At the sight of yet another keystone device, she tried to slam the door shut. "Go away." Jason, however, had slipped the two-by-four into the crack as soon as the door moved. Hua saw the door was braced open and leaning toward the crack held the pendant inside for all to see. "I have come with this," he said again.

Niu saw the keystone and another thing the general had said came to mind. A second hubot was on the loose and might show up—one for redundancy. This would produce an interesting situation that would help tick away more minutes. "Let the man come in," he said. "He has come for the test, too."

Cindy and Jason didn't understand what Hua had said, nor the responses from inside. When the door was released, they all came in. Everyone was on their feet thinking it was an invasion. Niu was taken aback as well, not suspecting there was anyone besides the man with the keystone.

The clock showed seven minutes to eight.

---

Breckon, too, saw the office sign and went in. The blood on the floor showed he had gone the right way. Peering into the office, he saw a lot of blood along with Chen's coat crumpled on the floor. There was nothing about the scene that gave him encouragement. The steps down the corridor were not as bloody, in fact, as he followed, he could barely discern that they had gone through the door at the end of the hall. Through it, he could see nothing of them. Instinctively, he looked down the shaft with the utilities passing up and down in it. No movement.

"Cindy," he called out.

No response. He started down continuing to the bottom. Here, all but security lights were off.

"Cindy," he called again.

Nothing. He retraced his steps up the long steel staircase, passed a landing and up again. Now he saw a space ahead of him he had missed coming down. It was dark where he was, but there was light further on in a larger open space. Moving ahead, he followed the more or less distinct walkway among the materials and equipment lying about. Coming to an area where the normal lights were on, he saw a newly constructed wall. It looked out of place since some of the construction was eons old. Approaching the door he noted the lock, but tried the latch anyway. It was locked. He tapped with his knuckles on the door. There was no answer, though, he thought he heard voices on the far side. After further futile attempts, he looked around.

To his left was another bay, or hall, not as well lit. Stepping over hoses, boards, and what not, he made his way into it. It was a workshop. Cautiously continuing on, he wove his way among workbenches, partially constructed equipment, and tools. The sound of flowing water seemed to increase with each step. He found the established walkway and soon came out on the far side of the newly constructed room. He glanced at the door but the lighting wasn't good so he turned his attention in the direction of the sound. Beside him was a river behind a transparent wall. He hurried several steps to where the water flowed down a sluice. There were probes with instruments protruding into the stream. His eyes followed the cables from the transducers to junction boxes and finally to an office computer at the side of the aisle beside the river. It was an experiment. All through the night, the "electronic eyes" would be watching the behavior of the water so in the morning scientists could study trends.

It was fascinating, but not what he was looking for. It was dark further up stream—unlikely anyone was working there. Turning, he saw the wall again. This time, he took an interest in the door. He turned that way.

---

The snow continued to fall. Muan Yingqu stood watching over the black barrel of his outstretched pistol as Breckon walked away. He saw him raise his arm, look at the time, and immediately break into a run. Why didn't he shoot? It all seemed so anticlimactic. Before he had time to reconsider, his chance was gone. Without realizing it, his focus shortened so he was watching the snowflakes landing on his gun. Most slid off, but some came to rest and laid there. They were so soft and harmless. The gun so lethal. A strange admixture. The arm muscles relaxed and the gun swung down so it hung at his side in the right hand. The dead man in the snow was still visible by his form, but as he watched, he was being covered by a blanket of pure white. Why was white associated with goodness and virtue? He doubted the man had been very good. He knew he hadn't been. He became aware of the snow making light ticking sounds as hundreds of white projectiles gently impacted his clothing. What was left to do? Kejian would have shown up by now if he were still alive. Yingqu sensed he was alone on his mission. What mission was that? *His* mission, that of bringing retribution on Breckon, was over, un-fulfilled. Both hubots were in the lab building. Supposedly, that's where they were intended to be. It was finished. He had no accomplishment, however off the mark, to bring to his superiors. He had failed. The future was bleak. The snow still fell.

Terrible earthquake! He holstered his pistol, and brushed off his clothing struggling to pull himself out of the torpor that had befallen him. What had Breckon said? It would kill everybody in the city? He even asked for his help. That lab was where Breckon and the rest of them went. Why not? He was off at a trot.

Between the buildings he followed the tracks but failed to see the sign for the office. Suddenly there were no tracks. He stopped. No one had come this far recently. He turned back. Still missing the sign, now above his head on the left, he discerned people had gone in to or out of the doors on either side. That made sense because he was certain several people had come this way in the last several minutes. He opened the door on his right. He froze where he was, seeing wet tracks on the floor. He hoped he could use them to determine where the others had gone. Care-fully, he stepped to the side of the hall and followed each step to where there were several and then no more. What had happened? Had he taken off his shoes? It took a moment and then he had it. They stopped by a door.

Through the door and he was on a landing at the top of a stairs. He could see no more tracks because the light was dim where he was. Plus, the steps were diamond tread steel plate and this far into the building the shoes would be leaving few marks of their passing, though, this was where the tracks seemed to lead. Down he went coming into a large room filled with something resembling a sandbox for adults. It was the space where river flood planes and similar waterways were modeled. There were a few lights, enough to make out the scene. The predominant sound was of trickling water. Yes, this was a lab, and this looked like a river that was being studied in miniature. He noted the plank bridges across the channel in places. Off to the sides were piles of sand. One had a shovel stuck in it. It was amusing. They could change the river at will. Make it narrower, dredge it, add banks, play with nature.

This was not the right place. He turned full around. It occurred to him that something was wrong. He could hear the water burgling along in the make believe river. In the background, there was a dull roar. At first he had though it was the passage of the water outside that flowed under the bridge he had used to get to the offices. But that should have been coming from above since he had come down the long stairs. This sound came from below. Was there a subterranean river running under the place? Finally, he spotted the start of a handrail. Another stairs. There was something below this.

# — 37 —

Peng flushed from the demeaning words spoken by Niu. It was too outrageous. That puke of an arrogant upper class piece of dirt, talking down to him! He was needed for the test. It was ordained that it should be that way. All the miles of travel and privation he had endured getting halfway around the world was the price he had paid to be a part of the test. What had that maggot ever paid? Nothing. He was simply born to luxury and advantage. Peng was at his post doing his duty. Glancing up at the big clock, he saw there was time to silence the irritation in the form of that detestable man. Peng took his first stride in Niu's direction when the banging on the door started. When the arm appeared with the keystone device dangling from it he knew it was HB-23. So, he had made it this far. No matter, he was wounded and weak. Might as well make an end to both Niu and him.

The door opened and three people appeared. Everyone from the Chinese team was standing and talking at once. Peng saw the pendant as his immediate threat. He advanced to Hua, grabbed him by the shirt, and threw him against the wall. Hua slid down in a cry of pain.

Cindy screamed as the rest looked on in horror.

---

Breckon heard the scream. Its frequency was far above that of the sound of the rushing water so it cut through with clarity. It came from the direction of the new wall. Hurrying to the door, he saw it had been forced. There was a plastic rope around the knob, and through the broken strike. He tugged on the doorknob. It was made fast with a rope. He pounded on the door. "Go away," someone shouted from the other side.

From being tossed off Peng like a dry leaf, he knew he was the man with the strength to account for the damage. He pulled out his pocket-knife and sliced at the cord that gave under his persistence. He pulled the door open and took two steps into the room. The door swung shut of its own accord. Peng was about to grab Hua again when Breckon shouted, "Stand away from that man, or you're dead! Do it now!"

---

Peng slowly straightened up looking toward Breckon who had a gun pointed at him. This man had jumped him, clasping his knees while still in the parking lot. He would not have done that if he had had a gun. Peng had the gun from the vehicle behind his belt in the small of his back under his suit coat. The gun he had shot Shorty with was empty. Shorty's gun had been fired six times. It too, was empty. This had to be one of those. Breckon was bluffing. A wicked smile came to his face.

"There are no bullets in that gun."

"I reloaded it."

The smile became a chuckle as Peng made a step toward Breckon. "No you didn't."

"Stop!" Breckon pulled the trigger and the hammer fell with a click on an empty cartridge.

Peng laughed as he took a second step.

Now that it looked like these two men would come to blows, Niu tried to inflame the situation further by shouting, "Quan Peng. Settle down. Don't be a hot-headed fool. You will do exactly as I say!"

If any words were able to unbalance Peng in his state of mind, those were the ones. In a swift fluid movement, Peng pulled his gun from behind his belt.

Oops! Niu had not counted on that.

The gun came up aimed at Breckon.

Niu, thinking the gun was aimed at Lu, laughed hysterically as he said, "There goes your test, and you with it!"

The gun shifted in a wink and discharged. Niu's brains were splattered on the wall.

---

As Yingqu approached the head of the stairs, the roar became louder. Halfway down the sound was coming from his left. Instinctively he looked that way. This was amazing. A torrent of water rushed along behind a transparent wall.

Continuing down the steps, movement caught his eye to the front, someone going through a door, the door swinging closed. He hurried to it. The sound of a shot. He pulled it open as Peng's gun was swinging back to Breckon.

From behind, Breckon heard. "Breckon! Freeze! Don't move a muscle."

"Oh, for crying out loud!" Breckon said. Yingqu was still after him.

The whiff of the bullet a half-inch from Breckon's ear came a split second before the report. He felt the hot gases from the burning powder on his neck. Peng lurched as Yingqu's bullet caught his right shoulder sending his gun rattling on the floor.

"No!" Lu yelled. Then taking in the fact that Peng was disarmed and still standing said in a lowered voice, "Peng. One minute forty seconds. Please. Go to your post." Lu guessed that Peng had been drawn to the test in a way he didn't understand. He seemed to need it. His giddy mien as he entered the room seemed to portray that. If the test were to be saved that man had to start it by inserting his keystone device. "Peng, your chance to access the energy will pass if you fail to insert your keystone at the appointed time." His voice was firm, but, he hoped, tinged with help-fulness. It worked. Peng forgot the rest in the room and started toward the keystone station.

Hua called out in a faint voice. "Ed. Come to me. I need you."

It was all happening so fast. Ed knew from the voice behind him that it was Yingqu who had shot Peng. He didn't know when the next shot, the one for him, would sound. He turned slowly and looked at Yingqu who stood in the open doorway. Yingqu, still holding the gun, shrugged with the strangest expression Breckon could remember having seen. It was as if he were saying he didn't understand it either.

"Ed," the faint voice said again.

Breckon looked past Lu and saw Hua on the floor with his pleading face turned his way. Hoping the threat from Yingqu was gone, he went to Hua. Beside him, on his knees, he said, "You're not looking so good, ol' buddy."

"Will die soon. You must prepare me die. You can do that."

"What? How?"

The weak voice came back, "Talked with Father Aldrich. You know him. Learned much. You must baptize me."

Ed absentmindedly rubbed his forehead. "Yeah, I know. Anyone can baptize anyone else. But, you have to know what you're doing."

"I know what I'm doing, and I know I will die in minutes. You know this saying? *Suprema lex salus animarum*."

"No."

By now, the others, except for Peng, were clustered around looking down on the drama of death unfolding before them. The members of the Chinese team all understood English enough to follow that was being said.

"That means," Cindy broke in, "something to the effect that at the time of death salvation is all important. Everything that can be done to insure reconciliation with God must be done. That includes baptism . . . I think."

"Okay, I'll do it. I need water."

"There," Cindy said pointing to a clear plastic bottle of spring water on a workstation. One of the team saw her point and handed it to her. She gave it to Ed.

Ed said, "Here goes. You want to be baptized, and I want to baptize you. The proper intentions are necessary. So, now, I baptize you in the name of the Father, and of the Son, and of the Holy Spirit."

Hua followed with a barely audible amen. "Death is now close to me . . . I reach out to it." After a labored breath he continued. "Death is not the end . . . it is a new place to start. A song of hope has become a song of joy." His eyes suddenly opened wide. "Oh . . ." he said in wonderment. "I see heaven open, angels come to greet me, and take me . . . it has never entered my mind what beauty and peace comes to those who seek God with a pure heart . . . I go to infinite good . . ."

There was a glow about Hua Chen that those who watched felt more than saw. It wouldn't cast a shadow or be seen on a movie film. It was other-worldly. For a few moments, the presence of God was close. The room was peaceful. Hua's eyes were still open and Ed reached over and closed them. It was over. The glow started to pass.

Jason was kneeling on the other side of Hua from Ed. "Wow." It was more an expression on reverence than an exclamation. "What happened? He died. But, it seemed so good. We think of death as bad."

Cindy padded him on the shoulder. "It's unlikely you'll see that again. It's rare. He died with that is called baptismal innocence. He passed from this life directly to heaven. Almost nobody does that, regardless of what most Christians will tell you."

"Yeah," Ed said. "The lucky stick. The rest of us are left to grope along trying to take the next best step . . . at least sometimes."

Dr. Luan had expected the hubot to be agitated by the decreasing strength of the pendant by the time he showed up for the test. Or, it was possible, he would be elated by the prospect of his pendant being re-charged. His instructions to Niu were intended to convert either of these states into intense anger and thus increase the dopamine and norepineph-rine in his blood stream. He had not counted on Peng's personality with his inflated ego. The state of euphoria about becoming a deity was never in the plan. The contradiction posed by the officious approach of Niu was compounded by him, not only getting prepared to kill, but actually doing it. This pushed the chemical response off the charts. This was fur-ther amplified by being shot which produced a real need for healing.

When Peng pushed his keystone into the receptacle at the appointed time it magnified his human energy field to feed the quantum process occurring at the edge of zero point. This was intended. Immediately the cylinder switched to self-generation. Circuits designed to sense this dis-engaged the sustaining power from the local gird. The system was oper-ating on its own. As long as it was properly regulated, it would continue generating power for the indefinite future. It had no moving parts, and the ceramic construction was immune to erosion or similar degradation. In short, there was nothing to wear out.

What was not intended was Peng's exceptionally high energy field and the effect it had on his keystone device. This ramped up power much too fast. Beyond that, the plan was to have the keystone removed after self-generation was established. At the worst, if the wearer of the pen-dant refused to remove it, he would collapse from pain, possibly dead, and thereby yank it out of the socket. In Peng's mind, the painful effects of having his pendant inserted in the system were interpreted as signs that he was being remade, becoming deified. In addition, the ill physio-logical effects came so fast that they stunned the muscles keeping him frozen in place.

---

Jianli Huang had been standing looking down over the shoulder of one of the men. She now returned to her station, still with some of the effects of her close encounter with eternity about her. She sat down and looked at the clock. The hour hand was on eight, the minute hand was passed the first minor increment on the dial, and the second hand was halfway around. "Time plus one and a half minutes," she screamed.

The jarring outcry electrified the team. Each one scrambled to his station, each scrutinizing data in his area of responsibility. Lu's monitor showed a vortex larger than anything intended. This translated to massive amounts of power being generated. Glancing up he saw Peng standing at his station with his arms extended. He was physically glowing. Then, Lu's eyes landed on the digital meter. "Delta-T! Three point two!" The decibel level of his exclamation got everyone's attention. Not only was it that high but it was climbing rapidly. The thousandths of a degree digit was changing so fast as to be a blur.

"Nucleate boiling detected on the ceramic, cavitation imminent," Jianli said in a firm voice.

"Reduce power," Lu said.

"Can't," Wu Zheng snapped contrary to his normal demeanor. "Nothing's responding. The keystone is too powerful."

Lu looked up to see the heat exchanger surrounded by a blue-green glow similar to that produced by Cerenkof radiation in nuclear reactors.

"Terminating test!" Lu yelled as the slapped his hand on the red mushroom-shaped "Panic Button."

"Cannot terminate with keystone in place." Zheng's words were tinged with dread.

---

The Chinese team's frantic statements, even if in Mandarin, caught the attention of the onlookers. Breckon looked up and, to the best of his ability, took in the situation. He saw the clock. The crucial time of eight o'clock was past. The apparatus in the water was glowing blue-green with the intensity increasing. His gaze fell on the Delta-T display. Being so prominently placed, it was obviously a key variable. Any time a critical value climbed that fast it would cause panic—something unmistakable in the voices.

"Look," Jason said pointing at Peng. His outline had streams of energy emanating from him like the discharge from a Tesla coil. "What's happening to him? He's getting fuzzy."

"The clock," Cindy said. "The second hand has stopped. I think it's starting to go backwards."

"Cavitation in heat transfer sector seven," Jianli said to the team.

"Everybody out!" Ed shouted.

Cindy and Jason raced for the door. The Chinese team was a little slow on the uptake being absorbed in their duties. Yingqu stood fixed to the floor watching Peng. He pointed not uttering a sound. The whole space around Peng seemed to be distorting.

Nudging Yingqu aside, Cindy and Jason rushed past him. Yingqu lost his balance and fell to one knee. By this time, the Chinese team was at the door. Not seeing their countryman, they tripped over him, scrambled up, and headed to the stairs closing in behind Cindy and Jason.

Yingqu groaned in pain as he rolled over grasping his knee. Breckon, the last one out, leaped over him and was about to dash for the stairs when he wheeled and stopped.

Yingqu was by now sitting on the floor holding his knee between both hands moaning. Breckon rushed toward him, grabbed him under the arms from the back, and jerked him to his feet. Yingqu cried in pain. "Guess you could have shot me a couple of times and didn't. Turn about's a bitch. I'm going to get even by saving your life."

Breckon swung Yingqu's arm over his shoulder with one hand and grabbed him around the waist with the other arm. They hobbled along, two men on three good legs.

Halfway up the first flight of stairs they heard a dull thud behind them. Stopping momentarily and turning, they could see the surface of the flume and the underwater ceramic cylinder surrounded by the heat exchanger through the transparent wall. The glow was brighter now. Streams of bubbles were erupting from seams in the shiny heat exchanger.

Yingqu grasped the iron handrail with his free hand, his breath coming in short rasping puffs. Breckon turned and said, "Come on. We have to get moving. That doesn't look good."

Reaching the floor above the one with the Chinese experiment, Yingqu lost his coordination and Breckon dragged him. Some of the others stopped and looked back. Breckon realized this was still under ground with the channel bringing water to the power plant a few feet beyond the wall on the right. Though he had no intimate knowledge of the facility, he was good enough at visualizing the layout of things to know this. If there were an earthquake, even a small one, they had to go higher, preferably get across the bridge and off the island.

"Keep going," he said to the others who had stopped. "Up to the top floor." After a pause, "Hey. One of you guys give me a hand here." His own breath was becoming labored. Ju Feng, the largest of the Chinese team, still several inches shorter than Breckon, came to help, grabbing Yingqu's other arm around his shoulder. Cindy was just ahead of the three men. Starting up the next stairs the whole place shuddered. The sound of things falling, clanking, twisting and splintering was obvious.

Breckon yelled to Cindy, "Get to the next floor and pull a fire alarm to clear the building."

She ran up the remaining stairs. Seconds later, the ringing of an alarm filled the air. She held the door open as they reached the top landing. Breckon pause to catch his breath. "How're you doing?" he asked Yingqu.

The man's eyes were wild and his face twisted, but he made no reply.

"Yeah. I'm fine, too. Thanks for asking," Breckon said as they started moving again. They almost fell at the next lurch of the building.

Once out the door the cold air felt good. The exertion caused Breckon to sweat profusely as he had been wearing his parka the whole time. He wanted to tell Cindy to run for it, but sensed it would be a futile effort. He said, "Go ahead and make sure the others get across the bridge."

As the two men carrying and dragging Yingqu approached the bridge, they could see everyone on the far side looking back. They had been joined by a half dozen others who had been working late. Three-quarters of the way across the bridge the third quake came and this time they fell. It was slippery from the snow, and the movement was much worse than before. Two of the men, one Chinese and one husky grad student, came to help. The wrenching of the steel support members of the bridge was unmistakable. The student grabbed Ju Feng's arm and dragged him along through the snow as Breckon and the other dragged Yingqu. The up-stream structure that adjusted the height of the gates to regulate the flow of water through the channel to the power plant was twisting and falling. Portions of the concrete deck of the bridge cracked and splashed into the water.

With everybody across the large student helped Breckon carry Yingqu. Breckon looked at the Chinese. "How much more of this?"

Lu responded in heavily accented English as the ground continued to jiggle, "The cylinder is still generating power. The big problem comes when it stops, and that could be any second."

"Great," Breckon rasped, still trying to get his breath.

They could see it was down a grade to the parking lot so the lot was obviously below the headwaters. "In that case, we've got to get to higher ground, at least to Main Street. Let's go." They started running slowly with Yingqu dragging his feet in the snow between the two men.

Before long, firemen finishing up with the meth lab were around them. They had felt the tremors and were concerned about all the old structures in the area. One man told three others to go down to the lab and see what was going on.

Breckon stopped at Main Street and said to his companion. "Let's set him down. I'm played out." As he straightened up, he saw the firemen start down to the lab.

"No!" he shouted. "That's not safe!" At that moment, the ground shook in earnest. They were all thrown on the ground. The building seemed to implode like all four sides wanted to get to the center in a second. Materials were thrown high into the air. The debris of the test facility as well as the power plant began being swept away by the onrushing waters as the dam structure gave way. The flood swept across the parking lot taking the vehicles including the Hummer with it.

"There goes our ride," Jason yelled above the din. In a couple of minutes, the debris was largely carried away. Small parts of the structure that remained continued to fall into the torrent as the water eroded its underpinnings. The raging waters continued to increase as more of the dam collapsed. The Excel Energy substation sparked and snapped. The hum stopped as it switched off line.

They were sitting in the snow and Cindy crawled over to Ed and sat close to him, real close. "You okay," she asked in a soft voice.

He put his arm around her, squeezed her tight, and said, "Never been better."

# — 38 —

Cindy and Ed stood together, Ed with his arm around her. Sitting in the snow will get you a wet behind no matter how cozy things are otherwise. Neither said anything. Muan Yingqu was lying on his left side waiting for help to arrive. Two firemen had put a waterproof coat under him and used another to cover him for warmth and as protection from the falling snow. His right leg had an unnatural angle to it. With the buildings gone, the only sound was that of rushing water seeking to relieve itself of the pent up potential energy it possessed by virtue of being held behind the dam.

Jason was nearby talking to his mother on his cell phone. Breckon said, "Tell her to be sure to have them send an ambulance. We have a man with a broken leg."

After Jason relayed the message Breckon couldn't help smiling as he overheard this end of the conversation. "Yeah, mom. Like I said, I'm fine. Some of the others aren't so good, though, like the guy who had his brains blown out." There was a pause. "No, that's not the one in the parking lot. That's another guy." Another pause. "Don't worry. I'm not standing here looking at them. They were swept away in the river. It's a long story. I'll tell you about it when you get here." After yet another pause, "Yeah. See ya."

Jason put his cell phone in his pocket. "Boy. Mom usually doesn't get so upset. Guess I should have called sooner."

Breckon looked at him. "It would have only meant that she would have been upset longer. There was no wining on that one."

Standing in the middle of Main Street two policemen were talking to Heng Lu. With Jian Niu's departure from this mortal sphere, Lu was now the lead man for the Chinese project. Breckon walked over to the officers and said, "Take my advice and don't talk to the Chinese people. Make sure they don't leave, but don't get involved in what happened. This is an extremely complicated case. The CIA will be here in a few minutes. Leave it to them. If the Asians tell you anything, you'll spend hours being debriefed. I've been there. It isn't fun."

To his surprise, the two officers took the advice. They identified all the players with Breckon's and Lu's help. Lu said to Breckon, "Thank you. I think you are right about the CIA. They will want to know everything."

Breckon leaned over to Lu and said in a low voice. "It looks to me like you were right. The conjecture *is* true."

Lu gave Breckon a strange look as if finding it hard to believe what he had heard. "What do you know of that? That is a closely guarded secret in China."

"We have had some of our best minds on it. By the way, I'm Ed Breckon. I'm nothing but an average citizen who's been caught up in this. I assume you are one of the lead physicists on this zero point energy project."

Lu was being guarded not knowing what he should say. Breckon could see from Lu's demeanor that he was right. "What I'm curious about is the first tremors. I thought the disturbance, earthquake I guess, would only happen when the device was shut off."

Without looking directly at Breckon Lu said, "The tremors were caused by power reductions prior to the total stopping of power production. You can see what would happen if many huge power plants were made. Eventually, it would break up the tectonic plates that make up the earth's crust. That would be the end of us."

"Some of our scientists thought the same thing. It was strange, though. It didn't just shake the ground. It seemed like it imploded. Why was that?"

"Very simply, it was like stretching a rubber band with your hands and letting go of both ends at exactly the same time. However, the rubber band represents only one dimension. Here we had three spatial and one time dimension doing that. In addition, there might have been a fourth spatial dimensions involved. In spite of what they will do to us, it was interesting to see."

"Yeah. That's something of an understatement. Let me thank you for bringing this to our attention with your test, even though in the process you sent that lab down the river. I doubt there will be many others who thank you."

Lu gave Breckon a wry smile. "I think, in that, you are correct."

Breckon continued, "Do you think this test was conspicuous enough to cause work on generating power from zero point energy to stop? It could be argued that the dam was old and its failure was only a coincidence."

Lu was nodding as Breckon spoke. "There is no question work will continue. The physicists that hold the view that the conjecture is false have too much to lose. Your dam is broken and the lab is gone. It doesn't matter, though, because in the end we will have accomplished nothing."

Then, staring at the river below them, Lu continued. "The three men . . . the contrast."

Breckon gave him a quizzical look.

"The three men who died in the laboratory. How different it was for them. Jian Niu had been making our lives miserable from the beginning. None of us would have minded seeing him removed from the project, by force if necessary. However, to see it actually happen in such a brutal, violent way was not expected. It gives me some feelings of guilt.

"Then there is the question of our umpire, Quan Peng. His coming along is hard to understand. Why he came or where he came from, or even what he was after, is a mystery. And, the thing I keep asking myself is, where did he go?"

Breckon was of a mind to interrupt and shed some light on the idea of hubots, but it didn't seem that was the purpose of Lu's recital. He was trying to get to something else so he let him continue.

"The wounded one . . ." he let out a sigh. "What is there to tell? I don't know words even in my native tongue that will say it. When he died it was full of peace." He looked at Breckon. "Did you see the nice light?" Then looking away, "Not really a light, a felt light on the inside . . ."

Lu looked down and kicked at the snow.

Breckon replied, "That was in the realm of the spiritual. I'm not the one to explain it to you, but God means for something like that to happen to each one of us—if we lead good lives. After the CIA gets done with us, if we can still remember who we are, we should get together and I'll give you some ideas about where to start if you want to learn more about it. As for Peng, there's an uneasy feeling in my gut that he isn't gone for good."

Lights flashing off the snow made them look up the street. A large ambulance led the way making a track in the snow with two black SUVs following.

# — EPILOG —

The first sensation Quan Peng remembered was filling his lungs with cold damp air. Flopping around in a current made no sense at all. The water was cold and the light dim. After two more deep breaths, it came back. Apparently, the energy production had been too great for the facility and in some mysterious way he had been flushed out of the place unconsciously holding his breath. He was looking to the dark outline of the river bluff through the still falling snow when something bumped him on the left. A foot thick chunk of ice was pushing him downstream. Looking in the direction of travel, he saw more ice that was not moving, and that he was about to be crushed. Sucking in air, he quickly submerged as the ice ground together. Swimming off to the side, he saw a change in the diffracted light indicating a place where the ice chunks didn't match. Thrusting up into the opening, he slapped his hands on the ice where it made a corner so he could heave himself up. Pain registered as he put pressure on his right hand. He remembered the bullet wound and wondered why he had not been aware of it when he regained consciousness. Pain or not he had to get out of the water. Forcing himself, he found the arm still bore the pressure of heaving him out of the water. He rolled in the snow away from the hole.

Up on his knees the scene around him had the familiar orange glow from thousands of sodium vapor streetlights of the city reflecting off the clouds and snow. The black spaces of open water were rapidly closing as more ice and floating debris came together around him. He was nearly thrown down by a jolt as a part of a building rammed into the stationary ice. He became aware of cracking sounds from upstream and understood that the laboratory building was being swept away. He was in the pool behind the second dam less than a half-mile down stream from the one at the laboratory.

Only seconds had passed from his regaining consciousness and he realized he had to get off the ice. The rush of water from the broken upper dam was causing the water to rise. It would soon send ice, debris, and

him over the lower dam. In addition, he had to get inside a warm building before he died of the cold.

He was up and running for the near shore on the east side of the river.
The ice heaved under his feet and then fell away as swells undulated
through the water beneath it. Timing his steps, he jumped over cracks as
they opened and then immediately closed. Finally, he was on shore
pounding through snow with tufts of tall grass thrusting out of it at intervals. As he ran across the relatively flat fifty yards, he noticed his pendant bouncing on his chest. It was still hanging around his neck on the
bead chain. With numb fingers, he dropped it behind his shirt.

Up a five-foot bank, he was at an eight-foot chain link fence. Here
too, there was a horizontal pole half way up as well as one at the top. The
halfway bar was on his side. The fence had been built with the intent of
keeping people away from the river, not the other way. Running to a corner twenty feet to his right he put his half-dead fingers through the wire
and pulled his feet up on the intermediate pipe. His leather soled shoe
slipped off on the first try. It wasn't going as well as it had earlier because he was tired and much colder. Shear desperation gave him the
strength to, at last, get up on the top bar and drop into the snow.

There was a road immediately past the fence with nearly erased vehicle tracks. Two hundred yards on his left was a large structure with four
tall stacks that looked like a powerhouse. Being a public facility, it would
have guards. He crossed the road and started up the thirty-foot bank.
Grabbing small trees and brush, he struggled up the steep slope slipping
and falling frequently. The leather shoes were not suited for this. At the
top, he saw a five story building a hundred yards in front of him.

With no time to think, he started for it. He crossed railroad tracks, a
road, knee deep snow, then a street, and a parking lot. He passed a sign
proclaiming Stone Arch Apartments. He slowed upon seeing a man
walking toward the entry. As quietly as possible he closed the distance to
him so he arrived at the door a few steps behind. The outer door was not
locked. The man had a key in his hand and unlocked the inner door. Peng
reached past the man and pulled the door open. This was the first the
man was aware there was someone near him. Before the man could bring
Peng into his field of view, Peng's left fist landed on the side of his head
sending him limp. Inside, at the end of the hall, there was an Exit sign
which meant stairs. Peng grasped the hands of his new acquaintance and
walking backwards dragged him to the exit door. In the stairwell he

dropped him and rifled his pockets. He took the wallet and keys. There was a letter with an apartment number on it—third floor.

He was too weak from the cold to carry the man that far, especially since that might not be the apartment the key would fit. He left him and started up. The key fit the door of the apartment closest to the steps. Inside he let the door swing closed and fell to all fours. He was becoming disoriented and knew why. He was still wet and was freezing. The wet clothes were frozen stiff. His legs were not working. He dragged himself to the bathroom with his hands and dumped himself into the tub. Fumbling with the handle, he got water to flow. At first, there was no sensation of the water on his numb hands. Then, he could feel it getting warm and put his head under the faucet.

Twenty minutes later he was drying himself in the infrared warmth of the ceiling heat lamp. His shoulder wound was blue and bleeding a little, though it only ached when he moved his arm. His pendant was working through his perineural system to heal the wound far more rapidly than normal.

This was perfect except for the man. He was still weak, but he knew what he had to do. The apartment's occupant was taller and slimmer than Peng as the clothes from the closet testified. They were ill fitting, but it didn't matter. A man carrying a body would not be remembered by the cut of his clothes. He hoped his assumption was correct that few people used the stairs in a building like this. Barefoot, he went to the man. Sitting the body on the steps, he folded him over his shoulder, and managed to stand up. The limp body was heavier that he imagined any man could be and going up made it harder. Struggling, he drew on the last of his strength as he drunkenly staggered to the third floor. At last in the apartment, he rolled his load onto the floor and sat beside him getting his breath.

The man groaned. Kill him. Had to kill him. It was only right. Peng deserved the warm apartment more than he did.

"Now, Mr. Quan, be nice!"

What? Was the flighty woman here? No. He had imagined the voice. Must have. But, it seemed so real. She couldn't be here. He brought a fist into contact with the man's temple again. No more sounds.

Peng found a roll of cord in a closet and bound the man, stuffed a dishcloth in his mouth, and covered his eyes with a towel. Finally, he set about bandaging his wound. He found what he needed and with some difficulty did a fair job. Safe.

The only sounds from the man were his uneven breathing. Why had he left him alive? Peng wasn't sure. His thoughts were disjointed. He was hungry and tired. This, taken together with the extreme cold he'd been exposed to, had put him off his game. That had to be it.

The events at the lab were never far from his mind. He knew his pendant had been recharged because his wound was healing so rapidly. Would it need another charging in time? If it did, he could only hope he'd find a more efficient, to say nothing of safer, way to do it. There were disjointed thoughts popping into his mind of his ordeal between the start of the test and his regaining consciousness in the water. If he could put the whole chain of events together, he might be able to work himself into a comfortable position with scientists working on the problem. For now, he found himself extremely tired. Future plans would have to wait until he was rested.

---

Too many stories in real life have, if not sad, at least less than happy endings. Why should a person have to endure that when reading for enjoyment, and where the author is free to make any kind of ending he wishes? With that in mind, the reader must know that Ed Breckon offered Cindy Thomas an engagement ring for Christmas which she happily accepted. Less than a stone's throw into the New Year they were married and lived happily ever after. Well, as happily as any two flawed human beings could. They kept their marriage on an even footing by taking to heart the little saying about true love penned by C. S. Lewis that goes like this:

> When I have learned to love God better than my earthly dearest, I shall love my earthly dearest better than I do now. Insofar as I learn to love my earthly dearest at the expense of God and *instead* of God, I shall be moving towards the state in which I shall not love my earthly dearest at all. When first things are put first, second things are not suppressed but increased.

# — End Notes —

There are, of course, nagging questions about zero point energy mostly dealing with the idea that "you don't get something for nothing." While the author does not have a working proficiency with the hard core mathematics of theoretical physic, it is interesting to speculate on a somewhat philosophical level about what the future holds. It is true that after little more than a century of steady advances from one theory to another, going from electrons, protons, and neutrons to a plethora of subatomic particles, string theory, and such, theoretical physics is presently stalled with no clear direction to go. There are many competing theories, but they all depend on more physical measurements to determine which, if any, is valid. However, the experimental apparatuses are increasing in size and expense at an astronomical rate. And then, once a new facility is built, it is primarily designed to measure a limited number of quantities that will prove or disprove one theory. If the data is inconclusive, another huge facility is needed to test another theory.

As the story tries to imply, there is the possibility that the next advance will have to be in the field of philosophy before the physics can proceed. It may be necessary to accept the premise that the only reason the universe is here, however it got here, is for us, and then develop physics from there. That may seem a little self centered, but consider the following.

Taking the simplest atom, that of hydrogen, we see that its nucleus is made up of a single particle, a proton, and it has one electron orbiting around it. Putting the size of these particles and that atom on a scale we can comprehend, we see that if the proton is the size of a B-B and it is placed on home plate of a baseball field, the electron is smaller than a spec of dust in far center field. All the rest is empty space. However, it isn't entirely empty. It is filled with the force fields caused by the two particles. The force is transmitted by virtual particles, so called because they are only mathematical constructs used to make sense of subatomic reactions. They cannot be observed because any such attempt changes the processes in which they appear.

All of the other atoms are similar to hydrogen, though with increasingly more complicated structures as one goes up the periodic chart of the atoms. This means that all matter contains very little in the way of "stuff" we can actually identify, and a solid wall isn't solid at all, but a web of force fields that no one really understands.

There is an hypothesis, called the zero energy universe, that has received quite a lot of attention. It says that the universe started from a unique instance where a particle and its mirror antiparticle popped into existence starting a massive inflation, something like a chain reaction, that produced an equal amount of positive and negative energy and our macroscopic universe came into being. The universe consists of essentially nothing, but, fortunately for us, in equal positive and negative parts. It's the ultimate free lunch; the universe is made out of nothing.

Few of the commentators on the zero energy universe hypothesis discuss the logical conclusion that if it came from nothing, it could revert back to nothing. With all solid matter little more than force fields made up of virtual particles, if these particles were in some way nullified the force fields they create would disappear and with them the universe and, of course, us.

It is the author's opinion that we will eventually find that life is quite common in other parts of the universe, but that we will be the only intelligent life. This statement needs further explanation. The human race has been in what could be called, for lack of a better term, a "scientific state" for only several centuries, certainly not more that a few millennia, depending on your definition. Unquestionably, most of our technical knowledge has come into our possession in the last hundred years. That is a miniscule amount of time when compared to the currently estimated age of the universe. If we continue advancing as we are for several more centuries, we will surely unlock the secrets of space and time. Part of this research will show, as mentioned above, that this structure is, after all, rather fragile. Human nature, being what it is, will cause us to make bad decisions with regard to the use of this knowledge. One or the other of those in power will make a fateful decision to use this information for personal advantage, or even for some perceived good cause, and will end up unraveling the structure of space and time and thereby destroying the universe. That's it, good bye, bring on the General Judgement.

The logic of this is that if there ever were another intelligent species they would have learned what we are about to learn before we did, and would have destroyed the universe before we had a chance to get as far as we have. Or else, this other species would still be back in the stone ages. However, due to the relatively very short time it takes to develop from there to a scientific state, it would be unlikely they would exist at all. Therefore, we should proceed as if we are the reason it's all here; we are as good as it gets. For some reason, that doesn't sound very encouraging, does it?

# — About the Author —

The author started writing fiction a dozen years ago as a diversion, and he still finds it an engaging activity. It is hoped that the basic premise of each story is uplifting even if there is a large dose of the all too common elements of evil. Including depravity of various kinds is, unfortunately, unavoidable to have a tale that has tension and holds the reader's interest.

The first book, *The Tiger's Fury*, was based almost entirely on heavily fictionalized events of the author's work experience. The theme, which might be hard to discern, is that all of the characters, both good and bad, that are after some worldly good for themselves end up not getting it. The only character who gets all of what he is after is the son of the rich Arab man because he involves himself in the plot to pay a debt to another man. A lesser theme is seen in the main character as he is dragged down to the point of praying only for deliverance.

The second book, *Dragon Fang*, touches on divine providence; if God is good, why is there evil in the world? It shows two men who, through severe trials, are touched in different ways by divine providence. One is saved from death at the last second because of a good deed he did. But, he has no way of ever knowing he nearly died. The other man must begrudgingly reason out and accept how terrible events worked to the benefit of all. In this story, too, many of the settings are based on the author's experiences.

The present volume, *Hubot*, looks at various aspects of what it means to be human. Along the way, some ideas are developed about what the future may hold for us. Having a Bachelor of Science degree in physics, the author has spent several decades applying these principles in his work, and therefore, has an ingrained interest in the science discussed.

The author is a life-long native of Minnesota who now lives with his wife in the Minneapolis St. Paul metropolitan area. He has six grown children also living in the state.

The little poem, *A Song of Hope*, is an original poem by the author published here for the first time.

It is hoped the reader will find enjoyment in these stories, just as it has been a delight writing them.

www.ingramcontent.com/pod-product-compliance
Lightning Source LLC
Chambersburg PA
CBHW032227010726
47494CB00002B/380